Destiny's
Road

*Destiny's Road

Larry Niven *

TOR®
A Tom Doherty Associates Book
New York

DESTINY'S ROAD

Copyright © 1997 by Larry Niven

This book is printed on acid-free paper.

A Tor Book
Published by Tom Doherty Associates, Inc.
175 Fifth Avenue
New York, NY 10010

Tor Books on the World Wide Web:
http://www.tor.com

Tor® is a registered trademark of Tom Doherty Associates, Inc.

Design by Basha Durand

Library of Congress Cataloging-in-Publication Data

Niven, Larry.
   Destiny's road / Larry Niven.—1st ed.
      p.   cm.
   "A Tom Doherty Associates book."
   ISBN 0-312-85122-7 (acid-free paper)
   I. Title.
   PS3564.I9D4   1997   96-53197
   813'.54—dc21   CIP

First Edition: June 1997

Printed in the United States of America

0 9 8 7 6 5 4 3 2 1

I turned in a draft of *Destiny's Road* in August 1996, four years overdue. I knew it was an ambitious project, and I flinched from it.

This book is for the people who waited, or advised me, or egged me gently on:

Marilyn, my wife, who reminded me of overdue contracts from time to time;

Tom Doherty, my publisher, who was quietly patient;

my former agent Eleanor Wood, with no stake in the book, who waited with the rest;

Jerry Pournelle, my frequent collaborator, who made numerous valuable suggestions as did Robert Gleason, my frequent editor;

and Michael Whelan who displayed his magnificent cover painting at the Chicago Worldcon five years ago. He has waited with no patience at all. Our landscapes no longer quite match . . . but the tree on the peak is his, and I snatched it up and made it the Destiny fool cage.

Thank you all.

Dramatis Personae

2493 A.D., Crew of the lander *Cavorite*—
James Twerdahl
Daryl Twerdahl
Robin Tucker, Second Lander Pilot
Willow Granger, Xenobiology
Oliver Carter
Will Coffey
Wayne Parnelli, Marine Biology

2711 A.D., Spiral Town—
JEMMY BLOOCHER aka TIM HANN, TIM BEDNACOURT, JER-
EMY WINSLOW
MARGERY and WILLIAM BLOOCHER, Jemmy's Parents.
The other children: MARGERY JUNIOR, BRENDA, THONNY,
GREEGRY, and JANE

the spring caravan
Doheny—infirmary and refuge. #1, front wagon.
Spadoni—ammunition and secret weapons, #2
Dionne—shark shells and other frivolities, #5
Lyon—cookware, #6
Armstrong—tents and bedding, #7
Ibn-Rushd wagon—cookware, #8
        Senka, Rian, Damon, Joker (Dzhokhar), and Shireen
Small—survival trade goods, #9
Milasevik—tents and bedding, #10
Tucker—yutz guns and shark-shooting ammunition, #11
Wu—#12

Dole—#13
YUTZES—   Dannis Stolsh
             Hal Gleeber (chef)
             Bord'n (or Boardman)
             Forry Randall (chef)
             Hal
             Tim Bednacourt

The Windfarm

Andrew Dowd
Barda Winslow
Shimon Cartaya
Amnon Kaczinski
Denis Bouvoire
Dennis Levoy
Rita and Dolores Nogales
Rafik Doe
Ansel Tarr
Jemmy/Jeremy Bloocher
Henry
Willametta Haines
Shar
Asham Mandala
Winnie Maclean
Duncan Nicholls (Duncan Nick)

Surf Rider

Harold and Espania Winslow
Karen Winslow
Karen's merchant child—
        Mustafa
Jeremy's and Karen's children—
        Judy Cole   married
        Eileen Wheeler   married John Wheeler.
        Brenda Winslow   married

the autumn caravan

Lall Wagon— Medical, #1
        Palava   Maiku

Hearst Wagon— Cookware, #6
    Glen Hearst
    Tanya and Angelo Hearst
    Harlow and Jeremy Winslow
    Steban, yutz chef
Miller Wagon— Cookware, #8
    Govert Miller

∗ Part One ∗

✳ 1 ✳

The Caravan

We have experience of the earlier interstellar colony, Camelot. Considerable information reached Earth from Camelot, describing both mistakes and success, before communication stopped. Destiny is our second try. Destiny will succeed.

—Naren Singh,
Secretary-General,
United Nations, 2427 A.D.

2722 A.D., Spiral Town

Junior at fourteen had grown tall enough to reach the highest cupboard. She stretched up on tiptoe, found the speckles shaker by feel, and brought it down. Then she saw what was happening to the bacon. She shouted, "Jemjemjemmy!"

Jemmy's eleven-year-old mind was all in the world beyond the window.

Junior snatched up a pot holder and moved the pan off the burner. The bacon wasn't burned, not yet, not quite.

"Sorry," Jemmy said without turning. "Junior, there's a caravan coming."

"You never saw a caravan." Junior looked through the long window, northeastward. "Dust. *Maybe* it's the caravan. Here, turn this."

Jemmy finished cooking the bacon. Junior shook salt and speckles on the eggs, sparingly, and returned the shaker to the cupboard. Brenda, who should have been stirring the eggs, and Thonny and Greegry and Ronny were all crowded along the long window—the Bloocher family's major treasure, one sheet of glass a meter tall, three meters from side to side—to watch what was, after all, only a dust plume.

13

*   *   *

They ate bread and scrambled hen's eggs and orange juice. Brenda, who was ten, fed Jane, who was four months old. Mom and Dad had been up for hours doing farmwork. Mom was eating poached platyfish eggs. Platyfish were Destiny life; their bodies didn't make fat. Mom was trying to lose weight.

Jemmy wolfed his breakfast, for all the good that did. The rest of the children were finished too. The younger kids squirmed like their chairs were on fire; but you couldn't ask Mom and Dad to hurry. They weren't exactly dawdling, but the kids' urgency amused them.

The long window was behind Jemmy. If he turned his back on the rest of the family, Dad would snap at him.

Junior emptied her coffee mug with no sign of haste, very adult, and set it down. "Mom, can you handle Jane and Ronny?"

Seven-year-old Ronny gaped in shock. Before he could scream, Mom said, "I'll take care of the baby, dear, but you take Ronny with you. He has to do his schoolwork."

Ronny relaxed, though his eyes remained wary. Junior stood. Her voice became a drill sergeant's. "We set?"

Brenda, Thonny, Greegry, Ronny, and Jemmy surged toward the door. There was a pileup in the lock while they sorted out their coats and caps, and then they cycled through in two clusters, out of the house, streaming toward the Road. Junior followed.

The younger three were half-running, but Junior with her long legs kept up with them. She wasn't trying to catch Jemmy, who at eleven had no dignity to protect.

The sun wasn't above the mountains yet, but Quicksilver was, a bright spark dim in daylight.

The line of elms was as old as Bloocher House. They were twenty-five meters from the front of the house, the last barrier between Bloocher Farm and the Road. To Jemmy they seemed to partition earth and sky. He ran between two elms and was first to reach the Road.

To the right the Road curved gradually toward Spiral Town. Left, northwest, it ran straight into the unknown. That way lay Warkan Farm, where four mid-teens stood in pairs to watch the dust plume come near.

The Warkan children had been schooled at Bloocher House, as had their parents before them. Then, when Jemmy was six, the Bloocher household computer died. For the next week or two Dad was silent and dangerous. Jemmy came to understand that a major social disaster had taken place.

For five years now, Jemmy and his siblings and all of the Warkan children had trooped three houses around the Road's curve to use the Hann computer.

The dust plume no longer hid what was coming toward Spiral Town. There were big carts pulled by what must be chugs. Jemmy saw more than one cart, hard to tell how many. Children from farther up the Road were running alongside. Their voices carried a long way, but it was too far to make out words.

His siblings had filtered between the trees. They lined the Road, waiting. Jemmy looked toward the Warkan kids; looked back at Junior; saw her shake her head. He said, "Aw, Junior. What about class?"

"Wait," Junior said.

Of course there had been no serious thought of rushing to class. Not with a caravan coming! They'd make up missed classes afterward. Computer programs would wait, and a human teacher was rarely needed.

Children began to separate at Junior's age. Boys spoke only to boys, girls to girls. Jemmy knew that much. Maybe he'd understand why, when he was older. Now he only knew that Junior would speak to him only to give orders. He missed his big sister, and Junior hadn't even *gone* anywhere.

If Junior went to join the Warkan girls, the Warkan boys would stare at her and rack their brains thinking of some excuse to talk to her. So Jemmy almost understood why the whole family simply waited by the elms while the wagons came near.

The wagons had flat roofs twice as high as a grown man's head. They moved at walking speed. You could hear the children who ran alongside carrying on shouted conversations with the merchants. There were deeper voices too: adults were negotiating with merchants in the wagons.

When the caravan reached the Warkan farm, the Warkans joined them, boys and girls together, it didn't matter. A few minutes later the troop had reached the Bloocher children.

It was Jemmy's first close view of a chug.

The beasts were small and compact. They forged ahead at a steady walking pace, twenty to a cart. They stood as high as Jemmy's short ribs. Their shells were the ocher of beach sand. Their wrinkled leather bellies were pale. Their beaks looked like wire cutters, dangerous, and each head was crowned by a flat cap of ocher shell. They showed no awareness of the world around them.

The wagons stood on tall wheels. Their sides dropped open to form shelves, and merchants grinned down from inside.

Jemmy let the first two wagons pass him by. Junior had already forgotten him; the rest of the children went with her, though Thonny looked back once. No eyes were on him when he reached out to stroke one of the chugs. The act seemed headily dangerous. The shell was paper-smooth.

The chug swiveled one eye to see him.

It was hard to tell who was what among the merchants, because of their odd manner of dress. As far as Jemmy could tell, there were about two men for every woman. They enjoyed talking to children. A man and woman driving the third cart smiled down at him, and Jemmy walked alongside. He asked, "Can't you make them go faster?"

"Don't want to," the man said. "We buy and sell all along the Road. Why make the customers chase us?"

A golden-haired woman with a trace of a limp, Mom's age but dumpier, passed money up to a dark-skinned merchant on the twelfth and last cart. That was Ilyria Warkan. The merchant reached way down to hand her a speckles pouch.

It was transparent, big as a head of lettuce, with a child's handful of bright yellow dust in the corner. You never saw these pouches unless a merchant was selling speckles.

Jemmy ran his hand down a chug's flank. The skin was dry and papery. Belatedly he asked, "Do they bite?"

"No. They've got good noses, the chugs. They can smell you're Earth-life, and they won't eat that. Might bite you if you were a fisher."

The merchants seemed to like children, but nobody ever saw a child with the caravan. Did they keep their children hidden? Nobody knew.

The Road was beginning to curve. More children joined the caravan: Rachel Harness and her mother, Jael; and Gwillam Doakes, a burly boy Jemmy's age; and the very clannish Holmes girls. No more adults came, unless you counted Jael Harness, who hadn't got enough speckles as a child and was therefore a little simple. Jemmy could see people walking away, far down the straight arm of the Road.

The merchant woman caught him looking, and laughed. "Too many people now." Her words were just a bit skewed, with music in her voice. "Serious customers, they see the dust, they come to meet us. Give them more time to deal. Now we get no more till the hub. How far to the hub?"

"Twenty minutes . . . no, wait, you can't take cross streets. They're too narrow." The caravan would just have to go round and round, following the curve as the Road spiraled toward Civic Hall. "More like an hour and a half. You could get there faster without the wagons."

"No point," the merchant woman said. "I would miss the cemetery too, wouldn't I?"

"Don't go in there," Jemmy said reflexively.

16

"Oh, but I must! I've heard about the Spiral Town cemetery all my life. We follow the Road around by almost a turn? It's all Earthlife, they say."

"That's right," Jemmy said. "Spooky. Destiny life won't grow where the dead lie."

The merchant said, "I've never seen a place that was nothing but Earthlife."

She was strange and wonderful, swathed in layers of bright colors. It was a game, getting her to keep talking. Jemmy asked, "Have you seen City Hall? There's painted walls, really bright. *Acrylic*, Dad says."

She smiled indulgently. He knew: *She'd been there.*

He asked, "Where do speckles come from?"

"Don't know. Hundreds of klicks up the Road when we buy 'em."

Hundreds of klicks . . . kilometers. "Where did they come from before the Road was here?"

She frowned down at him. "Before the Road . . . ?"

"Sure. We learn about it in school, how James and Daryl Twerdahl and the rest took off in *Cavorite* and left the Road behind them. But that was eight years after Landing Day. So . . . ?"

The man was listening too. The woman said, "News to me, boy. The Road's always been here."

Jemmy would have accepted that, accepted her ignorance, if he hadn't seen the man's lips twitch in a smile. In his mind, for that instant, it was as if the world had betrayed him.

Then seven-year-old Ronny was beside him, saying, "I'm tired, Jemmy."

"Okay, kid. *Junjunjunior—*"

One wagon ahead, Junior stopped walking. So did Thonny and Brenda, and the Warkan girls that Junior had been talking to, and the Warkan boys, all without consulting each other. Sandy Warkan said, "Twerdahl Street's just ahead. We can stop for a squeeze of juice at Guilda's and wait for the caravan to come round again."

"School," Junior reminded them.

"Can wait."

The Road itself was magical.

Bloocher Farm was soft soil and living things and entropy. Plants grew from little to big, grew dry and withered, changed and died. Animals acted strangely, and presently gave birth to children like themselves. Tools rusted or broke down or rotted or ceased working for reasons of their own.

Closer to the hub, you saw less of life and more of entropy. The

17

houses were old, losing their hard edges. New buildings were conspicuous, jarring. At night there were lines of city lights with gaps in them.
Things that didn't work were as prevalent here as among the farms, but
you noticed them more: they were closer together.

But the Road was hard and flat and not like anything else in the world.
The Road was eternal.

The Road was a fantastic toy. Things rolled easily on its flat surface.
Here, just short of Twerdahl Street and half a klick southeast of Bloocher
Farm, was a favored dip used by the high-school kids. Sandy and Hal
Warkan had showed Jemmy how to sweep the Road to get a *really* flat
surface, so that balls or wheels could be rolled back and forth over the
dip. They'd go forever.

No time for that today. They turned off at Twerdahl Street, and some
of the merchants waved good-bye.

Rachel Harness chattered to Junior, pulling her mother along. Rachel's
mother Jael seemed to listen, but answered rarely, and when she spoke
her words had nothing to do with what she'd heard. Jemmy liked Jael
Harness, but Junior and Brenda found her a little queer.

Children who didn't get enough speckles grew up like that.

But Rachel was a bright, active girl, Junior's age, who treated her
mother like a younger sister. Neighbors had helped to raise her, but
speckles were expensive. Rachel must have had a steady source of
speckles since her birth.

One wondered. Who was Rachel's father?

The Harness farm was to the right, and that was where Rachel was
pointing, Junior looking and nodding. Jemmy couldn't hear them, but
he looked. A silver bulge in the weeds . . . it was Killer!

The Council had sicced Varmint Killer on the Harness farm!

The old machine wasn't doing anything. Just sitting. Weeds and vegetation that had been crops ran riot here. It wasn't all Earthlife. Odd
colors, odd shapes grew in wedge patterns, wider toward the southwest,
toward the sea.

More than two hundred years ago, the great fusion-powered landers
had hovered above Crab Island and burned the land sterile. This land
was to serve Earthlife only. But the life of Destiny continued to try to
retake the Crab.

Weeds tended to cluster, reaching tentatively from an occupied base,
as if they did not like the fertilizer that made Earthlife grow. Black
touched with bronze and yellow-green; branches that divided, divided,
divided, until every tip was a thousand needles too fine to see. One
could rip up an encroachment of Destiny weeds with a few passes of a
tractor. One day the Harnesses' neighbors would do that.

But Destiny's animals were another matter. They lived among Destiny's encroaching plants, and some were dangerous. These were Killer's prey.

Killer squatted in the wild corn, a silver bulge the size and shape of a chug pulled in on itself. The children watched and waited. Older children bullied the youngers onto Warkan Farm's long porch, where Destiny creatures weren't likely to be hiding.

One would not want a child to come between Varmint Killer and its prey.

They waited, waited . . .

Ssizzz!

Even looking, you might not see it. Jemmy just caught it: the line flicking out like a slender tongue, snapping back; a drop of blood drooling down beneath the little hatch cover.

Junior's hand was on his arm. He obeyed, remained seated, but *looked*. Something thrashed in the weeds. Killer's tongue lashed out again.

The caravan and the crowd were trickling away slowly but steadily, off down Twerdahl Street. The Bloocher family gathered itself. Junior called, "Sanity check. If we skip Guilda's now, we can get through school time and still beat the caravan to Guilda's. Vote!"

Reality sometimes called for hard choices. They looked at each other. . . .

✳ 2 ✳

L e s s o n s

The planets
~~LOKI~~ DUICKSILVER
~~NORN~~ DESTINY
asteroids, a sparse and narrow ring
VOLSTAAG
HOGUN in Volstaag's trailing Trojan
point
HELA, black giant or brown dwarf
inner comets

Missing school was not a problem for the Bloocher kids, nor for the Warkans either. Computers had infinite patience. A teacher wasn't usually needed. Kids who didn't make up lost lessons would get a reputation, but delays would have been more serious at harvest time.

The Hann Farm was one loop inward from the Bloochers'. It was smaller than most. Maybe the first Hanns had been cheated. Maybe not. The land was fantastically fertile, and Hahn machines must have been among the best that had come from the sky.

Or else the Hanns made things grow by using intensive care, treating each separate plant as an individual; and maybe their machines lived longer than others because they were kept clean inside and out. There were things Jemmy would never learn, things nobody knew. He was already beginning to resent that.

Nine children trooped into the Hann front yard in late afternoon. The yard was a rich lawn with islands in it: round patches of dark soil three feet across marked with a big, strangely shaped rock and two or three Destiny plants, or driftwood and a cluster of multicolored irises, or . . .

20

Deborah Hann had a Julia set growing on a dwarf redwood. The Destiny vine wound around the straight Earthlife tree, spraying out green spines that bifurcated in fractal fashion into a nearly invisible lacework. Mrs. Hann smiled at the children and started to get up, but Junior had plenty of time to wave her back down. Deborah and Takumi were old. Their knees were going.

They entered the Hann house via the airlock.

Curdis Hann, at sixteen, fancied himself a teacher. "Hi, Sandy. Do you know why these double-door things are called *airlocks*?"

Sandy Warkan, the oldest boy and nominally in charge of the boys, said, "Keeps the wind out."

Curdis grinned. "In. Look it up."

The kids separated inside the airlock. Junior went with Marion and Lisette Warkan downstairs to the cellar. Sandy and Hal Warkan went upstairs to join Toma and Curdis Hann. Jemmy had never been up there.

That left Jemmy in charge of the younger ones, in the company room. Jemmy let Greegry log in. The kid was getting good at that. The rest read over his shoulder as he typed, find: airlock.

Diagrams, etymology . . . Airlocks were for spacecraft. They held air in against the vacuum of space, as long as both doors couldn't open at the same time. The first settlers had built airlocks into their houses against the ferocious coastal winds. Curdis had scored a point.

Jemmy asked, "Brenda, what've they got you studying? Path of the *Cavorite*, isn't it?"

"Yes."

Greegry said, "Hey, I'm supposed to be doing algebra."

Jemmy asked, "You like algebra?"

Greegry grinned over his shoulder. " 'Sorry, Dad, Jemmy wanted to know where the caravans came from.' Okay?"

"If he asks. I just want something to catch Curdis. Brenda, see what you can get."

Brenda reached past Greegry and typed, find: Cavorite∗caravan∗Road. Nothing.

"I think these records are older than the caravans. Let me try." Thonny typed, find: Cavorite∗ Road∗map.

The screen lit with visuals, and Thonny got up to give Brenda his seat.

Jemmy crossed to the smaller screen. "Greegry, let's get you going on algebra. Have you got a lesson on file?"

Greegry worked. Jemmy watched because he could use the brushup. The program was a good one, and Greegry wasn't stumbling much. Jemmy's attention strayed.

On Brenda's screen, *Cavorite* and *Columbiad* settled on pillars of flame: huge squat cylinders with flared skirts and bullet noses. Jemmy had seen this lesson before. It looked real, then and now, but Jemmy thought it must be a computer-generated cartoon. How could a camera have watched these first ships land?

Probes had been leaving Earth since the 1950s. Over the centuries they ranged farther, past the gas-giant worlds, over the sun's poles, out among the comets, ultimately to the nearer stars.

Humanity knew the local neighborhood well, long before they could build a starship.

Tau Ceti was a yellow dwarf star not far from Sol. One of its planets showed the blue of an oxygen atmosphere. Only living things can maintain an oxygen atmosphere.

Apollo was a star eight to ten billion years old, redder and smaller than Sol. There the probes found another blue world. They named it Norn. Norn, Apollo 4, held life . . . but Tau Ceti 3 was closer to Sol, and that world—Avalon—became the first interstellar colony.

The colonists aboard *Geographic* had settled on a great island and called it Camelot. Whatever lethal surprises waited on an unknown world, they could be restricted by choosing an island. That decision must have saved the Avalon colony from destruction, for a time.

Cryogenic sleep didn't quite work. Ice crystals formed in the brains of the first colonists. Some died of it. Some woke brain-damaged. Some lasted a few years, then died of strokes. Survivors faced local predators and weird weather cycles. Whether Avalon survived was in doubt: over the decades the broadcasts had slowed, then ceased.

The launching of *Geographic* had nearly broken Sol system's economy. All things considered, it was no wonder that Sol system waited two hundred and twenty years to send forth another colony ship. . . .

"She's blowing smoke," Jemmy decided.

Brenda tapped to pop up a window. The author of the teaching program was—"Allison Berkeley, Ph.D. . . . string of letters. You think she's lying?"

"More like confused. It bothers her. She's looking for reasons herself."

Brenda tapped, and the lesson's headings disappeared. She didn't need to say *We'll never know*. Allison Berkeley string-of-letters must have died centuries ago, light-years away.

In 2490 A.D. *Argos* arrived in Apollo system. The starfarers had already renamed the blue world. No longer Norn: Destiny was waiting.

They chose a narrow-necked peninsula with a ridge of weathered mountains, like Malaya in size and shape. As on Avalon, so on Destiny: they would isolate the problems.

Cavorite and *Columbiad*, the landers, were massive spacecraft designed to explore a solar system or a world. They sat low on ground-effect skirts. Riding the fusion drive alone, either ship could hover a meter high until the land beneath turned to lava; or above a lake, until the water boiled and rivers downstream ran steaming. It was thus that they cleared the Crab for farming and ranching.

Argos had been long in the building. The Apollo Project had sixty years to breed plants and animals of Earth for life on Destiny. Probes had shown them a shorter year, redder sunlight, a circular orbit and a mere ten degrees of axial tilt, stable wind patterns and no ice caps, a small moon that moved too fast to pick up much of a tide. Weather would not be a persistent problem. *They got that wrong!* But the dimmer, reddened sunlight would. The Apollo Project planners tried to breed plants to survive that.

Cavorite and *Columbiad* settled high on the wider, southwestern side of the Crab Mountains, fifteen miles inland. The settlers wanted easy access to the sea, but not too easy. There might be Bay of Fundy tides, despite the little moon, or amphibious sea monsters.

They dredged the sea for Avalon seaweed and used it to fertilize Earthly crops.

And *Argos* disappeared.

"I can see why *Argos*'s crew got bored," Brenda said, greatly daring.

Heads turned, but nobody spoke. *Argos* had betrayed them all, marooned the settlers and their descendants to the end of time. The crew of *Argos* had been tried and convicted of mutiny, in absentia. Later the lander *Cavorite* had abandoned Base One, Destiny Town. Lives that crossed between suns would drown in the mundane work of farming. Jemmy felt the same, some days.

Here is the farm, there is the Road. Take off, go. . . .

Thonny's screen showed something like an octopus made of clouds, curved arms, a body that bulged in the middle. An old view from orbit. Jemmy had seen that once and never found it again.

Greegry wasn't having fun. Nobody does algebra for fun. He kept leafing back through the text. There was a block to keep him from seeking the *Answers* file, but Jemmy had cracked that block long ago, and maybe Greegry had too.

The Hanns had once had a window like the one at Bloocher Farm. Eternal winds had finally cracked it. What they had now was brick set into the Roadside wall, and four panes cut from the old window and set in the brick. And nothing much was going on out there.

This room was not where Jemmy Bloocher wanted to be.

He wanted to be where *Cavorite* was, at the far end of the Road.

Columbiad became the colony's power source. Cables ran into the base, with a tent to protect the join. (Jemmy and Brenda were amused. The tent by their time had become a thick-walled building.) *Cavorite* was kept ready for an emergency evacuation of the Crab.

Inevitably, some of the half-a-thousand first settlers thought more like interstellar explorers than like farmers. Forty of them followed an alternative path—"the path less traveled by," in Groundcaptain Radner's words.

They waited eight years before the rest of the colonists had enough faith in their growing crops, and enough surplus to make the trip worthwhile. In 2498 A.D. there was a glut.

Cavorite had carried half the colony from orbit down to the Crab. Leaving Spiral Town, the same craft carried forty in roomy comfort along with a hydroponics garden, stores of seeds and fertilized eggs, considerable medical facilities and lab equipment. The animals were thriving too, but none would be left on this first trip. They'd have nothing to eat. The plan called for *Cavorite* to return, and eventually to make a second journey, scattering animals and birds along the path.

This trip, *Cavorite* would leave seeds and growing plants, and one thing more:

A road.

Sitting on the fusion drive alone, *Cavorite* would ride a meter in the air, with flame mushrooming out around the skirt, hot enough to melt rock. That was the idea. *Cavorite* would move off along the foothills of the Spine, the Crab's mountain ridge, leaving a snail's trail of cooling lava.

Jemmy recognized what was onscreen: a view from space taken ages ago from the mother ship, before *Columbiad* and *Cavorite* landed.

Water covered most of the planet. Destiny's core was deficient in radioactive elements. Its shell was thick. Ages ago it had cracked: an upwelling of magma had become a long, relatively narrow ridge of continent.

Most of the continent, Wrinkle, lay north, under the broad ice cap. One end reached south of the equator, then curled over. A constriction nearly split the end off from the main body. A spinal ridge ran along Wrinkle, along the constriction now called the Neck, and down the length of the Crab Peninsula, splitting the Crab into broad and narrow halves. That was the land that the settlers settled.

As he and Brenda watched, the computer drew the Road in neon pink. Down at the tip of the Crab, the Road curved out from *Columbiad* in a perfect little spiral. Where it got too big, where Bloocher Farm was now, it drew a tangent, a straight line that ran toward the mainland, parallel to the spinal ridge. As it approached the Neck it became a string of dots, then trailed off.

"Are those dots all we get?" Brenda asked him.

"They made the Road after everyone was down. There wasn't anyone in the sky to take pictures. Except *Argos*, and they don't talk."

Now the computer was drawing in Spiral Town, filling in the curves of the spiral and spreading off down the straight section . . . and fuzzing out into terra incognita.

Brenda complained, "Jemmy, it just trails off."

"They never came back. They were going to, but they never did." Everyone knew the *Cavorite* story. Nobody knew how it ended.

Brenda said, "The caravans must know where *Cavorite* went. The Road goes there and so do they. Why not just ask?"

"Okay," Thonny said obligingly, mocking her.

Jemmy tasted the idea. "Traders wouldn't tell anyone anything. But Brenda's right. They *know.*"

The Road was a spiral, and Radner Street was a radial path, not quite straight. The straggling line of children crossed the Road's next inward arc, and saw the last wagon receding. They crossed the next arc ahead of the wagons. Soon thereafter they walked between fruit orchards. The Road curved more tightly now. The intersection ahead was Guilda's Place.

Guilda's Place sprawled like three or four buildings pushed together around an open space, a courtyard. Bird feeders stood in the corners, and the courtyard swarmed with little birds. The buildings were old, of poured stone, with every corner rounded by two hundred years of winds; but the roof of the biggest building was new Begley cloth sheeting, dark silver-gray. Walks led through the fruit orchards out back.

The orchard wasn't enough to keep Guilda's going. The family had to buy fruit from farms farther out. The Bloochers supplied her with melons and grapes; their neighbors supplied other produce. And everybody stopped at Guilda's.

It wasn't as if farmers couldn't make their own juice. But Guilda Smitt sold sherbet. Guilda had a working freezer, and a storage battery, and a roof covered with Begley cloth to soak up the sunlight and turn it into electric power.

In the courtyard the boys and girls formed separate lines to get juice, then settled at four big round tables close enough for eavesdropping. Jemmy would have liked to listen to Junior reporting her conversation with the man who drove the second cart. But then his siblings wanted to hear about *his* conversation.

"She said, 'The Road's always been there.' And he laughed."

Eight-year-old Thonny scoffed. "*We* know better than that."

"They did too," Jemmy said.

Guilda's four daughters were replacing the juice. Junior stepped up and spoke to them. They listened, then moved briskly inside. Adults were gathering; the courtyard was filling up.

Other customers had gathered around Guilda's Place to hear Jemmy and Junior tell of the merchants. Turning heads and sudden quiet alerted Jemmy, and he saw what the rest had seen: a single chug pulling a small cart along the radial road, with a single merchant walking alongside.

He was more than twenty and less than thirty: hard to tell, with those pointed features. He had long black hair and a black beard trimmed short. Where other merchants wore several layers, this one wore only a woven vest, loose pants, and an elaborate cummerbund with a wide pocket in it. His feet were bare, and his arms and shoulders.

He seemed to speak to the chug, and the chug waited while he went inside. They saw him speak to a massive woman whose wealth of dark hair was piled into intricate curves: Guilda herself.

When the trader came out he was carrying a massive drum of sherbet. His arm and shoulder muscles rolled like boulders, and Jemmy envied him that. He didn't acknowledge the regard of the girls.

He set the big drum in the cart, all in one smooth motion, and drove back up along the Road.

Conversation started again when he was gone. "He'll meet the rest of the caravan coming the long way," an old man said.

Guilda herself came out. She clapped her hands for attention, then spoke rapidly. "Sherbet and coins for any of you who helps me this day!"

Jemmy downed his juice and stood up. Sibs and friends were doing the same. A horde moved into the fruit orchards. Wagons were in motion too, bringing fruit from markets nearer the Hub. The Bloochers, sticking together, fetched chairs and tables from nearby houses.

Guilda's contract was good, stated and implied. Guilda's neighbors knew. When the caravan was in town, chairs and tables were needed;

the loan would be repaid. For the labor of the children and young adults now spilling out of the courtyard, money would be paid tonight. Sherbet might come during a slack moment, or days from now, when the merchants were gone.

So chairs and tables were brought and stacked. The ancient freezer ran at its humming maximum, using power stored for months. Guilda's extended family occupied her huge kitchen, and there they turned fruit into juice and whipped it while it froze.

In midafternoon the caravan flowed around the curve of the Road. The wagons were nearly hidden within the crowd of customers. Every level of Spiral Town society had something to buy or sell or trade. Around the shell of customers seethed an outer shell of Spiral Town children.

Now Jemmy and his friends could deploy tables and chairs and silver umbrellas, competing for speed, competing for how many chairs a boy could stack and lift. In the wake of the wagons Guilda's sprawled across the square.

And suddenly there was nothing more to do. The caravan stopped near Spiral Town's hub, and business was being done there. Sherbet was ready, but the merchants were not.

The rules were known. Jemmy had never heard them. Perhaps they'd all learned them through osmosis. This was one: children would not interfere between merchants and the adults who wanted to meet them. The front of Guilda's was the square. The back was a slope of hill that became Endersin's Ranch at its top. Spiral Town's youth now began collecting on the grass behind Guilda's.

Guilda's daughters moved among them, serving minuscule cups of sherbet. Sheeko Radner, Guilda's eldest and as tall as most men, wove a contorted path, pushing a tub on rollers, doling out refill scoops.

The merchants were gathering out front. Yatsen's Far East would be gearing up to serve them dinner. The square must have filled with amazing speed, because merchants were already moving here to the grass slopes.

Four merchants. One was the brawny man who bought the drum of sherbet. Jemmy and the others made haste to make room, and the four traders sat in a circle.

Thonny, eight, was whispering to Ronny, seven. Jemmy couldn't hear. He kept his dignity for a long moment, then glared at them. *"What?"*

"They've all got guns," Thonny said, louder than he intended, his eyes invading the merchants' privacy. "See, the fat one has his in that loose jacket, and him and him have those holders in their pocket belts, and the guy with the muscles—"

"That's you, Fedrick," the fat one laughed at the guy with the muscles.

A wagon was pulling up in the radial street. More produce for Guilda's sherbet. Sheeko Radner waved prettily at a tableful of farmers. The six obliged: they followed her to the wagon and began lifting watermelons.

Fedrick grinned at Thonny. He pulled an L-shaped object from his belt. Jemmy too had been half-sure it was a gun. The brawny merchant made as if to hand it to Thonny, but he was pulling it back even as the fat one's hand blocked him. "I can't let you handle this, boy," he said, or something like that; his words were twisted almost beyond recognition. "I can show you, maybe."

Six farmers carrying six watermelons were trooping toward the kitchen door. The merchant named Fedrick fired at the sixth.

The watermelon in Davish Scrivner's hands exploded. It splashed in all directions, a sudden scarlet flower.

Scrivner stared at his arms, his clothes, hardly believing that it wasn't blood. For that moment he was too flabbergasted even to be afraid. Then, amid a sea of laughter, he turned.

He studied the tableful of merchants, and the roar in his throat didn't emerge. If it had been the fat one . . . well. But the grinning man now pushing a gun into his armpit looked like he could lift a *wagonful* of watermelons.

And he was coming forward with helpless laughter on his face and money in his hand. "It was for the children," he told the farmer. "Think, they'll never see a sight like *that* again! Friend, this should be the price to clean your clothes and a steam bath too. Really, I did look to see there was nothing behind you but hill. Forgive me! Come, share sherbet with us."

Thonny said, "*Damn!* Did you see that?"

In truth, Jemmy would never forget it. What the gun had done to a watermelon, it could do to a man. Davish Scrivner could have exploded like that. Would the merchant still have been laughing?

It never faded, never lost a trace of color: the watermelon exploding in Scrivner's arms, the pulp splashing every part of him like blood, the horror in his face as he gave up his hope of life. It was there in his mind eight years later, on Jemmy Bloocher's last night in Spiral Town.

✳ 3 ✳

Warkan's Tavern

"Dr. Maners, do you represent the crew of *Argos*?"
"I do."
"How do the defendants plead?"
"On the charge of mutiny, not guilty. On the charge of sabotage, not guilty. On the charge of treason, not guilty. On the charge of grand larceny, not guilty. . . ."

—Eric Maners, advocate for the crew of *Argos*

2730 A.D.

The Bloocher clan gathered in wilderness for the third time in three days. Mountains stood above them, the spinal ridge of the Crab. A stream ran foaming over rocks. The water had cut a shallow channel across the Road below, and somebody—merchants—had built a bridge across that.

The New Hann Holding would be here, four kilometers down the Road from the Bloocher Farm on the inland side.

Two hundred and forty years ago, Earthlife had been seeded over the entire peninsula in a random mix. You could make bread out of these waist-high grasses, corn and rye and wheat and a sprinkling of sesame. Apple and orange and pomegranate groves grew randomly. The tallest trees, twenty and thirty feet high, were both redwoods.

An early-morning fog had burned off. The Bloocher clan rested beneath a handful of oaks, the girls around Junior, the boys around Curdis Hann. Jemmy tended a cage that held Destiny tree lace and a pop-hopper. The pop-hopper was a Destiny burrowing creature, and nobody knew how to take care of it. After two days it looked to be dying.

Here and there were patches of darker vegetation, black trunks and branches and lacy extrusions touched with green and yellow-green and bronze. That was local life, Destiny life. Three patches below the clump of oaks had merged.

Varmint Killer rested within that patch.

Killer's surface was very like poured stone, Jemmy thought, pocked with small apertures for light-threads, tiny glass-bead eyes, whips and pellets, all retractable into an ovoid shell. It sat like a statue or a rock, but it had moved in the night.

Killer had siblings.

A myriad tiny machines, specks just bigger than speckles, turned rock and ore into Begley cloth within a cave in Mount Apollo. Similar machines made Earthtime watches in Mount Chronos. Jemmy had looked at both kinds under a microscope. In the places where tools branched out, and in the ovoid shell itself, Jemmy saw an artistic relationship to Varmint Killer. Then again, he'd known in advance: these machines had come from Sol system aboard *Argos*.

The Bloocher clan watched for a time. Then Greegry got bored and tried to climb a redwood, and Thonny began taking bets on when Killer would move again.

Junior had married Curdis Hann.

She was twenty then and twenty-two now. It was time and past time, and Curdis was a good man and a boyhood friend to all of them. Still, it made things awkward.

Two years had passed since the communal tractor failed. Most of Spiral Town thought of it that way, and blamed the driver and his ill luck. But the terrible machine had sent its lightning like an ancient stored flame through William Bloocher's nervous system. Dad was a helpless cripple now, his mind damaged too. And Jemmy, his oldest boy, was only nineteen.

So Junior had charge of the Bloocher farm, and Junior's husband must live with the Bloochers for now. They must call Junior *Margery*. Now *the* Margery, Margery Junior's mother, was *Mom* to everyone, even Dad, even Curdis. Curdis Hann became another brother, at twenty-one an *older* brother who didn't have property yet.

In a year Jemmy would be twenty. Curdis and Junior—*Margery*—would have their land, the New Hann. Then Bloocher land would be Jemmy's to farm.

They'd picked a plot not far beyond the last reach of Spiral Town's farms, where a stream ran down from the mountains. It was infested with Destiny weeds, of course. In the lazy days of midsummer they'd leased Varmint Killer from the Council.

Killer didn't require much supervision. It didn't take orders anymore. Jemmy had led it here by offering it Destiny prey wiggling in a patch of Destiny weeds. Now it just sat in the weeds and waited.

It would not harm life of Earth. It sensed Destiny life, somehow; Jemmy had never heard an explanation that made sense. It wasn't smart enough to see what a human being would: that Destiny life didn't have proper leaves. Photosynthesis went on in lacy extrusions from the branches, and on the branches and trunks themselves.

If a creature of Destiny moved, Killer killed it. When no prey surfaced for a time, it would kill some weeds, then move on.

It wasn't doing much right now.

Greegry had actually reached the top of the redwood. His perch didn't look comfortable, and Jemmy wondered if he was afraid to descend. There weren't any branches on that long, smooth trunk.

Greegry called, "Hey!"

Jemmy waved languidly.

"There's a dust cloud way down at the end of the Road. Jemjem-jemmy! Curdis! I think there's a caravan coming!"

"Great!" Curdis called.

Caravans came three times every two Destiny years: midsummer, first days of spring, last days of autumn. This was midsummer, idle time: neither sowing nor reaping season, a good time for a caravan to visit.

Killer's long tongue lashed into the bronze vegetation and out. Then Killer itself lurched into motion. "Something must have come out of a burrow," Thonny said softly. "It wants the rest of the family."

Jane called, "Thonthonthonny! You owe me four checks!" Jane was only eight.

Greegry called, "Curdis, there's someone on a bike. He's stopping near our bikes!"

"I'll go see," Curdis said. He stood, and Junior joined him. Jemmy got up too, but Curdis gestured him back.

Killer was in the Destiny weeds. They heard the snap! snap! snap! of Killer's whip tentacles. Jane had crawled close to watch.

Thonny was probably right: it was trying to reach prey in a burrow. A whip could be trapped that way.

The whip sounds came less frequently. And here came Curdis, jogging. "We've got to move Killer," he panted. "Jemmy, see if you can get him to follow the pop-hopper."

Jemmy picked up the cage. The pop-hopper didn't look good. "What's up?"

Margery was in range by now. "That girl was from the Council," she called to all. "All fees forgiven if we take Varmint Killer to the Tavern before sunset. The caravan's come early."

They could use the money! Jemmy moved toward the Destiny weeds. Killer had to be approached with respect. He stopped twelve meters away and lifted the cage into view. You *never* got closer than ten meters, because that was the range of its whips.

Killer was motionless.

So was the pop-hopper.

The wind would be out to sea, and that meant he was downwind. Jemmy began to circle, the cage held high. Dad swore that it didn't matter; Killer couldn't smell; it sensed Destiny life by some other means.

Curdis lost patience. "We'll have to catch another one. Greegry, get down from there. Thonny, find a stick. You get to the far side of that clump—*that* clump, way away from Killer—and you beat your way through. Anything jumps up, whack it. You're trying to scare it this way, right? Greegry! Find a stick and go help Thonny. Jemjem-jemmy?"

"It's dead, Curdis."

"Dump it and stand by with the cage. Get your gloves on."

Jemmy opened the cage and dumped the little shelled corpse and the withering weeds he'd put in with it. He began picking fresh yellow and bronze lace.

Killer wailed, a long, loud cry of warning. Then its whips began flailing around it, lashing the Destiny plants at root level. It slid slowly through the dark patch, lashing everything in its way. Though it was not moving straight toward Jemmy, Jemmy eased back.

The decrepit machine didn't take orders anymore. It sought Destiny weeds and Destiny animals. When they were not about, its tropism was weak and it went where it would.

A tree-sized Destiny plant balked it. Killer pulled in its whips until it had rolled past. Plant life was only part of Killer's job. A human—Curdis—would pull up the stumps Killer left behind.

"Hyah!" Curdis bellowed, and three boys leapt on something that tried to sprint out from under them. Jemmy ran toward them. Thonny trapped its beak in a bag. The others were sitting on the shell; its short legs scrabbled in futility.

The Destiny thing was a bit big for the cage. They pushed its bulk in with the butt of a stick. "Good enough. It's jammed in, it can't crawl out," Junior said.

Killer had slashed away most of the weed patch. It rested now. Curdis picked up the cage and walked toward it.

Killer began to move.

Curdis retreated. Killer wasn't fast. They moved down toward the Road, Curdis and the cage, the old machine following.

The heavy cage was passed to Jemmy, then to Junior, and back to Curdis before they'd crossed three and a half kilometers to Warkan's Tavern. Curdis had Thonny and Brenda making bike runs to get lemonade to the others.

The sun was still high, and Quicksilver a bright spark above it. The dust plume that must be an oncoming caravan was closer now, but not close. Other young adults were beginning to gather.

The Warkan place was the Bloochers' neighbor, down the Road on the seaward side. It was still part farm. The four Warkan kids and their parents ran the tavern in the evenings. They kept a distillery and a truck garden going, and an extensive orchard. They did less weeding than most, and parts of the Warkan farm were often overgrown with dark Destiny plants.

The Tavern's waiters and waitresses were in their mid- and late teens. They had to talk to each other, if only to coordinate their tasks. Jemmy had worked through two caravan visits. He hoped to again.

Land that was allowed to become infested was subject to confiscation by the Council. But the Warkans could afford to lease Varmint Killer frequently. Likely they would pay the Council a premium to get Killer to Warkan's Tavern by sunset, for the entertainment value.

Mom and Dad weren't as friendly to the Warkans as in time past. They preferred Harry's Bar, near the Hub, that catered to an older crowd.

But Warkan's Tavern felt like home.

Youngsters in the gathering crowd danced near Killer, or hovered well back and shouted advice, while the Bloochers led the machine through the garden gate and around back.

Destiny life hadn't gained much of a foothold here. Jemmy had visited as a kid. He knew this place better than Curdis did. He took the cage and led Killer to the near edge of the pear grove.

Earthlife found Destiny's sun a little cool, a little red. It was Destiny life that sought shade. These trees of Earth had overly black shadows around their trunks: Destiny weeds.

Older men and women were finding vantage places across the Road. There was plenty of room on the ridge. A bonfire was a pale glitter. The Martinas were roasting potatoes up there. Curdis found people for a murderball game.

From the ridge you could see down to the shore and farther, out to where Carder's Boat had been anchored since Dad was a boy. That had been the fastest thing on water before the motor died. Dad's generation used to swim out to it with lunch bags, use it as a raft. Then Destiny devilhair weed moved in. Now weed blackened the water from the boat to the beach and further.

In a time now lost, Carder's Boat would carry a child anyplace he could dream. Now there were only the caravans, and that too was a dream.

They were all on the ridge when the dust plume arrived.

This had changed since Jemmy was a boy: caravans no longer came into Spiral Town. Merchants did, but not with their wagons. Caravans stopped about where Bloocher Farm began, where the Road turned. It was better for everyone. Here the chugs had a straight run down to the ocean, and chug droppings need not soil civic pavement.

The wagons began stopping along a kilometer of Road. They stopped well apart. Then the wagonmasters went among the chugs and released their harness.

Twenty chugs pulled most wagons, with here and there a chug missing. From his high perch Jemmy was able to count eighteen wagons. Close to four hundred chugs streamed across black salt grass, then sand, toward the ocean and in.

There was not much to be seen after that. The merchants were opening their wagons. That was of interest if you had money. The teens on the ridge were generally disappearing in the direction of dinner, and so did the Bloochers.

Jemmy took the speckles shaker down. He measured a careful half-jigger and kneaded it into the bread dough, pulled it into two loaves, and put it in the oven. He shook the speckles jar again, reached up, and put it away.

"Curdis," he said, "we need more speckles."

"Margery?"

She'd heard. "It's a big caravan this time. Wait till tomorrow. They'll go cheaper."

Mom had three pots on the fire. She asked, "Margery? Can you handle this?"

"Yeah."

Mom went into the dining hall and sat beside Dad.

Margery reached for pot holders. Curdis moved up beside her and whispered something. She moved aside so that he could pull the heavy casserole out of the oven and take it to the table.

Dad said, "Saw the dust plume."

"Caravan's in town," Curdis said, and talked about moving Varmint Killer.

Dad nodded and nodded and presently asked, "Master Granger there?"

"I saw him," Jemmy said. Master Granger was an older man, proprietor of the lead wagon, though a younger woman drove. He and Dad had been friends. Jemmy and Dad had taken Granger and his driver to Harry's Bar, before Dad's accident.

Dad nodded and didn't suggest doing that again. Some days his mind worked better than others. Dad could barely get out of the house.

He wanted to know everything about today. Jemmy talked, with some help from Thonny, while Mom helped him eat.

The New Hann. The caravan. Chugs in a sand-colored wave rolling down the sand into the ocean.

Mom and the girls were talking about marriages, crops, weather, prices.

Jemmy had heard this too often, endless permutations, endlessly the same. He waited for an instant's pause and jumped into it. "Dad, how far down the Road have you gotten?"

"Oh, hell, Jemmy. Not far. We used to visit the Warkans, swim there, when the Warkans were the farthest. I hear tales, but . . . I don't think I ever got as far as where you were today."

The Road. He might never learn more of the Road than he'd learned from the schooling programs.

"Your uncle Eezeek had to go down the Road for awhile. Folk at Haven took him in—"

"Eezeek died years ago," Mom said.

But the merchants knew. Maybe somebody could get them talking.

Quicksilver glowed among lesser stars, just on the horizon.

A cart moved silently past the Bloocher clan toward Warkan's Tavern, moved by electricity and an old motor. It carried huge rolls of Begley cloth sheeting from the cavern in Mount Apollo: the most important product Spiral Town had to sell. It ghosted past the tavern and stopped by the lead wagon.

Normally roomy for the crowd it pulled in, Warkan's was just adequate when a caravan was in town. It wasn't just the merchants. Every human being between fifteen and twenty-five was at Warkan's Tavern tonight.

The older Spirals wore dancers on their feet. No room to dance in here. Outside, later, on the Road, in the dark—

Rooms normally closed had been opened. The big bar would be inhumanly crowded, and Jemmy led his brethren into one of the outer rooms. They'd be able to breathe here, and Varmint Killer was sparkling, darting, spitting threads of green light, and putting on a fine show outside the big windows.

Tunia Judda was here, far across the big room. Tunia and Jemmy had been watching each other for years. Their parents were friends, and something might come of that, but they hadn't spoken of anything permanent. They'd dance on the Road later tonight.

Jemmy played at catching her eye. Never worked. Women probably did the same thing men did: get a friend to do the looking.

A few merchants were already here. Jemmy knew he shouldn't stare, but . . . They dressed in layers, in bright colors and patterns. Each man carried a gun, and each woman too.

Rachel Harness had grown up lovely and a little twisted. She'd been feeding herself and her speckles-shy mom since she was a little girl. When the rest went to their homes for dinner, Rachel and her mom had stayed on the ridge to picnic and to watch.

"We didn't see a trace of the chugs for over an hour," she told the girls at her table, unmindful of the clear fact that boys were listening too. "The merchants were all settling in, pitching tents, setting up cookfires. They didn't look worried at all. Then here came the chugs, a great long wave of them, all the chugs at once. The merchants all dropped what they were doing and climbed up on their wagons! They settled on their bellies and pulled their guns out."

The merchants waited for service with more patience than locals did. They were listening to Rachel Harness with discreet amusement, men and women both.

"Now here came—I don't know any word for them," Rachel said. "They look like big toothy fish swimming through sand—"

A merchant, a man, turned in his chair and spoke to Rachel. "Sharks. They're all along this coast."

Rachel didn't quite know how to handle that. She pretended she hadn't heard, but she was blushing. "—Fins all along both sides of them, low down along the belly. Nasty beaks. They were faster than the chugs, but the chugs had a head start. They came plodding back to the wagons and hid under them. The merchants started shooting. For ten minutes they shot at the, the sharks. They killed maybe ten before the rest turned tail. Warkan's Beach is going to *stink* in three days' time."

Next to the man who had spoken, a merchant woman spoke to Rachel. "Willy's new to the train. Forgive him."

Rachel nodded graciously. "But sure. I'm Rachel."

"Hillary. It's a good bargain for the chugs, Rachel. Pull our wagons, get our protection. The lungsharks are the reason we carry guns—"

"Will anyone sell me speckles?"

The merchant woman turned in some annoyance. The noise level had dropped. Many were turning to the doorway, or turning away, pretending nothing had happened.

Everyone knew that merchants didn't sell when they were at dinner.

But everyone knew Evleen. She was nine when her dad died. After that she didn't get enough speckles, until someone noticed. Deprived late like that, she didn't have the look of a speckle-shy. She looked like any eighteen-year-old girl. But it had touched her mind.

The merchants were trying to ignore Evleen. So were the Spiral women. Wouldn't any of *them* stop her? But no man could speak to her, so Jemmy turned back to his table. Look for conversation, start a quarrel, any kind of distraction.

But his attention snagged on a familiar face—a merchant, he'd seen that man before!—as the man reached out and pulled Evleen into his lap.

The merchant was big and brawny. His speech was slurred by a merchant's accent, and something more. Hard to believe that he could get himself drunk so soon after shooting down a pack of, what had the woman called them? Sharks?

Evleen's response was friendly. She and the brawny merchant said a few words to each other. The merchant pulled out a transparent pouch of speckles.

Jemmy was on his feet. He had to *do* something. He had no idea what he would say to the man. Suddenly it didn't matter, because Thonny was shaking the man's arm, shouting into a thick silence, and then the man's arm swung out and Thonny went down with his arms across his face.

Jemmy's hand closed on the merchant's shoulder from behind.

Evleen went flying. The merchant was up and turning, one hand under Jemmy's chin, and he *lifted*. His scruffy-bearded face was half the universe, and now Jemmy remembered him.

Eight years ago. He'd carried a tub of sherbet from Guilda's Place. He'd blasted a hole through a watermelon for all the children of Spiral Town to see. Vivid as Hell, Jemmy remembered the watermelon exploding like blood all over Davish Scrivner.

Fedrick. He was hideously strong, and Jemmy hadn't ever been this frightened.

Evleen was trying to get up. She cried, "Nooo, Jemmy, I don't want to be like Rachel's ma!"

His feet were off the floor. A wall was against his back. In an instant his throat would be crushed. Fedrick was in his face, and he remembered.

Remembered the gun.

In Fedrick's belt.

Here. Jemmy had the gun butt. Jemmy had seen what such a weapon could do to a melon. He lifted and turned it and pulled the trigger.

The sound was deafening. The gun lurched in Jemmy's hand. Fedrick gaped in horror and let him loose.

Jemmy dropped to the floor. He looked down at what he'd done, and it was worse than he could have imagined.

There was a hole in Fedrick, in his left side, pumping blood. Blood spilled down his shirt and pantaloons. A man Fedrick's size had Fedrick by the shoulder, and that man's horror was a match for Fedrick's.

Fedrick's eyes turned up and he started to fall. The other man took a moment to ease him to the floor. Evleen gibbered in fear, staring wide-eyed at Fedrick. Now the big trader let go of Fedrick, and Fedrick fell, and Jemmy saw what Evleen saw.

The hole in Fedrick's back looked as big as Jemmy's head.

The silence was ending, and men were starting to stand up.

Jemmy ran.

The near door was past several merchants, and they were all getting up. Jemmy ran through tables of Spiral women instead. A lone merchant gaudy in gray and yellow had his belt for an instant before Jemmy ripped loose.

He almost took the stairs; pictured how many guns would pick him off if they all had a clear shot; ran around and out the Warkans' front door.

The window above the front door was one that opened. He remembered Addard and Sandy and Telema Warkan shouting through it, heads together, long ago.

Jemmy jumped and had the sill; pulled himself up, pulled the window open and was back inside on the landing halfway up. Flat on the floor, catching his breath, while traders and Spiral men swarmed below him and outside.

He crawled the rest of the way to the second floor. Through Addard's room to the balcony, down the outside stair to the truck garden.

The truck garden was a jungle in spots. Killer was busy at one end. Jemmy worked his way through shadow and weeds at the other end, into the less cultivated regions of the Warkan farm, making away from the Road.

✳ 4 ✳

Leavetaking

Probes have gone before. We expected an Earthlike world, Norn, and from orbit it seems all that we hoped. I've renamed it Destiny.
—Daryl Twerdahl, Defensive Ecology

Warkan farmland trailed off toward the sea. The land was barren rock and sand. It would barely support Destiny life and it barely hid Jemmy Bloocher.

The old fence was another ancients' miracle. Corrosion had not touched it in more than two centuries. It ran for over a mile between Bloocher and Warkan land, all the way into the shallow waves. The fence was three grades of mesh laid over each other, filters to stop anything from seeds to sharks to chugs.

Spiral children learned early: those fine strands would cut flesh.

The first settlers must have been anal-retentive about property rights. Or was this another attempt to confine Destiny?

The fence would cut a chug's mouth. Merchants never released chugs close to the fence.

But the fence didn't stop Destiny seaweed.

Here at the shoreline a grove of black and yellow-green devilhair ran into the sea and out as far as Carder's Boat. Weed had nearly swallowed the boat; had entirely swallowed the fence. By using the fence as a frame, the weed gained access to sunlight and the sea's nutrients too.

Jemmy reached the beach at a run. He swarmed over the humped weed onto Bloocher turf and kept running. Adrenaline raged in his blood. He

40

wanted to run until the breath seared his lungs . . . but every Spiral knew where he must come. Any of them might tell a merchant.

He spared a moment's glance for the settler's miracle offshore. They'd never find him there! and for good reason. A swimmer would never reach Carder's Boat. He'd be tangled in the weed and drowned.

He stopped, his chest heaving. Then he made himself crawl through the rows of wheat, uphill toward the house.

It seemed quiet. Merchants would have flooded the house with light and noise.

Jemmy went in through the root cellar, then up into the kitchen, softly, softly.

Loaves of bread were still in the oven. He left them for the moment.

More stairs, well lighted. There was light under his parents' door, and under Junior's. Margery's. Margery and *Curdis*. He eeled into his room and stood in the dark, thinking.

The Warkans had their reasons to let the fence go like that, but the Bloochers had no excuse for such slovenliness.

Not his business, now. Jemmy Bloocher wasn't going to be running Bloocher Farm after all. What could he take? Just the backpack and the hiking gear in it. Real shoes. A flash, a canteen, blankets; thick hiker's gloves, because much of Destiny life was armed with thorns or poison. He added underwear and socks and shirts, going by feel in the dark. He was already wearing a jacket. What else? Anything he left behind now was gone forever. Pen and a pad of paper—

He heard the front door slam. Only minutes now, he thought—and his own door slammed back against the wall and light blazed in his eyes.

Jemmy was standing with his hands spread wide and showing empty when the ceiling lamp came on. Curdis lowered the flash. "Jemmy," he said. "Thought it might be some thieving merchant."

Jemmy said, "I've killed a merchant."

Curdis's eyes only narrowed, but Jemmy heard Junior's gasp. She wedged herself around Curdis and squeaked, "Jemmy!," swallowing the scream because they'd wake their parents.

Curdis turned out the lamp. "We're too close to the Warkan place," he said.

"Why would you—even—" Junior caught herself and was silent.

The dark was welcome. Jemmy said, "I have to run."

Thonny's voice spoke from the hall. "He was trying to save me. Even so, Jemmy, that was *crazy.*"

"I know—"

"*Crazy,* Jemmy!" Brenda.

41

Curdis said briskly, "Just hide for a while. Get your camp gear and—you've got it already? Hide in the hills. Wait for the caravan to go away. We don't know anything, didn't see anything, can't guess—"

"They come three times every two years. Everyone knows where Bloocher Farm is. Everyone knows who I am!"

"Three times every two years, you just aren't here. Caravans come, you go. Bloocher F-Farm—" Curdis stopped.

That was the sticking point, all right. Margery was Bloocher Farm for now, but in half a year she and Curdis Hann would be farming the New Hann Holding. The head of Bloocher Farm *had* to deal with merchants, if only for speckles.

Jemmy said, "Curdis, I want to take the speckles bread that's in the oven. Okay? Thonny, you'll have Bloocher Farm when Curdis and Margery move out." They'd have to postpone moving, he thought, until Thonny was older. Curdis must see that already. "If merchants want to search the farm for a fugitive, go them one better. Lead them down to where the fence goes into the sea. It's covered with enough weed to feed a caravan, the chugs would have a head start on the sharks, and we'll get the shore cleaned off to boot."

Thonny nodded, eyes glassy, mouth open.

Curdis said, "Hold it. Jemmy, caravans use the Road."

Jemmy hadn't thought quite that far.

"The merchants only just got here. They'll stay awhile," Thonny said. "Jemmy, if you can get around them they can't catch you. Chugs don't move fast."

"They'll send someone to block the Road," Curdis said.

Thonny and Brenda and Margery came into Jemmy's room and found seats on the bed, the bureau, the footlocker. This was going to take some thought.

"One step at a time," Curdis said. "The merchants will search Spiral Town. They'll demand that, and nobody will stop them. You can't hide in town."

"I've got to leave."

"Have you thought of just hiding in the hills?"

Jemmy said, "We hike the hills, but merchants must know that whole range end to end. And if they found me—Curdis, they wouldn't have to take me to trial. *Bang* and plant a tree. Who'd know?"

"You'd be pretty conspicuous on the Road, too. How do you think you'll get around them?"

"It's our Road too," Thonny said tentatively.

Brenda said, "Yeah. Let's go for a walk."

In the dark one could just see Thonny's disgusted look. But Curdis tasted the notion. "Go for a nice long walk down the Road? Me and Thonny? Jemmy, you go over the hills. You can stay hidden in the brush for a few days, can't you? Meet us—"

"I'm coming too," Brenda announced.

Curdis ignored her. "Meet us somewhere down the Road, Jemmy. Then I'll trade packs with you. From then on, you're Curdis Hann: *me*. You come back by Road, with Thonny. I'll come back through the hills. If I'm caught, hey, I'm just off camping. I'll—"

"Come back by way of the New Hann," Margery said. "You're tending our own land."

Curdis nodded. It would give him legitimacy if he were caught.

"I'm coming too," Brenda repeated.

Margery said, "All right, Brenda."

"Margery—"

"Darling, you'll need her to talk to merchant women!"

Thonny suggested, "Bicycles?"

"Good," said Curdis. "We can let things settle for a day or two and *still* beat Jemmy to . . . where shall we meet?"

"There aren't that many bicycles on the Road. I'll find you," Jemmy said.

Curdis sat in the dark, moving his lips, while they watched him. Presently he said, "The merchants search Spiral Town and don't find you. Your camping gear is gone. So's our store of speckles, so you buy some more, Margery—"

Jemmy said, "I wouldn't take your speckles—"

"You would if you were going forever. Instead, we can bring you home after the merchants have searched the farm and Spiral Town. You take my place here. They're searching the hills by then, but at worst they find just me, camping on my own land. After they're gone you can grow a beard or something. Lie about your age, marry someone, move to another farm. We'll have time to work that out."

"I like it," Junior (Margery!) said. "I wish I could come—"

"You're in charge here," Curdis said gently.

They were deciding his future.

Margery said, "Okay. Thonny and Brenda and Curdis on bikes. Don't look at me like that, Thonny, you're brother and sister! *Not* betrothed. Oh, *hell!*"

"What?"

"Curdis, you can't pass for Jemmy."

Curdis had straight black hair, yellow-dark skin, eyes with an epicanthic fold. Hmmm? Jemmy said, "I only have to pass for Curdis coming back. Going out is when they'll be looking to be sure he's not me. Me, escaping. Going out, you're innocent. Let them look."

They closed the curtains and turned on the lights. Margery posed Jemmy next to Curdis, examined them and said, "No."

And Brenda was a girl.

But Thonny moved up next to Jemmy, shorter by three inches, and Margery said, "Maybe on a bicycle."

They took all of Jemmy's clothes out of the bureaus and carried them in armloads into Thonny's room. They began putting together matching outfits.

"You can switch scarves and hats," Margery said, and they tried it. "Right. Thonny, you stay on the bike. When you're not on the bike, you don't lean on the bike, don't lean on a wall, don't *lean.* Stand up like a man. Be careful coming back. Camp out on the New Hann land until someone comes for you.

"Jemmy, coming back, you're Thonny. You *always* lean on the bike, or a wall. Don't be seen standing straight up. Curdis, you wear those dancers going out, but you put those high-heel shyster-stomper boots in your bike bag. You're taller than Thonny going out, you'd better be taller than Jemmy coming back."

Curdis nodded in the semidark.

"Now, how did it happen, the killing? *Hush,* Jemmy. Brenda?"

Junior wanted Brenda's version, then Thonny's, and never bothered with Jemmy's. Then she told them all, "Take your time going and coming. Stop and talk to everyone. Thonny, Brenda, if a merchant asks you about the killing, you tell him. 'I was there, I saw it all.' Babble! But you haven't seen Jemmy since then, and you don't think you ever will. Jemmy, you heard everything Thonny said? You tell it that way coming back. . . ."

Once again Jemmy moved along the shore. Two more fences to cross. He went back up through rows of lettuce, the Wayne Holding. Where he crossed the Road it was deep into its first curve.

Gasoline Alley, then the next inward loop of Road, then Baker Street.

The graveyard had been well beyond the town for two good centuries, but Spiral Town had reached it at last. Jemmy stepped from the empty shops of Harrow Street into a grove of willows.

Destiny life wouldn't grow among the graves. The Spiral Town graveyard covered more than a square mile with nothing but Earthlife: long, lank grass, clover, and trees up to 240 years old.

Jemmy drifted like smoke among the trees. There was cover to hide him. The eyes he expected might be imaginary after all.

A lifegiver of Spiral Town would be buried with a handful of seeds. His will might name the variety of tree. If several sprouted, tenders would transplant all but one, and a marker would be fired into the bark for the lifegiver within its roots.

The oldest trees were huge, chosen for majesty: oaks, banyans, redwoods.

Majestic trees hadn't always survived well, and variety had come into fashion. For a long lifetime the lifegivers bore nut trees and fruit trees. Then someone had decided that the practice was disrespectful or something.

But an extensive grove still bore fruit and nuts. Jemmy picked a handful of cherries, a few plums, an orange. He stuffed his pockets, then settled in the shadows of the gnarled old trees to eat.

The markers around him were all above eye level. Jemmy tried to read them, but they were only a glitter in the dark. Holograms need light.

When the holomarker gun failed it would be a major tragedy. It was settler magic, irreplaceable.

On an ordinary night Jemmy would have been asleep by now. Though he felt that he might never sleep again, he was weary. His life had lost all direction in one deafening blast. Now the bark against his back was too comfortable. It would be easy to stay where he was.

Thonny's hat was a bit small, a bit tight. He took it off and waved it at the flies buzzing his ears. The buzzing went away, then came back, sounding like sleep.

Had he been dozing?

He surged to his feet, swung his pack onto his back, and was in motion. If he sat down again, they'd find him asleep in the graveyard come morning!

The slopes above Spiral Town resembled chaparral, the dwarf forest of California. It was Earthlife laced with surviving Destiny life, too thick and too hostile to hike through. The bare rock above would not hide a fleeing murderer.

But plants only covered the slopes up to fifteen hundred feet above the Road, and stopped quite suddenly. *Frost line*, the teaching programs would have called it, but Destiny never got that cold. The Destiny plants ran out of something else: air pressure, water, soil nutrients, something. Earthlife grew higher up, but sparsely.

Jemmy was at the frost line when lights came on above him.

He'd ducked back into the chaparral before his mind quite caught up.

Lights glared and men moved around a great ragged hole in the side of Mount Apollo. The lights within the cavern showed great dark silver-gray sheets peeling away like the pages of a thousand books, everywhere along the walls and roof. A man moved to the back of the cavern and pulled. Then, nearly hidden under layers of Begley cloth sheeting, he staggered toward a cart.

It was Jemmy's first sight of the Apollo Caverns. Children weren't allowed here, even older children.

Argos had carried several experimental von Neumann devices . . . a phrase every child learned and few could define.

Begley cloth was one. A handful of self-reproducing machines just big enough to be dots had been dropped into a hole in a hillside. For two and a half centuries they had been eating into Mount Apollo, carving out a fairyland underground as they followed veins of . . . silicon and some small set of metals; he'd seen the list in one of the teaching programs . . . and made it into sheets that would turn sunlight into power, fringed with wires to carry the power to machines.

Also, the dots made more of themselves.

The sheeting was Spiral Town's most dependable trade good, and the caravan was in town. He should have avoided Mount Apollo at all costs. But he damned well didn't dare wait for daylight!

He scuttled along the border between the chaparral and the bare rock above, hunching like a chug until he was out of sight of the Apollo Caverns, and far beyond.

By night the New Hann Holding was just another patch of wilderness, and Jemmy couldn't tell where he crossed it. It might have made a nice resting place. Merchants might see it that way too. Jemmy kept moving.

He walked through the night. Rarely did the Road come in view. At daylight he crawled into a manzanita grove and let his mattress inflate.

On tilted ground, in a glare of sunlight sieved through red manzanita trunks and the branches and lace of some tall Destiny tree, sleep was hard to find. He slept with evil memories. *Eyes and mouth wide in horror: Fedrick felt what Jemmy Bloocher had done to him. Blood flooded his vest. The fist-sized hole in his back—*

From time to time he woke and, with his eyes closed against the filtered light, thought how much he had lost.

Somewhere around noon he ate half the speckle bread. It was his last speckles for the foreseeable future.

What would satisfy the merchants? Just how badly did they want his blood? Would a face-saving gesture satisfy them? Or his exile? Or would they take reprisals against Bloocher Farm?

Grow a beard or something. Lie about your age, marry someone and move to another farm.

They'd been pressed for time, trying to decide what to do *now*. Even so, Jemmy hadn't liked hearing that. Even if it worked, even if the merchants let it work . . . how was it better than just moving on down the Road? Either way, the man who had been Jemmy Bloocher was gone.

Better, maybe, if he died here in the hills.

Many forms of Destiny life were poisons. Hadn't that been trollhair, the last time he'd stopped at a stream? It was hair-fine silver stuff, soft-looking threads with very sharp tips. He'd given those clumps a *lot* of room. Being scratched by trollhair was an easy death, a long slide into sleep.

His family need never know. *Jemmy never came to meet us.*

What had sent his thoughts straying toward suicide?

Jemmy realized with a start that he was sleeping in the shade of a fool cage.

There were fool cages growing among the manzanita, all around him. Four feet of trunk flared into a thorny oval cage of black wicker decorated with bronze and scarlet lace, and a few tiny bones in the cage.

A Destiny bird could perch on any of a number of Destiny plants and find lace to eat. Some plants grew gaudy lace displays so that birds would transport their seeds. But the lace within a fool cage was a lure and a trap. A bird could perch on the upper branches of a fool cage, but any breeze that rattled the branches would cause them to trap a bird's feet, pull it in.

Most Destiny birds had learned to stay away. These bones belonged to Earthlife.

Curdis and Thonny and Brenda would expect to find him on the Road. Jemmy rolled his mattress, got his pack on, and crawled until the plants were thick enough to hide him walking upright.

The water table was lower now: the plants reached no more than three hundred meters above the flatland and the Road. Jemmy traveled by night. By day there were plants to hide him. He slept away from water. A stream might make him a target.

At night the star fields were gaudy, gorgeous. Quicksilver was brilliant but tiny and only showed for a few minutes after sunset. Kismet, Destiny's massive little moon, cast no more light even at the full. Any meteor might be *Cavorite* in reentry, or *Argos* among the asteroids, making a few seconds' burn. The land at night was black; a man could hurt himself thinking he saw more detail than was there.

He could only glimpse the Road in patches, and the sea far beyond. Once he saw a boat moving parallel to shore. Once, a house or shed that looked abandoned. He hadn't yet seen a human being. Then again, he didn't intend to.

There were Earthlife birds everywhere, a hundred varieties of song at morning and evening, hawks hovering on updrafts by day, owls hunting by night. He'd seen the shells and bones the predators had made of Destiny birds. And he'd seen fool cages everywhere, with Earthlife bones and beaks in them. The coming of *Columbiad* and *Cavorite* had been good for the fool cages.

They were good for Jemmy. Any bird still flapping inside a fool cage must be fresh and edible. He found a smallish turkey on the second night, and he pulled on his thick gloves and reached in through the thorns and strangled it. After dawn he felt safe building a tiny fire in a circle of rocks. The perpetual wind was enough to whip the smoke away.

On the third night he collected three little birds, pigeons maybe.

At the fourth dawn he crossed above a waterfall, then crawled down-hill into brush. The stream had cut a gorge that ran down to the Road and through it. Someone had built a little bridge over the water.

Three men and a woman had set up camp near the bridge. The chugs were gone—in the water, likely—but the wagon nearly blocked the bridge.

Jemmy slept away from the water. From time to time he crawled back to the waterfall to spy on the merchant guards. Their eyes would see only the falling water; a tiny, distant moving man would be lost in all that motion. *Right?*

They weren't cheerful as merchants usually were. The woman was middle-aged and snappish; the younger men obeyed her with little grace.

He was moving back to the stream in midafternoon, careful as ever, when he heard a familiar shout.

"Brenbrenbrendaa!"

He crawled to the edge of the falls and looked down.

The falls drowned out speech. Thonny and Curdis were talking to the guards, to the men. The woman was talking to Brenda. The merchants' manner had grown cordial.

He crawled closer, staying in the thicket of fool cages. He got down to where the water wasn't so loud. Then sage and tumbleweed were growing too close together and he feared merchant guards would see them wiggle.

He heard Thonny shout, "Curdcurdcurdis! That's the last coin we've got!" And the sound of merchant laughter, and Brenda's laugh too.

Three bicycles moved on, across the bridge and down the Road.

Now all Jemmy had to do was catch them.

They would have gained from better planning. How on Earth was he going to catch bicycles?

Jemmy was seething with impatience, but he'd have to be crazy to move now, in daylight, with merchants just below him. He crawled back among the fool cages and tried to sleep.

They must know they'd have to wait.

The next stream. They were past the merchant guards; why not stop? They'd wait at the next stream, and he'd see them and know it was safe to come down. And if he didn't see them?

No way could he sleep. He crawled up to where plants thinned out to bare rock, and he kept crawling.

Where water next crossed the Road, they weren't waiting. Jemmy made sure of that, then moved on.

What stopped him next was more than a stream.

The plant interface dipped, an arrowhead shape pointing at the Road. Jemmy's gaze followed the tree line down along rock that had run like wax. Frozen lava ran up to the ridge a thousand feet above him, and down almost to the Road itself, ending in a broad patch of green Earth-life trees and water gleaming between.

Interesting.

Jemmy could picture the giant landers *Cavorite* and *Columbiad* hovering on either side of the crest, moving parallel on pillars of violet flame bright enough to blind any witness, burning off the life of Destiny. Then return to seed the slopes with Earthlife. One of the ships must have paused here . . . yes, and he could see why. Above him the ridgeline bent by forty degrees.

Cavorite on the broad side had waited for *Columbiad* on the narrow side (or vice versa) to round the curve.

Water at the point of the lava triangle, then a thick stand of Earthlife trees, then the Road. The far side of the Road was a thriving village. There were shops along the Road, and a setback wide enough and long enough for a whole caravan, and a wide stream running to the sea, spreading into a delta at the end.

Who were these people? It had never occurred to Jemmy that there was this much of civilization beyond Spiral Town. Somewhere the merchants went for their goods, and to trade what they got from the Spirals. And in between . . . ?

And how could he cross bare and slippery rock?

He couldn't. He was going to have to go down.

✳ 5 ✳

On the Road

Twerdahl and his idiot crew are running away. We isolated ourselves on this island for a *reason*. Whatever our problems, we'll solve them *here*.
—Julius Radner, Council Chairman

Where the wall of ancient lava converged to a point, there was a shine of water, then leafy Earthlife trees. From high up it appeared that the forest ran right to the Road. As Jemmy descended, it became clear that he was approaching a swamp.

He wasn't eager to wade into that.

The trees were cypress and mangrove on a wide spread of shallow water. There were no competing Destiny trees, but the trees were festooned with what he first thought were snakes. Snakes everywhere . . . motionless black snakes winding through webs of yellow-green lace.

Vines. One was a variety he didn't recognize, but the others were Julia sets, the same vine the elder Hanns cultivated. The Hanns must have played the bonsai trick, stunting the plant by pruning and by keeping it half starved. These were huge. In places they were strangling the mangroves.

Something rippled along the water. A snake, a real one this time. Another moved among the vines. Something bigger shied from it: a man. Jemmy sank slowly into a crouch, then tried to ease behind a tree.

The man—boy—broke through to the open with evident relief. Looked around. Didn't see Jemmy. Jemmy stepped out of hiding, and Thonny jumped.

"You all right?"

"Fine," Thonny said. "How was it?"

"Easy going. How did you make out?"

51

"There are merchants at the bridge!" Thonny was excited, enjoying himself immensely. "They asked about a merchant that got killed in Spiral Town. We changed the story a little."

Fear rose up in Jemmy's throat. "Changed *how?*"

"Uh, well, we talked it over. Curdis says I'm the traders' best witness. I mean *Thonny Bloocher* is. I'm your oldest brother and I saw it all. Brenda wouldn't see as much because it was all men and Brenda's a girl—"

And so she wouldn't have watched men quarreling. "Right. So?"

"So they would have turned us back and how would you find us on the Road? So I didn't say I'm Thonny Bloocher. I'm Tim Hann."

"With those eyes?"

"One of the merchants said that. I got insulted."

"Curdis's idea?"

"Yeah. The real Tim Hann would have been Curdis's older brother, but he died a year old."

"Tim Hann. I'm Tim Hann. Great. Anything else?"

Jemmy's fury rendered Thonny mute.

If he couldn't get Thonny talking any other way, Jemmy was ready to hold him under water. This was his *life* they were playing for! He said, "Look, if I'm Tim Hann, I have to *sound* like Tim Hann. Did Tim Hann *see* the killing?"

Thonny nodded.

"Where were you?"

"Across the room, near the fireplace."

"Did Jemmy Bloocher do it? Fine. With the merchant's gun? What does he look like? What did you *change?*"

"I didn't *lie.* It was just a better fight."

"Curdis was listening? I can ask him?"

"Yeah."

"What were they like, these merchants you met?"

"We saw three men at the bridge, with a woman. They searched us. We bought some stuff from them. They lost interest when we said we were broke. You're still broke going back, okay?"

"They'll expect me to know them coming back?"

Thonny thought it over, then shrugged.

"Okay. Where are we? What are all these people doing here?"

"I don't know. *Living* here. I peeled off before we got close to anyone."

"Uh-huh."

"Four or five of them saw us together. Older people, Mom's age. They dress like, well, like Jael Harness."

"Did they wave? Throw rocks? Do they think we're weird?"

"They pointed at us and started shouting, maybe at us, maybe at the houses. Women too. Curdis and Brenda went on toward them, but I did what Curdis told me. I peeled off. Didn't let any of them get a close look. Tied the bike to a tree. You just go through the swamp, get on the bike, and go join them."

Jemmy began to wonder if he sounded properly grateful. He said, "Sounds like it all went like somebody planned it," and smiled and hugged his brother.

That pleased Thonny. He asked, "How did you make out?"

Jemmy tried to tell him. "There's practically nobody on the Road. I mean at night, I only went at night. Stay with the frost line and you won't be seen. There's plenty of water, springs. If you see a bird flapping in a fool cage, that's your dinner. If it isn't moving, leave it."

"We trading backpacks?"

They did that. Jemmy said, "I made some fires. Did you see anything? Smoke?"

"No."

"Tiny fires in rock pits. I left some fire pits. You break them up when you finish with them."

They looked at each other.

Jemmy said, "Thonny, thanks."

"It's okay." Thonny adjusted his backpack, grinned at his brother, and began to climb.

"Hats!" Jemmy shouted.

He sailed Thonny's hat up to Thonny. Thonny sailed his down to Jemmy. It flew over his head and settled on the water.

Jemmy waded into the gloom. The water was knee-deep and tepid.

Jemmy's hat was sinking out of sight. Jemmy retrieved it and put it on. It streamed water, soaked like a sponge, but he had no other way to carry it. He was glad to have it back.

The air smelled alien: wet and thick with greenery and rot. He crawled over tremendous roots. The water was thigh-deep now, icy around his ankles.

Crotch-deep. Was this the right direction? Seen from overhead, the grove hadn't seemed this big. Now he feared he'd never reach the Road.

Something limbless slid through the water. Again, nearer now. Julia sets hung thickly from the branches. From time to time a vine lifted a wedge-shaped head and flickered its tongue, to watch and sniff for clumsy prey.

Bright and colorful they were, and they shied from him too. Some snakes described in teaching programs were poisonous. Interstellar travelers wouldn't have *brought* poisonous snakes, would they? These were Earthlife, brought for decoration. Someone in Sol system's planning section must have liked snakes.

But Jemmy didn't, and the thought of being *touched* by such a thing—

He'd reached the Road. But the dark water was waist-deep, and the Road was a smoothly curved rim of gray rock at eyebrow level. His hands slid over it. He couldn't get the grip that would pull him out.

Cursing, he wrestled his way up a banyan, then far enough along a branch to drop to the Road.

He rested on his knees, panting and dripping, his hands on its warm surface. The Road. He was home. By its look, by its feel, this was the Road that ran past Bloocher Farm.

But the houses on the far side were angular little boxes with drastically peaked roofs.

Three girls were coming toward him. They looked much alike, pale skin and narrow noses and hair the color of butter. Sisters or cousins, Jemmy's age. They dressed in older clothes of mismatched color that didn't quite fit.

Who were these people? Where had they come from?

Exiles from Spiral Town? *When?*

And where had Thonny left his bike? The girls shouldn't get the idea that this new Tim Hann didn't know.

Could be worse: boys would ask him embarrassing questions.

Tied to a tree? That would be down in the swamp! But Thonny wouldn't have left his bike that way. And if he'd peeled off as soon as they saw locals, he must have left the bike up the Road toward Spiral Town.

Up the Road by nearly a mile, it tilted. Four big robust trees seemed to be right up against it. Jemmy walked toward them, followed at a distance by the girls.

The huge roots of five . . . seven banyans were actually lifting the edge of the Road.

There: Thonny's bike.

"Hello," one of the girls called. "Are you Timmy Hann?"

Jemmy freed the bike and wheeled it around. He didn't know what to do. But they'd spoken, they couldn't be much surprised if he talked back. He said, "Tim Hann," correcting their pronunciation.

"I'm Loria. Everybody's down by the beach." She was Jemmy's height, the tallest of the girls. Narrow nose, narrow chin, wide eyes that held his own. Her clothes looked like she'd dressed in the dark, in garments borrowed half from Spiral Town, half from merchants. "Can I ride your thing?"

"Bicycle."

She waited.

They'd never seen a bike before, had they? On whim Jemmy handed it over to her. He held it steady while she got on, and showed her how to set her feet on the pedals. He avoided touching her. They talked to boys, but they might take *that* more seriously.

He rolled the bike forward, gave her a chance to find the feel of it, then let go. She stayed up. He ran alongside. Still up, learning to steer but not quite fast enough. She was going to fall into the swamp!

He lunged for the seat of the bike, brushed her where she sat, tried again and had it. Pulled back, leaning into it, and stopped her short of the edge. His fingertips burned. "I f-forgot to talk about b-brakes," he said.

Loria listened, looked where he pointed, nodded, and tried again. A few false starts and she wobbled in among the houses, laughing, faster than he could follow.

One of the girls said, "I'm Tarzana. That's Gl—"

"Glind Bednacourt. We're all Bednacourt—"

"The Bednacourt sisters." Narrow noses, narrow chins, wide dancing eyes. Tarzana took his arm, Glind took his other arm, and they walked him between the houses.

The houses were two deep, with truck gardens between. The mudflat beyond grew black Destiny sandweed that thinned out near the ocean. Fifty or sixty people were milling around braziers set on the bare mud. Others were down by the water.

Jemmy felt the blood freezing in his arteries. *They were all strangers.* He'd never seen so many strangers together. He hadn't guessed what that would do to him.

But the girls were urging him forward.

A few were examining Thonny's bike while Loria turned the pedals and the handlebars. Brenda— *There!* He'd found his sister.

Half a dozen men were out on the water, riding floating slabs. "Glind, what are those?"

"Boards."

Brenda was with other girls at the shore, and a couple of men too, watching them. Some of those had boards, and two of the men on the water were women. It was confusing, an optical illusion. He'd seen them as all men because they were together, all wearing sleeveless shirts.

Curdis was in a group around one of the braziers. He waved enthu-
siastically and called, "Timtimtimmy!"

Thanks for the reminder. "Curdis! There's a thousand kinds of trees
and a thousand kinds of snakes, and Destiny vines you could build a
city on." *And that gives Timtimtimmy a reason for going in there.*

"Typical. You dive into a jungle and ignore the people. Drew, you
really surprised us. We had no idea you were here. Tim, this is Drew
Bednacourt."

"Pleased," Drew Bednacourt said, smiling. He was white-haired and
muscular, Dad's age, and a white scar ran down his dark chest into his
short pants. "You surprised us too." His handshake was hard, horny.

Curdis said, "You're not *that* surprised."

Jemmy saw what he meant. Most of the locals weren't talking to the
Spirals. They were fishing or cooking or floating on boards in the water.

Drew said, "We've seen merchants all our lives. The caravan went
through two weeks ago. They'll be back in a week with whatever Haven
and the Spirals leave."

Tarzana looked Jemmy over. "He's already wet, Dad. Tim, want to go
for a swim? Do you know how to ride?"

Jemmy asked, "Ride?" Then he saw two men stand up on their boards
while a wave hurled them forward.

He *had* to try that.

They sat in a circle on the sand, eating in near darkness. The red of
sunset had faded. The only light was Quicksilver, a brilliant spark at the
ocean's rim.

Jemmy was exhausted. The long day might have worn him out, but
the surfing lesson was the finishing stroke. In the morning he was going
to hurt.

He listened, half-dozing, while Curdis and Brenda talked to the
Bednacourt girls and Cloochi boys. The girls were sisters born a year
apart, Tarzana nineteen, Loria eighteen, Glind seventeen. Drew, their
father, was cooking over the brazier with their mother, Wend, who
had been surfing. Harl and Susie Cloochi were older, Wend Bednacourt's parents.

The girls began passing out food. Jemmy didn't guess how hungry he
was until he bit into a chicken leg. Then he ate like a starving wolf,
whatever the girls brought him, chicken and corn and Earthlife fruit,
Destiny crab and Destiny seaweed.

Quicksilver disappeared in a blink. Now the only light was stars, and
a funny blue glow in the rolling waves.

Harl Cloochi said, "I'm an old man, Curdis. Is Quicksilver brighter than it used to be? I can never be sure. It's like Quicksilver disappears in a blink, and then the night's as black as inside my stomach."

"I'm only twenty-two," Curdis said.

"You're Spiral. You've still got machines that teach, they say."

"They're wearing out. Tim? Brenda? Remember anything about Quicksilver? From the schooling disks?"

Brenda did. "Quicksilver's closest to the sun, that must be why it's so bright. It's not very big. Quicksilver, Destiny, Volstaag, Hogun, Hela."

There was something else about Quicksilver. Something Jemmy had read and forgotten, and now it wouldn't come.

"How did you come here?" Curdis asked.

Susie Cloochi answered. "My father told me his family got in a fight with the Spirals. Mother was carrying me already. They took some seeds and stuff and came down the Road and found Twerdahl already here."

Jemmy exclaimed, *"Twerdahl?"*

Laughter. Susie said, "This place, we name it Twerdahl Town. After the Founders, the ones who took *Cavorite* and disappeared."

Jemmy laughed at himself. "I thought you meant the Twerdahls themselves."

"Your turn. You're the first Spirals we've seen in ages. What are you doing here?"

The silence stretched. Brenda or Curdis might have answers ready, but Jemmy couldn't know that, and in the dark he couldn't see their faces. He took the chance and said, "Following the path of the *Cavorite*. I want to know where they went."

Tarzana breathed, *"Cavorite!"*

"But you've got the teaching machines," old Susie Cloochi said. "Don't they tell you?"

All fatigue fled, Jemmy said, "Some. *Cavorite* left with forty crew. I know some of the names. Twerdahl, Tucker, Granger, Lyons, Doheny . . . Spiral Town was founded in 2490, but they called it Base One then. *Cavorite* left in 2498. You know they left a spiral of Road behind them? They never came home. Maybe they never planned to. Maybe something killed them."

Susie Cloochi said, "My family never went home. A good many families here never did. Folk do leave Spiral Town from time to time. Might it be that the *Cavorite* crew just wanted to get away?"

"Snakes," Jemmy said.

They looked at him. *"Snakes*, Tim?"

His mind had wandered, then closed its teeth on—"Snakes in the swamp. It just came to me, Miz Cloochi. *Cavorite* must have left those. Someone aboard *Cavorite* must have liked snakes."

"And swamps," said Brenda.

Jemmy looked back toward the swamp. "Can't you see it? They're drifting along. Flame mushing out violet under the skirt." He couldn't really picture that; he'd never seen a flame that hot; nobody had. "They could go faster if they were just trying to get away, but they're just drifting along, leaving a trail of melted rock behind them. Suddenly they're looking at a swamp.

"What can they do? They can boil the water, kill the Destiny weeds, but that won't make it into Road. They could go around it, uphill, but that wouldn't leave a Road for anything with wheels."

"Rocks," Brenda said. "They'd have to roll a line of rocks down across the water."

Curdis said, "We had tractors in Spiral Town, big machines for pulling a plow or pushing down a tree. They don't go anymore. *Cavorite* might have taken one."

Jemmy nodded, putting it into the picture. "Push a row of rocks across. Like stepping-stones. Then hover till the rock melts and the water boils. Wait till the swamp cools down, then seed—"

"No, T-Tim, that's a humongous thermal mass. You don't throw seeds in boiling water."

He nodded. "Right. They go on, making Road. Week or two later they come back and seed some trees—"

"Maybe a year."

"—and leave the snakes and anything else I didn't see. Damn."

Curdis said, "All right, what *damn?*"

"They weren't just runaways, the *Cavorite* crew. I always knew forty crew was too *tidy*. When you're running away, you don't wait for your numbers to come out *neat* like that. The Road was the point. If *Cavorite* came back this far to seed a swamp, why not come all the way back to Spiral Town?"

The Bednacourt sisters led them to a structure that was all one big room. "A lot of us slept here after the storm washed away some houses two years ago," Loria said. "Elsewise it's the House of Healing."

There was nothing like a bed. The Bloocher clan slept on the wide expanse of floor, covered in their own clothes.

In a moment when Brenda was surely asleep, Curdis spoke in the dark. "I had to turn down an offer from Loria."

Offer? Ah. "What did you say?"

"I said I'm married and Brenda's too young, but Timmy's not."

Jemmy's ears burned in the dark.

*   *   *

The sun hadn't risen over the mountains yet. The morning was cold. The water was colder for the first moments; then Jemmy's body stopped noticing. He and Tarzana fought their boards through the waves and paddled out to where others were sitting six in a row.

They waited, talking little. Sound carried very well over the water.

Jemmy asked, "Don't you get sharks around here?"

The pause lasted long enough that Jemmy thought nobody had heard him. Then one boy said, "I don't think they like the taste of the river. Sometimes one comes around. We get a lot of sharks when a caravan stops and three hundred chugs get their attention."

"Wave," Tarzana said.

The idea was to be moving as fast as the wave when it arrived. Paddle without falling off. When the board catches the wave, stand up. Jemmy had tried standing up yesterday. Today he didn't. Kneeling on a board as a wave hurled it toward the beach was tough enough.

Curdis asked the Twerdahl folk for work, and work was found. He and Brenda and Jemmy (make that *Tim*, start thinking *Tim*) knew how to garden, knew how to pull Destiny weeds.

"If we leave about now," Curdis said in midafternoon, "we'll get to the guarded bridge about sunset."

"I think they like us here," Brenda said doubtfully.

"Uh-huh. I don't guess Margery's worried about us yet, but, Brenda, I told the *merchants* we'd be coming back today."

Jemmy held up a hand. *Hold it.* "Sunset?"

"They saw Thonny around noon. Let's let them see *you* around sunset."

At noon and sunset, two views of "Tim Hann" could look quite different. Curdis continued, "Sunset, not dawn. They'd never believe we marched in the dark."

"Did the merchants tell you about Twerdahl Town?"

"Not a word," Curdis said in some irritation.

"*Nothing* about people living down the Road? Big surprise?"

"Big joke."

"So," said Jemmy, "we found a surprise and stayed an extra day. *That's* what they'll expect. Give them another day to forget what Tim Hann looks like."

Curdis grinned. "I like it here too. I didn't have the nerve to try those boards, Tim. How is it?"

Jemmy shook his head. "It's like, I can't *tell* a Twerdahl how to ride a bicycle. I can't *tell* you what surfing is like. Want us to show you? Brenda?"

"Yeah."

Brenda showed an aptitude for surfing. Curdis gave up early. He didn't like falling off in front of strange males.

The Bednacourt girls returned to the House of Healing with them that night. When the Bloocher clan curled into their blankets, the girls didn't leave.

Voices in the dark, men and women talking together. That was Loria: "You're good people. You have things to teach us. Some of what comes off the Road are parasites."

"We all do farm work," Curdis said. "We learn to look for what needs doing."

Glind: "We don't let anyone stay a *minute* if he's alone. Any man alone must be running from something."

"A woman?" Curdis.

"A woman alone might be running from, well, a man." Tarzana's voice.

Loria: "The only women we've ever seen on the Road were merchants. But there was a man called himself Haines—" And he was a murderer who hid in the swamp. He stole from the truck gardens when he could, until Destiny food and no speckles turned him into a skeletal zombie, and then they flushed him out.

"Sounds like Mattoo Haine," Curdis said. "He killed his wife and oldest son when I was little."

Nobody wanted to tell Twerdahls that if criminals could get past where the Road straightened, Spiral Town let them go. There was a silence Jemmy savored. Then he spoke into the dark. "It must have started this way."

"Tim?"

"Tarzana, grown men and women don't talk to each other in Spiral Town. When your grandparents came, maybe they didn't bring lights. They could talk together in the dark where they could be just voices."

"Mmmm."

He must have fallen asleep soon after.

Jemmy taught bicycle riding all morning.

Cooking over a grill fascinated him. He helped some, but watched more.

In midafternoon they retrieved their bikes from Twerdahl riders. Again Curdis said, "Time to leave."

Jemmy said, "I'm not going."

"What?"

"Tell the merchants Tim wants to know where *Cavorite* went. Tim Hann is on the Road."

He saw Curdis studying him and guessed his thoughts. *Is Jemmy crazy? How crazy?* He didn't know Jemmy like a brother, and the Jemmy Bloocher he thought he knew wouldn't have killed a merchant.

Curdis said, "They'll take a harder look at Tim Hann if Tim comes back alone."

"I don't think I'm coming back, Curdis. I can't run Bloocher Farm. I can't talk down a merchant's price while I'm hiding my face! And if Spiral Town gets in another face-off with the caravans— You see?"

Curdis did. "They'd have to stand without the Bloochers. You'd stand for the Bloochers, but you'd be hiding."

"Curdis, it's unacceptable. Give Thonny two years, he'll be fine running Bloocher Farm. Thonny doesn't have to hide anything."

"That's two years before Margery and I can get our own farm."

"Forgive me."

"Uh-huh." Curdis's eyes were unfocused: still thinking. "Okay, the caravan'll be starting back this way tomorrow or so. I figured we'd meet them just when they were getting organized, and we'd get you through that way. If you stay, they'll be here in, oh, four days. Tim, are you staying here or pushing on?"

"I don't know."

"You could keep ahead of a caravan. Even on foot."

"Sure."

"Or let them catch you in a few weeks, but now you're a Twerdahl with itchy feet."

"Mmm."

"Is this really your choice?"

"Yes."

"Me, too," Brenda said.

Curdis blew his top. Brenda shouted back, then cried.

Jemmy watched them dwindle, pedaling hard, up the Road.

When he returned to the House of Healing that night, Loria came with him.

✳ 6 ✳

Oven Maker

The northwest coast is mountainous. The southeast coast is wider, and rich
in beaches. We'll set down at the far end of the peninsula and explore.
—Anthony Lyons, *Geology*

Twerdahl Town didn't seem to know about bread.

There was grain growing along the Road. There were rocks about.
Children of all ages found Tim Hann strange and interesting, and some
would do what he suggested.

He showed the younger children how to gather grain. The older
helped him carry rocks. Upthrusting banyan knees had flaked a great
flat shelf of lava from the Road. Four were able to move that. It became
the base of Tim Hann's oven.

His first experiments came out scorched, but two days after his sibs
left him, Tim Hann served bread at dinner.

The morning of the third day—

The first of the board riders took their boards from where they were
propped against the long wall of the House of Healing. Tim Hann trailed
the others, watching them, trying to balance the board on his shoulder
as they did.

The board was a few inches shorter than Tim himself, carved from
wood that grew in the swamp. It was heavy and awkward. Playful gusts
of wind kept swinging it about.

Far up the Road toward Spiral Town, there was dust.

Jemmy stopped and squinted. A plume of dust, far off. He thought he
knew what it meant.

Wend Bednacourt carried her board like a wand. She wasn't stronger than he was, but she had the balance. The other riders were running, but Wend trailed back a little. She said, "My daughters have taken an interest in you, Tim."

"I know. But all the others—" It had taken Jemmy two days to notice that the Bednacourt women were the only women who would talk to him. In Spiral Town that was normal, but here? "Is it something I'm doing?"

"Tim, do they say *marry* in Spiral Town?"

"Yes. Of course."

Wend shied back a bit to avoid the wild swinging of his board. "How's it done?"

"There's a ceremony. You invite—"

"Tim, how do you decide?"

This was no casual conversation. Jemmy set his board down and sat on it, thinking it through.

"We kids all pretty much know each other, time the girls stop talking to us. If I'm interested in a girl—" He decided not to mention Tunia Judda. "—why, maybe I've got a friend who dated her, or knows her, or a friend of a friend." He'd learned quite a lot about Tunia and the Judda family. "Or my sister or maybe a cousin probably knows her, can tell me—"

"You don't talk to *her*?"

"Her. No, not until we're dating. That's—" He'd never thought of it this way. "—like a contract, like you're buying seed corn or a rooster. Like we buy each other on spec."

The older woman also sat on her board. "So, two nights ago, Loria spoke to you—"

He could feel himself blushing. "She did."

"What did she say?"

"She told you?"

"We talked," said Wend.

He couldn't lie. He wouldn't know what to hide. He said, "Loria came with me back to the House of Healing. She brought a blanket. I rolled up in mine. I was tired. There wasn't any light, of course, so I couldn't see her face and she couldn't see mine. Talking's easier that way some- how. I just thought we'd talk until I fell asleep.

"She said, 'Do you want to make babies with me?' "

"What did you take that to mean?"

He looked at Loria's mother. "It means rub up against. F-fuck. How could it mean anything else?"

"Yes. Tim, we say that when we want to talk about marrying. Raising children. How to take care of them, how many you can afford—"

"No, look, *she* touched *me*. I would have, but I was a little slow, maybe. She was a little distance away and I couldn't see her face. I didn't see it coming. 'Do you want to make babies with me?' and then a hand came out of the dark and had my knee. I pulled, and she came to me, and we did it."

The other board riders were all out on the water. Leaving them alone. Pointedly?

Wend Bednacourt was smiling, but not at him. "And last night?"

"I couldn't *find* Loria. All day."

"She went with some others, spice hunting."

"Avoiding me? I *told* her it was my first time. Wend, there are things we're not born knowing. It's dark in the House of Healing. I hit her jaw with my elbow before I got the knack."—of moving slowly, touching everywhere. Darkness had its good points.

"She wanted to let you talk to the rest of us. What happened last night?"

"Tarzana. She came back to the House of Healing with me after dinner. I didn't know what she had in mind, so I didn't push. I was hoping she'd tell me why Loria, if she didn't *want* to see me. *Why*. But I didn't know how to ask.

"She said, 'Tim, do you want children?'

"I reached out and got her hand and she said, 'No, Tim,' and I stopped." His memory raced on ahead. Tarzana's voice in the dark: *You do want children, don't you?*

He'd laughed and said, *What, from way over here?*

Aren't you interested?

I was, he said lightly, hiding disappointment. It was as if Tarzana blew hot and then cold, offered and then pulled back. Loria had done that too, then relented. He'd have been angry if a Spiral girl did that. Here, he might be missing some signal, some custom.

Loria says she asked you, but you didn't answer, Tarzana said.

She asked, he told Tarzana smugly. *I think I answered—*

He snapped back to the present. "We weren't talking about the same thing at all, were we?"

"No," said Wend.

"Uh-huh." How could he not be flattered? And horrified! These waters were deeper than he'd expected. "Loria *knows* I didn't know anything. She just . . ."

"Went ahead with it," Wend said.

"Why didn't she just leave? When she knew I had the wrong idea."

Her mother's lips twitched upward. "Maybe she *liked* the wrong idea. A girl might. She's seen every Twerdahl boy and man every day of her life. She could wait for a caravan, but that's so . . ." Wend smiled. "Everyone does that. You're different. You can do things we can't. Not just the bicycle, Tim, that only *came* with you. But the oven."

Are all Twerdahl women like this? He chose to ask instead, "So why didn't Loria tell Tarzana?"

"Why don't I ask her that?"

He couldn't stop grinning. "Big joke. On her sister. So why didn't Tarzana leave?"

"Big joke?"

On Loria? On Tim Hann? "Wend, where does that put me? I can't be dating both of your daughters." A weird impulse made him add, "Can I?"

"No, but you don't have to make up your mind right away."

"Good," he said. "Wonderful," meaning it. Then he said, "Wait. Yes, I do. Is *that* what I think it is?"

The dust plume had settled some while they talked, but it was still there.

Wend said, "They'll be here late tomorrow. Speckles are cheap after they leave Spiral Town, if they've got any left. We usually wait. Unless we're out."

"I never told you why I left Spiral Town."

"Not just following *Cavorite?*"

Jemmy told her.

Caravan. Merchants' guns. Fedrick blowing a watermelon to bits.

Eight years later: caravan. Fedrick again, Fedrick's gun, Fedrick dying on the floor.

Tim Hann was the mask that hid a merchant-killer. Nobody in Twerdahl Town knew that, but they all knew he was a stranger come straight down the Road ahead of the caravan. Anyone in Twerdahl Town might blurt that out to any merchant.

He didn't tell her his name.

She listened and nodded. He was expecting her to shrink from him, but she didn't.

"I think I'd best keep moving down the Road," he said. "Even if they send someone ahead, I can outride him on a bike."

"How will you feed yourself?"

"I found you. Further down the Road, maybe there are people too."

"Speckles? You can't go to merchants, Tim. What do you think you'll do, trade for speckles with locals? They had to buy theirs from merchants. *I* don't keep more than I need for my family. Most people don't."

"Okay, I get stupid and die. At least it's not right away. Wend, I don't . . . really want to leave."

She said, "Marry Loria or marry Tarzana. Marry into the family. We'll tell them you're one of us. Do you mind changing your name?"

Huh?

"When a wanderer marries a local—"

"No, I don't mind."

"It's rare, but it has happened."

"I don't mind."

"All right. Three days now you've been a Twerdahl. Let a merchant see you on a board first, he'll see you as a Twerdahl whatever you do next."

"Am I good enough?" A clumsy Twerdahl would catch a suspicious eye.

"I've watched. Tim, you're *good* with the board."

"And cooking? Let me do some of the cooking."

"Right."

"I need to buy some things. I don't know what you use for money."

"Money?"

Jemmy was only carrying a few coins, the price of three or four meals. He showed them to Wend. When she shook her head, he gave them to her. It would be bad if merchants found those on him. Then he asked, "What do you do if you want something?"

"Ask. Give something back."

"With a caravan?"

"With them too, but they want to know what they're getting."

"I bet they do!"

"What do you need?"

"More clothes. Shoes. Speckles. A board, I guess."

"Nobody has all of that."

"I need the whole town to cover for me, to make the merchants think I'm one of them. Wend, what if I give Twerdahl Town my bike?"

"I'll talk to them," she said. "Over dinner."

The dust crawled toward Twerdahl Town.

The ovens in the Bloocher kitchen outclassed Tim Hann's first pile of lava chunks. Jemmy was sure he could improve his oven. Sitting on his board, his feet wiggling in the sand, he started making sketches.

A few boys watched over his shoulder and made comments.

The Bednacourt girls came to him, all three. "We've been talking," Loria said.

"With Wend," Tarzana said.

"Mother," amplified Glind.

Men of Jemmy's age surrounded them, and they were all listening. Loria pulled him to his feet. "Let's surf."

The town's teen boys followed them into the water. Once beyond the waves, the boys who tried to join them were somehow cut off, discouraged. They watched from a distance, while Bednacourt girls surrounded Tim Hann like three predators.

Tim preempted the conversation. "Your mother explained some things. I guess I was a fool."

"A fool doesn't get what he wants," Loria said.

"We talked it over," said Tarzana.

Loria: "You're fianced. Both of us."

Tarzana: "Dating us, you'd say. But that can't last forever, Tim."

Glind: "So no sex."

Tarzana: "Until you make up your mind."

Tim smiled at Glind and said, "That's easy for you to say."

Glind's eyes dropped. Tarzana hastily said, "No, now, Tim, you shouldn't even be fianced to *two* women. It's only because you're from up the Road."

Loria: "Hands off Glind."

Tim: "I never asked Glind to make babies with me. Why bring her? I'm not as tough as I look," meaning that two girls should be able to ward off an attack.

Glind's hands thrashed water, turning her board. Tim called, "Big joke, Glind! Glind, I don't mind you talking for your sisters. I don't mind waiting either. I want to know what you're like. Both. What I can't figure out—"

Glind turned her board to face him again. He said, "I can't figure how you and you, and you too, Glind, decided I'd make a good husband. How do you *know?*"

They didn't answer.

"I told Wend. Did she tell you? The merchants want me. If I can pass for a Twerdahl, they'll pass me by. Did she tell you why they want me?"

"Tell everyone," Glind said coldly. "At dinner."

An arc of strangers faced him as they carried their boards in. Surfers straggled in behind him. Jemmy felt like a bug on a pin.

He saw no point in waiting. He began to talk.

It went better than he'd expected. There were faces like masks, people who wondered when Tim Hann would next loose violence about him. But many more grew raucous as Twerdahl Town worked schemes to befool the traders.

Tim Hann joined the Bednacourt girls. He had wondered if his problem would solve itself at this time, but Loria and Tarzana set themselves at his sides, and no other woman of Twerdahl Town wanted his company. He was fianced. Twice.

In early afternoon wagons began moving past. Twerdahls clustered about the open sides. Jemmy watched from a board on the water.

Loria, floating beside him, waved broadly out to sea and shouted, "Outside!"

Green water was humping out there. Big wave coming.

For his ears alone Loria said, "We surf when the merchants are in. Dad says it distracts them."

"Merchants are hard to distract."

"You want them to remember you like this. Surf!"

Kneel. Arms in the water, sweeping like oars. Sliding down, down the great green hill of water, Tim Hann stood up and held his balance.

He heard Loria shout "Walk it forward!" and didn't have strength to laugh. He could feel what she meant, though. He was too high on the wave, he needed to point the board *down* to slide *faster.* The problem was that he couldn't move his feet!

He got a fair distance, he seemed to fly forever, before the wave rolled over and flipped him and the board.

He'd never glanced at the wagons.

The wagons parked far down the Road, nearly out of sight. The chugs were an ocher wave rolling down the sand, raising dust in a great khaki cloud.

"They'll stir up the sharks," Loria shouted, and waved him toward the beach. The surfers were getting out of the water.

Jemmy went to help with the cooking. Faintly from down the Road they could hear the popping of gunfire.

Harl Cloochi had managed to hook some huge delta-winged Destiny fish. Younger men came running when they saw it flopping in the shallows, wrestled it into submission, and brought it up. It covered one of the grills from end to end.

The merchants returned on foot. They brought no wares, but some of them carried fruits and a great yellow squash: produce bought in Spiral Town.

The merchants had noticed Tim Hann's oven. Master Granger wanted to use it to cook the big squash. Jemmy guessed that they would ruin the oven if they weren't careful. It was nothing but lava chunks held together by their own weight.

So he made them wait while he punctured the squash with a big fork to let steam out, and helped them roll the squash in, and built up the fire again, smiling like an idiot and trying not to shy away from Master Granger. Master Sean Granger was an older man, proprietor of the second wagon, though a younger woman drove. They'd shared dinner with Dad and Jemmy at Harry's Bar, twice before Dad's accident.

Jemmy didn't dare *not* meet his eyes.

"That should do it. Thank you," Master Granger said to him.

"I should get back to cooking," said Tim Hann.

He had set himself in charge of watching the great fish cook. He saw too late that in the cool of coming night the merchants were all standing around the cookfires. But their eyes passed right over Tim Hann the cook, or through him. He'd made the right move after all.

"What would you call this thing?" Master Granger asked of nobody in particular.

Berda Farrow said, "Hell's angelfish."

"Nice."

She said, "I didn't make it up. That's its name. We see them a lot."

"I miss sub clams," Granger said. "In a month the Otterfolk'll have a mess of them for us."

Jemmy smiled. More people, down the Road? He called to Wade Curdis, trying not to overdo the accent. "Berda, Wade, we should turn this monster."

" 'Kay."

Wade was a strong man in his thirties. He and Berda and Tim Hann turned the fish easily. The merchants backed up to give them room.

"We're lucky there," Granger said. "If Otterfolk were people, they'd eat the best fish themselves."

Wade turned to stare. Tim Hann didn't look around.

Twerdahls didn't like to interrupt merchants, but Wade spoke anyway. "These Otterfolk, who are they? We never see anyone but you and us."

The merchants laughed inordinately. Jemmy looked about him, at merchants mingling with Twerdahls—any of whom could blow his secret to bits—and contrived to be busy. Destiny fish was tough and chewy unless it was cooked slowly. Cooking was creation itself; it seemed to put the universe in perspective.

"The Otterfolk, they're not people," a younger merchant said. "They live in the ocean. We trade them tools and stuff for fish. There are some Destiny fish we can eat, and they tend the Earthlife fish too."

"You only come through three times a year," Wade persisted. "Why don't they come trade with us?"

"Can't. They hate sub clams, though. Used to kill them, till we came along. Sub clams eat Destiny turtles, but they're good eating, for us, that is."

Tim decided the fish was done. He'd never seen Hell's angelfish before, but like many Destiny fish, the meat came apart in layers. Tim Hann cut and other Twerdahls served.

A merchant's accent said, ". . . Criminals."

Tim Hann served a perfect strip of fish to an exotic and lovely merchant woman. "Boiling potatoes now and the big squash in a bit," he said to her, precisely because Spiral men didn't talk to women. But Jemmy Bloocher had heard that younger merchant's voice before, barking some order at Fedrick.

And the other voice was old Harl Cloochi. "It's just a damn rumor, of course, but we almost never see a Spiral, so how do we know?"

"There's some truth in it," the merchant said. "Spiral Town takes care of their own criminals. I spoke as witness once at a trial in Spiral Town. They banged the yutz afterward."

"Ah. All right."

"But, Harl, if a killer gets to the Road before they catch him, *how can* they chase him down? Most Spirals never get out of town at all. A runner doesn't have to stick to the Road, and even if he did, how far did he go? It's a long, long Road."

"So they just let him go?"

"I suppose they chase him awhile. Longer if he did something sticky. Then they just tell us and let him go."

"And leave him for us! Let the Road towns deal with their dregs!"

"Well, that and speckles deprivation."

Appreciative silence.

The merchant's voice said, "A lot of the communities along the Road think the same way. Thing is, Harl, we're not executioners for someone else's dregs, and some of what they call crime isn't all that serious. When a yutz wants to ride the wagons, sometimes we see if he'll work out."

"Even criminals?"

"A man on the run can make a damn good labor yutz. . . ." And they'd walked out of range.

Late in the night, after the merchants went back to their wagons, Harl Cloochi took Tim Hann aside. He asked, "Was the man you killed a labor yutz?"

"I never heard the words until tonight."

"Well, there was a labor yutz killed in Spiral Town a few days ago."

Jemmy waited.

"He came from way down the Road. Merchants won't talk about that, drunk or sober. But Kashi says he had the manners of a shark, and that's why he got himself killed. They kept him around because he could lift his own weight in gear and shoot the teeth out of a lungshark one at a time."

"Labor yutz," Jemmy said, tasting the words.

"See the point? Nobody killed a merchant. They won't search that hard for whoever killed a labor yutz, and they may even think he earned it."

"Uh-huh. Thanks, Harl. From bottom to top, thank you."

"So what're you going to do?"

Tim Hann drew a deep breath of smoke-tinged salt air. He said, "Stay."

✳ 7 ✳

The Old Surfer

Destiny circles a cooler sun. Our year is only three-fifths as long as Earth's. We've divided it into eight months of four weeks each; the days run nearly twenty-five hours. Our descendants may well choose a different calendar.

—Henry Judd, Planetologist

Twerdahl Town's entire male population took twelve days to build them a peak-roofed house no bigger than the family room at Bloocher Farm. In Spiral Town a marriage was made by recording it in computer records; but here, the building of a house was a marriage. Tim Bednacourt saw how the house could expand under the overextended roof, once he and Loria began having children.

Autumn moved into winter.

It was a busy time. Everything edible seemed to be ripening at once. Everything must be picked and stored or preserved. Working refrigerators were rare in Spiral Town, but in Twerdahl Town they didn't exist. Fruits could be boiled for preserves, vegetables blanched, meat smoked. And any of it could be eaten at once. They ate like chugs.

Winter was colder than winters in Spiral Town. They lost some of autumn's fat. They kept a cauldron simmering for tea on a small fire pit that never went out. There were blanched vegetables, smoked meat, snakes from the swamp (Tim never got used to that), and Destiny fish. A dozen kinds of jam were eaten straight or with meat or on bread from Tim's oven. The sea was too cold for swimming or surfing. The water of the cypress swamp stayed tepid.

There were three funerals that winter: two elders whom Tim had barely met, and a little girl who sickened and died in two days. Twerdahl

Town set them in the swamp, along the edge of the Road. The first time, Tim got the shivers. But the dead were feeding Earthlife trees and creatures; what matter if those were denizens of a swamp?

Tim Bednacourt had no warning. Come dawn of a bright morning in early spring, Tarzana and Glind were pulling him and Loria out of bed.

The house they'd built had no locks and the sisters had no sense of privacy. Loria had Tim's arm and Tarzana had the other and Glind was talking too, and there was no resisting. Loria explained, breathless, as the laughing girls pulled Tim into a run.

There were near three hundred Twerdahls. There were fifty-two weed cutters. Once there had been sixty. Twerdahls were more careful counting knives than each other, Tim noticed, but the point was that there weren't enough knives. So they ran, knowing that their elders would wake later and follow at their leisure to take the knives away.

It looked like all the teens and twenties of Twerdahl Town were swarming toward the toolhouse. They raced to be first through the big doors; they pushed past each other clutching weed cutters.

One elder, at least, was up: Julya Franken was standing benevolent guard over blades heaped on a table. Early arrivals had picked them over. No seven were alike, though there was a set of six and there were several sets of five that had been six. Some were just big enough to use for cooking or eating. A few were big enough to swing two-handed.

Tim and the girls snatched up blades and ran for the swamp.

The youth of Twerdahl Town left their clothes in neat piles and scrambled down into the water. They slashed exuberantly at thick green hawsers fringed with lacy spines: the Destiny Julia sets and python vines that were killing Earthlife trees.

Tim could hear shouted warnings from elsewhere in the swamp. Not everyone had learned to stay clear of slashing blades. Tim disengaged himself even from Loria, who made joyful howling noises as she swung a quarter-meter serrated kitchen knife at the biggest vines.

Tim slashed, slashed with a midsized broad-bladed knife, moving straight inland through the hip-high water. Snakes avoided him, but there were too many for his comfort. He slashed loose a branch to prod them away. Now orange daylight glowed through the trees ahead, until he faced a rising lava slope.

He was alone.

If Thonny and Jemmy Bloocher had left evidence of themselves, a third of a year ago, it was best that Tim Bednacourt find it first.

Nothing?

Nothing of Jemmy Bloocher showed here.

He turned back toward the voices. Glind was gathering head-sized spongy clumps of fiber and stuffing them in a net bag. "Fairy loofa," she told him.

"Got enough?"

"I think so."

Cutting vine was exhausting work. When they got tired they worked nearer the Road, so that an elder could claim the knife. Twerdahls in their thirties and forties were arriving in clumps, and they took their time taking up knives.

It was a game of showing off strength, and Tim couldn't quit until Loria did. But the Road came nearer and nearer. They saw Tarzana pass her blade to her father.

Two older women who tended the bean gardens, Sharlot and Emjay Clellan, watched them for several minutes, then jumped down and claimed their knives. Tim and Loria crawled up onto the Road and joined Tarzana and Glind and a host of bodies lying and drying on the sun-warmed surface of the Road.

The vines would recover, of course. Twerdahl Town made no serious attempt to exterminate them.

Everybody quit around noon, gathered and stacked the blades, jumped back into the water, and bathed and scraped each others' backs with fairy loofas. It was fun, the first break they'd had from work in some time. And it got them clean before the spring caravan arrived.

At last night's sunset they'd heard distant gunfire.

The wagons cruised past while Twerdahl Town did business at their windows, trading harvest fruits for speckles and tools, chatting to learn what the others had. Prices would be cheaper coming back from Spiral Town.

Tim stayed in the house while Loria dealt with merchants.

The summer caravan was long gone. Who would know him here? But Loria took it for granted that Tim would not confront the spring caravan.

Windows were scarce in Twerdahl Town. This house had only two. Tim watched through the dining-room window as the wagons drifted off up the Road.

Loria was back. "I got speckles for fresh corn. I didn't want to wait. We were nearly out."

"It feels like I'm hiding."

She looked at him. "You are hiding."

*   *   *

The sun was low, and Quicksilver had already blinked out, when a rattle of gunfire drifted down the Road.

An hour later the merchants were back among them.

Tim was stir-frying vegetables in a wok big enough to bathe a two-year-old, using a spoon as long as his forearm. An elderly merchant woman tried to strike up conversation, but gave up quickly. Who could possibly expect him to pay attention to anything but cooking?

Loria was unhappy.

Why? He was hidden in plain sight. In the house he would be missing dinner, in hiding, in the dark. It wasn't *her* they were hunting, if they were hunting anyone at all.

The vegetables were done. The nearest man wasn't as strong as Berda Farrow, a middle-aged mother of four with long limbs and stringy muscles, so it was Berda who helped him move the wok aside. Tim pulled the big omelet pan onto the fire.

He poured eggs in, a quart or so. Berda stayed a moment to watch him work, then smiled and went off to chase children.

Berda had taught him this. Under her eyes Tim had made two-egg omelets all one morning, until there was no feeling in his arm. The eggs stuck at first, or burned. He used too much oil or too little. Under Berda's supervision he began adding fillings. She watched him perfect his technique, then graduated him to a wok with a double handle, ten eggs at a time.

All the territory around Twerdahl Town was infested with chickens. They nested out of range of sharks. Nothing else seemed to hunt them. Wherever you went there were nests. Twerdahl Town ate a lot of omelets.

He tilted the pan, then lifted the omelet's edge to let eggs run underneath. He tipped cooked vegetables across the omelet. The corner of his eye caught a grinning merchant woman holding a shaker. He took it, sprinkled the omelet with speckles, then handed the shaker back with a nod and smile.

Twerdahls put speckles in almost anything made with eggs; but Twerdahls wouldn't trade for speckles and then give them back. Merchants would get none in their dinner if they didn't bring their own.

Tim flipped the omelet over itself.

"—*Cavorite*—"

He finished the maneuver before he looked around. Who had spoken?

Two merchants didn't notice him. "The Otterfolk saw it come past. They remember. I got one of them to draw it for me."

"It's not easy to tell," the older man said. "When you don't know how it works you don't know what to draw either. Anyway, they were just drawing in sand—"

"I copied it."

"Sure you did, Joker, but they drew what they thought you wanted and you copied what you thought you saw—"

"*Skip it.* Yutz, isn't that omelet ready yet?"

Right. Tim briskly turned the omelet onto a plate. "Should be perfect. Jean, cut this up for us, will you?"

A half-grown girl began cutting the huge omelet and serving it onto plates.

Loria came out of nowhere, set a slice of broiled meat beside Tim, and took a stack of empty plates. She brushed sensuously past Tim and breathed into his ear, "I am so *sick* of hearing about *Cavorite*," and was gone.

Tim poured oil and more eggs into the pan.

In the morning the wagons went on to Spiral Town, and Twerdahl Town returned to the work of harvest.

Two weeks passed.

Loria was at work on a tossed salad. She brushed past him, back to back, slowly, a suggestive caress. *Yum.* The Bednacourt kitchen was bigger than the Hanns', but two at work still had to touch. Two could make a virtue of that.

Tim drained the rice. Brown rice with flecks of color in it, bell peppers and onion and bits of bacon. No speckles today: they'd all had enough last night.

Lunch for four including Wend, who was somewhere about, or five, if Tarzana showed up.

The Bednacourts were a close family. Loria was closer to her mother and sisters than to her husband. It didn't bother him. Spiral men were cliquish too. *That* was Tim's problem: he was a clique of one. He didn't have quite the same concerns, didn't speak quite the same language, as Twerdahl Town.

Had he chosen Loria? Or had the Bednacourt women played some complex game with Tim Bednacourt as the prize? Loria had taught him surfing as he'd taught her the bicycle, while Tarzana drifted with other men. Glind had never been alone with him at all. Loria had become the default option. . . .

"Caravan's in sight," Glind said.

Tim felt Loria stiffen. "We've already got our speckles," she said.
"You didn't wait?"

No answer. Glind turned from the Road and said for Tim's benefit,
"They like to travel at harvest time. The feasts are wonderful."

"Where's Tarzana?"

"Met a merchant man, I think."

He asked, "Not a labor yutz?," to see if she knew the term.

"Merchant."

"How will Gerrel feel about that?"

Loria looked at him queerly. Glind, serving out salad, didn't notice.
"Feel? Tim, anyone can mix it up with the merchants. Hey—" She
looked up. "They tell us about something called hybrid vigor. We get
better babies if we don't make babies with just each other. Did they
teach you about that in Spiral Town?"

"Sure, hybrid vigor and gene drift." Tim grinned at Loria. "Was that
it? Was that what you saw in me?"

She blushed. Glind, grinning, said, "We wonder. It's such a good
story, maybe it's just—"

"No, I read about hybrid vigor and gene drift in the teaching programs. I could go off with a merchant woman? And nobody will care?
And I wasn't supposed to know that?" He was watching his wife's face.
She was irritated and unamused. "Loria, you *know* why I can't get close
to merchants."

She nodded.

"Even so, I'm glad we lock up the knives," he teased her. His mind
ran on. *When did Twerdahls start doing that? Why? Was there a time of
knives and blood? And now they pass them out to cooks every evening,
and count them—*

Better not ask.

Abruptly, Loria asked, "Where did you hear that? 'Labor yutz.' "

"Last summer."

"Have you ever talked with Haron Welsh?"

"What, the old surfer? The one who does stunts?"

"He was a labor yutz. Twice. Once before I was born. Talk to him."

Haron Welsh wasn't cliquish. Tim hadn't seen him at the vine-slash. He
lived alone; he worked his own patch of garden; he surfed alone.

In late morning he was a small dark silhouette in a cold drizzle, alone
on the water. Tim waited on the beach. The old surfer let several good
waves pass. He must be watching the endless passage of the caravan.

Haron caught a wave. Finally! As the old man stood up in the shallows

77

Tim shouted and waved: a towel in one hand, a fat mug of silver fern tea in the other.

The old man thought it over, then pulled his board to land. He used the towel and dropped it, then took the mug.

"You were a labor yutz," Tim said.

Haron drank the hot tea down straight and handed back the cup. Only then did he speak. "Who're you?"

"Tim Bednacourt."

"You don't know anything." Haron picked up his board and turned toward the water. Stopped. "Spiral?"

"Yes."

"They got teaching things in Spiral? You learn?"

"That's right."

"Huh. What do you know that I don't?"

"Well—"

"I've been as far as the Neck!"

"Tell me about it."

The old man started to turn away. Tim said, "Ever seen *Columbia*?"

The rest of Twerdahl Town had no interest in *Columbia* or *Cavorite*.

". . . No. Tell me about *Columbia*."

Tim spoke to the back of Haron's head.

Columbia was a huge squat tower in a nest of cables, with a brick building against its side to protect the join. The original cables were as thin as angelhair pasta. Replacement cables were as thick as a man's fingers, made of copper or silver bought from merchants. Clusters of black conical pits each the size of a boy were attitude jets. Once they had spit fire. The hatch ten meters up, and the old stairway built to reach it, were made of poured rock, wonderfully precise.

Power had flowed from *Columbia* for two and a half centuries. Tim spoke of Spiral Town's machines all wearing down, getting less and less power as *Columbia*'s energy grew more sluggish.

The old man listened and gave nothing back, and Tim spoke more than he intended. He spoke of boyhood dreams: studying engineering and plasma physics, running the power system as apprentice and journeyman, until they would let him enter *Columbia*'s interior. To turn on the old ship's motors. And rise in a blaze of light and a tearing away of the ship's prison of cables, rise into the sky and *fly*.

The eldest Bloocher boy, the one who would inherit, could never do any of that.

The old man's attention was wandering. From some attic storage in his memory Tim pulled something random.

"Did you know that Earth's sun was hotter than ours?"

Haron's eyebrows arced. "Why didn't they fry?"

"Earth was farther away, of course. The sun probably looked *smaller*, and brighter, so it'd dazzle you quicker, and the light would have been more blue. Maybe the sky had more blue in it." Tim was guessing at some of this. "But Destiny's sun is a little smaller than Sol, and maybe two billion years older."

"Huh. And why would any of this crap make a fingernail's difference to anyone?"

Jemmy Bloocher had asked that too. There *were* answers. "Earth took almost twice as long to go around Sol. We have eight months in a year, they had twelve, but theirs were longer. The clocks still measure Earth days and Earth years."

"Yeah, the Spiral Town clocks. Can't anyone make a clock for Destiny time?"

"Nobody I know. Hey, have you ever been sunburned?"

Haron considered. "Few times, I've stayed out all day surfing. Next day I'm bright red and everything hurts. Can't wear clothes. Can't go outside. Next day, itch. Two days after that I'm peeling like a snake in spring."

"Yeah?"

"Yeah."

"On Earth you could do that in a hour," Tim said. "They had to wear hats and spread goo on their skins to thin the sunlight or they'd get cancer. Too much—" He'd never quite got this straight. "Too much of the light that's too blue to see."

Haron seemed to find that funny. "Too blue to see." He set down the board. Nearly naked to the wind, he didn't shiver. "All right. You know something. Not like these yutzes. What do you want?"

"Did you ever see *Cavorite*?"

"No."

"Did you ever find out where *Cavorite* went? Do the traders know?"

Haron's eyes went distant. His lips moved, but nothing came out.

"The Neck," Tim prodded.

"We got to the Neck. The Road goes right across."

"Is that where the Otterfolk are?"

"*Them*. They're all along the shore of the big bay. They don't talk. They can't go anywhere."

"You went twice? You must like it."

"Not so much that."

Tim waited.

"They don't *know* anything here. Surf in summer, gather and eat in fall, huddle hungry in winter. Time of year tells them what they're doing, *everything* they're doing. It feels so *cramped.*" Haron's voice was rising, but he caught himself. "Doesn't matter anyway. The merchants asked, I had to go."

"Why?"

"First time, they gave us two knives." Haron grinned. "Second time, I was trained already. Four knives."

Ah, he'd been *bought.*

"The Otterfolk, they can't go anywhere," Haron said. "There's only the bay. Anywhere else, they die. That's one reason. I'd go again, because the Otterfolk can't."

"What are they like?"

"We're not supposed to talk to them, but you can sneak away. They draw pictures in the sand. You try to tell them things that way, but it's—" Haron frowned. "It's not enough."

"For what?"

Haron shook his head. He picked up his board and ran into the water.

Merchants and Twerdahls mingled on the sand. Tim Bednacourt worked anonymous in their midst.

For a long moment Quicksilver burned at the edge of the sea, just below the cloud deck. Then it winked out. An hour of sunlight left.

Merchants watched Tim Bednacourt cutting onions, carrots, bell peppers, mushrooms picked in the cypress swamp. "That looks good," the older woman said. Tim smiled.

Four merchants came, all a few inches shorter than Tim, all exotic and elegant, dressed in many colors, many layers. He noticed the younger man first. Dark, with a thin mustache: Tim had seen him before. An older man with brown hair and a forked beard turning gray. A black-haired woman his own age; another very like her but no older than Tim. Skins browner than Tim's, all four. Their eyes were dark and a bit tilted. Parents, son, daughter?

He could be wrong about that, or their ages, or almost anything. Any fool might pretend to know all about merchants. Nobody really knew.

The young man said, "I remember you. We were talking about Otterfolk. I noticed you trying to listen and cook—"

"I remember. You're Joker?"

He nodded. The older woman asked, "Would you like to see them for yourself?"

Caught by surprise, Tim laughed. "Sure. It's not likely, is it?"

"I'm Senka," she said. "These are Damon and Rian, my husband and daughter."

"I'm Tim Bednacourt."

She was *examining* him. It made him uncomfortable. "How long have you lived in this place?"

"Twenty years. Born here," making himself a year older than Jemmy Bloocher.

The man asked, "Do you ever wonder what the rest of the world looks like?"

"Well, sure, sometimes I look off down the Road and—"

"Tim."

He jumped. *Loria!* She said, "You can't cook in the dark. You need help?"

It wasn't dark yet, but . . . "Yes, love, I got a little behind. You cut, I'll start these." An hour of light left. Tim added oil to the wok—already hot—then vegetables. The action became brisk. The merchant trio watched, then wandered off.

Loria asked, "What did they want?"

"They didn't say."

"But something?"

"Oh, yeah. Sounds like they need a labor yutz or two."

The big vegetable omelets had become almost reflex. Tim finished one and shouted for the nearest older child whose name he could remember.

"Did you talk to Haron?"

"Tried. What happened to him?"

"This batch is finished," Loria said, and went briskly away.

Food wandered toward him from other cookfires. Tim ate as he cooked: sausage, roasted ear of corn, half of a passerby's chunk of bread, a slice of his own omelet. When it was too dark to see he settled himself on the sand.

Heaven's fire still burned where sky met sea.

His arms and shoulders hurt. He didn't usually push himself this hard. Where was Loria? *Why?*

Hadn't she expected him to talk to Haron? It was her own suggestion!

Someone was at his side. He turned hoping to see Loria, or any Bednacourt who could explain what Loria was angry about.

It was a young merchant woman, her clothes still a patchwork of color in the dying light. She handed him the edge of a half melon. They broke it together; he kept half, the juice running down his fingers.

"Rian," she said. "You're Tim?"

"Hello, Rian."

Senka's daughter. She sat beside him. In the dark her face was all planes and angles, a lovely but abstracted shape. Eyes a bit tilted, like almonds. "This is my first trip," she said.

"From where?" he asked.

"We don't talk about that. We don't take labor yutzes past the Neck."

Too bad, he thought. Then he stared. Past the Neck? She'd been born on the mainland!

Rian leaned close enough that he could feel her breath on his cheek. "One of our cooks has died," she said. "We need another."

"Uh-huh?"

"Want to come with us?"

"As a labor yutz?"

"Yes."

Tim smiled politely. "Rian, why don't you tell me how your cook died?"

She hesitated. "Well. We were too far from the other wagons. Petey was a cowboy—"

"Say?"

"Cowboy. He liked to be right there on the sand shooting when the sharks came at us. Made us shoot around him. Few days ago the sharks got ahead of us a bit. They got Petey."

Tim said what he should have said first. "I've only been married two months."

"Yes, to Loria Bed . . . Bednacourt. She carrying a guest yet?"

This question seemed excessively personal, but Tim supposed it might matter to merchants interested in hiring a woman's husband. He said, "Not yet."

"So come."

Tim shook his head.

She was trying to study his face in the dark. "Nobody *has* to be down there on the sand with the sharks, Tim. Not a labor yutz, anyway. They never reach the wagon roofs."

She thought he was afraid?

"You know," she said, "the Otterfolk must have been the first unhuman tool users anyone ever saw. *Cavorite* wouldn't have just sailed past."

She was right, he thought. And— "They can draw pictures of *Cavorite*," he said.

He couldn't say, *Loria doesn't even want me talking to you, let alone*— Rian would wonder why, and Tim didn't know, but that left only a killing in Spiral Town as his excuse, and what would he tell her instead? He said, "I wasn't the only cook—"

"You have four. Van Barstowe limps. A caravan yutz has to walk, you know. Drew Bednacourt drops things, and he's surly. You and Van, you're the best. Do you like my company, Tim?"

At dinnertime there were knives everywhere you looked, and where was Loria right now? "No, look, Rian, we all grow up knowing about hybrid vigor, but Loria doesn't think like that. My life wouldn't be worth living if—"

He stopped talking, because the merchant woman was up and moving away.

He wondered if he'd jumped to conclusions. "Company," she'd said. Only that. He'd made an embarrassing mistake.

The house was empty.

Long after he was in bed, Loria slid in and tickled him awake. There was a ferocity to her lovemaking, and she wouldn't let him talk. She didn't want to talk afterward either. They made love again . . . unless he fell asleep first . . . but sunlight blazed through the bedroom window and someone was pounding on the door.

Tim pulled himself out of bed, squinting. Why didn't Loria answer? "Come," he called. He pulled on some pants and went into the common room.

Sharlot Clellan, Drew Bednacourt, Harl Cloochi, and Berda Farrow, all elders of Twerdahl Town, came in from the glare of sunlight. They ushered in three merchants wearing wild colors. Two men, one woman. Tim recognized the dark man named Damon.

"What's it all about?" he asked.

Harl said, "Tim, these are Damon and Milo and Halida, elders of the caravan. They came to us last night, not just to us, you understand, but to all of Twerdahl Town. Tim, this may sound odd—"

The door opened again. Loria and Tarzana.

Tim repeated, "What *is* this?"

"Loria, dear, we've had an offer," Harl said.

"Right. Did you know they came to Tim last night? Tim, what did they offer you?"

She could have learned that last night. "Job as a labor yutz. Cooking."

The elder Twerdahls stared at the merchants. "You went to him first?"

Damon smiled and shrugged. "We looked for a better bargain. He was reluctant."

Tim couldn't read Loria's expression.

The merchant woman, Halida, said to Tim, "Your elders and mine, they've been talking. We offer a long knife for every twenty days you're gone."

"Loria, is that a good price?"

"Dammit, Tim!"

"Tarzana?"

Tarzana said, "Yes."

"Sounded like it. Haron got less, his first time."

Damon said, "We want you cooking for us *tonight,* Tim. That means you join us now. You'll be with ibn-Rushd wagon, my family's wagon. Don't take too much with you, no more than you can carry. Don't take speckles. We've got plenty. And Tim—" He smiled. "The more we discuss it, the farther we'll have to chase the wagons."

It was happening faster than he could think, and he was still playing catch-up. "Loria, let's talk," he said, and pulled her into the bedroom.

Dawn light blazed through the window. It was easier to read her face in here. "What's going on?"

"Can't you *tell?*"

"Oh, a little. They'd have had me cheap if I'd gone with them last night. Now they've got to pay off the whole town, but Loria, do they think I'm for sale? I have a house and a wife."

And a secret that any of three hundred people might speak.

"The old people, they've already taken the knives," Loria said bleakly. She swept the blanket off their bed, flung it high and let it settle on the floor. "We have to pack. I *knew* they'd have you. You can do things nobody else can. Tim, didn't I try to keep you in the house?" He saw she was crying. "At least I gave you a great send-off. Didn't I?"

"I didn't know I was going."

"T—"

"Great send-off, damn right. Can you come with me?"

Her head snapped up, amazed. "You'd . . . ?"

"What?"

"Want me?"

"Yes!"

"No. No, I can't. Yutzes are always men."

"What do *you* want, Loria?"

"I want you to come back. But if you're coming back like Haron Welsh, then don't."

She'd stacked his possessions on the blanket. Coat and shirts. No hat; Twerdahls never wore hats. The skillet from Bloocher Farm had become Twerdahl Town property, and retrieving it would be a mistake. She took his pouch of speckles. "If a yutz carries speckles, they think it's caravan property," she said.

She considered, then added one of the few things she'd brought from the Bednacourt House. It was an old wooden toy model of *Cavorite,* vague in detail, worn by handling in places.

"That's yours," he said.

She said, "You'd have something like this, if you really grew up here. Take it."

"Loria, what *happened* to Haron Welsh?"

"The way he sees us . . . changed. He's Uncle Haron, but we don't call him that anymore. He thinks he's too good to talk to us. Don't come back that way. Tim, what's your *name?*"

"Jemmy Bloocher."

"All right." Loria rolled the blanket and tied it into a compact bundle. "Go on."

He could have smoothed it over, made his peace with Loria. He knew it then and he believed it later. But the caravan was already moving, and Twerdahl Town wanted knives, and Otterfolk remembered enough of *Cavorite* to draw pictures.

* Part Two *

✳ 8 ✳

On the Road

You don't stop your wagon to do business, not unless it's a favored mark or a decent offer. Stopping makes you look eager. Keep talking and let the chugs move on until the mark takes your offer.

—Shireen ibn-Rushd

The wagons were rolling steadily away from Twerdahl Town when three merchants and Tim Bednacourt walked into a haze of fine dust.

The morning wore on. Swamp trailed off into grass-covered hills. They crossed a wide and sluggish stream on stepping-stones too conveniently placed to be natural. Halida named it Whelan's Crossing.

The wagons didn't seem to be getting closer.

The merchants weren't hurrying. They ambled along, chatting among themselves. With his burden of possessions Tim was still hard put to keep up. Now they were asking questions about life in Twerdahl Town. . . .

Tim tried to distract them with questions of his own. "I've never watched merchants cooking. What do you use?"

"You will see. I am Damon ibn-Rushd. Ibn-Rushd is eight from the lead, six from the tail. We and Lyons family carry the cookware."

"Do you cook with the same kind of thing you sell to Twerdahl?"

"Yes."

"Good. Is there always firewood?"

"Always, except at the Tail."

A stone bridge arched over deep water. Tim asked, "Did you build all of these bridges?"

Laughter. "Who else?"

Gradually they drew alongside the last wagon. Now they were passing a line of chugs. Each chug spared Tim one long dismissive glance. They stood almost hip high. Those shells looked heavy. They'd weigh about half as much as Tim. The top of the beak was an extension of the skullcap shell, with a lower jaw to meet it. That beak would deliver a hell of a bite.

Tim suddenly realized that he was seeing the same odd blemish on each chug. They were marked with an E inside a D, carved into the shell on the right side.

"Dole," Halida said. "Dole Enterprises."

Nineteen chugs pulled Dole wagon.

Twenty pulled the next. They were marked with a bird of Earth, an owl.

Eighteen pulled the next, marked with an ellipse and a dot in the center. "Wu family had bad luck this trip," Damon said softly as he smiled and waved at two men in the driver's alcove.

"The wagons," Tim said, "they're all alike."

Damon nodded; Halida smiled.

Spiral children noticed early. Eggs were alike, seeds were alike, babies were alike, but crafted things were not. Things that were all alike were ancient machines from the time of Landing, "settler magic" like computers and microwave ovens; or they were the wood-and-iron wagons of a caravan.

Wagons were painted in flamboyant fashion, a match for merchants' clothing. When the side opened to form a counter and sunscreen, each wagon became a shop different from every other shop. But the counters were up, the wagons were closed, and this was Tim Bednacourt's first good look at wagons. They were identical down to the last centimeter, as if made all at the same time, from identical components, by identical workmen.

The drivers' alcoves denied their similarities. They were painted too, and furnished with pillows and little shelves and niches that held mugs or pieces of carved wood. From arcs of driver's benches that would be roomy for four, merchants watched Tim pass. They didn't speak, but they smiled.

"They smile for you," Halida said. "We might have had to eat our own cooking."

The chugs weren't paying much notice to passersby, or the Road, or anything but their own steady motion.

Fourth wagon from the end: the chugs were marked with two vertical bars on an S. Halida climbed four shallow steps to the driver's bench. The drivers shifted to give her room. She looked down at Tim and said, "Milasevik. We carry tents and bedding."

They walked on.

Ibn-Rushd was sixth from the end, out of thirteen wagons. A summer caravan would have been fifteen to twenty. Senka smiled at Tim from the driver's bench; Rian merely watched. The last chug was marked with a crescent and six-pointed star.

Damon ignored the steps. He was into the driver's alcove in a smooth pull-and-jump maneuver. A gesture invited Tim to do the same.

Tim dropped his pack into the alcove, then scrambled over the side. *Practice,* he promised himself.

Milo called up to him. "Milo Spadoni. Second in line. We carry ammunition, we and Tucker." He walked on.

The driver's bench would hold four, and it was full. Senka, Rian, an elderly lady Tim didn't know, and Rian's brother. Tim said, "Hello, Joker."

"Tim," Joker said.

Damon said, "Tim Bednacourt, this is Shireen ibn-Rushd. You obey her in all things. Mother, Tim is a wonderful cook."

"Very pleased," Tim said. The old lady smiled.

Tethers from each of the chugs were tied to knobs on a half-circle of rail, but the women weren't bothering with them. The chugs seemed to know what they were doing.

Damon ibn-Rushd said, "You're a yutz now, but not a labor yutz. Your rank is 'chef.' There are three other chefs and me and Marilyn Lyons. Lyons wagon carries the rest of the cookery. You take orders from me or Marilyn, but if any other merchant tells you to lift or carry something, you don't have to. You can draft a loose labor yutz if he'll put up with it, but any merchant might give him another job.

"And this is yours." Damon stooped and dug under the bench. Senka ibn-Rushd slid aside for him. He came out with what Tim recognized as a gun, and a broad belt in his other hand.

He handed the gun to Tim. "Have you ever fired a shark gun?"

Tim Bednacourt said, "No." He took the gun, suppressing the flinch, and held it as if he didn't know which part was the handle. It looked exactly like the gun that had killed Fedrick. He felt queasy.

"Hold it like this." Damon showed him. "Never point at anything valuable, and never at a person. Keep your fingers off the trigger unless you're serious. These are bullets." Bullets were the size of Tim's thumb: a ball of metal in a case made of what might be compressed vegetable fiber. "You load it like this. It doesn't work without bullets." The gun took eight. "Never be caught with an unloaded gun. Twice never at sunset or sunrise! Let's get up on the roof and I'll give you some practice."

Pull and jump, Damon was on the roof. Tim set his hands, pulled and jumped, lunged too far as the wagon rolled, and nearly fell off.

The roof was flat. At its corners were coils of rope. Cloth had been nailed along a ten-centimeter-high rim.

"Some of us like to get down on our bellies, prop up on our elbows and shoot that way," Damon said. "I'm not going to teach you that. You can't swing far enough. Something could come at you from the side. See that tree?"

Not far inland, a slender Destiny fisher tree leaned far over, tip almost horizontal, lace blowing and shredding in a brisk breeze.

"Suppose you want to shoot the tip off that. Stand facing right by a little." About thirty degrees right. "You're right-handed? Both hands on the gun. Fold your left fingers over the right, like this. Now your right arm is straight, but your left elbow bends. Lean forward a little, because the gun is going to kick back. Pull the trigger."

The noise was an assault. The gun kicked in his hands. Something burst into view from trees nearby: a caricature of a bird, feathery and two-legged and big as a man. It ran in circles, squawking madly, then off down the Road.

Tim braced his arms, pointed, and fired again. The gun didn't snap up as high.

"Arms pull against each other," Damon suggested.

Hmm? Tim tried that. It felt good, natural. The fisher tree was some distance behind him now, but he set his feet, held his aim on the tip of the tree, BLAM! it was flying dust.

He hadn't fired, the gun hadn't kicked.

"That Boardman yutz," Damon said, "on Lyons wagon. He didn't throw you off, did he? That's the first mistake you'll make. Something distracts you, you pull, shoot a hole in something. Here—" Damon took the gun. He set himself. The fisher tree was far behind them now. Damon fired and the chewed tip jumped. "Like that." He gave the gun back. "Pick something closer."

The Road swerved gradually inland and the land was drying out. Tim chose a lone thick-boled Destiny teapot, aimed for the bole, braced his feet, his arms, BLAM. Dust and splinters sprayed from the edge. He aimed above the bole, at a smaller target, the spout. He scored another hit.

"Good! and enough," Damon said. "Come sunset you can shoot sharks." He bent and lifted. A square patch of roof came up. "All the wagons have attic storage. If a predator ever got this far, here's refuge. We'll stow your pack here. And—" He reached into the hatch and brought out a transparent speckles pouch. "Here." Tim took the pouch.

Damon dropped a handful of bullets into it. "Close it like this. Keeps water out."

The space below the trapdoor might hold four or five friendly people, but it was packed with bedding, pillows, clothing, tarpaulins, and a big square box. Tim had to push to get his pack in. "Refuge? Damon, do I throw stuff out to make room for persons?"

Damon laughed. "It's never happened. We got used to using it for storage, but it's supposed to be a hidey-hole. All right, *yes*. Throw it to the sharks if they get this far." He thumped the box. "*Don't* throw away the bullets."

Damon showed Tim how to manipulate ropes on the wagon's roof to open the sides. Tim took it through the full routine while Damon watched.

"What's next?"

"Cooking. What do you do best?"

"Omelets. Stir-fry vegetables."

"Takes eggs?" Damon looked down the Road. Ground cover had grown sparse.

Tim asked, "Would there be nests around here?"

The old woman spoke unexpectedly. "Oooh, I'd think so!"

Why was that funny? But Damon smiled. "We'll send out some yutzes."

In midafternoon the wagons rolled drunkenly across wide, flat stones in a shallow stream. When the seventh wagon was across, they all stopped. Tim watched the women release the chugs.

He couldn't quite see how it was done. Loose a line from its knob on the rim of the driver's alcove, snap it like a whip, then retie it. It looked easy; it looked purposeless. Senka and Rian moved briskly along the arc of knobs. When they met at the center, several chugs could be seen to be loose and moving toward the beach.

The younger women stepped daintily down to the Road, then helped Shireen down. Damon and Tim stayed to open the wagon's side, then dropped to join them. Damon and the women were all armed, even Shireen.

All of ibn-Rushd's chugs were loose now. The other wagons, spread far apart up and down the Road, had released theirs.

"We've got time to set some fire pits," Damon said. He pulled shovels from the wagon. "Tim, come on down to the beach. The labor yutzes know what to do."

The sea was two hundred meters away. Most of the women, and not many men, walked down to the beach, taking no notice of two hundred and fifty chugs rolling down behind them in two slow waves. The chugs veered wide of the freshwater flow and its delta mouth.

There were old fire pits to be dug out. Men dug. Women supervised. Chugs flowed around them and into the waves.

Yutzes brought dry vegetation, Earthlife and Destiny trees and weeds. Tim saw two men dragging a lace-festooned log, and jumped to help. They set it on tinder in a dug-out pit.

One of the men asked, "You're Tim from ibn-Rushd? I'm Bord'n from Lyons wagon. Bord'n, not Boardman, whatever the merchants tell you. This's Hal, from Lyons too, but he's a chef."

The women were starting their fires.

"Hello, Bord'n, Hal. Are all yutzes men?"

Bord'n laughed. Hal said, "All I ever saw. A pregnant yutz could be awkward. You don't see children either on a caravan."

Still talking, the two men had him by the elbows and were walking him up toward the wagons before he could quite catch on.

With no discussion and no sign of haste, every human being in sight was ambling uphill toward the wagons. They climbed onto roofs and settled in. Senka, Damon, and Joker were already in place. Hal and Bord'n urged Tim up, and followed.

Damon greeted them; Senka passed around a pitcher of water flavored with lemons. Rian ibn-Rushd wasn't in sight. She must be visiting another wagon.

A forest rolled out of the water, black and bronze and yellow. A forest of seaweed, and motion working within it. Chugs.

Thrashing fish were dropping out of the weed, and chugs left the line to snap them up before they could reach water. Half-seen chugs were steadily pulling the beached forest apart, eating the crabs and fish and shellfish as they were exposed.

Tim watched in fascination.

As if at a signal, the chugs all began moving inland, leaving the weed behind.

Then things began coming out of the water.

They didn't look particularly scary. They were heavy and flat. The waves didn't topple them. They crawled onto land, paused a moment, then moved after the chugs faster than a walking man. There were twenty in sight when the first reached the beached seaweed.

The family ibn-Rushd, and their visitors, took their positions. "Save your bullets," Damon told Tim. "You too, Joker."

Tim had only been given six. It must be very natural, he thought, for a new yutz to waste bullets. So Tim held his pose and his fire.

A shark was three or four times the size of a chug, and flatter, built lower to the ground. Its shell was smaller and more simplified than the ornate points and edges of a chug shell. Its big head was mostly beak and shell cap and a backward-pointing prong for counterbalance. The beak was all points and curved edges, built for ripping. The eyes faced forward in deep recesses.

Even so, these were clearly the chugs' relatives. Chugs carried shields with edges and points that could gash a predator. Sharks carried weaponry.

The sharks paused at the seaweed forest. They were nosing into the weeds, seeking the same prey that served the chugs. The chugs were halfway to the wagons, moving as fast as Tim had seen them move.

One, then several sharks crawled over the weed in pursuit of the receding chugs.

Guns began to fire. Bullets thudded into the few sharks in the lead, poking holes in their shells or spraying seawater and blood from the rough gray-green skin below.

"Not many this time," Damon said. "That near one in the middle? That's your target, Tim."

Flat-footed, leaning forward just a bit, hands pulling against each other with the gun butt between . . . Tim fired. Bullets thudded into the beast's shell. Maybe one or two were his. He saw a shark still coming, swiveled, and used up his bullets on that one.

Four sharks were down, and the rest were running for the water. They weren't fast. A man could outrun them; but who would tire first, man or shark?

"You all stopped shooting," Tim noticed, "as soon as they turned tail. Why not kill them all?"

The yutzes looked to Damon, who said, "If we killed off all the sharks, who knows what we'd get instead? We don't know what goes on under the water."

"Think of us as priests of evolution," Senka ibn-Rushd said. "Another twenty years, they'll run at the first sound of a gunshot. Maybe they won't chase chugs at all."

"Here, Tim." Damon held out a handful of bullets. "You've got good self-control. Take some time tomorrow, get some practice. For now, we don't have much daylight."

Most of the merchants and yutzes began setting up tents. Those of ibn-Rushd and Lyons wagons set up to cook dinner. The evening was turning misty.

Marilyn Lyons glowed in the evening light. She was two centimeters taller than Tim and weighed more too. She dressed in brilliant greens and lavenders, dramatic against her white skin and black hair. She pulled cookware out of the storage compartments of Lyons wagon, hefting gear with no visible effort while she rattled off directions a little faster than Tim could follow.

"Teapot. Cook pot. Randall, Hal, get these on the fire and fill them with water. Add the turkeys when the big pot boils. You cleaned them? Good. Wok. Wok. Tim, you want both of these? And take this." She didn't hand it to him; she pointed.

Two flattened cylinders half a meter tall, both glossy glaring red, in a niche beneath Lyon wagon. Tim wrapped his arm around one and caught a familiar scent.

"The speckles always comes back here. Always."

Tim said, "Right."

"That fire, that's yours to work on. The yutzes have the eggs and the veggies are in Dodgson wagon. Boardman, you're with Tim. Tim, any questions?"

"Why did the founders thaw these flies?"

Laughter shook her whole body. "They must have been crazy. Anyone want ovens?"

Randall took the pots and moved briskly away. Bord'n gathered up cooking tools, forks and knives and spoons and spatulas, and set them in a flat shell that must have come off the back of a record-sized shark. He followed Tim, towing the shark shell.

Cookware stored aboard ibn-Rushd and Lyons wagons was little different from what Tim had practiced with in Twerdahl Town. That was a relief. Vegetables were what the merchants could buy in towns and carry in wagons. Meat was what they could kill. Yutzes and merchants had been out hunting while the wagons were in motion.

Lyons wagon's two woks were bigger than he was used to. No problem: a big wok could cook the same omelet as a small one. He was given oil. Yutzes from other wagons had the vegetables he needed. Bord'n had brought knives, spatulas, a whirring thing to whip eggs.

But the eggs were *tremendous*. He asked, "Bord'n, is this some Destiny sea thing?"

Bord'n grinned. "Ostrich eggs. Big bird supposed to be from Earth. Lot of 'em running around here. You maybe saw the mom, and maybe you'll eat her tonight, 'cause we shot three this afternoon."

"Damn. What do the eggs taste like?"

"Better cook one first and find out. Hi, Rian!"

"Boardman." The merchant girl nodded regally. "Tim."

He smiled at her. "Evening."

"How goes dinner?"

"Just another damn intelligence test," Tim said. "I never saw ostrich eggs before."

Rian smiled and moved on.

One ostrich egg was bigger than a ten-egg omelet. The taste was different, and Tim used more seasoning after his first attempt. Speckles, of course. A little lemon rind? Yes.

Veggies and eggs *never* stuck to the woks.

Other chefs were at work around other fires. Quicksilver winked out below the setting sun.

As in Twerdahl Town, people passed carrying food, gave him slices of fruit and big flat grilled mushrooms and ostrich meat, and carried away sliced-up veggie omelets. Ostrich was delicious. Heavier woks, heavier omelets: Tim was working harder than he was used to. He thought of himself as strong, big-shouldered, but this was wearing him out.

Shireen ibn-Rushd accepted a wedge of omelet. She tasted it. "Tim, isn't it? Yes. You have a nice hand with eggs." She put something in his hand, smiled, and wandered off.

Dried cherries.

He noticed tents being pitched and beds laid within. The tents were many-lobed, and flaps were generally left open. Some of the merchants were already asleep before sunset.

As in Twerdahl Town, cooking ended at sunset. He'd wondered. But now cookware had to be carted to the river, washed, part-filled with water, and set back on the fires to boil clean.

Damon led him away to the ibn-Rushd tent. He would not have found it on his own, in the dark. It was a cross, four lobes meeting at a communal circle of cushions, Shireen snoring in one of the lobes. In the center, a low table. Damon and Senka wanted to talk, but they must have seen he was ready to collapse.

He rolled himself in blankets in one of the lobes and persuaded himself he was asleep.

But their voices ran through his dozing mind, telling merchant secrets, and the memories came back in later years.

✳ 9 ✳

B e t w e e n   T o w n s

Rows of fin-contoured legs run down each side. Teeth rim the broad mouth, each splitting into a myriad points. A solid prong on the skullcap shell forms a beak or, more aptly, a ram: the cap butts against the main shell for greater strength. They're air-breathing. They can come right up the beach at you.

—James Twerdahl, Flightcaptain, *Cavorite*

In the morning Bord'n reached through an open flap and shook Tim awake to make breakfast.

Dawn was a red glare above the mountains. Tim was stiff and tired. He did what the other yutzes were doing.

Blow up the ashes and add wood. Wipe out the woks and add dough that has been rising through the night. Cover them. Set the woks on the coals. Now a Destiny seaweed forest is rising from the waves, and it's back to the roofs while the chugs feed.

Chugs move up the beach. Sharks follow as far as the seaweed. No shots are fired. When the sharks return to the sea, the chugs have reached the wagons and the bread is done.

The bread never sticks to the woks.

While merchants get the wagons ready and hook up the chugs, the chefs and yutzes put away the cookware. They pass out bread along a wagon train already in motion.

He met Rian walking back to ibn-Rushd wagon. Almond eyes, dark oval face, intricately shaped hair. Lovely and strange. She studied him, then said, "You look worn out."

"Where do we go next?"

"The Shire. Little town." She turned and was walking with him toward the front of the caravan.

"Does the Shire have a graveyard?"

"I'd think so."

"Just drop me off there," Tim said. "Here, have some bread."

"Thank you. Tim, you can sleep once the bread's handed out."

But the tents were already stowed. "Where?"

"On the roof."

He smiled. Two more wagons, four loaves to hand out, then sleep.

Just past noon, it rained. Six people crowded the wagon's dark, steamy interior amid cookware brought for sale and strange stuff collected in trade. The chugs plodded on while rain played flurries of drumbeats on the roof.

The rain left little time for hunting up dinner. Nobody found any eggs that day. Come evening, Tim and the other yutzes wokked vegetables with yesterday's red ostrich meat and served it over barley.

Wrestling the heavy wok was no easier the second night. When he tottered off to ibn-Rushd tent, yutzes and merchants were playing musical instruments and having a wonderful time. He wondered how they did it.

He felt his way through the tent by touch and hearing: toward Shireen's snoring, then turn left. Curled on blankets, eyes closed, he listened to the merchants' music. It came to him that he was learning more about cookery than about the path of *Cavorite* . . . and then it came to him that he was being watched. He opened his eyes.

Rian.

Just Rian. She asked, "Did you wonder why I didn't come to you last night?"

"No." She seemed to expect something more, so he said, "I thought you must be with somebody in another wagon."

She laughed. "Be with?"

He said nothing. Did merchants say that another way? Maybe a Twerdahl wouldn't know either.

Rian said, "It could have been you. I offered. Nobody turns me down more than once."

Flash of annoyance. Gently, superciliously, he said, "I'm a married man."

He couldn't read her face in the dark. He only saw her turn and move into another room of the tent. Tim let his head fall on his arm, and slept.

*   *   *

Moving up and down the wagon train looked easy. Anyone could do it. But the wagons never stopped moving. Tim was tired all the time.

The stored vegetables were running out. The only fruit left was apples. Chickens and ostriches were scarce in these parts.

The caravan's yutzes took the lack as opportunity. They fished or hunted, or went off into the chaparral to search for anything edible. It was more fun than the continual repair work on the wagons.

Where Earthlife grew, likely you could eat some part of it. Bord'n showed him roots to dig up, fruits to pick, spices. Sage and mustard, apples and pears and oranges, potatoes and yams. Watercress.

The Road ran a klick above the shore, more or less, never dipping very near. Sharks couldn't possibly get that high, and it wasn't convenient for tending the chugs. *Cavorite*'s crew hadn't learned about chugs when they made the Road, hadn't planned for caravans either.

Afternoon of the fifth day they reached land that looked half-cultivated, and twelve houses clustered halfway between the shore and the Road.

You couldn't call it a town. *Farther*, they called themselves. They were friendly to the point of effusive. The merchants supplied food and the Farther folk cooked it. Their style of cuisine was more like Twerdahl Town than Spiral Town. The merchants supplied the speckles.

Several men and women of the caravan didn't use their tents that night, but none of them were yutzes.

On the sixth morning, Tim Bednacourt was no longer tired.

Late afternoon. No ostriches, no chickens, no eggs. Bord'n had killed four rabbits; others had caught fish. Hal showed Tim how to prepare and grill a Destiny shieldfish on a grill carried from ibn-Rushd wagon.

The fish massed thirty kilograms. Its canoe-shaped shell was probably the dorsal surface. The fins on its flanks and underside were shaped to move water, but they bent in the middle and at the base: little legs with elbow and shoulder joints, tipped with twenty centimeters of horn blade. With those and its long pointed beak and the shell for a shield, the creature might fight one enemy while another wasted its efforts on the shell—

"Tim! Snap out of it! Let's get this on the grill."

They cut the fins off at the shoulders, but left the shell on. They set it on the fire, shell down, and trimmed off the fins while that side cooked.

"What's the Shire like?" Tim asked.

Hal said, "Hundred people. Tiny, but they'll cook for us and we'll trade our stuff for rice and nuts. Tim, *do not* try to sleep with any woman of the Shire."

Tim just nodded.

"They're very serious about that."

Tim didn't find that remarkable. "What if a woman asks?"

"Won't happen. Yutzes don't ever get asked. It's merchants who get the action, but not in the Shire."

"How far is it?"

Hal said, "We'll be there in four days, barring bandits."

"Bandits?"

"Guns aren't always for sharks."

The way Hal was grinning, Tim wasn't sure how much to believe. He asked, "How far away are the Otterfolk?"

"We get to Haunted Bay in another fifteen days. From Haunted Bay there are Otterfolk offshore all the way to Tail Town, another six or seven."

"You've seen them? Otterfolk?"

"Yeah."

Bord'n passed, handing out the last ear of corn. They ate, then turned the fish. The grills looked like iron, but they were frictionless settler-magic stuff. Nobody but Tim ever worried that food might stick. It never did.

Tim expected the level of civilization to drop with distance from Spiral Town. But wherever there was humanity, there would always be a few ancient, hoarded miracles.

"Ask Hal about Otterfolk. He's from Tail Town," Bord'n said.

"Oh?"

Hal said, "They're easy to like. Don't touch unless they invite you, because they bite. They can't help it. They like to hear us talk, or sing. They can't talk themselves. . . ." Once started on a topic, Hal tended to talk until some outside force stopped him.

Tim listened and wondered. Jemmy Bloocher was very far from his thoughts these days.

It had grown too dark to cook. Senka ibn-Rushd circulated with apples, and lingered to watch him eat. She said, "Tim, the families don't like quarrels in the caravan. Are you angry with my daughter about something?"

"Mph? No! I think Rian's angry with me. I turned her away, that night on the beach."

"Oh, Tim, that was just . . . I'll speak to her."

"Senka, don't. Ibn-Rushd family found me a married man, and that's what I told Rian."

She stared. "Were you *trying* to annoy her?"

"She annoyed me! Does she think I'm stupid? She rubbed up against me to get me at a lower price!"

"I see. I— Now, Tim, do you mean you're thinking of not . . . rubbing up against anyone until you're back in Twerdahl?"

"I *asked* Loria if she could come—"

"Tim, where are you *from?*"

She knows.

Now wait, she can't be sure.

Could she? In the flicker of firelight, what could she see of his face? Or hear in his voice over the breaking waves? She was his youngest aunt's age, and wise with the wisdom of merchants, and he couldn't guess where he'd made his mistake. What did Twerdahls know, that Spirals did not, that Loria wouldn't have warned him about?

Tim hadn't thought so fast since Jemmy Bloocher killed a labor yutz. He made an intuitive leap and rode it. "All right, I hear what they say."

"*What* do they say?" Senka demanded.

"Love a merchant, never get over it." He was guessing, but not wildly. It was a thing Loria might have concealed, and a thing a merchant woman might like hearing.

Senka was nodding. "But you can't spend the whole circuit wondering about *Cavorite* and Otterfolk, can you? You'll wonder what you're missing."

"Loria's wondering right now, back in Twerdahl Town."

She searched his face. "You asked her to come? She must be *flattered*, Tim. But we wouldn't take her."

"I wasn't thinking."

"Would you like a visitor tonight?"

She might not see his nod. "Yes, very much."

Her hand caressed his ear, and then she walked into the dark.

Haron Welsh had come home with no interest in Twerdahl women. *That* was Loria's fear.

A man wasn't expected to resist a merchant woman.

And Tim was burning to learn why. And yes, he was burning.

In the night a woman came to him. He knew a woman's rich scent that wasn't Loria's, that wasn't quite human. The dark hid everything but that.

She talked. *They* talked, voices in the dark, puffs of her sweet breath on his face. It made him self-conscious for a time, and then somehow it felt right. They moved together and peeled layers of gauzy cloth off each other. Then he was talking to a woman while they made love. It felt kinky, delicious.

Jemmy Bloocher was a virgin when he left Spiral Town. What he knew of sex was what the older boys told. Later he learned what the married men were willing to say.

Loria Bednacourt had taught Tim Hann. And all the glory and joy of the stories was real.

But Senka knew things he had never heard spoken.

They were making a lot of noise, his hoarse shouts, her wild laughter. In a moment of quiet he heard a distant chuckle, Joker's, and a querulous mumble, Shireen's.

In the morning she was gone and he must move.

Breakfast was always the same. Fires, woks and bread dough, chugs and sharks. Quicksilver didn't show at all: for these few days it would be behind the sun. Put the gear away, then share out the bread. The caravan was in motion before he saw any of the family.

Senka greeted him cheerfully from the steering bench. Shireen and Joker leered. Rian wouldn't look at him.

Tim Bednacourt had kept no secrets last night.

The morning looked like coming rain. He lay on the roof and thought.

When Loria let him go with the caravan, she hadn't asked him to be faithful. It seemed nobody would expect him to do that . . . nobody outside of Spiral Town.

Spirals and merchants never mixed. They even *danced* separately in the Road outside Warkan's Tavern. What was *wrong* with Spiral Town?

Hybrid vigor: merchants mated with everyone along the Road. They were trained at love, and everyone came to know it. Except in Spiral Town.

On the strength of that alone, for a moment Senka had guessed what he was.

It was the eighth day since Tim Bednacourt had joined the caravan. Something was different. The hunting parties never moved out of sight, and what they brought back was skimpy. The drivers released their chugs in order, first to last, so that they could bring the wagons closer together.

On the eighth night Tim fell asleep hoping that Senka would come; but he slept dreamless and woke alone on a gray and drizzly morning.

He'd half-expected that.

She'd acted to keep peace in the caravan. Now that problem was solved; and after all, the woman had a husband; and if Damon's knowledge of lovemaking matched her own . . . Tim Bednacourt had better make breakfast.

On this ninth morning the wagons got an early start. Chefs handing out bread must walk farther to reach the lead wagon.

Tim had trouble describing what he'd noticed, but Bord'n knew what he meant. "Open territory. They're thinking about bandits," he said.

Again the hunters stayed close through the day. And again the wagons released their chugs first to last, to draw the wagons together; but the first chugs slowed and waited, so that the entire line of chugs entered the water in a wave.

Again on the tenth morning the wagons, too close together, must hook up their chugs each wagon in turn. Lead wagons got an early start.

Tim mounted to the driving alcove. Joker, Rian, and Senka crowded the bench. Shireen must be resting in the cabin. Tim climbed to the roof. It had been cozy, all five of them huddling in the cabin with rain drumming outside. Better than this.

Joker climbed up to join him. He opened the hatch and burrowed within. The rain had become a steady fall, and Tim asked him, "Shall we go below?"

"No. Here."

Tim took what he was handed: two handfuls of bullets for his silk pouch, and then a hat with a brim half a meter across, with a great gaudy feather stuck in the band. No, not a feather: an orange-and-scarlet Destiny weed such as he'd never seen before, a stalk that split repeatedly into a tremendous plume.

The guns were crude cast iron, but these bullets showed sophistication. Bullets *could not* be carefully hoarded ancient treasures, after all. Somewhere on the Road, someone was making bullets.

The drizzle suddenly turned into a torrent. It was too noisy to talk. It wasn't cold, but Tim would have preferred the cabin. The chugs ahead faded into a silver blur. Chugs plodded out of the blur aft.

Joker waited for the lull, then bellowed, "This is bandit country. Bandits love to hit us in the rain."

"What do I look for?"

Joker stared. *Was Tim Bednacourt speckles-deficient?*

Tim shouted, "Joker, suppose I look out into that murk and I see something human. Is that a merchant or a yutz or a local or a bandit? How do I know? What do I shoot?"

"Oh. All right, look for the hats. A hat with no cockade is a bandit. Shoot it. These cockades molt, so they don't last more than one trip. Hard to steal. There aren't any locals."

"Can't bandits just pick their own cockades?"

"They don't grow here. Tim, if you see a cockade, don't shoot. We've got patrols ahead and behind. Father's in the lead patrol!"

"Could a bandit strip the hat off a dead merchant?"

Joker sighed. "I guess you just have to give him first shot. Or follow my lead."

The rain turned noisy again. Tim could see the wagon ahead, and a hint of the wagon behind and its chugs plodding endlessly out of the rain.

"What do you know about these bandits?"

"Tim, there's nothing *to* know. Whatever you learn, it won't be true the next time you come by. Now go guard the other side."

Tim crossed to the right side of the roof. Joker stayed on the left. The rain continued steady.

Rian climbed out of the driver's well and took a position at the aft edge of the roof, cross-legged, with a gun in her lap.

In the dark to the side of the Road: something moving?

The rain slacked for a moment. Clearly those were man-shapes running. Tim stood, aimed, looked again. Four men wearing broad-brimmed hats. No cockades. He fired into them as the rain blasted down, squeezing the trigger as fast as he could.

Rian was next to him, propped on her elbows and firing as his gun ran empty. Joker held his position on the left. One man was running for the edge of the Road. Tim couldn't see the others. Rian had stopped shooting. Tim was reloading when something twitched at his collar. Tim dropped below the rim to finish loading.

Too noisy to hear the roar, too rainy to see the flash, but someone was shooting back.

Tim could see bodies in the Road as the chugs passed them. He could count four. Oh, damn, one was dressed as a caravan yutz!

It was Randall! Randall was dead in the Road.

"They got us," Rian said.

Tim said, "Hell, no. We got them." Three to one or better.

Rian wriggled across the roof and was talking urgently to her brother.

Ibn-Rushd wagon was slowing, and, incredibly, the chugs behind were pulling Dodgson wagon around to pass. And now Tim saw that the line of chugs ahead of him was broken.

Fourteen ibn-Rushd chugs were pulling ahead of the rest.

Joker crossed to Tim. "We've got some time," he said. "The bandits cut our harness. They only need to do that to one wagon. The caravan can't wait for just us. They'll wait for the rest to pull ahead, then jump us. *Then* we'll have a fight."

They got us. They got ibn-Rushd wagon. Tim asked, "Have you got ten meters of rope?"

"For what?"

"Tie those loose chugs up again. I wouldn't need so much if they weren't still pulling ahead."

"There's a pretty good chance you'll be shot," Joker shouted, but he was already digging into the hatch. He came out with a coil of rope. "Double it up."

Tim took it. It was heavy; it was thick. Would a double strand of it hold the weight of ibn-Rushd wagon? Could he carry it that far? He'd need both hands. No gun.

"Hold up," Tim said. His mind seemed to be racing. The bandits had come from the inland side. But that was then and this was now, and the caravan was moving into a new position. Four bandits to cut the rope, at least one more to lay down covering fire; three now dead. A second group of bandits must be waiting ahead, to take advantage if the first group actually stopped a wagon.

"Just tell me how many bandits there are, Joker. Your best guess."

"Anywhere between, ah, six and fifteen."

"There have to be two groups."

"Right."

"I hope you'll shoot anything that tries to shoot me," Tim said.

"Yes. Don't lose your hat!"

Tim rolled over the left, seaward side. That second group could be anywhere between one and ten, and it could cover either side of the Road. Tim kept his eyes to the left as he dropped to a squatting position and duckwalked. The chugs would shield him from the inland side if he could stay low.

Six chugs were trying to do the work of twenty, and making slow progress of it. Dodgson wagon had come up from behind, and its chugs were moving alongside ibn-Rushd wagon on the seaward side. That would shield him too.

Tim glanced around ibn-Rushd's lead chug, saw no threat, and ran.

Fourteen loose chugs were following Armstrong wagon, moving no faster than they had pulling a wagon's weight.

He heard a whine, left and behind, and cut left before his mind caught up. Left and behind, a bullet grazed the Road and spun away. If that was aimed at Tim, the gunman must be right and ahead, and now Tim had the last pair of freed chugs between that gun and himself. He held for a moment, then shifted: now he was between that pair, and the one on the right was protecting him with its shell. That one grunted and looked at him.

Harness still linked the fourteen. Tying his rope to the harness was hard, clumsy work, until he realized that he could drop the coil of rope. Then it was easy, except that his squatting position was killing his knees. And now he must nerve himself to run back across that wet black empty space. Slip on that slick surface and he'd be meat for the taking!

But his hands were free now. He drew his gun, peered around the last chug, and fired three quick shots at his first glimpse of motion. And ran.

The coil of rope now trailed as far as the six chugs still pulling ibn-Rushd wagon. Tim scooped it up and tied it and pulled the knot taut, rolled under the harness and out between two chugs.

Past the caravan's tail, men in featherless hats were stripping Randall's corpse. One stood up with a gibbering yell and held aloft Lyons wagon's big glare-red can of speckles.

Damn! Why had Randall been carrying *that?* To protect it?

Tim moved back toward the wagon in an agonizing duckwalk he was coming to hate.

The bandits wouldn't let it go at that, would they? One lonely rope was holding ibn-Rushd wagon from disaster. Cut that and—

He'd reached the wagon, seaward side. Joker was looking over at him. Tim rolled underneath, between the wheels, and looked out from a prone position.

Here came the bandit, and he too was in a squatting run. He had a knife. No hat. Tim shot him and he rolled over, then backed away on hands and knees through the rain, leaving a knife as long as his arm. He collapsed before he'd left the Road.

The rear wheels were getting too close. Tim scrambled ahead of them, hands and knees. The bandit's knife came in range and Tim fished it up.

The rope held until the caravan made camp. Again they released the chugs a wagon at a time, to pull the wagons close.

When the chugs left ibn-Rushd wagon for the shore, one remained behind. Tim had never before seen a chug lying down. He went to look.

Its head turned at his touch. Under its cap of shell its eyes were too far apart to see in one direction; but the cap tilted and one eye studied Tim Bednacourt.

There were eight holes in its shell. It was the chug Tim had been hiding behind. Chug armor hadn't evolved to stop bullets.

Joker, Damon, and Rian set down what they were carrying: equipment to repair the harness. "Tim, you did well," Rian said.

"Thanks. Rian, will it die?"

"Yes. It can't feed itself."

"Shoot it?"

She shook her head, and set to work cutting harness.

Damon said, "There's no quick death for a chug. I saw Daddy try once. The brain, it's more a strand than a bulge, and bullets don't turn off its heart for a damn hour. It saved your life, Tim, and there's no way to pay back."

"But you saved ours," Rian said.

Tim glowed with the compliment. "I should do things about dinner," he said.

On the ninth night Tim Bednacourt stayed up far too late trying to learn the songs the merchants and yutzes sang. Joker was a singer too. Between songs they talked about the fight, and Tim bragged without embarrassment.

He listened when the others spoke. They were talking largely for him, enjoying lecturing the novice.

"This clan, they try to chop the harness on one wagon," Bord'n told him. "Then the rest of the caravan has to go on, but the tail guard stays with them. Maybe we kill some bandits, and maybe we lose a wagon. But this clan's only been here three years."

"So?"

Joker said, "Bandits all start as criminals. They're forced out of wherever they lived. Did something dreadful. People along the Road shy from strangers, so they wind up with each other. If they can steal speckles they can keep going. They don't care who they get it from, caravan, village, each other. Sooner or later they run out. Then they turn stupid. They'll attack anything. Then they die out and a whole new nest of the bastards has to grow up somewhere else. So whatever they have of techniques, it gets forgotten and then invented again, see?"

Tim saw. He'd had time to think. He didn't ask which among them had learned to shoot prone. He'd watch. He didn't ask about cockades, and nobody else even referred to them.

He'd never seen the gaudy sprays before today. When did merchants wear those hats? When bandits were expected, sure, and maybe when it rained. Spiral Town had never seen cockades, but anyone along the Road would know of them. He'd given himself away again.

He'd been trained, all of the yutzes had been trained to shoot standing up. Rian and Joker shot prone while the yutzes stood to draw fire.

The caravans had been at this a long time.

Lost sleep didn't hamper him the next morning. His body had caught up with the stresses of a caravan chef, and the morning was glorious.

✳ 10 ✳

Repair and Maintenance

Mankind's wastes have seeded potassium the length of the Crab. Birds and animals of Earth can survive on what gets into the plants. But how are the fish surviving?

My research shows that none of Destiny's predators have learned to store fat. I believe that they have "learned" to avoid eating Earthlife: those who did, starved. Fish and shellfish evolved on Earth are potassium-shy, but they're competing only with other potassium-deficient Earthlife!

—Wayne Parnelli, Marine Biology

By morning light the caravan assessed its wounds.

Two men and a woman of Wu wagon, #12, had bullet wounds and were being tended in Doheny wagon. The bandits who attacked Wu wagon had also killed a chug and damaged a wheel haft. The wheel was ruined.

Ibn-Rushd wagon had severed ropes and, again, a hacked wheel.

While bread was baked and distributed, the rest of the wagons hooked up their chugs and began to move. Two wagons remained behind with the damaged wagons.

Tim was reluctant to ask. "So, are we being abandoned?"

Three yutzes chortled. Bord'n said, "No, but Tim, the caravan can't stay in one place. Chugs wouldn't get anything to eat. So the wagons'll just roll down the Road by a caravan length, and then everyone will spend the day doing repairs."

"What about bandits?"

"We've got Tucker wagon. They've got Spadoni."

"Which are they? I can't tell the wagons apart yet."

"Oh, you'd better know *that*. In every wagon there's extra stores,"

110

Joker said, "like Milasevik and Wu carry tents and bedding. Doheny, that's the infirmary. Doheny is where you run if you've got time to run. It's a better hiding place than the shop sections of the wagons. You go there if you're hurt too. It's in front because anything dangerous hits the front of a caravan first."

"Doheny. Front wagon," Tim repeated.

"Spadoni and Tucker store arms—"

"Don't we all have guns?"

Bord'n hesitated. "Shark guns and ammunition are in Tucker. What's in Spadoni isn't for yutzes. Don't be caught wandering around Spadoni wagon. And of course every wagon is part shop."

Yesterday's bandits had a penchant for attacking wheels. Merchant men and yutzes came streaming back from the main caravan to help set up repair facilities; they did wheels first. Undamaged wagons wanted their wheels reground. Presently they were all rolling wheels back down the Road.

By midafternoon Wu and ibn-Rushd were ready to move.

They rolled just far enough to join the rest of the wagons. Then repair and maintenance work continued all up and down the caravan.

A few merchants were not to be seen. Tim had seen activity around Spadoni wagon. He might guess that they were somewhere about, armed, guarding the caravan. Armed with what? It didn't seem like a good day to stroll past Spadoni wagon.

In midafternoon the chefs dug their fire pits and the chugs ambled into the sea. Nobody had been particularly concerned about hunting. Dinner was skimpy, largely fish and stored vegetables.

Tim became aware that Rian was watching him.

She said, "I might have known Mother would have you if I didn't. I should have taken you on the beach. You would have come then."

Rian made him edgy. Hadn't she flatly rejected him, without his ever having offered? Tim said, "Loria would have brained us both."

"Why would Loria Bednacourt hurt you? Or me?"

"Hang on." Tim spent a minute turning two Earthlife salmon, and thinking.

Then he said, carefully, "You think Twerdahls are all alike? We aren't. Loria doesn't share. She wants her side of the bed, all of it. If she's in the kitchen, nobody else is cooking. Her man is hers from his heart out to all twenty-one digits." It was nearly the truth: Loria would share with her sisters.

"But she's not a merchant."

Again he saw how this would go. "Will you find me tonight?"

"I will," she said tartly, "if you don't stay up till dawn singing!"

When she was out of hearing, he sighed. She'd expected him *last night?* What kind of signal had he missed?

Better not to know than to guess wrong. A yutz could be in a world of trouble if he rubbed up against a merchant woman who didn't want him.

Loria was far behind him, and she would expect this of him, and hate it.

But Jemmy Bloocher still haunted him. Anything he did with a merchant woman might speak his secret. *Tim Bednacourt is a Spiral!*

But then Senka ibn-Rushd must already know. . . .

And he burned.

In the morning Rian was there, her back against his, sound asleep. He watched her for a time, savoring her touch without moving, smelling her hair, feeling good.

Rian was lean and flexible and smooth. She made love with her mother's ferocity . . . and her mother's perception for a man's erogenous zones and how they could be made to react. But Rian paid more attention to what she was doing. The taste of semen surprised her. He was ticklish just above both hipbones; she was delighted. She made momentary mistakes—an elbow whacking him just under the eye—and caught herself, like an apprentice.

Were merchant women *trained* somewhere? And the men too?

Faint noises told him other yutzes were awake.

Rian woke when he moved. Scrambling into his clothes, he asked her, "What's Spiral Town like?"

She looked at him sleepily.

"We wonder," he said. "It's so close."

"Why don't you go?"

He improvised. "I think the older people don't want the Spirals to *know* Twerdahl Town is that close."

"Why?"

"Maybe the Spirals would want to tell us how to live."

Rian yawned. "Maybe so. Anyway, I've never been in Spiral Town. They used to let us halfway in. They don't anymore, but they still buy from us. Not even Gran Shireen ever saw *Columbia*," she said wistfully.

Damon and Joker weren't in the tent. Tim thought nothing of that. While turning bread out of the woks, he noticed how many men weren't staying around for breakfast.

There were times when a yutz might ask questions, and times when he *must* listen. A fresh yutz must be taught. This seemed different. This morning the merchants moved in a closed and purposeful pattern, and a yutz could not make eye contact. Tim could see activity far down the Road, around Spadoni, the weapons wagon. Then men were moving uphill, and everyone was pretending not to notice.

Trader secrets.

It took longer to hitch up the chugs, of course, but—as yesterday—the caravan only moved one generous caravan length. Then all the women and yutzes (and no men) began a cleaning program. Wagons were emptied out and every compartment cleaned. Yutzes polished metalwork until, for the first time, Tim saw wagon trim gleaming. Clothing was laundered.

A handful of merchant women hung around Tucker wagon. They were still taking bandits seriously.

Dinner was skimpy again, but nobody seemed to mind. Everyone ate in a hurry, talking around mouthfuls of food. Tim never twitched anymore at the sight of men and women talking together. Still . . . something odd here.

Tim assembled a dinner for Shireen ibn-Rushd, who smiled down at one and all from her perch in the wagon's driver's alcove. She thanked him, and he said, "They all seem indecently cheerful."

"Isn't it wonderful? There's always a time like this once on a circuit. All the men gone. Just the yutz men and the merchant women, and no locals."

Oh. They were talking in *couples*, many of them.

The yutzes had cleaned up dinner before the sun dipped into evening clouds, with Quicksilver just behind. In fading dusk there was some singing, some storytelling, but a good deal of pairing up and disappearing into tents. Patriss Dole of Dole wagon sang with Tim, and taught him words and harmony to one of the ballads. Her own voice was very good. They'd never spoken until tonight.

They spent some time watching the sky. Patriss was sure she'd found *Argos*, a steady star with a blue tinge, in the plane of the planets. Wouldn't the *Argos* mutineers be carving up asteroids by now? Tim saw a meteor from the west, not blue-bright enough to match vids he'd seen of *Cavorite* rising to orbit, but still.

They went to Dole tent. Too late, too dark to be introduced to the other occupants. Just as well. They explored each other by touch in near-perfect darkness, made love, and talked, and loved again.

He'd hoped she would speak of where the merchant men had gone. She didn't, and he didn't ask.

*   *   *

113

Krista Wu had died of her wounds in the night. They buried her upslope, with a handful of apple seeds.

Thirty men didn't rejoin the caravan until near sunset the next night. They were tired and dirty and laughing among themselves, and again there was no eye contact for a yutz. They had shot a deer . . . or killed it with something stranger; it seemed chewed almost in half.

Grilling venison in the dusk, Tim could watch the merchants gathering at Spadoni wagon. The tools they were carrying, that Tim had never more than glimpsed, were gone when they broke into twos and threes to get their dinner.

Shortly after dawn, the caravan was rolling through tilted grasslands. Twenty merchants and yutzes walked past slowly moving wagons. Though they all carried shark guns, nobody seemed to be worried about bandits.

Eight were hunters. They carried the long knives Twerdahls called "weed cutters." The rest were fishers. Most of them carried line and poles, but Tim and Hal had been given long-handled nets.

When they were clear of the wagons, the hunters turned off, inland. The fishers continued. Now lifeless melted-looking bluffs loomed on both sides of the Road.

Cavorite must have crossed a ridge here, and recrossed and hovered, to carve a level path. When they reached the end of the cut, Tim peered over. He could see a path of gray rock leading steeply downslope through dense chaparral: a waterfall of molten rock, long since cooled.

Merchants spoke a murky jargon among themselves. Even long-term yutzes used familiar words in strange ways. Joker ibn-Rushd and Eduardo Spadoni talked at length in low, angry voices, both of them waving ahead and shoreward. The few phrases Tim heard didn't tell him anything.

When Tim got tired of that, he dropped back among the yutzes. They were talking about catching fish: a great weight of words for a task that seemed exceedingly simple. Tim listened and tried to learn, while they marched for most of a morning.

The Road emerged from between the bluffs. Now it split—

No, the Road ran straight ahead, miles from the sea. But just for a moment—

Tim looked away to rest his eyes. At the edge of vision, a curve off to the left suggested itself. A cut through the low scrub forest, away from the Road. Sparse vegetation was what he'd seen, nothing more; but he knew.

Cavorite had curved from its path, rising into the sky. Had flown downslope to explore, charring the soil. Returned and continued the Road.

They were approaching a river and a bridge. The wagons were two hours behind them. Hal was telling Dannis Stolsh, "We ran back as far as Doheny wagon. I had two bites in me the size of walnuts. Not one of us went past Doheny. We just swarmed up and in, you wouldn't *believe* how fast. It was *crowded* in there, and all men, too, and Bryne Doheny trying to bandage the holes. We could hear the little monsters batting against the walls—"

Tim didn't know enough to get a handle on this, and he didn't want to interrupt.

The merchants were still quarreling. Eduardo Spadoni waved down-slope and barked something sharp. He strode away fast, and Joker lagged to give him room. In a minute that put him alongside Tim.

Tim wanted to see his face. He asked, "Joker. Is it a nickname?"

Now Joker's anger wasn't showing. He wore that bland look: *secrets.* He pronounced his name, differently from what Tim had been saying, and spelled it out: "D-Z-H-O-K-H-A-R. An old name, not meant to be laughed at. My uncle's name is the same, but the family calls him Joe."

"Dzhokharr," Tim tried to imitate Joker's pronunciation. "What did Hal mean, *bites the size of walnuts?*"

Joker stared, then barked sudden laughter. "*I* remember that. Some turkey hunters ran into a hive of firebees in the salt dunes ten days down the Road from here. I could see men running back and climbing all over Doheny wagon and wedging their way in. Then the chugs, they all folded into their shells in a wave that ran right down the caravan. I just gaped, but Father, he got us inside. We all had to hide in the wagons, and some of us got bit. Stopped us for three hours. So, Tim, are you glad you joined a caravan?"

"Oh, yes."

Water roared around rocks, plunging down toward a sea lost to distance and mist. The river was wide here. The massive bridge was water-smoothed boulders embedded in smooth, homogenous rock: poured rock, like several structures near the hub of Spiral Town. Tim showed his awe and hid his recognition.

Over the bridge they went, then downstream, spreading out.

After that nobody got much exercise. The men with poles dropped their lines into still pools in the white water. They sat on smooth rocks and talked or dozed. When anyone shouted, Tim or Hal moved briskly to get the net under whatever was flopping on a line. The fish were Earthlife, three or four species. Dannis spread a sheet well back from the stream and cleaned the fish on that.

The mist cleared for an hour in the afternoon. Tim could see all the way to the sea. There was a rectilinear feature along the shore: houses, many.

"The Shire?"

"Right."

"Why didn't they build along the Road?"

"They don't like us," Joker said. "They'd die without us, so they keep their manners. They'll cook us dinner if we bring the food. They don't fish or hunt much, so they don't get enough fat. There's another thing about the Shire," Joker said. "You don't rub up against Shire women."

He'd already heard that. Tim said, "A yutz wouldn't anyway."

"Here, a merchant doesn't either."

The Shire was spread along five or six klicks of shore, four klicks down-slope from the Road. Over that distance a dozen men carried forty pounds of fish in a net hammock, following a worn dirt path that in no way resembled cooled lava.

There wasn't any beach. Waves smashed against rock cliffs, and only spray showed above the edge.

From a central building the houses reached two arms out along the bluff. They were squarish, with peaked roofs, like the houses of Twerdahl Town. Differences became clearer as they came near. These were smaller. Some had been shored up. They were all the same color: weathered wood. Roofs weren't as high. Walls leaned.

The hunting party beat them down. They'd killed something as big as a small man. Its head was shot to shreds, and puncture wounds showed along its body too. They were showing it to admiring Shire folk when the fishers arrived.

"Boar pig," Hal told him.

A score of children swarmed around the carcass and the hunters from the caravan. Adults hung back, except for a dozen elder men. Those elders came to meet the fishing party.

The merchants' bias against haste might have worked against them. Fresher fish would have made a better gift. The Shire elders chose not to notice. They exclaimed over the fish as they had the boar, gave both to the women's care, and took the merchants off to the big central building that Tim had already dubbed City Hall. It was older than the other houses, and better built; and it had once had windows.

The Shire women were setting up to cook dinner. When Tim announced himself as a chef, they just looked at him, then closed a circle with Tim outside.

Tim was starting to feel left out. The children didn't want to talk, only to look. He watched the women at work for a bit, ignoring Hal's grin. Did they think, did *Hal* think, would *Rian* think that he was interested in *them?*

The Shire women enveloped themselves in shapeless robes. It was hard to see what they were like. One woman seemed bent and twisted, and too young for it. One or two who might be in their teens and twenties moved like they were in their thirties and forties. The way they moved and stood formed groups, with merchants and yutzes and Shire men outside. They closed themselves off from strangers, men and women alike, and only the Shire elders spoke to the elder merchants.

Joker's warning, Hal's warning, seemed superfluous.

The Shire had agriculture, at any rate. There were mushrooms big as a man's hand, corn and squashes and potatoes and unidentifiable flowery green stalks. It was all set steaming between blankets of Destiny ferns over a bed of coals.

The pig got the same treatment. An hour later, the fish did too.

The Shire men were settled in conversational circles, idle but for their busy hands. They ignored the men of the caravan, and Tim respected their wish. But Hal stood above one old man for a time, then called, "Tim? Bord'n? You've got to see this."

The old man was seated against the tilted wall of a house. His skin was dark and seamed, his curly hair gone nearly white. His legs were thin and knobby. There was something distorted about him. Maybe something about the line of his jaw? He'd been working on the pale inner surface of an oval of hard gray stuff nearly a meter long, using tiny pointed picks. Now he grinned up, showing good white teeth set nearly at random, basking in Hal's admiration.

"This's Geordy Bruns," Hal said.

The picks left dark scratches, or else Geordy Bruns had rubbed lampblack into them for shading. He'd carved a seascape: clouds and sea and dark bluffs, the same bluffs Tim could see to the northwest. A man in the middle distance, his back turned, looking up at a tinier human shape on the bluff. Tim turned the picture in his hands. A woman?

"It's amazing," he said, "how much you've shown with so few lines."

Geordy Bruns nodded happily. Tim handed it back, carefully, and asked, "What is this?"

The Shireman's voice was rough, his accent twisted. "Scrimshaw. This's a lungshark's backplate."

Tim studied it. The polished surface had a pearly iridescence. Hal said, "They're littler, but elsewise they're not so different from a chug's. You can go to a caravan's campground and pick up a hundred."

Most of the Shire men were working scrimshaw carvings. Scenes differed; skills did too. Geordy Bruns showed a finished plate, a line of bas-relief skulls, all Destiny life, all clearly derived from some common ancestor. The middle one was certainly a chug. Another man had carved a crude view of Landing Day, as two featureless cylinders descended on inverted candle flames. A man Tim's age was instructing a younger one in technique, practicing on a chipped shell. They stopped uneasily until Tim stopped watching them.

The rest of the caravan arrived near sunset.

The men of the Shire distributed dinner. Some of them ushered the children into their own circle. When Geordy Bruns stood to take his meal, Tim saw that his back was twisted.

These women might know only one way to cook, but it worked. Fish, pig, potatoes and mushrooms and greens, they all tasted wonderful. Tim became certain that they'd used a different Destiny plant to flavor each coal bed. He should have watched more closely.

And finally it came to him to wonder—"Bord'n!"

"Tim?"

"Where on Earth are the chugs?"

"Well, they can't use the bluffs, can they? We turned them loose a couple of klicks up the Road, where they can get to a beach. It's still a good run for them."

"Sharks?"

"We stayed to shoot a few. That's why some of us are late."

Quicksilver was gone, and the sun was a last sliver of light on the sea. Against the dying red sky the silhouettes of human shapes showed their origin clearly. Tim saw it, the common thread. In their stance, in their walk, the Shire folk were distorted. Too many were sick, one way and another. Like Jemmy Bloocher's father: crippled, twisted.

He'd been seeing it half the afternoon: how they set wide privacy bubbles around traders and yutzes both. Beauty being in the eye of the beholder, did they think outsiders were the twisted ones? And the traders were being meticulously polite—

Tim watched Rian and Senka together. Senka's walk was always an invitation, and Rian's too. Not tonight! Senka's walk was clumpy, jarring. Rian tottered alongside, imitating her, two cripples keeping their balance with each other's help, with jaws set in anger against what the universe had done to them. Rian caught him looking, and winked.

The Shire elders and the merchants emerged from conference. Master Tucker and Damon ibn-Rushd accepted fish from two Shire men, then vegetables from another pair. Arms well extended with their plates. Keeping their distance. The senior yutzes knew the drill too.

Whatever was wrong with the Shire folk . . . was it contagious?

That was in the teaching programs too. Humankind had evolved alongside tens of thousands of parasites. The parasites kept pace easily: they died faster so they evolved faster. In Africa and Asia the parasites ruled. Mankind had come later to Australia and the Americas and the polar ice caps; parasites that preyed on humans, were fewer there.

The Destiny expedition had brought no parasites at all.

But disease and parasites would evolve eventually, given enough prey. Ways to fight infections, diseases, and plagues were in the teaching programs.

He couldn't ask a merchant, of course. Tim Bednacourt had never seen those teaching programs. He could hardly ask the children. Boys and girls were moving among the yutzes and merchants, and Tim couldn't shy from them: they were friendly and curious, unlike their elders. But he couldn't quite make sense of their accents.

So Tim Bednacourt began to sing.

He picked a song the yutzes had taught him, a ballad of terror and courage, "Grendels in the Mist." No sex in it, no gender references. A simple chorus shouted at the top of one's voice. It sounded splendid in the dusk. Other voices joined him one by one: yutzes, a few merchants, now a woman's voice, now another, now a girl. . . .

The full moon had risen above the mountains. Quicksilver would have been brighter, but the moon cast as much light. Quicksilver was a point; the moon showed a clear disk. In its light you could walk around obstacles and make out human shapes, but not faces, not even body language. Communication wasn't easy.

But they could sing.

Now the Shire women were singing, and the men listened.

City Hall was crowded, and blazing daylight outlined the door. With the wagons six klicks uphill, the entire caravan had stayed for the night. The building was one huge room with alcoves at the corners. The sleepers all tended to gather at the center.

Tim wriggled his way out of a knot of women and men and made his way out. Children cheered as he emerged into the morning, and he waved back. And froze.

He was in the crater left by *Cavorite*.

It hadn't showed yesterday evening. It showed vividly in daylight.

City Hall had been built on a foundation of melted and recooled lava, a concave dish.

Cavorite must have come straight down.

Cavorite's crew had examined this site and found it good. . . .

But why not bring the Road right down to the Shire?

He was on their track. One day he'd know.

The caravan cruised past the Shire the next morning. Of the Shire's alleged hundred people, nearly forty adults and fifteen children had climbed six klicks uphill to walk alongside the wagons, to haggle or just to watch.

Tim moved up and down the line, passing out bread. He'd wondered if Doheny wagon would be empty, but Bryne and Lucia Doheny were selling toothbrushes, dental floss, bandage cloth, and crudely blown bottles of clear fluid.

Tim recognized these. The bottles held flavorless, nearly pure alcohol. Merchants sold them in Spiral Town as antiseptic. Kids too young for it watered it with fruit juice and drank at secret parties.

The Shire folk were paying off in scrimshaw.

One artist left a carved plate at Dionne wagon and staggered away with a stack of uncarved shark plates as high as his eyebrows.

Geordy Bruns had traded a plate for flour and dried meat and another for dental tools. Tim saw him dropping back as if tired. The trouble with the merchants' way was that some good customers hadn't the strength to keep up.

Tim joined him to see what he still had.

It was the plate with the skulls on it. Geordy pointed them out proudly: platyfish, juggernaut, chug, lungshark, sand trap shark, Otter-folk.

Tim said, "Wait," and jogged ahead.

Sixth from the end was ibn-Rushd wagon. Damon looked at Tim curiously as he clambered through the driver's alcove to the roof. Tim dug into the roof trap and had what he wanted.

Geordy looked through Tim Hann's worldly possessions. They weren't much. Any valuables of Jemmy Bloocher's had stayed in Twerdahl Town.

He said, "This."

It was an old wooden toy model of *Cavorite*, vague in detail, worn by handling in places.

Tim said, "Done," and took the plate of skulls.

✳ 11 ✳

H a u n t e d   B a y

. . . interesting rectilinear formations on the floor of this body of water, like a buried city nearly crumbled to dust. . . .
—Wayne DuQuesne, Systems Integration

In a clearing in a wood of beech and elm there lived two families and a still. The Hornes and Wilsons lived on opposite sides of the Road. The Wilsons made cheese from sheep and goat milk. The Hornes made alcohol.

They didn't bother with glasses. They passed around big wide-mouthed jars of a whiskey as good as any Jemmy Bloocher had tasted in Spiral Town. It went fine with yellow cheese and roasted mutton. When it ran out, they switched to raw-tasting fruit brandies. *That* seemed to be in infinite supply.

Tim missed being drunk among drunken companions, but too much would set him talking. When a bottle passed, Tim tilted it to his mouth, gave it a few seconds, then talked nonstop while hanging on to the bottle until someone yelled for it. His cousin Farank drank like that, hogging the bottle.

Younger merchants were pairing off with younger Hornes and Wilsons; the elders stayed to play host and hostess. Joker ibn-Rushd was finding pleasure in Layne Wilson's company. Astrid and Carol Wilson, sisters, were holding court among the yutzes. The two yutz surgeons from Doheny wagon were topping each other with stories of weird injuries they'd treated. Tim was, as usual, listening.

Bord'n noticed. He spoke of autumn rites in Twerdahl Town. He hadn't seen these himself, so he asked Tim for details and Tim obliged.

Good man, Bord'n. Tactful. He'd helped Tim's cause without meaning

121

to. Tim gave the best description he could of Twerdahl Town's weed-cutting and bathing ceremony, but he didn't know enough of the rationale behind it all to sound quite sober.

Tim enjoyed himself greatly as the hours passed. Being half-sober among drunken friends was a kick.

Younger merchants had gone off with Horne siblings and cousins, but Layne Wilson and Joker were the heart of a raucous one-up punning contest. Tim made a clumsy pass at Layne, took a backhand swing from Joker, fell sprawling, rolled and scuttled back on all fours, mumbling apologies as he went.

That was probably enough of *that*. He joined a singing circle among the yutzes. It covered sounds that were coming from the huts and tents and bushes, and it held until Astrid Wilson lost interest. Carol Wilson had gone off with . . . someone. Where was Hal?

Tim showed off the scrimshaw plate he'd bought in the Shire, pointing out each skull for Astrid with help from several other yutzes, and listening contentedly as they described the creatures from life. Tim might look like he was drinking more than he was, but what he'd had still set his mind buzzing. He looked about him at yutzes and merchants and locals, and none of them seemed the least interested in just another yutz chef.

It could make a man wonder.

The guilty fly where no man pursues. Jemmy Bloocher had killed a yutz during a murderous quarrel. Did any merchant even remember? Did any care?

So Tim Bednacourt pretended to be something he was not, and it seemed he had the knack. But Jemmy Bloocher had never had the chance! Most men, most women, in Spiral Town and anywhere on the world of Destiny, would live among a few hundred people. All would see them growing up; all would know their every secret.

Loria knew who Tim Bednacourt was.

He missed Loria terribly.

Rian ibn-Rushd was in a cluster of Horne cousins, looking hemmed in. Tim wondered if she needed rescue. She caught his eye, and he went to join them.

By morning light Rian looked hungover and disheveled, but her smile was enchanting, conspiratorial. "You look like something pulled out of a pickling vat," she told him.

Tim felt fine. Rian was seeing what she expected.

Last night had been wonderful. *Different*. He had thought Rian would end up with one of the locals, but they'd wobbled off to the tent together. Then Rian had forgotten that she was a skilled . . . was there a word? Sexist? She'd lost a bit of dexterity, and she'd lost herself in sensation. Sex was a game nobody lost.

She helped him into his clothes, and he enjoyed being just a little clumsy.

Yutzes and merchants and locals all looked a bit seedy. The caravan got a late start. They left a variety of goods behind: new tubing for the still, melons and rice, pouches of speckles. They went away with fruit brandy and little clear bottles of alcohol antiseptic, and big wheels of yellow cheese. Mason Horne from Dionne wagon stayed; Anthon Wilson joined Milasevik wagon as a yutz.

When next Tim saw Rian she was asleep on the roof.

Above and below the Road were shallow grass slopes dotted with sheep, the source of the cheese they'd eaten last night.

The Road had angled inland since before they reached the Shire, three days ago. They were a good two klicks inland now, and half a klick above sea level. The shore ahead and below curved around in a vast half-circle. Tim couldn't judge its actual size.

"Rian," Tim asked, "what if you got pregnant on the Road?"

"Then I get a baby."

"Raised by the caravan?"

Her eyes opened. "Tim, it's a secret."

By now he knew better than to probe further. "Rian, do you think *Cavorite* was avoiding the sea?"

Rian mulled the question and presently said, "Maybe."

"Why?"

"Maybe not. Go get us some tea, Tim."

Being this far inland gave access to the grassland, grazing for sheep and/or forage for goats on the hills beyond, whatever *goats* might be. Last night he'd eaten what he was told was goat cheese.

But this must have been a blackened, lifeless slope until *Cavorite* seeded the land with grass, and returned to leave half-grown sheep and goats.

Tim reached back into memory for the map of the Crab. A composite photograph from eleven hundred klicks high, the text called it, with sketches of Spiral Town and the Road overlaid. Those added lines were fiction, though, drawn by people long dead who never knew where *Cavorite* had gone. It was worth remembering that *Cavorite* had *flown*, that the crew had seen patterns a bicyclist or merchant could only guess at.

What *had* they seen, that they put the Road so high? Level terrain *here*, suitable for the Road. Bluffs at the sea's edge, or a color in the water that matched a breeding ground for lungsharks, or worse. The lessons said that you could see sea-bottom contours through many meters of water, if you were high enough, looking straight down.

Two hundred-odd years ago. Best to keep *that* in mind too. Was the sea higher in that age? Were there storms to make the shore a death trap?

Something had persuaded *Cavorite* to leave the sea.

Water and tea leaves and a glass jar were kept on the wagon roof. During the day it would be warm and fragrant and ready to drink. Tim filled five big mugs and shared them out, then refilled the jar.

Merchants had their secrets, and questions about *Cavorite* were not welcome. Tim kept his silence. He'd learn about *Cavorite*. He'd learn why merchants would rub up against anyone along the Road, except in the Shire and Spiral Town. The secrets in Spadoni and Tucker wagons didn't interest him, but he'd learn why merchants kept them hidden. There were questions he hadn't thought of asking yet, and he'd learn those too.

A river ran in S-curves, broad and shallow, across the caravan's path. Tim could see no sign of a bridge.

Tim lay on the roof with his head over the driver's alcove. He pointed ahead and asked, "How do we pass that?"

Damon looked up from where he was cleaning their guns. "The Spectre? You'll see."

They were all clutching big mugs of sun-warmed tea. Joker was driving, Shireen beside him, their heads a little below his. Neither looked up as the old woman prattled.

"Lucia Doheny? She doesn't have a family. It's just her—"

"She did, though," Joker said.

"Oh, yes. Doheny wagon was the infirmary before I was born, but it used to be at the tail, until Lucia's man and father and boy and girl were killed by . . . I can't recall."

"An animal?" Tim asked. "Bandits?"

"Bandit *town*, I suppose—"

"Wasser Township!" Damon snapped without turning around. A few moments later he said, "They're gone now, of course. That's their graveyard upslope. It's what reminded me."

There was nothing to mark a graveyard here, and nothing to mark a town ahead or behind, unless . . . a certain linearity to the chaos downslope.

"Yes, Wasser," said Shireen. "They were buying stuff as we went past.

Not buying much. All crowded around Doheny there at the tail, but we
didn't notice anything until they all pulled knives. Lucia was on the roof.
That saved her. Brenda Small saw what was happening back there and
we came. They killed Morris and Boris and tore their way in and got
Wendy and, and, I can't remember, the little boy. But we got there in
time to save Lucia."

Damon: "So Lucia reinforced Doheny wagon. Built it like a safe.
Turned it into a refuge. Oh, and it's heavier than the rest of the wagons,
so Doheny always has twenty chugs even if they have to come off another wagon."

Shireen: "A lot of Wasser Township got away. They bothered us for
years after."

Damon: "We burned their village, though. Most of their graves weren't
marked, but we flattened those too."

Both front wheels went over a bump.

When the rear wheels bumped, Tim was at the roof's edge to see
what happened. The Road humped, just a bit, in a little ridge. *Cavorite*
must have stopped here and then resumed, and what was the ship doing
in between?

But Doheny wagon was arcing around, off the Road. Spadoni wagon's
chugs were following Doheny around one curved arm of the river. That
seemed far more interesting to Tim.

"Damon, what are they doing?"

Damon looked around. "Turning off for Haunted Bay."

"Damon, is that whole stretch of coast Haunted Bay?"

"Sure. Baytown is just downslope."

The bay stretched around in a ragged arc, and Tim remembered the
maps. He suddenly realized what he was seeing.

The arc was a hundred and ten klicks around, he remembered that.
The middle of that arc, unseen, was the Neck. Beyond that . . . he was
looking at the mainland.

The trail down didn't match the curves of the Spectre River, but it had
its own switchbacks. It was unplanned, not made by *Cavorite*'s flame.
The Road ran straight beneath the river and on out of sight, as if there
had *been* no river when the Road was made.

Tim wondered if they would leave the wagons. But the chugs must
be fed, and they were two klicks uphill from their clientele, so the whole
caravan came picking their way down.

There *was* a bridge. Doheny's chugs were already plodding past it.
The river was wide here, and the bridge was too, with two sturdy feet

in midstream. This didn't look like *Cavorite*'s work. Impressive, but crude.

The nearest houses were not far below the bridge.

They'd been noticed. Women and children were coming up to meet them. Joker and Senka and Rian descended to keep shop while Damon drove.

The river splayed out into a salt flat cut by bifurcating streams, twenty or thirty before they reached the sea. Near a hundred houses crowded this side of the river. On the far, northwest shore was nothing but sand beach, and a line of posts, and an eroded shape like a shallow dish set on the sand. Tim knew that shape. *Cavorite* must have settled on its drive flame.

The southeast shore was sand. Inland was a stand of Earthlife trees, just a bit too green and regular, as if tended: possibly a graveyard. Better leave that alone, but there were scrub trees growing elsewhere, dusty green among the Destiny colors. Tim saw that he could make fire pits and find firewood.

That was how they would cook, no problem, if Haunted Bay didn't cook for them.

Out on the water . . . those tiny shapes were boats. Twenty, thirty, more: narrow, pointed at both ends, with white sails above.

The houses spoke a community of two or three hundred. They were squarish, well made, built wide of the river delta and well back from the sea, leaving a beach scores of meters wide. Tim counted more than thirty boats. None were on the water.

Now, where were the men?

"Tim," Damon said, "keep the children occupied, will you?"

"Mmm. So their mothers can buy in peace?"

"They buy when we're leaving. Now they just want to see what we've got."

In Twerdahl Town and elsewhere they might have wanted that too. Their wish had not been granted there; why here? But Tim only asked, "What are they expecting, a magic act?"

"Can you do that?"

"No. I could show off my surfing? Nope, not that either." There were no surfers on the water, and in fact Haunted Bay was as flat as a sheet of glass, barring the boats and a thousand white riffles.

Show off a bicycle? Tim Bednacourt didn't have one and perhaps shouldn't know about them.

He shrugged elaborately, and Damon grimaced. "Get them to lecturing you. You're good at that."

*   *   *

The children exclaimed over Tim's scrimshaw. Three or four had seen Otterfolk skulls, or claimed to, and one said he'd seen a shark skull. He got them talking about themselves.

A little girl pointed. "That's where we live, see? The little house between two big ones."

Tim asked, "Why are they only on this side of the river?"

She stared at him, astonished. An older boy said, "We can't build houses on the other side. That's where the Otterfolk come to trade. Mother says they like the water near river mouths. Salty, but not real salty."

Tim watched, and nodded. Houses along the river had access to fresh water. Southeast, that stretch of beach would feed the chugs. In between was the delta: diluted salt water. "Is that where the Otterfolk live?"

The girl nodded vigorously. An older girl said, "There, and *there*," waving toward thousands of square klicks of water, west and northwest.

Joker was suddenly among them, dropped from the wagon roof. "Won't have to worry about sharks here," he said. "Water's too fresh for 'em. Hi, Carlene!"

"Hi, Joker!"

Joker set to stowing items that ibn-Rushd wagon was getting in trade. Tim asked the little girl, "You know Joker?"

"Since I was little. Mom says he's my father. What's it like, being a yutz?"

"So far so good. I haven't really had time to find out. Carlene, what's that huge dish?"

"Dish?"

He pointed. "On the other side—"

"Oh, *Meetplace!*" The girl laughed so hard that all the other children started laughing too. "Meetplace is where we trade."

"In the dish itself?"

"Yes. Kids get to go too sometimes."

"Where're the Otterfolk now?"

The oldest boy pointed at the bay. "Watch," she said.

They watched. Boats running back and forth, and riffles of white, and "There!" cried the boy, and Tim saw nothing. Then a white riffle appeared and Tim saw a black dot in its center, only for a moment, just as the boy said, "Their heads pop up and make a little wave."

He asked, "When do you trade? Is it soon?"

"Oh, no, not while the caravan's in."
Damn!

Merchants and yutzes, local women and children all pitched in to dig out fire pits and fill them with twisted wood from upslope. Coals were burning nicely, and vegetables were cooking, when the boats came in.

It all happened in some haste. Thirty-odd boats ran aground while the men pulled the sails down, then jumped into waist-deep water to pull them up onto the sand. That looked like fun, and Tim plunged in to help.

There were men on either side and he did what they did: grip one of four handholds set at water level, lift, and pull. Fish flopped around two peculiar objects in the bottom of each boat: a flat wooden fin with a bar for a handle, and a bigger heavy flat thing with no handle.

You couldn't sail a boat with those things lying in the bottom. They'd get in the way. Hmm?

The merchants and yutzes only watched as the sailors, and Tim, pulled the boats ashore.

Now the sailors pulled straight up on the masts, pulled them out and set them on the sand, and set the big wooden fins there too, to get at the fish. They spread the sails on the sand and began scooping fish onto them.

The smell of fish was everywhere.

The women began to clean fish and array them in fire pits.

The men flocked off, not toward the houses but toward the mud-flats below. Two came jogging back to get Tim, who stood dripping wet.

Two fishers, mid-teens, jogged up toward the houses. The rest plunged into the several channels of clear water that ran through the delta.

The boys came back with armfuls of towels. Fishers were taking off their clothes, dipping them, and wringing them dry.

The boys were setting their towels on . . . trays? Not on the mud. Tim hadn't seen that as a problem. And the fishers were setting their wrung-out clothes on those same trays, narrow things near a meter wide, scores of them sitting everywhere along the flats. They didn't look carved and they weren't quite flat, and Tim manfully resisted the urge to turn one over.

The fishers were staring at him, not unfriendly, just curious. Tim looked back. They were built like he was, and they must have seen the same, because they were turning away, curiosity satisfied.

Damn, he'd guessed right: he was the first naked man they'd ever seen from a caravan. What had the Haunted Bay women been telling their men?

The smell of dinner lured them back. As they passed a boat Tim pointed at wooden fins lying on the sand. "What are those?"

"That's the rudder," one of the youngest fishers said. "You steer with that. That's the keel, it keeps the boat moving straight when the wind is from the side."

Tim had learned not to ask twice. He studied the boat instead. He could see that there were mountings on the bottom of the boat and hinges at the stern. Fins to guide the flow of water?

The locals cooked; the yutz chefs served. Tim found several merchant ladies in a crowd of local men, in the silver glare of Quicksilver. He served out the vegetables he was carrying. He took the chance to ask Senka, "Have you ever seen Otterfolk?"

Senka smiled at him. "Not close."

He went away, and thought, and came back with a sizable Earthlife fish deboned and cut up for serving. Senka and her grandmother were perched on dunes to eat. Tim asked Shireen, "*You* must have seen Otterfolk."

The old lady grinned at him. "Pictures."

Senka laughed suddenly. "You think they're a hoax? A *joke?*"

He hadn't. He remembered the grendel hunts in Spiral Town; the new kid was always told he would be the bait . . . but Tim Hann wouldn't know about those. He said, "Joker once told me I'd see Otterfolk."

"You did."

"From high up?" He'd seen a momentary black speck in a sudden white riffle on the bay, and a shape carved on a shark's shell.

He came back to serve a corn pudding. Senka ibn-Rushd studied him without humor, and this time he didn't speak.

"You don't go near Otterfolk," she said. "Fishers took you to the mudflat because you swam with them. Don't do that again, and don't think it means you can go there alone. Don't cross the river until the caravan does. Tim, we *never* have to say these things! Most yutzes are afraid of Otterfolk. Why aren't you?"

Tim shrugged that off. "I know people who are afraid of guns. And swimming." What tales did children hear about Otterfolk that never reached Spiral Town? Dangerous topic. Change it. "Senka, doesn't *any-one* go near the Otterfolk?"

"Well, yes, here and at Tail Town. But they know the rules."

"Can't I—"

Shireen spoke. "Not rules you write down. Rules you learn from when you're a baby, if you live along this shore. Boy, it isn't the locals who make the rules. It's the Otterfolk. Stay clear of the Otterfolk."

✳ 1 2 ✳

Tail Town

Cavorite blew up on the Neck. Half the crew got out in time, and they moved back up the Crab. Yes, it's only a story, but can't you see how the whole Neck was fused?

—Tail Town tale

Tim crawled around the tea table and out of the tent. His sleeping hosts didn't stir.

Why had Senka assigned him the alcove farthest from the entrance? Come morning, a yutz chef *had* to crawl past everyone else. He hadn't wondered until now, but—

Had there been yutzes who robbed merchants?

Dawn flamed off the mirror-smooth water of the bay. The mirror broke in a frothy wave as an army of chugs pushed a jungle of weed onto the beach. No sharks appeared. Only the Tucker and Spadoni merchants even bothered to draw their guns.

The chugs finished feeding and straggled into position.

The wagons began moving away from Baytown. Their sides dropped open to welcome the younger men and women of Haunted Bay. Older folk must be staying with the children. Chefs moved bread, yutzes moved merchandise, merchants bought and traded.

The locals weren't holding out for bargains today. The upward slope was robbing them of breath.

It didn't slow the chugs. It didn't slow Tim, though once it would have.

The locals followed the caravan onto the bridge and across the Spectre. Thirteen wagons and hundreds of people, but the bridge never quivered. At the far end they turned back, every one.

The caravan continued along a rising path.

In the afternoon, merchants went out to hunt. A dozen yutzes were sent to harvest what was to be found. The chefs went with them, armed with shovels.

The way continued gently upward. It might have been a cow path widened by wagon wheels, but picks and shovels had shaped it in places, and here a landslide had been cleared away.

Along the way were fruit trees and fields of grain half-strangled by Destiny weeds. Without weeding parties, Destiny life would have won. Tim was sure they must exist. He was glad not be drafted into one.

The chefs didn't stay with the pickers. Hal held rank here, and it was Hal's task to make ready for dinner.

They stopped at a spring-fed stream. They found wood for fires. They found traces of old fire pits on the slope, dug them out, and shaped the detritus into seating arrays. Beds of coals were glowing orange by late afternoon, when the yutz and merchant parties arrived.

The chugs pulled to a halt and the drivers turned them loose. The beach was more than a klick downhill, with a two-hundred-meter drop. The chugs seemed to crawl forever before they reached the sea.

Nobody followed them down to guard them.

Cooking on a slope of rock and dirt was awkward. None of the current crop of chefs had done it before, save Hal. Mistakes were made. Dinner was late. They served some potatoes raw in the center. Bord'n fell while carrying a haunch of boar. The meat rolled until it disappeared into chaparral, and Bord'n's ankle swelled to the size of a grapefruit. Most merchants didn't seem angry or even surprised.

Tim watched dying red light on the bay. A school of lungsharks would find a good meal here, if they could tolerate diluted salt water for a bit. But the chugs flowed out like a long wave breaking, and dined undisturbed in the ruins of a seaweed forest, and presently crawled uphill to the wagons.

Next day the path rose to rejoin the Road. They had to stop earlier because the chugs must travel farther. Otherwise—well, dinner went better for last night's practice, even with Bord'n incapacitated.

The slopes below the caravan were bare of houses and structures of any kind, for that whole day and the day following. Meals were red meat and chance-met vegetables.

The third day fizzed with suppressed excitement. Marilyn Lyons supervised dinner and cleanup, then pulled Tim *and* Hal into the Lyons family tent.

She'd never touched either of them before, and Tim didn't ask why she chose to now. She no longer feared that rubbing up against a yutz or two would cost her respect or authority. They must be nearing the end of . . . something.

On the fourth morning it was clear that the land was narrowing. The Road dropped again. It could hardly do otherwise, though the wagons were riding the rocky crest of Crab Island as it sloped down toward Tail Town.

On the maps Crab Island had broad and narrow sides, unequally bisected by the Crest. The peaks here at the northwestern end of the mountain chain had melted like wax. The Road ran almost level, angling down; but its width pulsed like a heartbeat, wide where peaks had been, narrow where there had been a lower crest.

The range looked like a candle castle. It was ugly as sin, and *Cavorite*'s crew must have known it even as they were melting mountains into Road.

Where lava had run from melting peaks, the Road's edges angled up. In the narrow places the edges angled down to sheer cliffs. It would be easy to fall.

Heights didn't seem to bother chugs, low-built as they were. Tim, riding cross-legged on the roof, tried to put it out of his mind.

Below and ahead was a community bigger than the town of Haunted Bay. Houses sprawled off down the shore, but the bulk of the town crossed the ridge to touch both shores. Its pattern was angular and ordered. Tim couldn't make out individual features yet.

Yutzes ambled along the Road, stopped to talk, walked on. Others perched on rocks and let the wagons go past. Yutzes learned that from merchants. Let your goal come to you! Merchants didn't hurry, and a yutz worked hard enough.

But why were there so many?

A split boulder was moving placidly toward him, and Hal was on it. Tim waved, but Hal was watching the town below. Hal would be getting off there.

—Oh, *that* was it. These five or six yutzes must be from Tail Town. They were saying good-bye to friends.

Beyond Tail Town the land narrowed. Unmistakably he was seeing the isthmus and the mainland beyond. It was hidden in distance and mist, but he was seeing the mainland with his own eyes!

And missing an opportunity, too. He'd view Tail Town and the Neck in detail when the caravan drew near. Tim got up and crawled (the sheer drop was getting to him) to the wagon's aft edge, and that was his first sight of the narrow coast of the Crab Peninsula.

Cliffs ran straight to the sea, sheer rock in a sixty- to seventy-degree slope, with glossy runnels where lava had flowed from the peaks.

He was not seeing very much of the hidden coast. The Crest curved a little, and that curve hid everything but . . . hmm . . . forty klicks of beachless coast facing north. If it was all like this, then small wonder that the colony had set Spiral Town on the Crab's fat side. But he was seeing more than any Spiral had seen!

Springs flowed out of the mountainside; a hundred waterfalls merged on their way down. A big, blocky structure intercepted the biggest falls. At the mountains' base the falls joined in a river that flowed northwest into a tiny perfect circle of blue water, just inland from the bay.

Hal's rock was below. Hal got up. He spoke a few words to the ibn-Rushd family, then drifted back.

Tim waved ahead. "Hal? That's your home?"

Hal pointed along the shore. "There. They all look alike, but my home is tenth along Bayshore Ride from Tucker's Lake."

Tim looked. "The circle."

"Right, where the Last Drink runs."

Tucker's Lake was just the size of the crater across from Baytown: a landing crater left by a hovering *Cavorite.* The river must have filled it afterward. Tenth along the widest street . . . well, they did all look alike, peaked two-story houses, but they were bigger and finer than the houses of Baytown, with wider streets.

Tim chose his words carefully. "Don't other towns along the Road seem a little, well, crude?"

"Tim, they do. I thought I'd been had. But they're all different, you know, and I knew I'd get home with tales to tell."

"Those are boats, aren't they? Do you fish?"

"Some."

"Are the fish different outside Haunted Bay?" Tim's eyes flicked forward, just for an instant. No merchant was in sight.

"Sure. Cooking style's different too. You've noticed? And we don't get bandits here."

At this aft edge of the wagon he'd be out of earshot. He said, "Or sharks."

"Nope."

Not *"The Otterfolk kill them."* So: "How about Otterfolk? No, hell, you live with Otterfolk."

"Well. Not *live*," Hal said, and caught himself.

Worth a try. Now change the subject. "Where do we camp? Who cooks?"

"I'm going home. You, you'll trade off this eve, and you'll eat with the autumn caravan. You go through town and camp on the Neck. We do the cooking, I mean the locals. The merchants, some of them like the restaurants—"

Autumn caravan? Puzzled, Tim looked toward Tail Town again, and then beyond.

The Road crossed the Neck, or became the Neck, and continued inland, following neither shore. Along the Road just beyond the Neck he saw a dark line.

The *next* caravan.

Tail Town didn't huddle like Haunted Bay. The streets were wide enough for thirteen wagons pulled by more than two hundred chugs, and customers to walk alongside. Along the low ridge that the Crest had become were structures bigger than any house. At the outskirts were big boxes with no windows: storage places. A lot of trading must go on in Tail Town. Nearer the center were public buildings with wide stretches of grass and gardens around them. Pipes, aquaducts must be fed by the Last Drink River.

Tim had come to expect that the level of civilization would drop with distance from Spiral Town. Tail Town was nearly a match for Spiral Town, and Hal seemed to take it in stride.

Tim didn't notice when Hal disappeared.

The houses ended suddenly, and the wagons were slowing. Inverted boats lay in a line along a beach of fine white sand. Twenty-two boats of the same type he'd seen in Baytown, with handholds at the waterline, and detached wooden fins lying beside them. Tracks ran out of the water into a shed, and the nose of a twenty-third boat poked out.

"We lose you here," Damon said.

Tim jumped, and the merchant laughed. He sat down cross-legged on the roof. "We'll cross the Neck, and the wagons will be repaired, and the chugs will be turned loose. You'll join the autumn caravan and go back. Tim, a yutz goes around the full cycle. You'll see some of Spiral Town before you turn back, if that's what you want. But you could just go as far as Twerdahl Town."

Tim pretended to think about that. He asked, "What's Spiral Town like?"

"Like they don't want us, but they want speckles," Damon said. "We used to take our wagons deep into Spiral Town. Now they stop us at the first curve, but there's a wonderful inn. You really should see Warkan's Tavern."

"I'll ask Loria." Damon grinned. Tim asked, "We don't cross the Neck? I wanted to do that. It'd be a rite of passage."

"Tim, we shoot anyone who crosses the Neck unless he's a merchant."

Tim had guessed as much. "That's one serious rite of passage. Now, Hal says the town serves dinner for two caravans. Do we help cook?"

"The locals do a seafood grill. You'll *love* it. Anything else comes from us, and we serve. Two caravans is one serious cookout. If Tail Town wasn't so big they couldn't do it at all. What have we got?"

"Root veggies. Not much fruit, but some. The boar meat's gone. Pickings have been skimpy since Baytown. Rabbits—"

"Use it all. Now, tomorrow there'll be a few new yutzes. They'll have to learn."

Jemmy Bloocher had fled from the summer caravan.

In Twerdahl Town he'd stopped, and married, and when the summer caravan caught up, he'd been Tim Hann of Twerdahl Town, cooking in firelight and fading sunset.

Winter came and went, and the spring caravan brought strangers who picked up Tim Bednacourt and carried him the length of the Road.

—But the Road continued an unknown distance into the continent, and *Cavorite*'s trail went with it—

And the autumn caravan would carry him back.

Should he let Rian give him a gorgeous send-off? Or Senka? Or would they be busy in Tail Town tonight? Or should he wait to meet the women of the autumn caravan?

His mind could see no threat. He'd serve these strangers as he'd served the spring caravan, and live his life out in Twerdahl Town.

His adrenal glands were screaming bloody murder.

Senka set him a few errands up and down the caravan while the wagons ran onto the Neck for two klicks and a bit. The wagons stayed on the broad side, the bay side of the midline hump. They were a hundred meters apart when Damon loosed his chugs to join the others, a little early today, with the sun still half up the sky. The autumn caravan had turned theirs loose too. Half a thousand chugs all flowed into Haunted Bay, spreading out so that one long wave entered the water.

Had a chug ever investigated the other ocean?

Haunted Bay continued around, the shore curving into distance and mist. Otterfolk must be out there, all the way around the curve of island and mainland both.

Lines of wagons faced each other across the Neck.

The Neck was Road: softly contoured gray rock crazed with cracks. Big cracks served for the barbecue fires; little cracks could break an ankle. A frozen lava pool ran from sea to sea. Rounded edges dropped into two oceans. A ridge ran down the middle, the last remnant of mountain range. There was no trace of life save for the wagons.

Cavorite drifted back and forth until the whole of the Neck glowed red and orange, to bar any living thing that might cross from the mainland. Humanity's rule of the Crab was not to be challenged.

Under direction of the chefs, yutzes carried the caravan's stores of fruit and vegetables to the midpoint. Tables were arrayed there, a permanent feature. The chefs laid fires and started root vegetables and pots of beans. Gaudy merchants watched them from the far caravan.

Where were the chugs? They'd been underwater too long.

A woman walked across to join them. She was hefty, formidable, like Marilyn Lyons. Her robes blazed with color: cloth that had not yet felt the dust of the Road.

"I'm Willow Hearst." She had a carrying voice. "Randy and I work Hearst wagon. Hearst and Jabar wagons carry the cooking gear and the chefs. Go back to your wagons and get your possessions. We'll sort you out when you come back. We'll still have plenty of light."

Three more merchants had left the autumn caravan. Would they give further orders? But they were swinging wide of the cookfires, headed for town.

Joker—"Joker? Where are the chugs?"

Joker smiled and pointed toward the fog-shrouded mainland. "See, they can't climb back out. They can walk underwater against the current. There's better forage on the mainland, where fisher boats haven't stirred things up. And then they're home to stay, Tim, with a hell of a tale to tell, presuming chugs could talk. The autumn caravan won't take chugs that are marked."

"It's beautiful," Tim told him.

"We've done it this way for two hundred years. The autumn caravan picks three hundred or so. You'll see them straggling in all night. They haven't learned yet. The ones that get here last, they won't be taken."

Willow Hearst had told them to leave, and the yutzes were all going back to the spring caravan. Could they abandon dinner at this stage? Hal wasn't here to tell him. Tim was senior chef. But the vegetables were cooking nicely, the fruits were arrayed and some were stewing, and what remained could wait.

The party of three was close now. They were all older men. Elders of Doheny, Spadoni, and Tucker were coming to meet them. They would dine in Tail Town and talk of things even the younger merchants shouldn't hear. Tim looked again and recognized Master Granger.

He let his placid yutz's face turn gently aside while his eyes followed the old man. Yes, that was his father's sometime friend, Master Sean Granger.

Tim's adrenal glands had known all along. His mind was only just catching up. Not three caravans. Two. In summer it was twenty wagons; in autumn and spring, some were left for repair. The people of the summer caravan, whom he'd eluded once, had come back as the autumn caravan.

Tim mingled with the other yutzes.

Villagers were passing the spring caravan, pulling a string of little man-drawn wagons. Tim sniffed great masses of sea life. The merchants swung wide; Tim edged close to inspect the fish, pulling other chefs with him. "Good haul," he told one of the men.

"We say *good catch*," the Tail Towner said.

—And the elder merchants were past, and the yutzes were among the wagons.

Tim climbed into ibn-Rushd wagon and onto the roof. Opened the trapdoor, pushed his head into the dark and set the tea bowl under him, before he let the terror have him. He felt like he might throw up.

Sean Granger was no threat. The old man would remember Jemmy Bloocher as a little boy, and Tim Bednacourt as a Twerdahl Town chef. But younger merchants had seen Jemmy Bloocher kill a man in Warkan's Tavern.

He'd kept his possessions in his carry pack. In a moment he could snatch it and run . . . where?

Anyone caught crossing the Neck would be shot.

The far side of the Crab would kill any swimmer.

Tail Town sprawled from Haunted Bay to the other sea. There was no path back that didn't run through Tail Town.

He couldn't join the autumn caravan. He couldn't run, not until dark: there was nowhere to hide. Did he dare to serve them dinner? Yes, with dark falling, but be ready to run at a moment's fright.

Run where?

Fingertips stroked his arm, wrist to elbow.

Tim straightened to kneeling position. He didn't look around and he didn't flinch. He reached back and let his fingers trace a slender neck and jaw and nape. Smooth. He leaned back. Rian. *Good.* Senka was just too good at reading minds.

He asked, "Do I get a spendid send-off?"

"Hey, didn't Marilyn Lyons use you up?"

"I damn well needed all the help I could get," he admitted.

She laughed. "Tim, there are women in the autumn caravan too."

"I haven't met them." Witnesses. Women who would look straight at a murderer and know him half a year later. "Can I give *you* a splendid send-off?"

A breathy laugh. "You might not impress a lady if I get to you first."

"Given the choice—" He turned. Their breath mingled. "It's a choice? I'll risk it then." He wasn't just randy, and it wasn't because he'd never see Rian ibn-Rushd again. Never see any woman until he could reach Twerdahl Town and Loria. But he would have done it just to forget the risks he'd face tonight.

It was a splendid send-off she gave him. They'd never made love in the open, or in daylight. Perhaps they were even seen from other roofs. Even now he didn't see Rian naked: they kept most of their clothes on.

As his breath slowed it came to him that this was the lesser risk. The darker the better when he joined the other caravan, and if he had a decent excuse for delay . . . well, an indecent excuse was better than none.

An unworthy thought.

"Tim," Rian whispered, "time."

He nodded, and kissed her, and reached into the trap for his pack.

"Don't take the gun," she said. "Guns go with the wagons. You'll get a new one."

"What about these clothes?"

She laughed. "They're yours."

He pulled the gun from his tunic pocket and dropped it into the hatch. He pulled out his travel pack, opened it, and spilled it across the flat roof. "Better see if I've got everything." *No second gun, see?* The bandit's long knife, his trophy from the attack, was wrapped in spare clothing. The carved shell was too. He unwrapped it—"I bought this with something of mine." *No speckles either, see?* He wrapped the shell again and shoved it into the travel pack, donned the pack, and dropped over the edge of the wagon.

Run now, or serve dinner?

Rian dropped beside him, flushed and lovely. She took his hand, and off they went across the Neck with the other stragglers. She'd made his choice. What the hell, he was ravenous.

✴ 13 ✴

All at Sea

If these creatures are anything like sapient, they must be left alone. Willow Granger is most emphatic on this point.

—Cordelia Gerot, Xenobiology

Willow and Randall Hearst met them as they arrived. She was even more large and magnificent close up. Her husband was shorter, slender, and dapper. Rian was amused and hiding it.

They showed him to Hearst wagon, third from the front. Tim and Randall climbed to the roof. Randall ceremoniously passed him a glare-red shaker of speckles, then a gun and some bullets. "Sharks don't get this far into the bay," he said. "Still, nobody likes surprises. Stow your pack. If you need a rest stop, it's over the hump."

"I'd better."

What remained of the Crest was shallow, but taller than he'd thought. Tim paused at the top. He was seven meters up, and the Neck and the bay and the far ocean rolled away to infinity.

The bay was flecked with white. The wagon trains, the fires burning in cracks in the lava, the tables in the middle, were all on the bay side of the hump. The far side was narrower, and dark.

How long had caravans been using this place as a toilet? And a garbage dump too. Even since *Cavorite* passed? Ever since there were caravans, surely. The smell wasn't intense, but it was inescapable, and ancient.

Along the Road there was always concealment to make a rest area. Here, nothing but distance. No problem, really. If people stayed apart, what could anyone see? But it seemed strange that nobody had put up a building or a wall.

No hiding place. *We shoot anyone who crosses the Neck....*

As he rejoined the cookforce, Randall Hearst joined him. Randall wanted to know about bandits; about his impressions of the Shire, the health of the various communities, and recent news of Twerdahl Town. Tim answered as best he could while he served out toast spread with red fish eggs, then roasted potatoes. If Randall wanted to know what had changed since he'd last seen the Road, then his questions might tell Tim something.

The fish eggs would go well in an omelet, he decided. He hadn't seen bird eggs in many days.

Chaff covered the bay to left and right as far as he could see. It hadn't been there when last he looked. Tim remembered the chugs. Twice the usual number of chugs had pulled up a forest of seaweed on the mainland side of the Neck. It had floated back.

Now, which way did the current flow on the *narrow* side of the Neck?

Riffles broke on the bay, raised by a brisk wind or by dark heads rising. The heads stayed, dark dots on the water, watching.

Merchants were eating apart from the yutzes, trading news of the Road, no doubt, and keeping merchant secrets. Hearst, Miller, ibn-Rushd, and Lyons families discussed cooking and the chefs. Merchants from the weapons wagons fell silent when a chef approached.

Tim ate as he served, as any chef must. Sliced orange. A potato. Bord'n was hobbling around with a stick. He and Tim ripped apart a big Earth-life crab and shared it.

These yutzes had all come with the spring caravan. They knew Tim Bednacourt, and none had been at Warkan's Tavern. In the fading light, all he had to do was avoid notice.

Locals must have brought this barrel of fresh water. Tim drank deeply. He'd need it.

He carved huge fillets of tuna and gave head and bones to a yutz to dump over the hump. He sliced up one fillet and ate a slice and carried the rest of it among the benches.

A merchant gaudy in gray and yellow caught his eye.

Tim knew him instantly: he'd snatched at Jemmy Bloocher as he ran from Warkan's Tavern, and had his belt for an instant before Jemmy tore loose.

Tim Bednacourt's reflexes kicked in ahead of his mind. "Tuna?" he said, offering the platter. "And the sweet potatoes are ready. Did you get any of the fencecutter crab?" looking at other folk of Milliken wagon, the weapons wagon, making it a general offer.

"We got some." The merchant helped himself to a tuna fillet. "If there's more, we'd love it. Is anybody making tea? It's getting chilly."

"I'll start some."

Tim was sweating as he walked into the growing dark. A merchant would starve if he couldn't catch a chef's eye! Tim couldn't avoid notice. There was no help for it but to *be a chef.*

He set a big pot of water on for tea.

The speckles can was as big as a five-month-old baby. There was no color like it on Destiny, barring murals in the Spiral Town Civic Hall. It couldn't be opened. The caravan considered it unstealable, and Tim felt they were right.

He shook speckles over a pot of beans. In a spare moment he over-sprinkled a bowl of beans and ate it fast, wincing at what the excess did to the flavor. Merchants used a lot more speckles than Spiral Town did, or anyone else they'd found along the Road. That bowlful would keep him healthy for a while.

The fishers had brought in a clamshell the size of a grown man, armed with siphon/tentacles each the size of Tim's arm, that had curved teeth in the ends. *Sub clam.* Tim sliced it into strips, ate one (Wow! Delicious!) and carried the rest among the benches. He set the empty platter aside and walked over the hump.

Quicksilver had set a quarter-hour before the sun. Mere traces of red still lit the west, and the hump blocked that. Yutzes dumped their loads at the midden. Tim walked a distance away from them before he did his private business. Then he kept strolling toward the autumn caravan.

The sea was black and empty. He couldn't guess which way the current flowed.

Tim had dropped his pack over the back side of Hearst wagon instead of stowing it. Here it was. Tim donned it, crawled under the wagon, and, with nobody about, walked toward the water. If anyone saw him, he'd be fifty meters away and running hard.

Nobody saw. He slid down the smooth lava slope and entered the bay without much of a splash. The water was warm after the first instant; warmer than the wind on his ears. Taking his time, he put his shoes in his pack, then began to swim.

If he stayed right up against the Road, nobody could see him without walking right up to the edge. But how would he explain himself then? He chose to swim well out into the bay before he turned southeast.

It seemed to take forever to swim past the barbecue. Had he been missed? Fires were the only light, and they were almost gone. Tents were up. If he was seen, he'd be taken for a wind riffle or an Otterfolk.

The rim of the Neck was unclimbable. Tim would have to swim all the way to the Tail Town beaches, and so would anyone who came in after him. Tim hadn't seen anyone swim, merchant or yutz, since he'd left Twerdahl Town.

He'd have felt quite safe but for the Otterfolk.

Otterfolk were a mystery. He'd been led to believe that they were fanatical about their privacy. Now a creature had invaded their home. Drowning him would not be much trouble at all.

But their heads had kept popping up to watch the caravan.

It wasn't as if he had a choice. He swam.

A current was helping him along. There was still no sign of pursuit when he crawled onto a pebbly beach in a line of boats. He was shuddering with cold.

He'd planned it out, this part. He crawled among the boats and began to examine one, as he hadn't been allowed to do in Baytown. In the shadows of boats under a starless sky, he was quite blind. He explored with his hands.

The flat piece with the handle, the tiller, would fit *here* in notches at the tail end of the boat.

The other flat piece would fit *here* in the middle of the underside. It slid in from the pointed end.

If he put them on now and tried to get out into the water, they'd break off against the sand. The tiller, he could slide it in after he was afloat. The other? That would have to be inserted from underwater.

He saw that taking a boat would leave a gap in the line. The boat in the shed? No, it was probably in there for repairs! So—

A heave uprighted the last boat in line. No gap. He set the tiller and the centerpiece in the bottom.

It was a heavy sonofabitch. Four handles on the bottom meant four men could lift it. Could one man drag it?

He could if he was desperate. The boat moved in surges. He dragged it down the sand until it floated, then pushed it out hard and swam after it. Clambering in was harder than he'd expected, but he made it.

He'd thought of swimming around Tail Town and then ashore. He'd still have to do that if he couldn't control the boat. The boat would be easier travel. Now he felt very conspicuous, one lone stolen boat on this great flat expanse. Get the sail up and get *going!*

But he needed the tiller to aim the boat.

So: mount the tiller in the dark, using the mountings he'd felt out so carefully, in the dark.

The sail was bound against that horizontal beam. He hadn't spent enough time feeling the lines out, and it cost him. *This* line would raise it after he untied *these.* Then tie it down. Where?

He got it up.

The boat had turned under him to face the wind. The sail hung slack. He felt conspicuous as hell. He moved the tiller. It wasn't steering anything.

He lowered himself off the stern and kicked until the bow came around, reached up and swung the tiller hard over.

The sail billowed as sails did at Baytown, and he heaved himself into the boat as it *flew* back toward shore. He turned the boat into the wind, kept the tiller turned when the boat wanted to just stop and drift, and now he was *flying* back toward Loria and Twerdahl Town.

Yes! But how on Earth did fishers do this?

Okay, it took four men, one on the tiller while three raised the sails. . . .

Most of Tail Town was quite dark. Torches still burned in the larger buildings. Tim searched the water for Otterfolk, but there were none in sight. Did they sleep?

As dawn showed above the Crest, boats were putting out from the beach beyond Tail Town. Tim had sailed past Tail Town in the night. He watched them, having little better to do.

Sails came up. Five, six boats took to the water, raised sail, then foreshortened, turning toward his position. It looked choreographed.

Merchants armed with guns might be aboard, but Tim didn't believe that. Fishers would be dangerous enough. He was a thief. If they caught him, the least he could expect was to be turned over to the caravan.

The autumn caravan would know him by daylight: *Jemmy Bloocher.*

A row of dark heads appeared ahead.

Their eyes glittered black, facing forward at water level. As they neared he saw that their heads were as big as his own, capped with a shell that dropped to form the upper part of a beak, like a chug's head. Their beaks were cable-cutter traps, more like a lungshark's mouth than a chug's, but they were clearly related to both species.

He watched for a bit. They did nothing. He waved; nothing.

"I'm—" He hesitated, then shouted, "I'm Jemmy Bloocher. That's one small step for a man—"

They were waiting for something.

He was about to sail past.

He couldn't see it, but he *felt* how the boat slid sideways across the water, losing forward momentum. Those fishers would catch him unless he could get the centerboard down.

He was tired of banging his shins on it.

He swung the boat into the wind and saw the sail go slack. The Otterfolk flicked into motion and were with him again. He picked up the centerboard and slid it into the water, hanging on to it until he felt hands take it from him.

Then it was a matter of waiting. He watched more boats take sea room and turn toward him. The floor of the boat thumped and bumped.

The boat began to turn by itself.

The Otterfolk knew how this worked. Tim twisted the tiller to help them put the wind in the sails. The boat took off, but sluggishly. He looked down to see what he'd expected: four Otterfolk, their short, thick forearms wrapped around the handholds at water level.

Damn, he could reach down and *touch* them.

He didn't. But he leaned far over to look, his arm far back to hold the tiller in place.

He'd half-expected to see smiles. Their beaked faces were immobile, yet it was clear they were having fun.

They were smaller than he was, but he'd known grown men as big as the Otterfolk. Sixty kilograms, he judged, and very alike except for their shells.

Left and aft was the one he was studying. Its legs were short, ending in big splayed fins. Its arms were short too. They pulled its body hard against the handhold. Its body hugged the hull. It twisted to look up at him. It seemed wonderfully agile where the shell didn't bind it.

Its shell was smooth, streamlined—and painted! Painted in unreadable hieroglyphs, in brilliant scarlet and orange and green.

The other riders were painted too. Tim couldn't read the patterns, though they looked more like simplified pictures than an alphabet. But he'd seen those colors before. *Where?*

Forward left, that one had been injured. Tim could see a healed split along his shell, under paint that turned the crack into a coat of arms. The accident had bent the shell, and bent the Otterfolk's body too.

Tim believed he had known they were sapient the instant he looked into their eyes; but the paints told a more emphatic tale. They were *artists.*

A creature barred from using fire could never make such paints. Wait, now, that was the red of a speckles can!

Settler magic. The walls of Civic Hall in Spiral Town had murals in those colors, and others too.

The Otterfolk would have used more colors if they'd had them. Somewhere was a source of red and orange and green acrylic paint, and the Otterfolk had access.

* * *

Twenty or more sails were chasing him now. Tim wasn't really concerned. Those other boats must be carrying Otterfolk too, to slow *them*. The handles on a boat weren't placed for fishers' convenience, after all.

The day passed like a dream. This was sensory deprivation: lying in the bottom of a boat, holding the tiller in one position, sometimes finding the will to lift his head, look over the side, check his position. Once he looked just as the left-forward rider reached out, snatched a platyfish from the water, bit off two big bites, and dropped it to be caught by the rider behind him.

Then one of the riders flipped a big Earthlife bass over into the boat.

Around midday the rearmost pair dropped off. The boat picked up a little speed, and then he had another pair of riders. Later the front pair dropped away and were replaced.

He was hungry. He was thirsty. He'd eaten and drunk as much as he could hold last night, and it wasn't enough. When Quicksilver blinked out his arms were racked by cramps. He tried steering with his feet and found he could make it work.

That left his agonized hands free to fillet the bass into sashimi.

The fleet came ever closer.

The sun sank, the sky darkened.

In an hour he couldn't tell the land from the sea. He could tell where the wind was. Once, staring into the dark, he perceived the land far too close. He steered hard about, and sensed that the wind was blowing straight at the land. He could keep himself aimed, if Destiny didn't change the rules on him.

Sailing an unfamiliar boat was dangerous enough in daylight. Sailing at night was suicide. Would he even know if the shore was about to smite him? If he'd seen a way, Tim would have surrendered. But the fishers would smash their boats and his if they caught him in the dark.

And in the morning, would they have him surrounded?

Quicksilver peeked above the mountains, a brilliant point against a sky already showing yellow-white.

Sails had come very near, but they hadn't surrounded him yet. With Quicksilver's added light, Tim angled closer to the beach. Closer yet, as the sun itself glared between peaks.

Tim didn't intend to be caught. He'd beach the boat and run when they came close enough.

The waves were tiny, twenty centimeters high, breaking only ten meters from shore. He was sailing only a few meters beyond that point, and that was very near the beach. He could see an endless reach of sand without a shack or wall or footprint anywhere, nothing but sand and weed and painted shells.

Otterfolk shells. A score in view to left and right, now that he thought to look.

Tim edged the boat closer yet. That wasn't an Otterfolk graveyard, was it? Sharks had bones; chugs had bones; but there weren't any Otterfolk bones on that beach. Just shells painted in acrylic colors, all set on the beach beyond the tide line, like headstones maybe, until one shifted suddenly, and again.

The boat rocked. Damn, he was too close, his centerboard was grinding against sand! He turned hard, and back a bit as the sail tried to go slack. The centerboard wasn't grinding anymore because his four riders had dropped off and the boat was riding higher. He angled for open sea before he thought of the other boats.

They were all turning.

He had some sea room now, and he looked back for the particular shell that had moved.

It covered a hollow. Shapes too small to see crawled out from under the edge.

Otterfolk were riding waves to shore. He saw them clearly for the first time, four limber shapes with short finned limbs and long bodies. He half-recognized the markings. Those had been the riders on his boat.

He worked it out later, thus:

Fishers were too skilled, and a fisher boat was too predictable. Boring.

A thief in a boat he didn't know how to use, making mistakes and learning as he went, made for an exciting ride.

Four riders piling on a thief's boat would slow it. Fisher boats chasing it, being less interesting, would carry fewer riders. *Of course* the thief would be caught.

Otterfolk might choose to ride two at a time to give a thief a longer run; but Tim always believed that the Destiny natives had minds but no language. Negotiation had to be basic.

Threatened, the thief sent a basic message. Tim had threatened to beach his boat on the birthground.

The Otterfolk must respond. Perhaps they fouled the fishers' centerboards or tillers, or clung to the handholds in hordes, until the boats couldn't move.

At the time, Tim couldn't guess why the fishers had abandoned their chase. But sailing near shore now seemed a very dangerous thing.

Otterfolk shed their shells: that was clear. They made nests in sand, and left the shell to shade the emerging young: that was a likely guess. Otterfolk would kill any creature found on that shore: that seemed *very* likely.

He stayed well out to sea until he was nearly to Baytown.

The sky was red with after-sunset, and Quicksilver burned right at the water. Baytown fisher boats were at sea ahead of him. As he came nearer they all turned toward him.

Tim aimed his boat inland, toward where a dish-shaped crater lay on the beach.

The wind was blowing out to sea. He couldn't aim directly toward shore, but he could approach in a switchback pattern. When the centerboard grounded and heeled over, he went overboard. The lightened boat bobbed up and righted. He swam for shore with boats converging behind him. He crawled out winded, and ran for the crater on rubbery legs.

He paused once, and stooped to lift the rim of a painted shell that would almost cover his chest. His vision grayed and he went to his knees. But the cavity under the shell was empty; the Otterfolk children gone. He heaved himself up and kept running, chest heaving, and half-fell over the rim of the fused sand dish.

Arcs of wooden bench lined the inland half of the dish. The wood was ancient and weathered. Soft sand lined the bottom on the sea side, and the slanted rim had been painted with hieroglyphs in yellow, orange, green, scarlet, indigo.

The shell he was holding was very like those he'd found scattered over the mudflats that held towels and soggy clothes for the Baytown fishers. Would he have found paint, if he'd turned one over?

It was too big for his pack. He shoved it up between his shirt and rain tunic, against his chest.

He was burning priceless seconds. Fishers had gone overboard. They were in the water, trying to save his stolen boat by attaching lines: they meant to tow it. A few shouted at him, the words blurred, the tone unfriendly.

The five-color cartoons along the rim of Meetplace were old but still vivid. If he studied them he'd see what those simplified figures represented.

But Baytown women were wading the mudflat in his direction, and Tim thought it best to leave.

✳ 14 ✳

The Speckles Can

Think of us as priests of evolution.
                              —Caravan proverb

He climbed as far as the caravan trail before he looked back. They wouldn't follow him in the dark . . . ?

It was already too dark to tell.

Thirst was near killing him.

Well, he was new at this. He followed the caravan trail to the Spectre River. He watched from cover while the last of the light died, before he crept to the water and drank his fill.

Then he kept climbing.

He woke sheltered in bushes, just below the Road, on the wrong side of the Spectre River. He woke joyful. He was free! Anyone could outrun a caravan.

He watched Baytown wake. He watched the boats put to sea. Any tiny fleck of white on the water might be Otterfolk. It was all a wonder, but the thing he wanted most was to go down.

Did he do wrong to run? He was frantic to question them. All those discarded Otterfolk shells! Fishers must be in constant contact with Otterfolk.

Why did the merchants let Baytowners inspect their wares the day before they bought? They didn't do that anywhere else along the Road, except in Tail Town itself. Did the *Otterfolk* tell the locals what *they* needed?

How?

All his traveling had only bought him more questions.

He saw no way across the Spectre. The bridge lay too close to Baytown. Baytown knew that he had stolen a boat. They knew he had landed on the forbidden beach. The shadow of the mountains was withdrawing from Baytown, and sunlight would soon touch the mountains where he hid.

The flat Road itself hid nothing and grew nothing.

If he tried to hunt what lived in the brush, Baytown fishers would see brush moving on the mountain. He didn't dare even reach up into a fool cage.

But the slopes above the Road bloomed with Earthlife crops that hadn't been harvested since *Cavorite* passed. He crept among them like a snake, and gorged on fruits and berries. He collected beans, several kinds of nuts, and a few root vegetables. The beans he set soaking in a bottle.

He cooked after dark in a rock fire pit tall enough to hide the light.

Then he climbed in the dark until he reached bare rock.

In the morning the Spectre had become a thousand springs. Crossing was easy.

Now there were none to spy on him at all. Nobody lived on this long stretch between Baytown and the distillery. Tim stayed high, at the interface between Earthlife growth and bare rock.

Fruits and grains grew here, and the occasional fool cage with something trapped inside. Rotten bird meat would still make bait for catfish. He didn't hunt; someone might hear gunfire. He walked wide around the occasional wild pig. Once he speared an unwary rabbit with his weed cutter. He was never able to do that again.

He'd traveled this way before.

He watched the Road for signs of pursuit. Merchants must know about bicycles, and Tim couldn't outrun those. He'd be wary for a while.

But nobody followed. In ten days he was halfway home.

He'd been seeing birds as big as men. He hadn't seen one fly, but they ran like the wind. *Ostriches.* The land was flat up to an abrupt "frost line," where bare rock suddenly rose nearly straight for five or six hundred meters.

He was halfway between the Neck and Spiral Town, he judged, high on the spine of the Crab. A klick's stretch of chaparral, of tiny Earthlife oranges and berry bushes and Destiny thorns, barred him from the Road. Far ahead he could see a vertical white thread of waterfall.

The long stretch of lonely coast was ending. The Hornes and Wilsons were friends of the caravans, and so was every community beyond. How would they treat a yutz found wandering loose? Tim would have crept past the distillery and dairy; but it seemed to him that he was becoming clumsy.

Nothing serious. He'd left the Otterfolk shell behind, three mornings in a row. The shell was proof of some terrible truth that he hadn't yet fully understood. It served as a platter too: it kept food out of the dirt. He needed it.

This morning he'd lost time doubling back to get the shell, *again,* and he'd found his fire pit sitting like a signature. He threw the rocks into the bushes, as usual, but this was getting scary. He didn't want to end like Jael Harness.

There was no sure way to recognize speckles deficiency.

He could keep track of the days, eleven now, and so what? He could move more carefully, look around himself more often, avoid some mistakes that way. More likely he'd just forget the question, and gradually all the patterns in his mind would go too.

He was a couple of caravan-days downRoad from the distillery. For now he'd keep to the heights. He'd reach the falls tonight and go down in the morning—hide the gun first—approach the distillery by the Road, unless they found him first.

Every child knew that planets glowed by reflected sunlight. Quicksilver was brilliant before it passed behind the sun. These last few days, with its shadowed side turned toward Destiny, Quicksilver had been nearly invisible; but now it was crossing the sun.

Half an hour before sunset, Tim could just glance at the westering sun and glimpse a black dot on the solar disk before he snatched his gaze away.

Children did that. Adults yelled at them for it. A child who tried such a thing with Earth's hotter, brighter sun would blind himself. *Tim* could blind himself if he blinked the sun too near noon. If he let the sun get too far down the sky, the dot would blur out.

But he'd caught it.

So he sat on a boulder and waited for his vision to come back, and wondered why he was wasting time. Loria waited ahead, a caravan was crawling up his tail, the falls he'd seen was still ahead, and Tim Bednacourt sat on a rock waiting for dark.

. . . Because he needed rocks to build his fire pit, and water to cook.

He hadn't seen loose rocks earlier in the day. Here was a convenient spring near a convenient landslide, a raw cleft in the rock spilling stones just small enough to lift easily. This boulder would do for a backstop, and when he brushed the coals away it would stay warm for hours: he'd sleep with his back against it.

He'd stopped to gather berries and blink at the sun. He'd washed himself thoroughly, and his clothes too, to make himself presentable. Dawdling here rather than hoping to find more rocks ahead.

His vision was coming back. Tim looked down and saw char marks.

He slid off the boulder and into the brush to think it through.

Marks of a fire.

Of course he hadn't looked for char marks on the rocks he used. He made his fires in the dark!

Vulcanism and landslides made these stonefalls. But he'd found stones conveniently clustered these past ten days, spaced a scant day-walk apart for a man carrying a pack and stopping to hunt and gather and cook.

He'd been pulling his fire pits apart after use, and so had someone else, it seemed. Someone who built much bigger fire pits. Not just a wanderer. Several men together.

Now what?

Don't hunt. He'd gathered fruit and some barley. Did he dare cook the barley? Nobody had seen his fires . . . had they?

He'd been more than careful. The mountain was bare above where he built his fires; no human lived there. Someone close might have whiffed smoke, but nobody had seen it rising in the dark. He built his stone circles tall. Nobody could have seen fire within Tim Hann's fire pits, not unless he were floating in the sky.

At dusk he built his stone circle and his tiny fire. There was the risk that he *had* been seen, that he was being followed or tracked. Best he remain predictable until he could see another way.

He lay not against the fire-warmed boulder, but in the bush, where he could watch it. A tiny moon silvered the crest and left all else black.

The bandits he'd fought had been up the Road by many days, past the little distillery and past the Shire too. So the scorched rock he'd found might mark a wanderer or two, he told himself, but not one of that band of bandits.

But any wanderer *must* attack caravans for their speckles.

Tim Bednacourt carried no speckles. Could he buy a bandit off? With what?

Or evade them? The only way to evade bandits was to know where bandits were.

Here were two faces of one problem. How could Jemmy Bloocher avoid being found? He'd taught himself to do that. How could Tim Bed-nacourt find bandits who didn't want to be found? They'd be living as he lived, but more of them. Taking refuge at the frost line? Changing identities?

Tim waited for sleep, with his eyes on six hundred meters of split rock above him. He tried to picture bandits . . . not bandits attacking a caravan three times a year, but living between caravan passings, settled in little groups, gathering and hunting, stealing speckles from locals or fighting each other for a dwindling supply. . . .

His mind must have gone on working while he slept. He woke in darkness. He felt quite lucid.

He donned his pack. He moved to the stream and drank until his belly was taut as a drum.

Then he began to climb.

The Crest Mountains were glossy-smooth wherever fusion flame had touched rock. But the cooling rock had split. Here a vertical split ran nearly to the peaks. The spring flowed from the split.

He'd been looking up at the rock face for so long that it was branded in his memory. Good thing, too. He couldn't see! But he could follow the split by touch.

No telling how high he was when he began to be afraid.

Climbing in the dark was crazy. The notion had come to him in his sleep, fully formed. He was climbing in the dark because he would be conspicuous in daylight, against gray rock with no plant growing any-where.

The little moon continued west. A trace of light touched the mountain face now. The cleft narrowed, but Tim was able to pick out handholds and footholds. Then those ran out. All his muscles were shaking with fatigue. They'd *throw* him off the cliff if he kept this up.

Down a bit and over, a rock face was trying to split off, leaving a ledge.

Not as wide as he'd hoped. He lay with his back pushed hard against the rock, and was asleep before the trembling stopped.

Dawnlight and terror. He'd forgotten where he was. The slope stretched a vast way down. He was exposed and conspicuous on a rock cliff, hunted by men with guns.

Far away, the shadow of the Crest Mountains crept steadily from the sea onto shore.

In early summer he'd been on shore looking up at where he was now. What had he seen? Backlit by a rising sun that hadn't cleared the peaks, this whole face of the mountains would be *black*. He would be invisible. Nobody would look this high anyway.

Tim Bednacourt began to climb again. Cracking had put ledges over his head to block him, but cracking gave him handholds and footholds. He rested on the trunk of an incredible scrub-oak tree that had sunk roots into the last of the main split. When the sun lit the southwestern face of the range, he was on the narrow side of the Crab Peninsula.

Nothing grew at the crest, and little grew lower down. Flame had scoured this side of the range too. Nobody had since bothered to weed out Destiny life. This was the steeper side, a straight drop to angry waves, and not many plants had the tenacity to cling to the rock; but some did. Tim could make out Destiny colors, black and bronze and yellow-green, but Earthlife greens too.

He couldn't see a way down.

There was nothing to eat up here.

He found a flat spot to sleep out the noon hours. He made several klicks that day, picking a way along the crest, his eyes on the alien beauty of the wild shore. At evening he didn't bother with fire. He chewed a handful of barley, and waited for full dark.

Then he slipped between two peaks and looked down.

A bright orange light glared below him, just at the Road. Left and above, a mere orange spark glowed too.

He blocked the fires with his hand and let his eyes adjust.

From world's end to world's end, the Road was a gray-black line through black rubble. The shore was more vivid: there was white phosphorescence in the waves.

A faint yellow smudge far to his right: fires along a beach. The autumn caravan must be past Tail Town by now. If the caravan had sent out a yutz-hunter, Tim would have seen his fire too, and closer. It wasn't there.

The caravans hadn't sent hunters.

That bright fire must be huge, to be so steady. The distillery? It would be just below him, their dinner fire.

As for the orange spark, he must be looking down into somebody's fire pit.

He'd found what he sought. Two cookfires burned on the mountain this night: the Hornes and Wilsons gathered at their dinner, and a handful of wanderers above, dangerously close to the first. The Hornes and Wilsons would have to be warned. And surely they'd feed a wanderer some speckles?

*   *   *

He slept on the mountain, cold but quite safe in a cleft between two peaks.

Dawn gifted him with an amazing view. Shadow covered the Crab's broad side, but here were details never seen by a caravan.

Below the Road was a wide stretch of meadow. Destiny black was not having much luck against Earthlife green. Half a hundred head of sheep grazed. Four big buildings near the Road must be the Wilson dairy, barn, and dwellings.

The caravan had partied on Horne turf, that big cookout area in a horseshoe of one large and several small buildings. Around the Horne establishment was more meadow, but it was the yellow of wheat. High on the mountain . . . were those goats?

Of wanderers and bandits there was no sign.

He was hungry, but he delayed going down. He'd fought hard for this view, and it was very pleasant.

He could follow the line of Road a long way before the curve of the Crest hid it. Far to the left: the Shire? He couldn't be sure. To the right, nothing, nothing . . . the line of a caravan, far, far away.

At the western edge of the Horne meadow was a single monumental tree in a regular array of white dots.

Tim heard a gunshot.

Faint and distant, crisp and clear, the sound jerked his head straight toward brush that was mostly Destiny black. Three man-shapes were charging downhill behind a gigantic bird.

Tim started down the rocks. At the edge of hearing were voices quarreling in shouts and gasps. He kept his mind on not falling to his death, and only spared the occasional stolen glance for men dealing with a wounded bird.

The ostrich was stumbling now, slowing. The men would have caught it if it weren't running through clumps of vengeance thorn.

It turned suddenly. (Tim hugged rock so he'd be free to look.) One man froze, one tripped, and as the bird came at them screaming, the third man steadied himself. Tim heard another gunshot. The bird fell over and thrashed.

Tim couldn't hurry and he couldn't hide. He kept moving.

The men pulled the bird downhill a good distance to the nearest tree. There they hung it and tore the feathers off, and butchered it. As far as Tim could tell, not one ever glanced his way.

He climbed down as far as the plants grew, and rested.

Guns belonged to caravans. A gun not in the hands of a caravan meant bandits. It seemed to Tim that the surest way of avoiding bandits was to know where they were.

Here was a most convenient trio of bandits. All Tim had to do was follow them.

Burdened by the butchered ostrich, restricted by lesser brush, the bandits weren't making any great speed. He could hear them; he could almost make out the words.

". . . Two bullets!"

". . . get more . . ."

"Months till we . . . weed cutter next time!"

They were circling four or five acres of green-bronze-black thorn. One of them wanted to chop it out tomorrow. The others thought that a joke: too much work.

". . . Get the next caravan to do it."

Vengeance thorn was nasty stuff. The fractally dividing thorns could punch through shirt or pants, then leave invisibly small needles embedded in flesh. Tim had marked this patch from above: it reached right to the Road.

He could follow these bandits as far as the Road, but what then? Watch where they went, of course, but he'd be seen if he followed. But following bandits wasn't the point, was it? Knowing where they were, *that* was the point.

Going the other way around the patch would bring him to the brook that fed the distillery.

Tim wanted a drink. If he met someone named Wilson or Horne, he could tell a tale of bandits, and maybe get something to eat.

He drank his fill and filled his bottle and washed a little.

The stream ran past a stretch of green grass and a huge, ancient Earth-life tree, and stones in lines and rocks. Not fire-pit rocks, but . . . the Horne and Wilson graveyard? Many communities along the Road used headstones instead of holograms.

The graveyard intrigued him, and he waited there, hoping to see a familiar face. Somehow names and dates had been written into the stones. The oldest dates were sixty years back. The lifegivers weren't all named Wilson or Horne. Wanderers marrying locals would take local names, but a bachelor from a caravan would keep his own, and a married couple would keep theirs.

Nobody had come. Sating his thirst let his hunger shine brighter. He could smell cooking now. He followed the smell downslope.

He was following the sour smell of the distillery too. *Here.* Tim had passed this building, had glanced inside, months ago. The big doors were open now, and Tim stepped inside to see the huge tanks and arrays of pipes.

The distillery was deserted. Maybe it didn't need much tending.

A woman came out of a smaller building next door and turned away, her long soft brown hair flying. She hadn't seen him in the shadowed building. Layne Wilson, even at this distance, the first familiar face he'd seen. Tim was about to announce himself when he saw the red flash in her hand.

There was a window: not glass, but a wood plank propped open near the ceiling. He had to climb on a cask to see out.

A dozen people were at work around the fire pit. Three men were setting up an ostrich to roast while chatting with Layne. Tim knew the men.

He knew the butchered ostrich.

And the brilliant red can Layne Wilson was shaking over a pot.

First he hid. There was space behind the distillery's huge pressure vessels. He crouched with gun in hand. If anyone discovered him—

Think, now:

Was there a legitimate reason why three Hornes and/or Wilsons might camp high above a dairy or distillery?

Was there any way an honest distiller or dairyman could put his hands on a merchant's gun?

Or on a speckles can?

The possibility that Tim Bednacourt was behaving like an idiot grew stronger with every hour shy of speckles. What he couldn't figure out might only mean that his cranial nerves weren't firing. What would *he* look like if they found him now? Living where no human lived. A spy hidden in shadow with a bullet for anyone who saw him. Might these dairy keepers and distillers take him for a bandit and execute him out of hand?

It crossed his mind, now, that goats might require tending, and Wilsons would need to gather their milk. That a gun dropped by dead merchants, or dead bandits, might be held for the next caravan by honest men, or might migrate up and down the Road as barter.

Would it be better to simply ask for help?

But Forry Randall, yutz chef with Lyons wagon, had been carrying the Lyons speckles can when he was shot dead. Tim had seen a bandit whoop and raise it high and run with it. Now Layne Wilson was using a big flattened acrylic-red shaker in her cooking.

Roasting ostrich kept getting into his brain and scrambling his thoughts. Likely his brain wasn't at its best anyway. But the more he thought about it, the less crazy it seemed:

Caravans passed three times a year. Who were the bandits when there were no caravans to rob?

Did they rob locals? But Tim had heard no horror tales, seen no elaborately barred doors. Was there some kind of treaty?

What if a caravan came late or charged too much for speckles or brought too little? What could locals do about that? Twerdahls would give or trade whatever a merchant wanted, as they'd traded Tim Bednacourt.

He eased out from behind the still and caught a scant cupful of what was dripping from the spigot, and moved back into place. He sipped, and thought.

Bandits couldn't run around with that great red can. That was the point of it. Where could they keep it safe?

Layne Wilson returned with the speckles shaker. She entered the smaller building, and left without the shaker.

Waiting for dark would make sense.

But it had grown noisy out there: dinner was well in progress. They'd never notice anything. If they saw him they'd—

He was still dressed as a merchant. He took the time to turn his tunic inside out, and turned the collar down. Now his color was gray-brown and the big pockets were hidden. From a distance it might serve. He should have done that days ago. Now they might take him for one of their own.

Now, all in one smooth glide, he—pulled himself back barely in time as a man and a woman wobbled into the distillery, poured a half-liter of whiskey from the collector pail into a jug, and went out with their arms around each other.

Now: out from behind the still, get his balance, adjust the shell and backpack. Walk out through the open door and straight across to the other building and in.

It smelled of metal. A smithy. That didn't take genius: he was looking at an anvil.

Dark as it was, he wouldn't have missed the speckles can. It must be in a cupboard or something. Something easy. Layne had been quick. Then again, caravans did come three times every two Destiny years. There had to be a hiding place, something hard to find and hard to get into.

Damn. He didn't have forever. He'd be lucky to get out of here alive, let alone— Wait now. That anvil was on tracks! And behind it, below floor height, something bright red.

The weight of an anvil would guard that cavity. It was hard to open and hard to close, but they were between caravans, so Layne just hadn't bothered. Tim picked up the speckles shaker. He ignored four guns that must have come from caravans, but he took three speckles pouches full of bullets. He wrapped it all in his tunic and walked out.

He hadn't thought beyond this. It came to him that his patterned green shirt wasn't any less conspicuous. He was running now, into the graveyard, known turf. Could he get up into the tree?

Noise behind him hadn't changed: they weren't after him yet. But terror was in him, and he kept running.

Past the vengeance thorn, walking wide around thorns he couldn't see in the dark. An ostrich leapt to its feet and ran squawking away. Damn, if anyone was already looking, they'd come straight here!

Chop a hole in the thorn patch with his weed cutter? A hiding place? While his mind toyed with the notion, his body was still running uphill, flat out. Despite starvation and speckles deficiency and whiskey and terror, his mind was catching up, and his body was right. He had to go *up.*

Up, because he had to build a fire. To cook.

He didn't need to build a fire pit. The three goatherds hadn't torn theirs apart: an ostrich had distracted them. They'd even abandoned a can of milk! He set some barley cooking and used the speckles can liberally, before he drained the milk. Earth, he was *hungry.* Was it sour, or was that just how goat milk tasted?

Dead of night. Nobody seemed to be coming after him.

Then again, he couldn't carry the speckles can.

There was no clear way to open it. He'd never tried pounding it on a rock. He tried it now. He couldn't even dent it.

He couldn't steal the speckles inside without stealing the whole can, even though the damn thing was nearly empty. To be seen with it was to be guilty, *guilty*, GUILTY! and how could he not be seen?

He couldn't wait any longer. He ate the barley half-cooked. Then he lay on his back and waited for his intelligence to come back.

It would take days, of course. Sometimes it never returned. But the answer he needed was looking down at him.

How could anyone not be seen with the Lyons speckles shaker?

By being where there were no eyes.

✳ 15 ✳

The Shire

Obedience be damned. We're not on a ship anymore.
—Suzanna Barnes, Astrophysics, *Argos*

He was where the springs began to join into waterfalls, not far below the frost line, and several klicks above the Shire.

Just below was a fool cage knocked down and torn apart, and feathers around it, on a hillside covered with tiny Earthlife oranges and berry bushes and black Destiny weeds.

A klick-long stretch of such stuff barred him from the Road. No problem: he could follow the falls and rapids down, and then the switchbacks of the caravan trail. Two klicks farther, houses spread out along the shore.

Tim's first impulse was to creep past the Shire. The Shire had nothing he needed. The caravan didn't seem to be chasing him. No telling when pursuers from the distillery would catch on, though.

At least he didn't have to wrestle that damn speckles can.

It wasn't that you couldn't get speckles out. There were holes in the top for the tiny seeds. You couldn't get them out *fast* . . . and it wasn't *that* slow, because the chef holding the can had to feed seventy people. On the other side of the Crest, Tim had spent most of an hour shaking speckles into his spread shirt.

Then, finally, he'd thought of firing a bullet into the can. *That* worked.

Now he had four times what he'd need to get as far as Twerdahl Town. He had left Lyons wagon's empty speckles can in plain sight for anyone who could get to the blind side of the Crab.

He'd watched bandits fanning out from the distillery. Eight of them, split into pairs to cover the Road and the heights in both directions. None at the shoreline.

What did the distillers think had happened to their shaker? They seemed to suspect a lone thief. But if Lyons wagon's shaker marked the thief, then Tim Bednacourt didn't have the shaker.

And he *still* didn't want to be caught alone, on the Road or off it.

He'd been traveling at the frost line. Seekers from the distillery were ahead of him, traveling by Road and above. He didn't want to catch up with them. The question wasn't how to get around, but how to approach the Shire.

He picked out another fool cage knocked down and torn apart amid scattered feathers.

Now that he was looking for them, he could follow a broken chain of them down along the falls. Some big carnivore had learned to find food this way.

Time to move.

Tim was not trying to hide now. He followed the broken fool cages down. He rather hoped the Shirefolk would approach him.

He was on a slope, fighting through waist-deep brush while he circled a stand of fisher trees being strangled in Julia sets, when he heard brush crackling. A moment later he saw a disturbance in the brush. He dropped below the branches, among the trunks of the low bushes, while he wriggled the gun free of his tunic pocket.

A huge dark shadow came at him out of the fisher trees in a thunder of broken branchlets, head held low, tiny mad eyes. Tim, squatting on his haunches, fired until the gun was empty. It fell thrashing before it had quite reached him.

Four men conspicuously armed with spears and fish clubs came to meet him.

Tim had time to hang the heavy carcass from the tip of a sizable fisher tree. It was a boar pig, and he'd cleaned it. "Yours. Dinner," he said loudly, and smiled.

They didn't smile back and they were still advancing. Tim shrugged out of his pack, no sudden moves now, hands in sight. The shell fell too.

"And I'll bet you've never seen *this* before." One hand held high, he lifted the Otterfolk shell and turned it to show the paint.

That got a reaction, a chorused "Ooo!"

"Feed me," Tim said, "and I'll tell you all about this."

"Otterfolk!" said one.

"Yeah. I seen those colors—"

Tim said, "Geordy Bruns?"

The old man studied him. "You're one of those yutzes from the spring caravan. I traded you a shell."

"I still have it."

Geordy set down his spear and came forward. Tim gave him room, and he searched through Tim's pack. He found the carved shell and inspected it for damage. He searched further, and said, "You run from the merchants. You take any speckles?"

"No. You can't steal the cans. I ate some before I went."

"Pouches?"

"They lock 'em up."

"Where's the gun?"

They'd heard the shots. He said, "Hidden."

"All right. Come."

Two of the others took the carcass. Geordy led off. The fourth man trailed behind Tim, spear in hand. Geordy suddenly whipped around and said, "In the morning you're gone."

"All right."

"We can't give you speckles. We need what we got."

"All right."

Shirefolk still formed circles: elders, younger men, older children, women with children, women without; smaller circles within the larger groups, circles of opportunity. Women-without were chefs. Women-with drifted from their circle to help or give orders. Elders were an arc around Tim Bednacourt, and the circle of men was a loose arc around those. Men left it to fetch or carry under direction of the women/chefs.

They seated Tim Bednacourt on a dune and expected him to stay there. Several of the women-without took their turns bringing him food.

Dinner was pork and a variety of vegetables. Tim tasted speckles in the rice pilaf. He talked about the Road, but not about bandits. He described Tail Town and the Neck.

They were watching him.

They hadn't done that when he was with a caravan. The elders and the young men and the children would meet his eye. The women would not. But they lingered near when no task called, listening.

He told of dropping into the bay and swimming back to Tail Town. That made even the women stare for just a moment.

He wasn't being treated as a caravan yutz. The women were watching him askew, not a gaze, just a mutual awareness, as with women and men in Spiral Town. Did the merchants see Spiral Town this way? Genders and cliques forming defense perimeters against the stranger?

"I think the boats are for giving rides to Otterfolk," he said. "Then the Otterfolk pay off in fish." And he told of shells along a beach, and newborns crawling into the world while Otterfolk warriors swam ashore to defend them.

In the dark of Quicksilver there was only firelight. Women-with-children had gone to their beds. Older children were gone too, and women-without drifted off to the river to clean cookware, and the few remaining elders were all men.

Tim taught them a song he'd learned on the Road. Then the men escorted him off to the big building in the crater.

It was one big room. Seventy merchants and yutzes had all slept on the floor in a tangled pile when the caravan was here. Now he had it all to himself. He stretched out in the middle of it all with his pack for a pillow, until the men bade him goodnight and were gone.

Then he left his pack and moved himself into a remembered corner. He lay down again with two walls to guard him and his weed cutter under his hand.

He'd slept some during the day. For the first in many nights, he wasn't cold. The painted Otterfolk shell no longer scratched his back. It had served his need.

The question was whether to run *now*.

The Shire seemed uncommonly friendly to a man alone.

From the midpoint of the Crab Peninsula to the corner of Haunted Bay, there were no dwellings. Single men or women, couples, whole families running from failure or crime or politics or boredom, must have filtered down the Road in the wake of *Cavorite*. The distillery/dairy was as far as they'd got except for two sizable communities on Haunted Bay.

But that was one serious leapfrog.

Why wasn't he finding a house or three every step of the way?

Because only *strong* communities could treat with bandits as equals?

Bandits didn't seem to bother the Shire. And the Shire was friendly to a man on the run, though they watched him like a possible thief. Had they been similarly friendly to messengers from the distillery?

When he heard the rustling, *bandits!* was his first thought. He stood up in a crouch. They were in here with him!

The giggles—two, three?—didn't sound dangerous. But he hadn't heard the door or seen moonlight. There must be another door, hidden.

A woman's voice spoke with just a trace of impatience. "Runner?"

Another voice: "He's gone," bitterly disappointed.

"No. Why would he?"

A nearly incoherent wail. "Oh, who knows what lives in a stranger's brain? He knows the merchant women! We don't dress like they do—"

Tim had been tiptoeing toward the center, toward his pack. He'd gambled his life when he brought a butchered boar to the Shire, and the bet still stood. He asked, "What's it all about?"

A third voice, much calmer, didn't speak directly to him. "We can hope he'd like some company?"

Tim said, "Sit down with me. I have a thousand questions. Shall we make a light?"

Laughter and protest. "Oh, no!" The rustling came close; circled him.

It was seriously dark. He guessed at anywhere from four to a dozen. He slid his weed cutter under his pack and sat on that.

He said, "I know not to touch you, but I'm wondering how this all started. People along the Road don't all do as you do."

Silence. Ragged breath. Then, "The merchants tell us we can't rub up against a stranger."

"Ever since the first caravan came."

"And Rashell Star turned down Wayne the speckles man."

"Rashell *the* Star. And she slapped him."

"Bobbitted."

"A hundred years ago."

"More."

"So we keep ourselves to ourselves, men and women both, and we teach our children too. We know what happens if the merchants don't bring speckles." The woman who had spoken was quite breathless, and a silence followed.

Tim said, "Look, they told me *you* don't mix with strangers."

Four hands reached out of the dark. Tim jumped at the first touch. Then he patted the hands (five, six!) and asked, "It's the merchants' idea?"

Laughter. Someone took his hand, and guided it under clothing, and that was a woman's breast, *big*.

What on Earth—?

They were swathed in layers of clothing. It came off in great soft piles that made a fine extensive bed. They stripped him insistently, and explored him first with their hands, whispering to each other. He never knew if he would touch clothing or skin, and now it was mostly skin.

Once he got the idea, Tim began searching shapes in the dark. His wandering hands found delight—and perfection. No twisted spine or twisted foot. Here a nose like the prow of a ship; here an ear that protruded interestingly; he knew them both, women-without-children who had served his food without meeting his eyes. Regular features, no strangeness, no flaws.

Wasn't that what they were looking for too? No point in making babies with a flawed or twisted visitor.

He counted six. And they still wouldn't talk to him, though they whispered to each other.

Tomorrow he wouldn't know them. Tonight the shapes and scents of the women were his whole environment. Tonight they were taking his genes.

Maybe he dreamed it. A hand shook his shoulder and a voice whispered, "Merchant man. Why did the Founders wake the flies?"

Without opening his eyes he asked, "Am I supposed to know?"

"You're supposed to know everything."

He'd thought that about caravaners. He'd thought about flies too. "Meat has to rot," he said, and was asleep again.

He woke alone, and stiff everywhere.

He dressed in customary haste, as if he must bake and serve breakfast. Then he took the time to search out a second entrance. It was set in a corner, a miniature maze baffled against light from outside.

He hesitated before going out.

The first caravan, she'd said. There never would have been a first caravan without customers already in place. So the first caravan found this isolated community halfway along the Crab—

Rashell the Star? Wayne the speckles man? Likely two or three or six merchants had tried to make babies with the wrong people. In Spiral Town men and women married before they got pregnant, and it might have been that way in the Shire. Then, merchants hadn't yet earned their current reputation. The Shire's need for external genes didn't show yet.

Somebody got slapped, or bobbitted, whatever that was.

Then what? Today the Shire was not dying, but Tim had *seen* some effects of inbreeding here. The merchants and yutzes weren't getting laid. What did anyone gain by continuing this nonsense?

He stepped outside knowing that there would be nobody to ask.

The men were gone. The women wouldn't meet his eye, any more than they ever had, and they wouldn't let him help with breakfast. They fed him fruit and speckles bread, then watched him walk off along the beach.

*   *   *

Along the beach until it curved out of sight. Then up into Earthlife trees, a tiny version of the graveyard grove in Spiral Town. He stuffed his pack with citrus fruit and kept moving.

He retrieved his gun and speckles-filled bullet bag. He hadn't stopped moving for an instant. Anyone who tried to follow him would be blowing hard. If someone was waiting above him, well, now he had the gun.

Speckles was in his system. He expected to feel more alert, and he did. Just his imagination? Too much of that could make him careless, make him miss something.

So think it through—

Four days up the Road, that was where the spring caravan had been attacked. Two days at the rate he was traveling. It now seemed that bandits' turf ran all the way from there to the distillery.

Two pairs of thief-takers ran ahead of him, traveling by the Road and by the frost line.

He might have tried a boat, or gambled that they couldn't swim. Instead, he climbed. He climbed until he'd reached the crest. Bandits might know the blind side of the Crab, but he'd seen no sign of them. He'd travel that way until he was past Farther.

✳ 16 ✳

Twerdahl Town

Columbiad is losing temperature, ionization, and humidity controls. We'll have to hold public meetings elsewhere.

We feel betrayed when a subsystem fails us. Anything worth bringing across interstellar space was meant to last forever.

—Ansel Milliken, landholder

He traveled at the frost line. At dusk he dipped into the snarl of plants below for fruits and any vegetables he could eat raw. A fool cage gave him a pigeon the second night: he risked a fire, and a gunshot for some spiny Destiny beast that thought he looked edible.

Two days, two nights, and at noon he'd reached the naked **V** of frozen lava above Twerdahl Town.

Two lines of houses ran for several klicks between the mudflat and the Road, with acres of cultivated land between. Twerdahl Town hadn't looked this big the first time he'd seen it, coming straight from Spiral Town.

Falls ran down the **V**, converged in streams, then ran across the flats into green and black swamp. Tim hadn't noticed, the first time he'd seen this place, how gradually the swamp formed. A wide band of dark, wet topsoil bloomed sparsely in a flood of sunlight, black touched with bronze and yellow-green.

Rice. Rice would grow well here. He'd tell them to plant rice, if he could find seed rice or buy it from the caravans. Pulling up Destiny weeds would be no trouble. They didn't like this much light.

He found a memorable place to hide a gun and bullets. He secreted his three speckles pouches in the hidden pockets a merchant favored. For the rest of the day he watched.

Surfers rode the waves. People worked the gardens, and fished. A man rode a bike along the Road. Three people came out of the swamp carrying a snake. Fires burned along the salt flats.

No sign of messengers from the distillery. Twerdahl Town might not be involved in that, but . . . wait for sunset.

After sunset Tim discovered that he wasn't willing to go down. Quicksilver gave no light; it was merely the brightest star. Climbing down slick lava in the dark could get a man killed, but wading through a snake-infested swamp . . . insane.

He'd go down in the morning. He'd been hiding too long. It was becoming a reflex.

At dawn he started down. There was brush to cling to along the edge of the lava shield. He could see boards out on the water. He hadn't surfed in a long time.

By the time he got down, sunlight penetrated even into the swamp. He waded in.

Black Destiny vines were growing all over everything. High time for another weed cutting! Of course that only meant that the autumn caravan was coming soon. Meanwhile he must crawl through black vines and black water, slashing at snakes with his own weed cutter.

At the Road he washed as best he could. Then he climbed out and dripped.

The bicycle was coming back. Tim watched it come. Had it gone as far as Farther? He didn't recognize the man on the bike, but he would when the man got closer.

The biker saw him. Tim called, "Hello! I—"

The bike wheeled hard right and disappeared among the houses.

Tim strolled after it along a dirt path between houses. No chance of catching a man on a bike! He was yelling. Suddenly Tim knew the voice: one of the Grant boys, the oldest, a skinny nineteen-year-old.

Two rows of houses, and cultivated land between. Tim turned downRoad. He knew his own house, there at the end, and he started to trot.

Loria came out. Tim called, "Loria—"

She froze. Behind her came a man, a *big* man carrying a baby. Behind them, Tarzana Bednacourt, pregnant; and then Gerrel Farrow.

The man touched Loria's arm and spoke. The four moved briskly between houses and were gone.

Tim gaped.

Now what? Go into the house to wait? Whatever was going on, it would be over presently. Meanwhile Tim could clean himself up and get fresh clothes. He hadn't given much thought to what he must look like.

But he had to *know*. This all felt very wrong. He walked between rows of orange and grapefruit trees, between houses and onto the mud-flat.

He was facing half of Twerdahl Town. Most of them were carrying farming or fishing implements, and that wasn't strange, but they carried them like weapons.

He thought again: what must he look like? He dropped his plumeless hat and combed his hair back with his hands. It might help.

"I'm Tim Bednacourt!" he shouted.

Men and women (no children, no elderly) moved to put Tim Bednacourt at the center of an arc. Loria and the man with the baby were standing *way* too close together, mutual protection in frieze. The man was Ander Cloochi, son of the town's master farmer.

Tim was moving from exasperation toward panic. "Berda Farrow, you taught me to cook! Tarzana, don't you know me? Loria!"

"We know you," Susie Cloochi said. "Tim, what happened to you?"

"Long story. But I—look." He dropped his pack and was about to open it when everyone took one step forward.

"It's a shell," he babbled. "Scrimshaw."

Ander motioned him to go ahead.

Tim untied the pack, one-handed, and dumped it. He didn't need to conceal anything in the pack. He fished out the shell and pointed out the pictures. "Chug. Shark. This is done on a lungshark shell. That's an Otterfolk. I had an Otterfolk shell too, but I gave it away. What happened to me? Everything you can imagine, Susie, and then some. I've sailed a boat. I can cook in styles you never imagined. I've seen the blind side of the Crab."

"You don't *seem* to be speckles-shy," Susie Cloochi said.

And suddenly he *knew* what he looked like.

He was wearing a trader yutz's glare-bright clothing, though it hung in rags and dirt. He'd traveled on the far side of the ridge for a long, hungry time. He was gaunt. Worst of all, he was *here*, with the caravan twenty days away. A wanderer not following a caravan was a bandit.

And a thief; but they couldn't know about the stolen speckles can. In a way that made it worse. A speckles-shy bandit might do anything.

The corner of his eye caught motion, way upRoad around the tool-house. He couldn't spare the attention. "Test my mind," he said. "Test my memory. I gave you the bicycle Tedned Grant was riding. Ander,

Gerrel, you helped me build that oven. I taught you bread! I remember getting married, Loria. Ander Cloochi, is there something you'd like to tell me?"

"We're married."

"Now, I'm still new among you," Tim said, "so I have to ask—"

Loria burst out laughing. It didn't seem she could stop. Ander said, "No, Loria can't have two husbands."

"But you both, you *all* knew I'd be back."

"But not *now*, damn it, Tim! We'd—Loria would have had time to decide."

"Is this what happened to Haron Welsh?"

Loria's laughter had trailed off. She wouldn't meet his eyes, now, but she nodded.

"Went off with a caravan. Came back. Found out he wasn't married? And you thought he'd tell me?"

Nod.

Ander put the baby in her arms, and stepped in front of her. "So, you're here. What happened to you, Tim?"

"At the Neck they trade yutzes. The autumn caravan was every trader who ever—" He was so tired and so miserable. Tim felt he was about to faint. He didn't dare. "—ever watched me shoot a man. I had to run. I took enough speckles to get me here."

At the corner of his eye, motion. Three or four older people at the door to the toolhouse. He recognized Julya Franken by her long white still-lovely hair, and remembered when he had last seen her.

She'd been handing out blades on the day of the weed cutting.

The four went into the toolhouse.

"You're not speckles-shy," Susie Cloochi decided. "You took enough speckles—"

Tim stooped and picked up his open pack. And ran straight at Tedned Grant.

"—from who? *Tedned!*"

Tedned was a skinny boy/man who flinched from big waves, or wrestling, or quarrels or confrontations. Still he was no runt. With all eyes on him, he tried to get his fists up. Tim knocked him aside and dodged between houses.

He emerged between high rows of corn, with nobody in sight. Paths ran between the garden plots. He pelted upRoad, counting.

Tedned was behind him, not catching up.

Tedned had run his bike between houses rather than meet Tim in the Road. There ahead, *those* houses. When Tim had next seen him, the bike was gone. Tedned must have dropped his bike and kept running, yelling into every house he passed. And *here* were the houses, and one was the Younger Grants' house, and the bike was leaning against a wall.

Tim was too late to board the bicycle as Tedned came running up.

It wasn't as if Tim had choices. He couldn't make for the water, not yet. He left the bike and ran at Tedned. Tedned got his arms up and Tim punched between his elbows, a quick one to the solar plexus, the heel of his hand to the nose.

Now the bike. They had let grit get into the gears. It started slow. He pedaled past Tedned, who was curled up and trying to find his breath.

Twerdahl Town's defenders were pouring between the houses now, and others would be running along the mud, but Tim was ahead and moving considerably faster than a running man. He could see the toolhouse, the last building upRoad.

Well short of the toolhouse, he turned again. Between the houses. Out onto the mud. Off the bicycle before it got mired, because Tim Bednacourt was no thief.

DownRoad, a horde was running toward him, though they seemed out of breath. UpRoad, only four, and they all looked as old as Julya Franken. But they bristled with weed cutters.

He might have escaped them, he thought, if he'd turned toward the Road. But then what? He'd stopped alongside the surfboards lined up along the wall of the Elder Bednacourts' house. Tim snatched up the biggest and held it over his head as he ran for the water.

They tried to follow him, of course. A few were better surfers than he was, and they were hot on his tail, but he wasn't surfing now. Once beyond the waves he need only paddle.

Paddle for his life, slipping over the water, on and on. The ache in his shoulders grew until it swallowed everything else, while the current carried him southeast.

Ultimately his pursuers were too far from Twerdahl Town for their comfort, too close to Spiral Town, and they turned back one by one.

✳ 17 ✳

C a r d e r ' s   B o a t

Black for photosynthesis. Sagan and Schklovskii were right.

—Gerot, Xenobiology

He thought he was going to die.

He thought he didn't care.

There was nothing to drink. There was nothing chasing him anymore. There was nothing to do but paddle.

A thousand times he turned his eyes toward shore. A wave would carry him in. He could live between Twerdahl Town and Spiral Town . . . live like a hunted animal, until his mind turned animal too.

When he could make his arms move, he paddled. When he rested, the shore still drifted past him by infinitesimal degrees. His shoulders were one long moan of pain. The sun burned into his neck and his arms and the backs of his calves.

He lay in salt water. The board floated two centimeters below the surface. If he let his head rest on the wood, he could drown. The off-balance weight of his pack drove him crazy, but never quite crazy enough to drop it overboard.

When he remembered this part of his life, he never knew how long anything took.

He was drifting in a stupor with his chin propped on his arms on the second night, or the third. He was flying *Cavorite* in his mind. . . .

The long, slow drift from the landing site down to the Neck and beyond. Day and night shifts? Stop to rest, or to shed the heat from riding a fusion flame, or to look at anything interesting. Side jaunt to Haunted

Bay, because cameras in the sky found seabed geometries suggesting an undersea city. . . .

. . . Trying to see why they ran the Road so high.

Twerdahl Town filled the whole space between the Road and the beach. *Cavorite* had flown close to shore when it made the Road there. As it moved down the coast, the Road ran higher. Near the Neck it ran as high as it could get, right along the crest . . . as if Twerdahl and his crew had become afraid of the sea.

He toyed with an odd notion. When had *Cavorite* learned of the Otterfolk?

Teaching programs named thousands of extinct species of life on Earth. All species die or change over millions of years. A meteoroid impact had rendered all the dinosaurs extinct, barring those that sired the birds . . . but many species died because Man was good at changing his environment.

There was a shadow among shadows ahead of him. . . .

Had *Cavorite* laid the Road to protect the Otterfolk?

He remembered, though, that the Hub in Spiral Town was far, far inland. *Cavorite* was hovering over burnt-out alien wilderness when it drew the lines of Spiral Town. The Twerdahls must have run their loops of Road to within a klick of shore, stayed near the water for forty klicks farther, then eased upslope toward the peaks again. . . .

Avoiding the sea.

The landers had charred the land and boiled the lakes, but a flame couldn't reach below the sea. Future generations would follow the Road, spiraling outward until they gradually approached whatever came out of the sea. They'd have time to prepare.

Cavorite's crew feared the alien.

. . . *Ahead of him, then passing on the left.*

He moaned and tried to work his arms.

He could make them move, but he couldn't paddle.

He slid far back, half off the board, and kicked. Against the current, toward shore, gripping with dead arms and kicking with all his remaining strength, his breath a stuttering moan. A raft of Destiny devilhair with an angular shadow in the middle was trying to creep past him. He gained a centimeter at a time.

Then the current was pushing his board not past the vastness of black weed but into it, and he could rest.

Hours later the cramping in his arms faded. He found he could grip the board with his knees and pull handfuls of weed toward him, sliding the board across the weed, until floating devilhair lifted his board above the water. Now he could let his head rest on waxed wood for the first time in two days.

By morning light it looked tremendous. It loomed far above him, shaped like two slender fisher boats with a deck across their tops.

Carder's Boat, sure enough.

Sunlight's touch turned the heat in his neck and arms and calves into a flame. He pulled himself and the board across the black weed into the shadow of the boat. That pain eased, but what was hurting his hands?

Destiny devilhair had covered his palms with myriads of black needles barely big enough to see as specks.

Carder's Boat loomed vast. He could not imagine such a thing stowed in a starship's cargo hold. Settler magic was compact, never bigger than it had to be.

He used his shirt to shield his hands. He dragged his board across the devilhair, around the stern and into sunlight.

Children had used this as a raft before the weed grew too thick. They must have left a ladder somewhere! But the weed hid everything. On this sunlit, seaward side the weed had grown right up the side: a black shroud marked with yellow-green, and a boat half-visible beneath.

He climbed the weed with bare hands and feet.

It didn't quite reach the rim. It kept ripping loose. Somehow he got a hand on the rim and pulled himself over. The impact of his fall was so strange . . . but what mattered was the cabin, and the steps down.

The weird surface gave back no impact. He crawled like a ghost, down into the cabin, into shadow.

In shadow the burning went away and he could think about his thirst. There was a sink.

Water ran. He twisted his head under the spigot and drank. He remembered to be afraid of it, old water in an old container, but it tasted like spring water: like life itself. He drank until the weight of his belly pulled him to the weird floor. He didn't want to die.

On a table he found what must have been lunch for six or eight, then a garden of Earthlife yeasts and bacteria, then this dead powdery residue.

There was nothing to eat aboard Carder's Boat.

Carder's Boat was not of this world. The floor and walls of the cabin ate his footfalls and gave back no sound and no recoil. Carder's Boat was nearly massless, an airy foam under a taut skin.

They *hadn't* stowed Carder's Boat aboard an interstellar spacecraft. They'd stowed a tank of something that foamed up and hardened, and maybe a boat-shaped membrane to foam it into, and a few compact settler-magic machines, like this sink that seemed able to make drinking water, and the lighted interior walls. The hull's silver-gray surface was Begley cloth sheeting from Mount Apollo, pressed into place after the boat was inflated.

His hunger had subsided to a dull ache. His fingers and toes were black with tiny needles; he could barely move them for the pain. Climbing the weed had cost him.

There was a bath. Water still ran. When the salt was off him some of the itching went away. He left his clothes soaking and moved naked about the cabin.

A small patch on a counter almost burned him. It glowed dull red with heat. He found a dial to turn it off.

A teapot and a frying pan were both chained to the wall above the counter. There were hooks for more cookware, but the cookware was gone.

He found boxes and chests of Spiral Town workmanship, here and on deck. One held a big stack of towels that shredded in his hands. One held fishing gear, sturdier lines and sturdier poles than the caravan used. He looked over the side and saw only black devilhair. How could he fish through that?

And one chest held clothing: floppy knee-length swimsuits and elbowlength windbreakers in a strange old style, tinted in shiny pastels. These had held up very well. Jemmy tried to pull one apart, hoping he'd fail; and the seams held, if there were seams. He couldn't find them.

Carder's Boat was a small frog on a wide lily pad.

Events came isolated. Afterward he was never able to order them properly.

He was still wandering naked about the boat when he found the fishing gear. He'd kept his weed cutter. He put that together with a jointed fishing pole four meters long and some translucent line, and had a four-meter weed cutter. He began to chop devilhair.

It hurt his healing hands. Flying mites lived in the weed, and the blade set black clouds rising.

Something leaped. He stabbed, and had a Destiny amtrak eel on the point. A moment later it wriggled free. *When?* The gap in the weed wasn't very big then.

The gap was bigger before anything leapt again, and he jabbed and flung—heavy!—and a little lungshark flopped on dry weed. He worked the blade under the shell and was able to flip it into the boat.

He killed it and filleted it and cooked it with speckles. It fed and calmed the ravenous animal in his belly. He lay on deck to watch the fires of sunset and, briefly, Quicksilver.

It must have been next morning that he baited a hook with the shark's remains . . . thought it over, and threw the offal overboard. Destiny life would not keep a man alive. He didn't want to catch more.

He went back to cutting weed. He perfected the jab-and-flip. He got another amtrak eel that way. He was ready when a flounder appeared—Earthlife!—and he got it aboard. He baited three hooks with what was left after he'd eaten. There were sockets in the deck to brace a fishing pole. He lowered the lines into the great open patch he'd cut in the weed around Carder's Boat.

Earthlife fish lived deep down. He ate himself stupid, and remembered to add speckles.

The skin on his neck and legs peeled off in flakes.

Later—it had to be later—he was wearing swim trunks and a windbreaker and a floatation vest fished from a locker. He slept through noon and worked at night. Quicksilver had become a white glare.

He kept chopping. Every day there was less weed around the boat. It was trying to grow back, but he stayed ahead of it. There was a ladder after all, under the thickest part of the weed. He cleared it.

A few people watched from shore, day after day. Then a great crowd came down from Warkan's Tavern, when Quicksilver was almost behind the sun, brilliant at sunset. They never waved, they just watched, day after day.

One day they were sparse; another day, gone.

He found the anchor cable by chopping devilhair from around it. He tracked it up from the water to a housing in the boat's nose.

There was a switch.

He flipped it.

The housing hummed to itself, gearing up. Then it pulled, and the boat's nose sank. He watched, fascinated. The boat was too light to sink, he thought, but could it pull itself underwater? right to the floor of the ocean? He never thought of turning the motor off.

Something in the sea bottom gave first. The boat surged savagely; the deck slapped him silly. The anchor lurched up while he was still too dizzy to care.

Later—Quicksilver was rising well before dawn—he saw that the weed that linked the boat to shore had stretched into a line. The current was pulling him southeast.

He chopped weed until all that was left was the little patch on the starboard side on which his board still rested. At some point the boat tore loose and he drifted free.

He had no way of rowing or steering Carder's Boat. Nonetheless his life had changed. Jemmy Bloocher was moving again.

Tim Hann had lived ten days. Tim Bednacourt, Loria's husband, had lasted half a year. Tim Bednacourt, the caravan's chef, was a hunted bandit.

He couldn't remember when Jemmy Bloocher came back. It just felt right.

The land slid northwest, then away.

The current along Haunted Bay ran southeast toward Spiral Town. Jemmy had thought the water would carry him around the point and down the Crab's barren shore. Those cliffs were unclimbable—he'd seen that—but he could wait, drift down along the Neck, see what the shore was like along the mainland.

The mainland. There was nothing left for Jemmy Bloocher on the Crab Peninsula, but the mainland . . . *Cavorite* had gone there, leaving Road for others to follow. The caravan's home was in the mainland.

He came to understand that he'd guessed wrong.

He was far out at sea. Mist hid the land but for the projecting peaks of the Crest. Those slid northwest, then away—north and east—then, very distant now, drifted southeast again. He was moving in a great curve.

The sea flowed like a wide bathtub whirlpool of which Haunted Bay was only the drain.

None of this bothered Jemmy Bloocher. His speckles and the ocean would feed him for a while. As the days passed, he watched a vast sea and a serrated edge of land, and a towering black storm far down the coast. In his mind he traced *Cavorite*'s path.

He was noticed, of course. On all of Destiny there couldn't be two objects like Carder's Boat.

One morning a few Otterfolk had him in view.

The next morning there were more. He couldn't tell how many because they spent most of their time underwater, but he could see five or six at a time. At noon they drifted away, or drifted deep to fish. He came to believe that Otterfolk didn't like direct sunlight.

On another morning he came on deck into a flurry of Earthlife flatfish. He ducked two and another smacked him on the cheek. There must have been a whole school flopping on deck. He stood at the edge of the deck and raised his arms and shouted, "Stop!"

They stopped. He brushed flopping fish overboard, picking those who might live to swim away. He kept a dozen. Otterfolk watched for half a day while he filleted and cooked the catch. He didn't have to fish for a while.

Another day, his line pulled a sub clam up to the surface. There were beaked faces all over the water, watching.

The thing was heavier than he was, too heavy to lift into the boat.

Did Otterfolk play practical jokes, or were they testing an alien intelligence? How was he to free his hook?

He pulled the sub clam onto the remaining patch of weed. It rested on its shell, its siphon/tentacle writhing as it fumbled at the slick fishing line, trying to tear it.

If he climbed down there, the weed would drown him.

Could he balance on the board while he worked? Weed surrounded the surfboard, but he could pull the clam into reach of it. But if he did find some way to get the sub clam up to the boat . . .

Otterfolk knew that humans ate sub clam meat. They might not know that it wouldn't keep him alive.

He used his four-meter weed cutter to chop at the meat around the hook until some of it came free. He pulled up twenty pounds of sub clam. Then he compromised. He sliced two pounds of it free and threw the rest back into the weed alongside the shell, where scavengers swarmed around it.

The Otterfolk got the idea, or else they didn't like waste. He was never offered another sub clam.

He could remember the sub clam shell in view beneath a blazing Quicksilver, long before dawn. An Earthlife duck was flapping in the shell with both its wings broken.

It took all of his will to cook it before he ate it.

Afterward he wondered if there was a way to teach mercy to Otterfolk using gestures alone. . . .

The Neck was where the peaks disappeared below the mist layer. Beyond they rose again, marching into the mainland toward a distant storm.

Storms formed and went away, didn't they? This one didn't. He was still drifting toward it after . . . he couldn't remember how many days. The clouds towered higher than the peaks of the Crest. At night he could see lightning playing within.

How old *was* that storm? He fantasized that it was a permanent feature of Destiny. Jupiter's Red Spot had lasted centuries. Destiny storms didn't normally do that, but if one had . . . then *Cavorite* would have gone to see.

He was passing the Neck, then, the morning he found that the picked-clean shell of a sub clam held a neatly placed tuna still flopping. They couldn't have thrown such a mass, could they? They must have guided and chased it across the weed and precisely onto the shell.

Neat!

He was working out how to hook it when he saw sails.

He'd thought the mist would hide him. Maybe it only hid him from the Neck, while a fisher at sea could still see his mast. Maybe they hadn't told the merchant guards on the Neck. But Carder's Boat was conspicuous.

The fisher sails showed clearly now. They'd get here hours before sunset.

He raised the ladder.

From above, weed half-enclosed the surfboard. From a boat they'd never see it.

He'd left his mark in chopped-away weed, but a fisher might think it just grew this way.

He gaffed the tuna, pulled it up, took it into the cabin's shadow, and cleaned it. He threw the offal onto the weed to draw scavengers.

Lying on deck with only his eyes above the rim, he watched four sails come closer. He didn't know the men in the boats. None of them wore merchant's clothing.

Jemmy took his four meters of weed cutter to the cabin, and waited.

He could hear them moving about. He heard their voices, querulous and awed. Otterfolk watched from afar.

The fishers were gone at sunset. They hadn't been able to find a way up.

More boats came the next day. Carder's Boat had drifted by then, but they'd come straight as arrows. They threw something over the side: a rope ladder with hooks on it. When one of them started to climb up, Jemmy cut the ropes and heard him splash.

They sailed off. The next day nobody came.

The land came near: an unfamiliar coast half-seen through mist. The storm came nearer too.

He'd eaten tuna until it went bad and he had to throw it overboard. Now he'd grown hungry enough to want it back. The Otterfolk had gone away. He'd caught nothing using tuna for bait. Earthlife fish must be scarce around here. But the current would carry him back toward the Neck, where Tail Town fishers didn't seem to go hungry.

But he'd be giving the fishers and the merchants another shot at him.

He could hardly hear himself think for the howling of the wind and, often, the pounding of the rain. He had to shelter in the cabin most of the time. But he thought about drifting back along the Neck, conspicuous as any fifteen-meter craft from another world, and he thought of *Cavorite* flying into a storm that wouldn't go away.

He couldn't remember making a decision. It was just there.

He took all the clothes he'd found aboard, though it was only short-sleeved windbreakers and trunks and a pair of work gloves. It all went into his pack along with fishing line and hooks. He showered: no telling when he'd do that again. He drank all the water his belly would hold.

He knelt on the board in a pelting rain.

The devilhair hadn't actually eaten into the wood. He peeled it away in big patches, wearing the gloves he'd found aboard. Then gloves and shoes went into his pack and he began paddling with great overhand sweeps of his arms.

He had imagined the path of *Cavorite*, but it felt very real to him. Had he imagined the days aboard Carder's Boat? Events in his head were isolated; he had trouble connecting them. He'd been on this board forever.

Rain lashed at him and withdrew and fell again. It could not be much past noon, could it? But it was dark as night save for the slashing of the lightning. Thunder and rain filled his hearing.

Now there was another sound, growing.

He couldn't see sign of a beach ahead, but he could hear, above the thunder and the rain, waves rising and smashing down, throwing spume. Storm waves. If this storm had been here long enough to draw *Cavorite*—

But he had no reason to think that was true, did he? The storm might be only weeks old. But if he'd guessed right, then there had to be a beach. Waves like this, pounding rock cliffs for centuries or millennia, would have smashed rock to sand.

The waves were lifting him and dropping him. He got to his knees. This oncoming mountain of water looked like *it*, and he paddled hard, then stood up and walked the board forward, sliding down, down. The nothing ahead was taking shape.

Alien-looking black cliffs.

He veered the board. The wave was trying to break.

Twerdahl Town surfers had given him a name for what he was doing now, but he couldn't remember. He rode the board parallel to shore with a wave breaking behind him and curling over him. He was losing ground, always closer to black rock, but that was *sand*, it *had* to be sand at the foot of those black cliffs. He veered straight toward land and ran ahead of the wall of water, as far as he could, before the wave broke over him.

He crawled onto a narrow band of black sand. He lay for a time, just breathing.

Choking on seawater, he'd still had the wit to hurl his pack at the rocks. It was beyond the waves. But the waves were playing with a shattered board, rolling it in and back out, shredding it. His four-meter weed cutter must be under the sea.

The border of sand had narrowed. When the moons lined up you could get tides a meter high. If this beach disappeared, he could drown yet.

The black cliffs loomed alien and dangerous, a type of rock he'd never seen on Destiny.

He donned his pack. It was incredibly heavy, the clothes within soaked with seawater. Presently he found something like a way up.

✳ 18 ✳

The Windfarm

Something in the ocean is absorbing or precipitating potassium. What it is doesn't matter: we couldn't possibly counteract it in time. We'll have to look elsewhere.

—Cordelia Gerot, Xenobiology

Ferocious winds and stinging rain held him crouched and crawling and nearly blind. Lightning sputtered continually, like settler magic gone bad. It was all black and gray rocks tilted at all angles, and it had gone on forever.

He slid on slippery smooth surfaces. In places he found a surface like foamy rock. Traction was good, but it lacerated his knees and would have torn bare hands and feet to ribbons. His shoes and gloves were worth his life here.

It was another world, as alien as pictures of Volstaag and Hogun taken by crawler probes.

Yet there was life all around him. The rocks were cracked everywhere; and wherever there were cracks, wherever mud could accumulate, dwarf forest clung to the cracks and the flats.

Jemmy found he could cling to the spiky plants and follow the cracks.

Shadows blew past him on the wind, like kites with broken strings. He couldn't spare attention for what must be fragments torn from Destiny plants. But he had to keep ducking to protect his eyes, so he never got a good look. Now flurries of shadows dipped and darted about him as if a malevolent whirlwind sought his death.

He ducked a shadow and it slashed his pack.

He'd barely glimpsed its shape. It was not an Earthlife bird.

He could huddle close to the black-and-bronze plants. Birds had to

183

veer from the plants, and Jemmy got a better look at them. What seemed to be feathers certainly weren't. They looked more like a chicken than an eagle: more compact, less likely to fly. He ducked slashing claws, and peered after the bird as it wheeled and came for him again. How many legs did that thing have?

Furtive creatures were looking him over from within the brush. Maybe his scent would keep them clear . . . but it wasn't stopping the birds.

A lovely, brilliant creature posed on a rock to watch him crawl toward it.

In the sputtering blue-white light it stood out like a bonfire, scarlet and yellow with bands of electric orange. When he came close it stood upright and spread short wings, and now there were threads of blue in the pattern. It looked too big to fly. It was patterned like a butterfly, iridescent in this light. It turned its head sideways to look at him, and snapped a beak like needle-nosed pliers.

He stopped a few meters away, wondering what defense could give it such confidence. It never gave ground. Destiny birds veered clear of it, and so did Jemmy.

He was crawling blind along a curve like a huge snake. He forced his eyes open and found he'd run up against a smoothly curved surface, a tube of rock.

He crawled into it, out of the rain.

It ran for meters before it became too narrow. As soon as he stopped moving, he was asleep.

Thunder shaped nightmares. He'd wake with a scream he couldn't hear, and remember where he was, and sleep again.

Later, slept out and hungry in a black coffin of rock, he wondered what built tubes. Human engineers built pipes, aquaducts . . . but here? He pictured huge worms that ate rock. . . .

He crawled out into a world much like the one he'd left, and kept moving. Water had drained from his pack. It was lighter, briefly.

Starvation and battered senses left him light-headed. It was only a day since he had eaten, but many days since he'd eaten anything but fish. Fruit and vegetables were a fading memory. There were potholes in the rock everywhere he went, and he drank rainwater to fill his belly.

He had no idea what he was crawling toward.

An orange glow . . . gone now, as he crawled along the edge of a patch of forest . . . there again, orange to his left and a touch of heat on his cheek. He crawled toward that.

The warm rain wasn't warm enough. It was draining the heat out of him, easing him into death. He was shuddering with fatigue and hunger. Lightning sputtered continually: the world was dark and blue-white, and it wasn't much better than being blind. He couldn't recognize a single plant or tree in the Destiny forest. The air stank. But orange flashed and drew him. . . .

. . . Until warmth bathed him, and he turned himself like a roasting boar carcass to soak it in. The wind went *up*, carrying the rain away from him.

For a while, then, he could stop.

Curiosity brought him closer to the heat. Crawling over naked slippery rock, he looked down into a sea of red-orange light. It made him back up. He'd found what was only found in teaching programs. Lava— molten rock—*volcano*.

Destiny's crust had ripped here. That happened often on Earth, but nowhere else on Destiny.

An alien place indeed, where no food grew for Earthlife such as himself. He should go while he still had strength.

Wind howled in his ears beneath the crackle of lightning. It wasn't easy to walk; but he just couldn't crawl any more. His whole body screamed if he tried.

He walked directly into the wind, peeking between his fingers. He didn't remember why. He'd figured something out . . . he couldn't exactly remember, but this was right. Keep the wind in his face.

Plants drew him, color against the dark.

They covered the shallow slopes ahead of him. They stood out like settler-magic paint: green, orange, black. Black stalks split and split again to become orange thorns whose tips divided down to tiny green needles. Bristly plants hugged the ground, knee high and twice as wide as they were tall. Nothing grew around or between them.

There were paths between the rows. The slope was gentle, and the rain had eased. Suddenly everything was easier.

Jemmy was too far gone even to be thankful.

The plants tore at his legs when he wobbled off the path. He bore it twice or thrice, then bellowed in rage and tried to pull one up. The plant's roots clung like a demon. He tried another, and a third, then quit.

And now he'd found a wider path, rock not too slippery to walk on. The broad band of smooth rock continued level, maintaining a constant width alongside the hip-high forest. Even blinded by rain, he couldn't lose his way.

Plants all in one variety, like something tended. If there were Otterfolk on the sea, could there be sapient natives on land? Farmers? A world older than Earth might have had time to father more than one sapient species.

He walked, his mind dreaming, disconnected.

He'd done this before.

It didn't dawn on him; it *seeped* up into his mind. From magma spilled from a ripped planet, he had wandered onto rock melted by fusion flame and refrozen. He was on the Road again.

Above the wind and thunder he heard his own wild laughter.

A pulsing yellow-white light began to intrude on the lightning, growing bright as he followed the Road. He couldn't even feel surprise when he found the door.

Someone fed him broth.

Later, a bowl of rice with vegetables in it.

In between he must have slept.

The stone walls felt thick as mountains. They blocked the thunder down to a suggestion, a background. It was one big room. Bunks ran away from him in an infinite rectangular array. The occupants slept, or talked quietly; he heard nothing of that. One moaned and protested in her sleep, just audible above the whisper of thunder, and Jemmy knew that he could hear again.

He kept falling in and out of sleep.

He half-woke when the lights brightened. He was too tired to move, but he watched as men and women rolled out of their beds. They all wore shorts, scarlet and yellow with a narrow orange stripe, and nothing above the waist. Most of them pulled voluminous slick-skinned blouse-and-hood garments over their heads, all in the same scarlet-yellow-orange pattern, with strings dangling everywhere.

They went out in little clumps. Storm sounds rose, then fell as the door shut, rose again and fell.

Two doors. *Airlock.*

"Who are you?"

He blinked up at a half-bearded, half-naked man. Had he slept?

The man shook him. "Who *are* you?"

"Jemmy Bloocher."

"From now on you're Andrew Dowd. Remember that."

"Andrew Dowd."

"No, no, *Andrew Dowd.* Have you been getting enough speckles?"

"Andrew Dowd." He tried to imitate the man's pronunciation. It wasn't quite Tail Town speech, but closer to that than anything else. *Dowd* was not quite *Dawd*, not quite *Dode. An*drew, not *An*der.

The man was hairy everywhere, a pelt of tightly curled black hair over chest and arms and face and head. His beard was half a finger joint long, too short to be a real beard. His hair was the same length. His ribs and muscles stood out like an anatomy diagram: wiry strength and no fat at all.

He listened carefully to Jemmy's pronunciation, then said, "Better."

"Why? Why am I Andrew Dowd? Why do you want to know I was Jemmy Bloocher?"

"Tell you later. When you were out there, did you see anything like pools of water glowing blue?"

"Nothing like that."

"Good!"

"Why?"

"There are pools where the water acts as neutron traps for uranium. We call 'em Oklo pools. They're radioactive as hell. We'd have to put you outside if—Willametta?" Half-beard stood up. He too wore shorts in screaming colors, and a stick shoved through a loop at the small of his back.

Willametta wore shorts just like Half-beard's, and the same brush haircut in blond, as he saw when he managed to pull his gaze away from her tits. She'd be Senka ibn-Rushd's age: late thirties. But Senka ruled a merchant wagon. Willametta was master of nothing, as lean as Half-beard, and worn out. He could see a sharp-faced patrician loveliness beneath the fatigue.

She lifted Jemmy's head and slid her knee underneath. In that position she fed him spoonfuls of vegetable stew. It was nice.

It might have been erotic too, but Jemmy was just too tired. His attempt to impress her by feeding himself got as far as trying to free his hands from under a sheet. Too weak. Too hungry to bother. He hadn't eaten much when his protesting belly made him stop.

He asked, "Where am I?"

"You're serious?" Smiling, Willametta curled over to see his eyes. "Yeah. This is the Windfarm."

"Who found me?"

"Henry saw you first," Willametta said. "I thought Andrew would be angry. He's a trusty. He keeps track of us. But then—" She stopped. "Maybe tomorrow you can feed yourself, Andrew."

Questions yammered in his head. *Two Andrews? Trusty? Where are the toilets?* "Where are my things?"

"Andrew, you were carrying speckles. Speckles means you're ready to run! The proles kill you if they catch you!"

He looked up at her.

"We stashed the speckles. Clothes too. The trusty will give you a poncho when you can work." She handed him an oddly shaped pan. "This you piss in until you can get up."

The room faded. When his strength came back he looked under the sheet and found that he was wearing scarlet-yellow-orange shorts, way too big, with a drawstring.

He woke when everyone came in glistening wet. They left their ponchos at the far end where the airlock was. The kitchen and tables were there too, and they ate without much talk, though Jemmy could sense eyes on him.

Willametta fed him again.

They dimmed the lights.

Jemmy snapped awake. The brightening of the lights was like dawn flashing through a curtain suddenly swept back. He'd never seen artificial lights this bright. The others were all tumbling out of their beds. A sudden whiff of bread: they were tearing a loaf apart. They ate fast while they dressed.

Voices: "I'd kill a prole for a jar of strawberry jam."

"What size?" and a trickle of laughter.

They pulled ponchos out of a box at the far end of the big room, a machine that had throbbed all night, just audible through the muted roar of the storm. There were glare-orange ovals on the backs of the ponchos, a blue thread along the sleeves. They weren't all alike, not quite. Half-beard's had a broader orange curve down the front, a bigger oval patch in back.

They flowed out through the massive airlock. Jemmy counted as they cycled through: five women and fourteen men including Half-beard. Three stayed behind. There was the woman who couldn't get out of bed and complained a lot. There was a small muscular man with straight black hair and a bristly-black angry jaw, and an older woman whose tunic markings matched Half-beard's.

The woman loomed over him for a time, studying him. She was tall and dark, broad across shoulders and hips. She must weigh more than Jemmy did, despite being just short of gaunt, her big breasts slack and empty. By her size and her air of command, she reminded him oddly of Marilyn Lyons and Willow Hearst of the spring and fall caravans. She was of their kind, but starved to the bone.

Jemmy found himself avoiding her eyes. He was just as glad when she and the angry man disappeared through a door.

He lost interest, and dozed. Later he remembered sounds like quarreling or lovemaking . . . or storm sounds mingled in his dreams.

The smells of cooking woke him.

The man fed the bedridden woman, who appeared to be pregnant, not sick. At the big woman's orders he fed Jemmy and took Jemmy's bedpan.

There was no day or night out there. Jemmy (*Andrew*. Why Andrew? They could have picked a name closer to his own, and they had another Andrew.) "Andrew" could hear thunder. It never quite stopped. But there was day and night in here.

He'd lost his sense of time aboard Carder's Boat. Maybe he could rebuild his memory of the voyage from the phases of Quicksilver. . . .

He'd guessed right about the storm. Heated air rises from a sea of molten rock, a rip in the world's crust. Air at ground level flows in to replace it. Air moving inward on a spinning ball, must spin . . . a hurricane pattern that must have been running for centuries if *Cavorite*'s crew had come to see.

Oh, *that* was it. Air flows in, so face the wind to get out. Take the easy way out and you'll end on the easiest path to run a Road . . . assuming that *Cavorite*'s crew meant to lead the Road right into a storm!

Why would they do that?

He'd found plants arrayed in rows; then the Road; then a plantation house. What would be grown *here?* He could feel the answer tapping at his mind. It was right on the tip of his tongue. . . .

$*$ 19 $*$

Prison Cuisine

. . . stable storm, like Jupiter's Red Spot or Uranus's Dark Spot, but we haven't had as long to observe it. There's got to be a heat source under it, and it has to be geothermal. It may be a potassium source.

—Alan Waithe, Geologist

Morning. The big woman and her paramour stayed behind again. The man gave Jemmy a fist-sized chunk of bread, then water. They both sat on Jemmy's bed and watched him eat.

"Get up," she said.

Jemmy rolled out of bed, landed on his hands and knees. Mostly he'd stopped hurting, but he was weak. She watched him pull himself to his feet. He asked, "Where's the toilet?"

"Shimon, go with him."

There were doors at this end of the room, marked with silhouettes of a man and a woman. Yesterday afternoon, these two had disappeared into the women's room for an hour or two.

The men's room was bigger than he'd guessed, with urinals, toilets, basins, towel racks, showers, and a tub. Partitions around showers, tub, and toilets had been ripped out and the marks painted over, badly. The walls were smooth stone like the rest of the barracks.

He turned a spigot. Burning hot water roared into the tub.

Shimon was amused. He helped Jemmy climb in. He even got a towel for him; and then he watched as Jemmy got himself clean.

"How'd you get that scar on your hand?" he asked.

Jemmy tried to explain. His voice was rusty. He'd almost forgotten how to form words. He'd burned himself holding a gun wrong when he fired at an advancing line of sharks, and now there was a ridge of pink between thumb and wrist . . . and Shimon nodded and gave every sign of being fascinated.

When Jemmy tottered back to bed Shimon was supporting him with a hand on his elbow, under the woman's critical eye. Lying down was bliss.

The woman said, "I'm Barda. You do what I say. You do what anyone says if he wears the orange."

"I call you Barda?"

"You call me Barda. I call you Andrew. Gatherers like Shimon, here, call me Trusty unless we're alone. They call *you* Trusty. You use their given names. It's good if you can learn their family names too. Barda Winslow," she thumped her chest. "Shimon Cartaya," she thumped Shimon's. "Willametta Haines. Amnon Kaczinski, the big guy. Duncan Nicholls, you call him Duncan Nick. Denis Bouvoire if you need some machine unjammed. There's a Dennis Levoy too, don't get them mixed up. Rita and Dolores Nogales, the twins. You noticed *them*."

"The huge pale guy, yes. Amnon? Twins, no."

"Most men notice Rita and Dolores."

"There's a dark guy who looks young and old . . . crippled, maybe, but quick—"

"Rafik Doe. Came here at fourteen, near ten years ago. He won't give his real last name to anyone. Records say he killed a whole trader family with a yutz gun. You notice anyone else?"

"No."

"What've you guessed?"

"The other trusty, *he's* Andrew Dowd." Barda slurred her speech like Half-beard, and he tried to imitate that. It might buy his life. Prison workers who asked a stranger to lie would want to be sure he could!

"You wear the orange too. You're both bosses, trustees. I'm supposed to be him. Is he supposed to be sick?"

"If he gets sick they make someone else trusty. If someone finds you now, you're just someone we pulled out of the storm. Naked. Can you walk?"

He felt fifty feet high and made of glass, but Jemmy walked down as far as the box (which was bigger than Barda, and chugging again) and back. He set his hand unobtrusively on a bedpost to hold himself up, and asked, "Pulled naked out of the storm, right. Where are my clothes supposed to have gone?"

"What d'you think?"

"Torn off by the wind?" Better—"Shredded by the plants."

"Good."

"What really happened to them?"

"Don't worry about it."

"I saw a big bird the same color as your clothes—"

"Firebird," she said.

"The biology lessons say that when something is colored like that, to stand out, it's a signal. Could be a horny bird making himself easy to find, or a flower calling a bee. Could be it's poison and it's warning all the bird eaters away. *Stop, I am inedible!* You wear the firebird's colors so the Destiny predators won't bother you."

She nodded. "Now, 'Andrew,' I want to know all about you. Come on down to the kitchen." She took his elbow and they walked.

Everything that wasn't beds or washrooms was down at the airlock end. There was considerable space here: the huge stove, a line of hanging cookware, locked bins, the dining table and benches, an enormous heap of black twisted logs drying for firewood, and the chugging box.

The box was bigger than a coffin. It was settler magic, but it bore signs of later crude repairs. Below a glass hatch was a churning storm of brilliant colors. It was a dryer for wet clothes.

Barda gestured, and he sat at the table. Shimon set out a heap of vegetables from a bin. Barda sat across from Jemmy and began to chop and peel.

"I can help," Jemmy said. "I was a caravan chef."

"You just watch. I don't want you fainting."

She listened while she worked. Her expression didn't give away much. He could watch her muscles tense and relax, and watch the knife move. She was very fast, running on automatic, and her emotions went straight to her knife hand.

He couldn't watch Shimon, who busied himself tending the stove, feeding the pregnant woman, and watching Jemmy suspiciously.

When Jemmy told of killing Fedrick, the knife didn't pause.

She knew of the caravans, but she listened sharply to what he had to say of towns along the Road, and cooking. At one point she said, "What you know about pit cooking isn't worth a fart in the wind, in the Winds." And she chuckled for a long time.

The pile of vegetables grew, and he asked, "Barda, are we vegetarians?"

"They'll bring a bird in tonight if they can. Everything else gets carted in. They don't give us red meat. I think it spoils too quick. When we take in enough kilos of seeds, sometimes they give us a radiated sausage. Keep talking."

The battle with bandits excited her. When he spoke of the Otterfolk, she was rapt, her knife hand slow and forgotten. She loved the theft of the speckles can. She looked queasy when he described sunburn.

She smiled (knife speed increased) when he spoke of swimsuits aboard Carder's Boat. "The boat must have been rifled for anything anyone could use on land. Even cookware. And somebody left a burner going. The towels had all rotted, but the older stuff must be settler magic."

"We wondered. Six baggy shorts and seven old windbreakers and no hat, no jacket. You were wearing three windbreakers on over each other!"

He drifted with the current aboard Carder's Boat, fed by Otterfolk. Barda looked wistful. He took his surfboard into the Winds and her knife action turned angry. "You must be some kind of crazy and some kind of lucky. We lose gatherers in the Winds every year."

"When I found the Road I knew I'd be all right."

"Not the plants? You didn't know the plants? Black core, orange branches, green tips?"

"Never saw them before."

"Yeah, why would you?" Barda stood and stretched elaborately. "They're speckles. We grow speckles."

"And you're prisoned here."

She didn't answer.

"Barda, you're faster than lightning with that knife. Can you cook as well as you carve?"

She shrugged. A silence grew, and then she said, "Daddy owns the Swan. It's the best inn and restaurant in Destiny Town, *he* says."

"There's a Destiny Town?"

Shimon laughed incredulously. Barda started to laugh, then changed her mind. "If you don't know Destiny Town, you're a big bright target, 'Andrew.' Just don't ever mention Destiny Town, okay? I can't tell you enough to fake it."

"Just tell me if the Road ends there."

"Yes, of course—"

"Have you seen *Cavorite?*"

His intensity startled her; then she laughed. Jemmy said, "I've followed *Cavorite* all this way from Spiral Town. Have you seen it?"

"Not up close. They take children through for tours, but Daddy—" She didn't say anything while she shaved a potato naked. Then, "Me and my four brothers, we were free labor. Daddy never took us anywhere unless it was for the Swan, or for cooking, or for customers. I did every part of making an inn work before I was twelve. I saw the top of

Cavorite once because we went to Romanoff's. *Cavorite* is right down the Road from Romanoff's. The top is round and there's a glitter from the windows. If you need to know more—"

Jemmy waved it off. "I've been through *Columbia.* That's the other lander in Spiral Town. Unless *Cavorite* was damaged or painted . . . ?" She didn't know. "Better not talk about that either. So tell me about Romanoff's?"

"That *is* the best restaurant in Destiny Town. When Daddy was a boy the Swan was outside town, just beside . . . I won't tell you where the Swan is."

Jemmy smiled. "What if I get hungry?"

"I don't want this . . . scum thinking they can hide out at the Swan. Anyway, Daddy thought he was going to move the Swan. The town was growing up around us, and we had to buy more and more of our food—"

"You used to hunt it?"

She sighed in exasperation. He said, "Tell it your way."

"Tell *what?* You can't pass for a citizen just because you somehow crossed the Neck! I should be telling you how to talk like a trusty."

"I'm tired, Barda."

"Get yourself a nap. Tomorrow you work."

The melee around the stormlock woke him. He walked down to watch Barda and Shimon cook dinner. It went fast. They set up a pot to boil rice, then a wok big enough to bathe in. He wouldn't be able to lift *that* for a while! Barda shook and tilted it to stir-fry the vegetables. Fans sucked the smoke and smells up into the ceiling: settler magic, whereas the stove was a wood-fired iron box.

Barda served herself, then Shimon, then Jemmy. They sat while Half-beard and the gatherers, fresh out of hot showers, converged.

"I never saw anything like that," Jemmy said. "Is that how they cook at the Swan?"

"It's how we cook vegetables. We served fish and waterfowl grilled and baked. I know other ways to cook, but I couldn't feed twenty people that way."

"You can feed two hundred with a fire pit."

"Not when it rains one day out of four, and that's how it is around Destiny Town. The settlers must have liked things wet. The spaceport's on a plateau, top of Mount Canaveral, and that's dry. Old Igor didn't want the noise—my granddaddy's granddaddy—so he built down below Swan Lake."

"How does the Road go? Spaceport, then Destiny Town, then here?"

Shimon's sullen silence cracked. He said, "Trusty, may I?" And he spilled some flour across the wooden table and began to draw in the flour. "The Road runs straight from the Neck along the coast to the Winds—"

"How high?"

"High?"

"Along most of the Crab, the Road acts like it's afraid of water."

"Oh. Yeah. High enough that nobody bothers the Otterfolk, except here." Shimon's fingertip grazed the line of ocean and veered away. "Then you have to go right past unless you get permission from the Overview Bureau. Then the Road branches *here,* about halfway, and the other branch runs inland. *Cavorite* stopped for a few years where this little town is now, Terminus, and that's where I was born. We grow up wanting to leave," he said. "Destiny Town is where it all happens, but they don't want you in Destiny unless you already got work there, and how can you do that? The damn Admiralty—"

"Shimon, stick to the point."

"*Yesss,* Trusty. Trusty, there's a little branch off the Road, here. It spirals around this bluff to the top. They flew *Cavorite* to orbit from Terminus a lot of times, then from Mount Canaveral just once. They gave it up thirty years ago. They only started flying again . . . Trusty?"

"Fifteen years ago. Those new ships have to land on the ocean. The port had to be moved, and that's what did it for Daddy." Barda reached past him. "The Swan is *here,* foot of Mount Canaveral. And now they launch the ships from somewhere this way. Clean it up now, Shimon."

"Shimon, wait," Jemmy said. "Barda, where were you thinking of moving to?"

"Moving? Oh, *Daddy.* Daddy wanted to build another inn *here.*" Her finger left an imprint on the other side of the Road's first branching, where the Road dipped to nearly touch the sea. "A day short of the Neck. We'd get all the caravan custom, and people who wanted to study the Otterfolk could stay there too. It wasn't just a whim. Daddy sent us to build the damn thing, Barry and Bill and me."

Shimon said, "There now. Is *that* everything you need to know?"

"Let's hope," Jemmy said, and Shimon began to clean the flour off the table.

Barda said, "It better be, Shimon. Tomorrow *you* keep him straight. Right at his elbow every second. If he starts to make a mistake, you cover for him. I can't. I've got to be watching the whole troop."

"Excuse me," Jemmy said, and he managed to reach his bed without falling over.

*   *   *

When the lights came on, Jemmy crawled out of bed with the rest. They eased out of his way so he could get to the bread before it was gone. Nobody seemed to want to talk to him.

Half-beard watched him. He said, "Take another day."

Barda said, "I wanted Shimon watching him."

"Oh, we can fix that. But *look* at him, if he tries to hold the pose . . . You taught him the pose?"

"No."

"I'll do it."

Barda and Shimon went out with the rest. Half-beard waited until they were gone. Willametta was tending Miledy, the pregnant woman, but listening too.

"The pose," Jemmy reminded him.

"It looks like this." Half-beard stood with his arms held high to the sides. "Do it."

Jemmy stood, feet apart, and raised his arms. Any speckles-shy could have done it.

"Hold it till I tell you to quit. Barda says you're smart."

"Good."

"You need to fool the proles into thinking you're me. Can you do that?"

"Not yet. Tell me about proles."

Half-beard studied him.

Jemmy said, "We're the, Barda said *gatherers*? You're *trusties*? Someone is trusting you. Your bosses. That would be the proles?"

"Proles."

"*Proles.* Keep talking, I need to hear you."

"Ten men and women. They rotate. We don't know their names. We don't ever have to."

"When you talk to them——"

"You say *Yes man.* If it's a woman, *Yes mam.* They sound alike, so if you're outside it doesn't matter if you can't tell. You know them 'cause——"

"They've got more orange. They *wear the orange.*"

"Right."

His arms were beginning to ache.

"Where do they live?"

"Down the Road through the cleft, not far. If you go there you don't come back. Andrew, Barda says you've fired yutz guns? What the proles have is worse. Don't ever go up against the proles. And when you talk to them you say *the Parole Board.* Like their main job is to let us go."

Jemmy bobbed his chin. His arms and shoulders were hurting now. He held his breathing deep, and *reached*.

"I'm going out tomorrow to farm in the rain," he said. "I'm a trusty. Proles come to check on us? But they can't see anything about me but a big jacket with a hood and an orange stripe, unless there's something funny about your legs—"

Half-beard laughed, a full-throated bellow.

Jemmy said, "Right. But you have to tell me what they think you'll be doing—"

"Sit down. *Lie* down."

Jemmy lowered his arms, then sat. "I don't know how to get speckles off a plant. Do I have a sack?"

"Backpack. You get your gear after you leave the stormlock. Gatherers get a pack and a scoop glove, this time of year. *You* get a bird gun. They strip the speckles with the scoop gloves. Come spring they'd be planting. Weeding takes a weed cutter. Proles don't give gatherers weed cutters, so *you* have to cut the weeds. But you still get the bird gun, and a pack too, but there's rescue gear in yours. You get your gun in the toolhouse and hang it back when you come home, and the proles replace the ammo while you're gone. They take the packs.

"Now, as far as the Parole Board is concerned, nothing, *nothing* stops us from gathering speckles, and that's how they pick trusties, so you better not show them anything else. Otherwise you don't have to know anything except to count gatherers and see they do the work."

"Count?"

Half-beard grinned. He said, "You met Shimon. He'll help you. You watch Shimon, don't make it too obvious, and he'll point the way if you get confused—"

"And what will you be doing while Andrew Dowd is leading a work party?"

"Leading a *shift*." Half-beard grinned. "And that's *my* problem."

Twenty-two prisoners, Jemmy thought. The trusties are prisoners too. Firebird shorts and ponchos would mark them anywhere outside the Winds. Go out without them and you're naked in a storm, and birds tear you apart.

But now the storm gives up a stranger. The Parole Board doesn't know about a twenty-third gatherer carrying shorts and windbreakers that aren't red and yellow with an orange stripe.

Now the proles can count twenty-two while the other Andrew Dowd is off . . . where? Gathering whatever might be needed when six prisoners disappear wearing clothes they shouldn't own.

Barda Winslow and Andrew Dowd and four others. *Not* Jemmy Bloocher, unless he can talk his way in.

Do the rest know?

Half-beard was watching his face. "Do you think you can be me?"

"There's no telling what I might have to know. I got Barda talking yesterday. Tell me how you got here."

Half-beard scowled and turned away.

Jemmy said, "The Parole Board knows how you got here, Andrew. When they ask me, *I'd* better know."

Half-beard spoke without turning. "Murder twice. They don't want to know any more. If they do, you killed them when they tried to rob you, okay? The damn tribunal didn't believe you."

"Transport?"

"Trans—? They walk us in. Felony tape around our wrists, crossed like *this* in front of us. There's a wagon sealed like a safe, with gun slits, and tugs to pull it. We stick close to that. We're already wearing firebird colors. If we run, serve us right. Andrew, I got to start dinner sometime. Come along."

"I was a caravan chef."

"Barda said."

He noticed more today. Food was stored in bins near the stove: grains, fresh and dried fruit, potatoes and carrots and other vegetables, a big bottle of cooking oil, some spices. Half-beard opened the bins with a key. Cookware was in there too, including heavy pans and cooking knives. The ovens and burners seemed to run continually, keeping the place warm.

Cooking was wonderfully relaxing. Jemmy helped where he could, peeling and cutting vegetables and feeding the fire, until he got tired. Then he watched. Willametta and Half-beard set up the wok.

Indoor cooking was most unlike the fire-pit cooking he'd learned on the Road. Suddenly, powerfully and painfully, Jemmy missed the kitchen in Bloocher Farm.

The gatherers brought a dead bird in with them and gave it to Half-beard, who passed it to Jemmy and Willametta. Jemmy was startled to find himself holding two raptor-clawed legs while Willametta took the other pair. Big wings drooped between. Eight kilos of Destiny bird!

Half-beard shouted, "We don't *stare* at it, Andrew, we cut it up and cook it!" Willametta smiled and showed him how to slice under the feathers. The bird didn't seem to have a distinct skin. The feathers were narrow fractal spikes based in muscle tissue. The blood was rich, dark red. This was no relative of the shelled varieties Jemmy had encountered along the Crab.

"I was expecting Earthlife," Jemmy said. He was surprised, now he thought about it, to find himself holding a knife. Twerdahl Town wouldn't trust a stranger so. "Where are the speckles?"

"You're gonna *love* this, Andrew. Barda showed me how to stir-fry Destiny bird with potatoes and onions. Speckles? We don't need speckles. The birds and turtles around here concentrate the elements in the meat."

"But is it *all*—"

"Sure. The wagons bring in Earthlife food, and we kill windbirds for the meat." He waved the cooking oil. "This is the only fat we get, and they don't give us enough.

"We were *real* glad to see *you*, Andrew. Just anyone wouldn't pass for one of us. It had to be someone who's been starved." Half-beard smiled. "I'd kill a prole for a rasher of bacon."

Willametta's lips twitched: a token of a smile. "*Fletch*. Say *fletch* of bacon. People will think you're easy."

The gatherers were piling their ponchos into the dryer, taking firebird-colored towels and trooping back to the showers.

Before the lights went out, Dennis Levoy cut his hair to match Half-beard's.

✳ 2 0 ✳

The Speckles Crop

You can't eat these seeds straight. On food they're almost salty, almost metallic. I hope we can get used to the taste.

—Dutton, #2 Hydroponics

Jemmy entered the stormlock first, with Shimon and four he hadn't met. He got their names: a trusty would know. Rafik, Shar, Denis, Henry—

"Henry? *You* found me."

Henry grinned. "You looked like a drowned dustbird."

"Trusty!" Shimon snapped.

"—Trusty," Henry said.

"*Door*, Trusty." That was Shimon again, reminding "Andrew" that the trusty was always first through a door.

He walked into pulsing yellow-white light.

It stopped him for an instant. A flood of raindrops flared irregularly as the light waxed and waned. Somewhere in his murky memory . . . hadn't he seen this before? Flashing yellow rain. Too tired to look up. A pair of skeletons took him by the arms and told him "Don't say bird-fucking aloud!" and led him out of hell . . . some kind of hallucination?

He didn't look up now either, because two bird-shapes and a cart waited outside in the rain. A cart pulled by a little smooth-shelled machine.

Jemmy lifted his hood and, as hood and arm hid his face from them, shouted over the thunder. "Proles?"

Shimon nodded violently.

Jemmy had thought they'd wait in the toolhouse, where it was dry.

The gatherers were all pulling their hoods up. Jemmy wiped his eyes

200

and looked around and had to throttle a laugh. The hoods had eyes and beaks!

The proles came near, one behind the other and a little to the side. The orange stripes on their ponchos were broader than a trusty's. Weapons dangled at their sides, belted over ponchos. Jemmy had seen merchants returning such things to Spadoni wagon after a bandit hunt.

They bore another clear sign of their power. Half-beard hadn't told him that proles would wear pants! Big loose pants and boots to keep legs and feet dry. *Luxuries beyond your wildest dreams.*

Jemmy stepped forward, eagerness over fear. "Yes, man?"

The lead prole's voice was rusty, and male. "Get on with it." He waved, and Jemmy saw the toolhouse, like the short arm of an L built onto the barracks building.

The gatherers were cinching the strings on their ponchos. None of them moved, not even Shimon, until "Andrew" took the handles on the high-wheeled cart and pushed it toward the toolhouse.

Wooden bed, metal wheels. A crude piece of work, very different from the low-built machine that had been pulling it, but it rolled easily. It held empty backpacks painted in the colors of a firebird, and one that held something massive.

The proles maintained their staggered position. Attack one, you'd be shot by the other.

The door was blocked by a thick metal beam with a big crude metal lock. A prole opened it. His sleeve hid the key; he returned it to a zipped poncho pocket. Jemmy pulled the cart inside, and the gatherers filed in after him.

He lifted out the heavy backpack. It was full of bullets.

Lungshark bullets (yutz bullets) were this size, but these looked wrong and felt light. Jemmy didn't pause to study them. He found the ammo bin where Andrew had said it would be. He unlocked it. It was near empty. He poured most of the bullets in. A handful went into a pocket in his poncho. He returned the pack to the cart.

The gatherers were picking up empty packs and big duck-foot–shaped gloves. There was a pack with a bigger orange patch. Jemmy took that, and glanced in before he donned it. Rope, and a big box marked with a red cross.

The half-dozen bird guns were shark guns, yutz guns, and nothing but. Jemmy loaded a gun and got his first good look at the bullets. The business end was a cluster of little pellets, not a slug. The gun took eight.

Shimon never stopped watching him. Jemmy wished he would lose that grin: it called attention to them both.

Still moving briskly, as if he had been here too often to find it interesting, Jemmy followed the last gatherer. He glanced back once. Blacksmith-level technology here; settler magic in the barracks—

"Snap it up, Trusty."

"Sorry, man." "Andrew Dowd" stepped briskly into the Road, leading his gatherers to their work site. Amnon took last place. The proles stayed to lock the toolhouse.

Twenty meters down the Road, Jemmy turned to look back.

Above the barracks, pure light flapped like a banner and blazed like a lightbulb, too bright to look at. Jemmy squinted hard and looked anyway. The roof might have been Begley cloth, but in this light he couldn't tell. The flagpole was three poles meeting in a narrow tripod on the barracks roof. The flag must have been at least ten meters by seven.

You couldn't get lost with that light to guide the way. But how much power was being burned here? How long had it been burning? Cloth that burned like a lightbulb, that was settler magic!

From the beginning Jemmy had seen a flood of electrical energy. Barda's kitchen would have fed a dozen times the Bloocher family. Hot water at the turn of a knob, and enough to wash twenty gatherers at once! All these ponchos and shorts and blankets cycling endlessly through the big machine that was never turned off. And this!

There wasn't enough Begley cloth to power a fraction of all this. Where were they getting their power?

A sudden downpour turned it all into a great half-globe of yellow-white rain. Rain hid the last of his line of gatherers, and the proles weren't in sight. Jemmy turned and walked on.

He looked back rarely. Rain and mist hid stragglers. He assumed the proles were mounting rear guard. They couldn't watch him fumbling with the strings of his poncho, snarling them in knots, until he finally managed to cinch wrists and neck and waist against the rain.

Shimon kept pace behind him. When he caught Jemmy's eye, Shimon's casual *push*ing gesture waved him straight ahead. Jemmy grinned at that. He was following the Road along row after row of speckles crops. How could he get lost?

Proles might guess something if he stopped where speckles plants had already been stripped, or led them past plants ready to harvest. But Half-beard was out with the gatherers yesterday, and he'd guided them to the end of the Road at day's end.

He felt/heard the rain stop. For a long moment the air cleared, and when Jemmy looked back, the last plodder was a shape too big to be anyone but Amnon Kaczinski. No proles.

And the rain resumed, and they marched on.

The Road ended in a muddy pond: a shallow crater. *Cavorite* had hovered here. When Jemmy was sure where he was, he waved into the plants. The gatherers moved in. *They* knew where they'd stopped last night. Shimon looked back once before he followed the rest.

The proles were in place. They followed Amnon in, then separated and began to circle wide around the little crowd of gatherers. The gatherers formed a line, one to a row, and followed the rows of speckles plants.

Jemmy Bloocher moved among them, watching and learning. *Andrew Dowd moves among the gatherers, supervising.*

With gloves built like pieces of an umbrella, they stripped the branches, holding their packs to let a rain of bright yellow dust fall in. Rain was turning the bottoms of the packs into a sludge of tiny yellow speckles seeds. The packs would be heavy, coming back.

He passed near Shimon. Head down, Shimon shouted above the rain. "Look around, not just at me. You're not just watching us work. You're protecting us."

"From what?"

Shimon looked up, disgusted. "Just pretend. Anything that pops up, the proles'll get it first."

Jemmy hadn't been told of any danger. Shimon went on, "They're seeing if the ground is clear. Any bird they find, they'll shoot it—"

"*Any* bird?"

Still annoyed, still obtrusively patient, Shimon explained. "Any bird that doesn't eat meat must eat plants, right? Any bird you see is after us or the speckles. So the proles do a circle, then they'll take a pass through the rows, then they'll go home and get dry. Home for lunch." He said it like a curse.

Jemmy moved on.

Winnie Maclean looked like an elf or wraith, very thin and fragile. She smiled up at him and then looked down again, working briskly. Eerily beautiful she was, if you could forget that she was starving.

He got a conspiratorial leer from Duncan Nick, to whom he had never spoken at all. Jemmy watched until Duncan suddenly remembered what he was supposed to be doing with his hands.

A woman's eyes snagged his own, though her hands didn't pause in stripping branches. A once-pretty face turned hard. Was that hatred? What had Jemmy ever done to her?

He was idle while she worked. Trusties must get a lot of this. Jemmy was going past when her head beckoned.

He moved closer. —And in the next row over, a face turned toward him within a gatherer's hood. Narrow head, narrow nose, yellow-brown skin, and Oriental eyes: the same face with a smile like sunlight.

The angry twin said, "They'll leave you. You know that."

Hmm? Jemmy asked casually, "Who's going, Rita?" This had to be Rita or Dolores Nogales.

"Not us either. We're not crazy. He wants to go over the mountains!"

"Who do I talk to if I want to go?"

Rita shrilled laughter.

"Who?"

"Willametta, bet. She's with *you* know."

With Half-beard: the other Andrew. "And Shimon's with Barda?"

"Nobody talks to Shimon." Rita Nogales looked down, dismissing him.

He moved on. The other twin smiled at him and said, "Good day for picking, Trusty."

He couldn't help smiling back. "Is that sarcasm? I wouldn't know, Dolores."

"It doesn't get drier. Gets noiser, gets windier, sometimes the air burns your throat. If there's windbirds you maybe have to hold the pose for half a day, and then the Board wants to know why your pack's light. You were a yutz?"

"Yeah."

"The trader women, they teach you anything?"

Dolores Nogales's eyes were direct and speculative. Jemmy's instinct was to back up a few centimeters. He said, "I think your sister hates me. You don't?"

"Rita's being stupid. You're *lucky*. Talk to me later."

He moved on, thinking pleasant thoughts.

What did trusties and proles get out of this? They got just as wet as the gatherers . . . but proles went home for lunch, and everyone took their orders.

Anyone but proles had to take a trusty's orders.

Of course you couldn't trust random felons to cook. There must be poisons to be found in the lava scrub, and cooking knives could kill, or a heavy pan. Might as well give the cook a gun and call him a trusty. But cooking meant trusties stayed dry one day out of two. And anyone a trusty liked would also stay dry one day out of two.

It was Andrew's day outside and Barda's day in. They'd had to arrange something to get Shimon out here guiding "Andrew." If Shimon wasn't with Barda, maybe Barda was rubbing up against another man?

She'd better be *doing* that. No wonder Shimon was irritable. But to-morrow would be "Andrew" 's day in. Was that what Dolores Nogales was thinking? "Andrew" didn't *have* to be with Willametta. . . .

Willametta was with Andrew, and Jemmy-as-Andrew was outside, so one of these identical shapes must be Willametta. Jemmy stopped by each gatherer for a time, looking around conscientiously for a threat he couldn't describe. The real threat, the proles, had closed their wide circle around the gatherers. They talked, then separated and moved in stag-gered fashion toward the gatherers.

Here was Willametta. Jemmy looked into her bag and said casually, "I'm told I'm not going."

Willametta had a couple of pounds of seeds in the bag with another three pounds of water. She said, "Going where, Andrew?"

"I have no idea." She returned his grin, and he said, "I'm trying to think of a way we can all go."

Willametta seemed to have the giggles. "Right."

"Six of us in shorts and T-shirts. Lucky I came in summer! Someone comes by, 'We were swimming at the beach and a freak gust blew all our clothes out to sea.' Couldn't six of us in swimwear tell a tale while the rest hide? I'm a *good* storyteller."

"Shoes and pack and all?"

"Freak wave?"

"Talk to Andrew."

"I'm *being* Andrew. Let's see, along the Road from the barracks there's fields this way and molten lava beyond. That's no good. Other way is the Parole Board housing and then what? Civilization? *If* you get past the Parole Board, which will be a neat trick, I guess."

Her hands were stripping speckles branches, head bent. He glimpsed a smile beneath the hood.

"But not if you leave seventeen gatherers behind you to answer ques-tions."

She looked up out of the hood and the smile was gone. She said nothing.

He walked casually on. Henry's grin was conspiratorial, or maybe proprietary. Rafik, last in line, looked starved and hunted, an aged youth who didn't want to meet Jemmy's eyes. His hand slipped twice, drop-ping seeds on the ground. Jemmy slapped his shoulder and said "Relax!" and walked on.

A slacking of rain moved across the field. Jemmy's eyes followed the wave across gatherers moving in an even line, one to a row. Well be-yond, the two proles were walking toward them, the second behind and one row to the side. Behind them two speckles bushes stood up and streaked toward them.

Jemmy's gun was out before his mind caught up. What moved like that was lungsharks!

The proles' guns moved. They were going to shoot *Jemmy!*

He fired his bird gun straight up and pointed with the other arm. One whirled around. Jemmy heard a brief ripping sound that wasn't thunder and wasn't a gunshot. The attackers slowed as if they'd plowed into invisible honey. Birds? Now they seemed to dance—

Jemmy turned away, looking for more attackers: away from some terrible secret he'd almost guessed.

Much closer, two black-green-bronze darts streaked along two rows of black-green-bronze speckles bushes, near-invisible and too far to shoot even with decent bullets, but coming fast at the line of gatherers. Someone yelled, "Pose! Pose! Spectre birds!" Shimon's voice, that should have been "Andrew" 's.

Jemmy took the pose as he'd been taught.

One row over, Henry said quietly, "No birdfucking allowed."

And a whispered chorus: "It's the law!"

He couldn't see anything else attacking. The proles had stopped firing. What had attacked them was gone. The gatherers were a row of statues, their ponchos drooping from raised arms, their hoods facing the oncoming pair of spectre birds. Jemmy stood last in line, arms raised high, a bird gun in one hand. *A field of firebirds spreads their wings to face an aggressor.*

Spectre birds were fast. Like proles, they came in staggered stance. The range was too great for pellets. Jemmy held his fire while they closed. The birds slowed as if confused, then made for the middle of the line. Why weren't they veering? Jemmy held, held . . . aimed and fired at the lead bird.

He hit it. The bird flinched back and lifted its head. It was as big as a small man, with oversized ripping foreclaws, the forward-facing eyes of a predator, and a beak that was a hooked prybar on top, paired prongs underneath.

It came on. Jemmy shot it again, then shot the trailing bird. He had their attention now—

The lead bird lunged at a gatherer's chest.

The gatherer whirled around at the last instant. The beak gashed his back, and he shrieked and tried to run. Then both birds were on him.

Jemmy yelled and charged them, firing. One ran. Jemmy fired at the other bird. Its beak was deep in the gatherer's torso. Four quick shots emptied Jemmy's gun before the bird dropped its prey and ran.

As each bird cleared the line of gatherers, Jemmy heard the ripsaw sound of the proles' weapons. Matter sprayed from the birds, blood and a chaff of feathers.

The proles' weapons didn't fire bullets: they fired *streams* of bullets.

Jemmy tore his gaze away and ran to the fallen gatherer. Blood was flooding through holes in his poncho, and Jemmy couldn't doubt he was dead. When a prole shoved him aside, he gave way.

But he'd seen. It was Shimon.

Jemmy reloaded, looking about him. Where there were four spectre birds, there might be six or eight.

A hand snatched at his shoulder and pulled him around. The prole was a man with a full red beard. He snarled, "What did you think you were doing, shooting at a spectre? Bird guns aren't for things that big!"

Jemmy protested. "He was going after my man, man!"

"Take the pose!" The parole's chest heaved. He must have run flat out. "How often do you have to be taught? Take the pose and the bird thinks you're a firebird. Firebirds don't run, don't shout, don't shoot!"

"Shimon was posed! We were all posed. Why did it kill Shimon?" *While I stood like a statue—*

"When the bird got close he tried to run." The prole heaved in a ragged breath. "Lost his nerve. Yeah. They could have killed you all. That's why we're here."

Jemmy had seen . . . but he said something safe. "Thanks, man. You took them out good."

Redbeard turned without answering. He and the other prole spoke for a time. Jemmy waved the gatherers back to work; and they obeyed, fortunately; and he waited for orders.

Redbeard told him, "Take your people back to barracks. Four of you carry this one. Wait for us. We'll look around a little. There has to be a report."

✳ 21 ✳

S u s p i c i o n s

If speckles can be farmed elsewhere, we must still extract potassium to feed it. Why bother? We'll grow it here.

—Will Coffey, Hydroponics

Of course the strongest men should have been carrying Shimon; but the ones who did were the first names Jemmy could remember. Dennis *and* Denis, Henry and Amnon.

Jemmy draped Shimon's nearly empty pack to keep some of the rain off Shimon's torn torso. The Parole Board might want a coroner to examine those wounds.

He walked alongside while four men carried the fifth. He'd told off two more to carry one of the spectre birds, for dinner and a chance to examine the wounds. And so the funeral procession straggled up the Road.

"Willametta?"

"Trusty."

"There was a joke 'Andrew' wouldn't have missed. 'It's the law'?"

Willametta guffawed. "Well, *I* wasn't here yet, but you can picture it. Nobody gets a bird gun except the prole. But there hadn't been any birds so they'd been eating nothing but rice and veggies for *weeks*. One day a crooner popped up in the field. It's as big as an ostrich. Well, the proles and the trusty were a little slow for Gordon Weiss. He didn't wait. He ran the bird down and jumped on it and tried to crush it in a scissor lock."

Jemmy thought it over. "Ouch."

"Of course those aren't really feathers. There's a reason the windbird

208

predators all have needle beaks. They've got to stab *through* the Destiny feathers to get at the meat. Because the feathers are nothing but needles.

"So picture it," she said. "Gordon's legs and arms are full of needles, and he rolls away screaming, and the bird is crooning and the trusty has finally started shooting, and somebody shouts," Willametta drew breath and bellowed, " 'No birdfucking allowed!' And someone else yells—"

Her timing was perfect. Six people behind them shouted, " 'It's the law!' "

"And ever since then—"

Light grew behind them, like a sudden dawn.

Drenched, exhausted, frightened: Jemmy could only wonder at the glare behind him that threw blurred shadows along the Road. He turned, expecting to see sunglare through split clouds. That would not be such a strange thing—

Whirling storm was still there, but the clouds flared too bright to look at. Lightning was only a faint sputter against *that.* Jemmy shouted, "Will-ya! What *is* that?"

"They're lighting the field. Looking for more birds."

"Lighting it with *what?*"

The other pallbearers laughed. Willametta said, "Quicksilver."

"Quicksilver how?"

"The power comes from Quicksilver."

And the long Road stretched away, and after a time the light behind went out.

It seemed to take forever. A white flicker became an intermittent white glow, and the rain blew it away, and there it was again . . . until a blazing yellow-white banner led them on, and on. . . . At the end Jemmy stood in the rain before the massive door and its massive lock, and couldn't remember what to do next.

Like the barracks, the toolhouse was built for giants. Generations of gatherers labored to move masses of rock, their lives as nothing to their Parole Board masters . . . *Nah.*

Jemmy had come to understand *Cavorite's* intent.

Find potassium! Get it back to the landing site before everyone on Destiny dies!

They must have come prepared to refine the ore, here or at Spiral Town. Speckles must have been a surprise: a plant that poisoned herbivores by secreting potassium and other trace elements that Earthlife needed.

So *Cavorite* brought the Road here, and *Cavorite's* crew farmed speckles. They came with interstellar technology and desperate intent, and they built massive forts of fused rock.

If the first settlers tried to stop them from leaving, and later remembered *Cavorite* as a ship of deserters, perhaps it was because they were already speckles-shy.

Today's gatherers lived in housing that settler wizards had built for themselves. Prisoners swaddled in luxury! Twerdahl's crew hadn't barred this door against themselves; the lock must have been added years later, or centuries.

And he didn't have a key. Oh, *that* was it. Jemmy couldn't get in, so four men were standing behind him still hoisting the dead weight of Shimon. Jemmy turned toward the barracks.

Willametta blocked his way.

"You've got to give over the packs and gloves first," she said urgently, "and your gun. They'll shoot you! Have some sense!"

"We can't just . . ." Two hours' walk through rain with lightning-blasted vision and thunder-shattered hearing and that damned ghostly banner ahead must have turned off his mind. *Of course* they could wait out in the storm for the proles' convenience. Yes, but they couldn't set Shimon down in the mud. Jemmy looked around him.

Two gatherers were half-reclined on an exposed ridge of bare white rock. Jemmy told them, "Move."

They stood, not hurrying: Rita and Dolores Nogales.

"Here," he beckoned the pallbearers, and they set the body down. Shimon was still dripping wet, and his pack no longer covered him. Jemmy looked around and found packs piled on another bare tufa ridge, and the dead spectre bird next to them.

He felt queasy, looking at the spectre. Its torso was chopped half through, raggedly, as if a big dull ripsaw had been used on it while it wiggled.

Warm breath in both ears: he jumped. Voices whispered:

"Trusty?"

"Could be a long wait."

The twins had him bracketed. Jemmy said, "Sorry. If I had a key we could wait in the toolhouse, but then I'd be a prole, so maybe I wouldn't give a shit."

"What we sometimes do—"

"—We go around the other side of the barracks."

"The corner? For shelter?"

The women brushed gently against him on both sides. Even through the poncho that felt nice, and practiced. One said, "Not everyone, just us. The rest, they know not to bother us because you're a trusty. And it's a corner—"

"Of course it's still wet, but it's not so cold."

"You could think of it as *slippery*." That twin *had* to be Dolores.

It was tempting. Jemmy's arms had reflexively moved around their waists; at worst they warded off some rain. Dolores meant it, he thought, but anger still smoldered in Rita's eyes. So what *was* going on?

He said, "You know they'll do a count."

He felt Rita go rigid. Dolores said quickly, "They'll want to know what spectres were doing there in the fields where there's no prey. So they won't be right behind us."

"But we might want to hurry, or just fool around now and then stay in tomorrow." Rita.

Dolores: "Have you seen the big baths?"

"There's the packs and there's us," Jemmy said firmly. "Three of us in the barracks, that hasn't changed. Andrew's gone but I'm here. I count eighteen of us out here including Shimon. But that should be *nineteen*."

Rita snapped, "He'll be back!"

Who? Jemmy asked, "And the pack? Piling them up is good, but he took a pack. I counted those too."

Rita touched Dolores's hand and they both faded back. Amnon Kaczinski asked, "You got a problem, Trusty?"

Willametta was standing beside the looming giant, and Jemmy spoke to both. "You tell me. A missing man, a missing pack, and a pair of proles coming closer every second. Those guns are like *hoses*. Then again, I don't have a problem, Amnon. *'Sure* I know we're one gatherer *short*, man, and he stole a pack of speckles too, but I can't chase *him* because there's just me to watch all of these *other* gatherers, including that big *dangerous*-looking one—' "

Willametta spoke. "*Yes*, all *right*, Rafik took Shimon's pack and he'll take a handful of speckles for the stash!"

Amnon said, "Willametta—"

"—And the Parole Board won't notice that little, all right? And you should have stopped him, Amnon! He's *crazy*—"

"We need the speckles, Willya!"

"We've got two man-years' weight of speckles stashed and what did we ever *do* with it? But now we've got something to wear, finally we've got clothes! What if Rafik gets caught *now*?"

Jemmy suggested, "Send someone for him?"

"We can't have *two* missing! He'll be back," Willametta assured herself.

"Good. I've got a few questions."

"Talk to Andrew—"

"The proles are going to ask me questions. We didn't know there'd be a dead man, so I wasn't told any answers. Why did the birds attack Shimon?"

"How would I know that?"

"Amnon?"

"Birds." Amnon shrugged massively. "You never know."

"But am I *supposed* to know?—No? Good. Will they ask me to guess? Willametta? Amnon?"

"Shut up, you!" The big man was going into a rage.

Willametta said, "Go away, Amnon."

"But, Willya—"

"Amnon, what do they do to you when you hurt a trusty? Go away! Go wait for Rafik."

"He's not— Oh." The big man went.

"Willametta? Just give me a guess that doesn't sound totally stupid." She was silent.

"Mating season makes them twitchy?"

"What? Windbirds don't have a mating season."

"He cut himself? No, that's—"

"Human blood? It'd drive birds *away*!" She was laughing at him.

"Try this then." Jemmy hesitated. The bird struck, *then* Shimon turned . . . the prole was *sure* it couldn't happen that way . . . so Jemmy *knew* that Shimon had been murdered. But how?

Did he dare to guess right? But Willametta was looking at him, waiting.

"Suppose one poncho out of all our ponchos wasn't the right color. Not quite the color of a firebird. There must be animals or plants that don't secrete potassium but that show colors, maybe a little off."

She was shaking her head. He persisted. "*Is* there a paint source? In the toolhouse?"

"That thing in the toolhouse used to make survival biscuits out of Earthlife garbage. Trusty, any trusty would *know* that."

"Well, that's why I'm asking, Willametta!"

She nodded.

"Let's see, you brought a bird home for dinner last night. Now, suppose Shimon was cold so he kept his poncho on, and he still had it this morning—"

Her hands gripped his arms hard. "Don't say that!"

"—with the blood of a windbird all over it. If some of those horrors whiffed *Destiny* blood—"

"Don't tell them that!"

"Was he a spy?"

Willametta's mouth stayed open.

Jemmy said, "The proles have to know what's going on in the barracks. They need a spy. They can tell a spy they'll make him the next trusty. Barda and Andrew, they're trusties now, but were they spies before?"

"Andrew was."

"So *he* knows how a spy gets picked. Did Shimon know you've stashed some speckles?"

She pulled him close and whispered in his ear. She was scared right through. "They haven't touched it. Yes, he knew, but he didn't know where. How could *you* know all this, Jemmy?"

"I guess I was waiting for someone to die. Barda and Andrew have to know who the spy is, or they can't hide *anything*. When the birds tore into Shimon, it all just fit, except the paint, I guess. Who gave him his poncho this morning? Barda?"

They were hood to hood, arms bracing each other against the wind. An approaching prole would see only lovers. Jemmy said, "Willametta, I need a story to tell the proles. They know something. They waited for us in the rain. This morning they stayed to search for something else before they caught up with us."

She said, "They'll search the barracks. Did Andrew tell you—" She looked into his eyes. "Damn him. When the proles search, *you* open every door and drawer. Don't close any of it. They do that. You go around the room—"

"Clockwise?"

"*I* don't know. Sure! Or watch their hands. If one points to something, you open it or move it or lift it. Try not to talk too much." The rain slacked and she looked around; they all seemed to do that. She said, "Rafik's back—" Her breath caught oddly.

Jemmy could see past huddled gatherers, far down the Road to where two rainbow birds walked like men. Two.

Willametta's hands closed like claws and she pushed her cheek against his and keened in terror. He whispered, "Not Rafik?"

"They're too soon! Where did they come from?"

"Isn't the Parole Board in that direction? No way could a runner get to them. Settler magic?" He remembered an old word from the lessons. "Phones?"

"Quick, around the side!" Willametta ducked and lifted the hem of Jemmy's poncho nearly to his chin. He guessed what she had in mind. The rain was back, a waterfall now, and he had to shout into her ear.

"We can't do that."

"It's a distraction!" Her hand found the waistband of his shorts and dipped in to cup his genitals, and squeezed gently.

He stopped her, hand on wrist. "Now *listen*. There's a man dead and proles coming to look into it. 'Andrew Dowd' is alert and scared and waiting. He *can't be* around to the side rubbing up against a lovely woman when he could be having her all day tomorrow in dry comfort! It'd be suspicious as hell."

Her hand stopped moving. He had her attention. He had an erection too, so he'd best talk fast. "Rafik went that way? Then the proles passed him, right? He's behind them!"

"Yes. Yes."

"We have to give him a chance to join us. Okay. You get— Let go now."

She did.

"You get Amnon and the twins. Send *them* around *that* side while the rain holds." The Parole Board direction. "The gatherers stay huddled so they'll be harder to count. I'm at the Road, ready to serve my prole masters but looking in the wrong direction. I don't know anything about prole phones, right?"

She gaped.

"Willametta!"

"I never *heard* the word!"

"Good, then Andrew didn't either. You, behind me, ready to spot anything weird and tell me. And let's drape a pack or two over Shimon."

The next break in the rain showed two pairs of proles converging. The pair from the Board direction was nearest, and Jemmy let them see him suddenly discover them. They plodded up to him and one said, "Trusty, some of your gatherers are missing."

Jemmy looked around wildly. "Oh, man, they must be around to the side. Can I check that out? I had to stay here, man. One of my people got killed."

"Go get them. Where are the packs?"

"We piled—"

"You're missing some of those too!"

The other prole had drawn his weapon. Jemmy shrank back, raised his arms. "No, man, we spread some packs over Shimon, over the body. I thought you'd want to look him over, I didn't want the rain to wash anything away. I still can't figure why birds would tear him up like that." Walking backward, Jemmy led them to Shimon laid out on white rock. There: two packs covering torso and face, and when

Jemmy lifted them, there were the terrible holes in Shimon's poncho and Shimon's corpse.

For an instant Jemmy glimpsed a bird-shape with a pack in his hand, behind the proles. A moment later he'd merged with the other bird-shapes. The second pair of proles, the ones who had been in the field, were bird-shadows seen through slackening rain, and Jemmy could only hope that they hadn't seen Rafik. Rita and Amnon and Dolores were coming around the toolhouse, obtrusively straightening each other's clothing, and Jemmy shouted and went to yell at them. When he looked around again the piled packs looked to be the right height.

The four proles closed on Jemmy. "Tell us how this man died, *now*. Don't leave anything out."

"I *swear*, man. The spectre bird jabbed him before he moved," Jemmy said, belligerent and tired.

Two proles shrugged and one had gone to open the toolhouse, but one, Redbeard, cursed. "What I saw was a bird getting curious and a gatherer losing his nerve!"

"Maybe you're right, man, but I saw what I saw." Jemmy had considered changing his story, but he judged this better. *Just stubborn, that's all.*

"Turn in your gear and then we're going to search the barracks."

The packs of speckles went in the cart. The gatherers returned their gloves to the toolhouse. Jemmy left his bird gun and bullets in there too. He watched the little smooth-shelled machine pull the cart away.

The three who remained directed their passage through the storm-lock. They were too edgy for anyone's comfort. Jemmy and the red-bearded prole went in with Willametta and Amnon.

Jemmy smelled stir-fry cooking. Barda Winslow looked around, and jumped.

"Go easy, Barda," Jemmy said. "It's a search." He pulled off his poncho and dropped it.

A woman moaned on one of the beds. Jemmy reflexively turned toward the sound.

Redbeard said, "You go nowhere, Dowd. Stay with the cooking, Winslow. Who's that?"

Barda Winslow answered defensively. "Miledy Waithe is pregnant and overdue. My assistant, Ansel Tarr, is standing by as midwife."

Ansel Tarr was a good-looking sixteen-year-old boy, white skin, straight black hair, just a touch of sullen. He was plausible enough as Barda Winslow's love slave.

Redbeard grimaced. "When the rest of the Parole Board gets in we'll do our search. I believe we'll start by searching under Miledy Waithe." He was watching Barda's eyes, and he wasn't pleased when she laughed out loud.

The stormlock door opened and he said, "All right, here come— Hell."

Here came two gatherers and a dead bird. Jemmy commanded them, "Take the bird to Barda and help her cook."

Miledy Waithe screamed again. Ansel Tarr murmured in her ear. Otherwise the storm-free silence was heavenly.

"You don't give orders when we're here, Dowd," the red-bearded prole said quietly.

Jemmy said, "We're all going to run late tonight, man. Last chance to search the bird?"

"Did."

"What are you looking for? Something you can talk about?"

"Hidden tools. Hidden speckles. Dyes. Any kind of cloth that isn't," the prole's fingers rubbed the cloth of Jemmy's shorts, "*this* kind."

Three gatherers and a second prole entered. Redbeard said, "Dowd, *stay!* Marta, when Horace gets in we'll search the bathrooms. Cover me, will you?"

"Go for it," the second prole said.

Redbeard pulled his wet poncho over his head and was bare to the waist. He ran fingers through his hair and flung the water away. "Ah! Better."

"My turn."

"Go."

Marta stripped off her poncho. She was, in Jemmy's judgment, exquisite. Males gaped at her, and she hoisted the gun and grinned.

Redbeard caught Jemmy's smile, and glared. "Men's room," he snapped. They began their search there.

The men's bath was bare of anything suspicious.

The women's bath was very like the men's.

When they emerged, the gatherers were all inside along with a third prole. He was a stocky, muscular man, and he stood guard while the prole Marta and the gatherer Ansel examined Miledy. Miledy certainly seemed about to give birth.

Jemmy ignored that. Moving clockwise around the room, he opened every door and drawer he could find.

He missed two that the proles knew were there. They took that seriously. The prole he'd nicknamed Muscles held him at gunpoint, Marta took position in a corner and covered the whole room, while Redbeard emptied a cabinet in the medical stores and tapped it for secret compartments, all in the sullen communal glare of wet and uncomfortable gatherers. They did the same later with a kitchen storage bin.

They watched carefully while Barda and Jemmy poured the elements of dinner slowly from one container to another. Nothing hidden.

Then Redbeard gestured toward Miledy, and wet and uncomfortable gatherers began to murmur.

Do this fast, Jemmy thought. He summoned Amnon with a gesture. They lifted the bed next to Miledy and invited the proles to examine that. Then, together, Amnon and Jemmy and Muscles lifted Miledy Waithe. They set her on the other bed before she could begin to protest.

For Miledy that was the last straw. Redbeard and Muscles examined Miledy's bed, ignoring the sounds behind them; but Miledy was giving birth. Ansel Tarr and Marta helped them tend to that. At the end they were holding a squirming red infant girl, and Miledy had gone from screaming into monotonous cursing.

Marta said, "So, there's your free ride out."

Miledy wasn't listening. She moved the baby a little, said, "Girl," in tones of wonder, and went to sleep.

The search was over.

But while the rest of the gatherers served themselves and ate, the proles questioned Barda and "Andrew" about housekeeping details. That was hellish. Jemmy didn't know most of the answers. He and Barda found a routine: he'd start to answer, then Barda would interrupt.

It seemed forever before the proles trooped into the stormlock and were gone.

Then Jemmy sagged and sighed, and Barda called, "Get your showers *now.* The Parole Board can check our water flow. Did anyone save us anything?"

There was still food. Jemmy was ravenous.

Most of the gatherers were showering. Miledy was asleep with the tiny new baby in her arms. Jemmy and Barda ate in silence for a time, in a silent hall.

Barda said, "Good routine, domineering bitch, wimpy male."

"Worked. We should practice."

"Yeah. It'd work better with a guy who wasn't so, mmm. Impressive. Rafik? This could have gone on all night, you know. Cooking smells helped. Proles get hungry too."

"Redbeard found something in the men's," Jemmy said. "He hid it."

"Paper?"

"Not sure."

"Message from Shimon. *That's* all right, Jemmy. I found it and took out the part about you."

"What now?"

Barda took her bowl to the sink. She hadn't actually eaten much. Nerves, maybe. "We wait for Andrew," she said. "Then maybe we run. I want to talk to Rafik, but let's get our showers first."

✳ 22 ✳

Plans

Destiny's ecology, after all, will have its own agenda.
—Dutton, #2 Hydroponics

He couldn't remember hitting the bed. Now something was pushing his toes down and the barracks was buzzing like a hive, and through his eyelids he felt the heat of a stare.

They were both watching him, the Nogales twins. They were on his bed, their weight pulling the sheet down on his feet. When his eyes opened one said severely, "Men don't turn us down. Most men *like* rubbing up against two women just alike."

Jemmy said, "You may be the best opportunity I never had. Who told you I needed distracting?"

"Willya. You weren't supposed to notice the pack or count heads—"

"—Just us," and a hand in his chest hair.

Jemmy felt damp and grungy. He'd been too tired to shower. He asked, "Am I getting another chance? Should I shower first?"

"Andrew's here. They want you."

"What time is it? Did I get any sleep?"

"They don't give us clocks."

They were down at the tables: Andrew, Barda, Rafik, and Willametta. The rest were staying clear. A few were asleep.

Andrew Dowd was wet and triumphant. "Jeremy Bloocher," he said—

"Do I get to be Jemmy Bloocher now?"

"The rest of your life," Half-beard said expansively, "and I get to be

219

Andrew Dowd. Jeremy, we need to know what the proles know. Did they get Shimon's note in the men's?"

"He, the one with the red beard, he didn't look at it. Barda, you said it mentioned me?" Because if *that* note didn't, then some other would.

"Yeah, it did. I copied it with that part missing."

Jemmy was still getting his brain up to speed. "They thought I was hiding something because there were two cabinets I didn't open, but they searched those. They'll look for bird blood on Shimon's poncho, but maybe the rain washed—" He saw the look that passed among them. "Barda? Shimon's poncho?"

The big woman shuddered. "No. I sucked the poor bastard dry and kept him distracted. I set him to keeping *you* out of trouble so he couldn't talk to proles. I did *not* put a bloody poncho on him. But," she whispered, "I would have."

Andrew said, "Couldn't. Rain would wash off bird blood. Rafik?"

Rafik grinned. "We soaked the inside of a pack in bird blood. We gave that to Shimon. He had to open the pack to gather speckles, and that let out the smell. The birds were in place—"

"Shells," Andrew said suddenly. "Rafik, tell me you didn't leave a mock-turtle shell for proles to find!"

Rafik shrugged. "What of it? Trusty, they know there were spectre birds in the field. They have to guess the birds went after something they could eat. *How* a mock turtle got there, that's the part they'll never know."

Andrew Dowd was nodding reluctantly.

Rafik said, "When we got back I took Shimon's pack, took out the speckles, turned it inside out, and let the rain wash it clean. They'll be looking at the wrong pack anyway."

"You switched the speckles?"

"Sure. Then Willya and the yutz, they got me back in."

"See, Jeremy, there's bird blood soaked all through the speckles in Shimon's pack. We can't let the Parole Board have that, so *those* speckles went in the stash and Rafik put speckles from the stash in his pack. Rafik, you didn't scant that, I devotely hope—"

"No, Trusty. Generous."

Andrew saw the heat in Willametta's cheeks and the glare in her eyes. "Willya, I didn't want you to know exactly what you were hiding. Be too much of a pointer." He waved it off. "So. The spy is dead, we changed the only message he left, the proles don't know we've got clothes and they don't know someone was loose today. Are we clear on that? Have I left anything out?"

Jemmy asked, "Who wears seven windbreakers and six shorts and a merchant's pack?"

"Barda. Me. Amnon. Shar Willoughby. Henry. You. We had to throw away the one you were wearing on top. It was torn to shreds."

They were grinning at him. Rafik said, "You don't get it? It's anyone with a trace of fat on his cheeks."

Aghast, Jemmy looked about him. *Of course. And we'll still look like—* "Well, it only works if there's only one," Jemmy said. "Andrew, what happens to the rest of us?"

"We take all but eight," Andrew said. "It's nine now, I guess. The baby."

"You're leaving them—"

"Jeremy, we'd never get past the Parole Board, not by Road. We're going over the mountains. We'll pick up the Road on the other side. Eight of us don't want to try it."

"Winnie Maclean?" *Too frail—*

"She wants to come. The Nogales sisters don't."

"I'll miss the twins," Rafik said soberly.

Je-re-my, not Jemmy. Have to practice. Later— "You're leaving eight people to describe how we did it?"

"The ones who aren't coming, I didn't tell them everything, and that's okay with them. They know there was a spy. Jeremy, we never *could* have taken Miledy Waithe and her baby, so what's the point? Too many of us are looking at a five-year hitch and four years gone already. If I tried to make them come along, they'd drop out somewhere in the rain and I'd never find them."

"That prole said something about a free ride—?"

Willametta said, "If you give birth in here, the baby goes back out and you go with her. Only twice, though. Then they char your tubes."

"But men don't get pregnant." Rafik laughed. "We're screwing for nothing."

"Fourteen of us."

"We're the maxers," Andrew said. "Destroy life support, it's seven years, and they're generous with that term, aren't they, Willya? Kill, it's seven years. I killed two, never mind why, the Board won't listen. Now, I scouted the mountain today. That place you found, Rafik? It doesn't work. I had to go farther. Six klicks toward the fields, then up. There's a channel up to a ridge that runs another two klicks back. Must be an old flow. Then another channel up, and that'll take us over."

"And down to the Road!" Barda didn't see Andrew's shrug, or ignored it. "On the Road we can pass. If anyone comes, the rest hide, we do the talking. But Jeremy's right, Andrew. Two of us together still look . . . gaunt?"

Jemmy said, "Like so many liches risen untimely from our graves. One of us at a time is only skinny, but two or three together— You can't see it? You've been together too long. Andrew, can we all climb?" *He* could. No thirteen felons could outclimb Jemmy Bloocher.

"Don't know," Andrew said. "I need as many as I can get. We're going to take over a caravan."

Jemmy sighed. They were crazy after all.

Barda said, "We need you to tell us what they're like. How they're armed."

Well, it had to be dealt with. He asked, "Where were you going to jump them? This side of the Neck? That way you're only fighting fifty or sixty merchants. Other way, you'd be fighting yutzes too."

"This side, sure. We'll be lucky to get that far. But we'll only be facing bird guns."

"That's *yutz* guns, Andrew. They're the same as bird guns but with a solid bullet for putting holes in lungsharks and bandits. When bandits jumped us we shot them with yutz guns. But when the merchants went off alone to kill all the bandits, they took stuff from Spadoni wagon that they wouldn't let us look at. I saw just enough. Prole guns, Andrew!"

Silence.

"The toolhouse is locked till morning. You've got no guns at all."

Andrew stood, turned, opened one of the bins with a key. He lifted it just into sight: a prole gun.

A shudder ran through him. Jemmy said, "We looked in there." His hand reached out without consulting his forebrain.

Andrew pulled it away. "I came in after the proles left."

"Bullets?"

"Two chains." Andrew lifted those too, and Jemmy stood to look. He had never seen chains of bullets meant to feed into a prole gun; but, standing, he could see that both loops were part empty.

It was suicide, and, more than that, it was murder. They'd end up killing as many merchants as they could before the merchants killed all of them.

He could rave against spilling blood all over the Road, but would it persuade these already-murderers? Or would they only kill Jemmy Bloocher? Try something else. He asked, "Do you know how to make a caravan move?"

Andrew said, "You do."

"I know how to tend chugs," Jemmy said. "I'm a chef. I did a little mending. I never drove a wagon. I can't do it all." Jemmy wondered if they'd believe that. "What time of year is it? The date tells us if we'll get a caravan on its way to the Crab, or coming back, or nothing at all. Willya, what's the date? Rafik? I've lost track myself."

"We can't wait," Willametta said.

Rafik said, "We'll find someone on the Road. Ask."

"Uh-huh. Then we'll know if we're between caravans. That could take months."

Murderous silence.

"Of course we might outrun a caravan. They can't move faster than a chug. But you didn't even know that much, did you? What you don't know, doesn't it scare you?

"Now, *if* there's a caravan, and *if* fourteen of us could take it, you'd lose some wagons just by shooting them up. Bullets kill chugs too. That gives you a short wagon train, and maybe eight or ten left alive to run it, and nothing to sell—"

Andrew released a bit of his fury. "Hold it, you son of a dirty bird! Why nothing to sell?"

"Andrew, a caravan full of trade goods is on its way to meet the other caravan! They stop on the Neck, nose to nose. They transfer all the yutzes and throw a big party. They see we're fakes and shoot us all dead.

"So you can't stop the outbound caravan. You could stop the caravan that's coming back and turn it around, but it'll be full of stuff they bought on the Road, and every little town along the Road is going to notice one caravan following another. With not enough people to defend it. And that, Andrew, is when your pitiful few survivors of that last fight get to die at the hands of bandits. By the way, there's no point in negotiating with bandits. They're speckles-shy. By then, I guess we'll be too."

Barda Winslow stood. She said, "Go away."

Jemmy went.

Hot water flooded over him. He stopped trying to think. Just let it happen. Ancient luxury. The water never had run like this at Bloocher Farm.

A voice shouted "Hey!" and a hand touched his arm. Then the twins were under the shower with him. He laughed and shouted into an ear, "What if someone wants the men's room?"

"Amnon's guarding."

"We asked Willya. She said you could use a distraction."

"If anyone else comes in, we break this up."

"Rita's mostly here to take care of me. Some men, they'd get rough."

223

They connected, he and Dolores, sitting in a thundering flood of hot water. Rita was massaging his back and shoulders, and that felt good. Jemmy found he could still shout. "Trying to get a free ride out?"

"Yeah!"

They rode.

In the aftermath glow he reached up along Rita's leg. "Hey. If Dolores gets pregnant but you don't, would they take her but not you?"

"Girl, move over. Hey, yutz, you got any of that left?"

"Weeks. I was saving it—" for Loria.

"Well, save it no more."

Then someone did come in, and the women rolled to either side and were on their feet, and Rita turned off the shower while Jemmy lay bedazzled and bewildered.

Three shadows seen through fog. "Just us. Down, Rita! Jeremy, we've talked. Can you join us?"

"Sure."

Barda and Rafik and Henry emerged from the steam. He was still short of sleep, he thought, but there wasn't any way to rest *now*. "Barda, do we have *time* to talk? If *I* thought of looking for windbird blood on Shimon's shirt—"

"They won't find it," Rafik said carelessly. "Come on."

Jemmy got his shorts on. He was talking as they walked toward the airlock end. "I shot both birds. Then they both chewed Shimon up. They must have gotten their own blood all over him. The proles *will* think of looking. The question is, did it wash off?"

Henry began swearing. Rafik's glare was the kind that kills. Barda took Andrew aside and began to whisper.

They broke. "All right," Andrew said, "we have to go. *I* have to go. I killed a prole tonight for that gun. Jeremy, for Earth's sake, when did you think of this?"

"Came to me while I was in the shower."

"What *can* we do? Steal one wagon? Do they ever separate?"

"They can *be* separated. There are stories. You need more than fourteen people for a bandit gang, though. Yet again, Andrew, what would you *do* with it? Even if we could peel off a wagon and kill everyone in it and take all their yutz guns, we wouldn't have enough firepower to hold off shark attacks. We'll lose our chugs in the first week! That's *why* they take so many wagons."

"Well, if it's that hopeless, there's no point in any of you going. I'm a trusty. You c—"

"*I'm* coming," Barda snapped without looking up. She was rolling the biggest of the kitchen knives into a pair of shorts.

"You couldn't have stopped me doing anything," Andrew told her. "Didn't know I was out there killing a prole and hiding the pack wagon. Can't stop me now, 'cause I'm holding that damned *hose* of a prole gun. So, Jeremy, do you have anything to say that isn't 'We're all gonna die'?"

Jemmy said, "I think we can become a restaurant."

✳ 2 3 ✳

The Run

Old sun, old planet, means less of heavy metals and radioactives. The crust
is too thick for plate movement and mountain building. Destiny doesn't
really have more water than Earth, but it covers nearly everything.
—Henry Judd, Planetologist

Andrew stopped them just outside the stormlock in the flapping white
light of the electric banner. "I forgot something." He grinned, and turned
to go back in.

Jemmy had him by the poncho. "No you don't. *Amnon!*" he bellowed.

The snout of the prole gun pushed into Jemmy's throat. Andrew
almost-whispered, "Just what d—?"

Jemmy screamed, "He's going to kill the ones who stayed!"

The crowd of refugees melted. Jemmy couldn't tell who ran or where
they hid, but Barda and Willametta moved immediately to Andrew's
side. They whispered urgent remonstrances, their hands caressing his
arms, while Amnon stepped up behind him and wrapped his big arms
around Andrew's head.

But Andrew pushed the prole gun hard under Jemmy's chin, and
Jemmy didn't try to move.

Amnon's arms began to tighten and twist. He asked, "The twins too,
you birdfucker?"

"We can't leave them to talk!"

Barda was holding the point of the biggest of the kitchen knives just
under Andrew's eye.

Andrew cursed and released the gun. Jemmy caught the heavy thing
and cradled it, pointing it at nobody. A tiny green light twinkled in the

226

butt. He said, "You never did have a plan, did you? Just kill and kill until something stops you."

"Nooo."

"Jeremy. Jeremy! Give me the gun a minute."

"What?" Jemmy swung round; the gun swung too. One of the twins shied back.

"Just give me the gun for a breath," she pleaded, laughing.

"I don't think so."

"Then you do it. Shoot up the toolhouse a little."

"Bad idea, Rita."

"Dolores. But look—"

Willya shouted, "Barda, don't cut him, it's all right! Let him go. Now what, Andrew?"

Andrew snarled like a beast.

"Plan," Jemmy said in disgust. Without Andrew the rest had no direction, but Jemmy Bloocher might as well be lost on another planet.

He said, "Push anyone stupid enough to trust you until he drops out, then kill him for it. Kill proles till they shoot everyone who's still with you. Keep it up till there's nobody left. *Plan?*"

Andrew wrenched himself loose, and they let him do it. He shook himself, and strode off shouting, "Follow me!"

The flapping yellow blaze dwindled into black rain.

In the rain and the thunder there was a rustling too, and motion that wasn't just trees in the wind. A big bird dropped from the sputtering sky and lifted again with a turtle-shape in its four sawtooth-edged feet.

Andrew had told them to keep their ponchos. He was right. The night was alive.

Rafik Doe recognized tree roots strangling a sharp-edged boulder, and fished Jemmy Bloocher's pack from underneath. Those on the short list stripped and donned the swim trunks and windbreakers from Carder's Boat, then wore their firebird colors over them. Jemmy gave his prole gun to Amnon before he pulled a windbreaker over his head, then his own old and battered pack. Amnon handed the gun back, somewhat to Jemmy's surprise, and got himself dressed.

They'd walked halfway back to the field where Shimon died. In a sputter of lightning they watched a battle between shadows of birds. Rafik complained in a continuous drone, until others took up the theme too.

"Here!" said Andrew.

He meant a line of spiky black-and-bronze foliage dug into the crack that ran up a near-vertical rock face.

There were exclamations and protests, and then they climbed. Jemmy waited to help the laggards.

Shar Willoughby got ten meters up and froze.

Jemmy climbed up to show her which plants would hold, where to place her feet. She shook her head and wouldn't look or move. "Get me down. Just get me down."

Andrew and Barda were high above him. He couldn't ask: *Do we need Shar?* She was wearing shorts and windbreaker! But she'd never make it, and she was blocking the path.

A ten-meter fall would break bones. He guided her down, letting her stand on his shoulders when he had to. She knelt at the bottom, panting like a dog. He made her strip and took her shorts and windbreaker.

The others were climbing. Shar plodded back toward the barracks.

Jemmy pulled himself along a row of Destiny plants. Or was it all one plant? He couldn't see a break, just a line of roots prying a mountain-sized rock apart.

Before that crack ran out there was another.

The world was all tilted surfaces, black and lightning-white, and roar of thunder. He remembered wandering in a daze, mostly blind and mostly deaf, pulling himself from nowhere to nowhere just because he wasn't dead yet. . . .

But this night was very different from the night he'd abandoned Carder's Boat. He'd been fed and succored, and twelve people had given their lives into his hands . . . gloves. Nobody else had gloves.

The plants ended suddenly. Other climbers started having trouble. Jemmy had to double back a few times to guide the others to foot- and handholds. The prole gun's strap left Jemmy's arms free. He could see Andrew watching from far above.

If Jemmy slipped, Andrew would have the gun again.

"Here," Andrew bellowed. "The ledge. Leave your ponchos here. Firebird shorts too. Use rocks to weigh them down."

Rafik exclaimed, "Now what on Earth are you playing at, Andrew?"

"Do it right!" Andrew bellowed. He'd left his own clothing where he was, fifty feet above the ledge, sleeves spread and wedged in cracks. "They can't see through unless the clouds break!" He scrambled back and helped Rafik, then Willametta, then Amnon place rocks to display flame-colored ponchos and shorts against dark wet rock. The others were getting the idea.

Andrew was painting a picture of climbers scattered over a cliff face.

"We're halfway up and frozen in fear, right? And that's the way it is until they get here themselves, and *look*. Right?"

"Andrew," Jemmy asked, "do you think they can see us?"

Andrew's teeth flashed in lightning. "Not yet. All set? Come!"

"Andrew, there's too many!" Andrew looked at him, and Jemmy shouted, "Me! I'm one too many! They're looking for thirteen ponchos, not fourteen, and if we meet a spectre or something, someone has to pose!"

And after they found Shar they'd be looking for twelve ponchos, not thirteen . . . still one too many . . . unless Shar talked.

Andrew said, "One of us should have started naked. Damndamn. Ansel, you look cold—"

Ansel Tarr dressed again in flame colors.

Jemmy looked around at them. "Willya?" He gave her Shar's swim shorts and windbreaker. She looked no more skeletal than the rest.

Andrew led off again, leaving twelve posed ponchos.

The ledge was straight, hard to lose in the flashing dark, but it wasn't a split in rock. It was a frozen flow of lava, naked of plants, and slippery. There were holes etched by rain for handholds and footholds. Jemmy stayed on hands and knees even where he could stand, because those behind him were copying his style.

Jemmy, Henry, Andrew, Willametta, Barda, and Amnon wore swim trunks and windbreakers. Ansel wore the last poncho. The rest were naked and not liking it.

He barely heard the scream, but he turned quick and shouted down. "Who fell?"

He heard: "I caught something. Caught a plant." Amnon's voice. "Thorn."

"Can you climb up?" Oh, Earth and Moon, Amnon was in a windbreaker and trunks! If proles found those on a gatherer's corpse, they'd guess there were more.

"I can't move! It's like two handfuls of hypo needles!"

"I've got rope, Jeremy." Andrew hurled a coil of rope at him. He leered at Jemmy and said, "Anchor me." *Plan? Where's* your *rope?*

Jemmy tied the rope to a low, knotted Destiny tree. He could hear Amnon whimpering. The rope didn't seem to be finding him.

The sky lit like a sun.

It hurt the eyes . . . like the light that burned over the speckles field after Shimon's death. Jemmy blinked. "What on Earth—?"

"Quicksilverrr!" Andrew's bellow was all triumph. He trolled the rope toward Amnon, who was clinging to a double armful of thorn on a sixty-degree slope. The rope was too short. "Jeremy!"

It was long enough when Jemmy had untied it from the tree, but the only anchor now was himself and Andrew. Amnon didn't want to let go of the bush.

Andrew shouted, "Take it, you damned fool!"

Amnon moaned and snatched at the rope, lost his grip and had only the rope. He clung and swung while Andrew and Jemmy pulled hand over hand. At the end he lay sobbing at their feet, his hands full of needles and blood.

And Jemmy asked again: "The light?"

"It's Quicksilver, you Crab-shy dropout! And the date is late summer, and Quicksilver rises just an hour before sunrise. And we are right on schedule, Jeremy, but we should move!"

"Quicksilver's bright, but *this* bright?"

"Settler magic. That's what you call it, isn't it? *Argos* flew past Quicksilver. They dropped a metal and plastic turtle—I've seen pictures—it makes solar-electric plates, and lasers to beam the power, and more little mining turtles. Now it's hundreds of years later and Quicksilver's covered in solar collectors. That's why it's so bright."

An entire *planet* covered in Begley cloth.

Jemmy began to understand that Destiny Town had power undreamed by the towns along the Crab. They could light up a mountain range. Launch ships into space. Andrew had *known*. Did they all know? Did they all take this for granted?

Lightning flickered dimly against a sky like a hazy noon. The rock slope was etched in detail. It looked to be four hundred meters to the ridge, and there, that crack might be a way up.

But—"They're looking at us. How?"

"Amnon? Got your nerve back? Ready to move?"

"Dammit, Andrew! How are they watching us? From the sky?" Light like this had burned behind them this afternoon, lighting the proles' investigation of Shimon's death.

The others gathered around Andrew and Jemmy and Amnon. Andrew said, "All *right,* Jeremy, but we don't have forever. Now, that light isn't for us. They're looking for firebird ponchos—Ansel, get that off now, ball it up and hide it!—and those are upRoad. They're looking through video—you understand video cameras?"

"In Spiral Town we still have a few that work."

"Video from orbit. So they can't see us unless the clouds break, but there's a way to split light into colors. They'll look for firebird colors. They'll match every firebird in the area, but firebirds don't gather the way our ponchos are gathered—"

Willametta said, "Andrew?"

"What?"

"The light's on *us*. It isn't on the ponchos. Can't you see? The mountain's lit up all around us, but it fades going back toward the barracks. Fades toward the fields too."

The others murmured. Jemmy saw that she was right. But Andrew said, "You're imagining that. Why would they be looking at us?"

"I thought they might be focusing on this." Jemmy held up the prole gun.

"Why?"

But Willametta asked, "Jeremy, how long has that light been blinking?"

A blinking green light in the butt of the gun. Jemmy said, "It's been doing that all along. Why? Because they wouldn't want a gun like this wandering loose! If they've got phones—"

"Prole guns don't blink when we're harvesting. They didn't blink after the proles shot the birds," Willametta said. "Andrew, when did it start blinking? After you killed a prole for it?"

"Maybe. Damndamndamn. It's sending a help call, isn't it, Willya?"

"Throw it away, Andrew!"

"Daaamn! Damn. Jeremy, do it."

Jemmy hurled the evil thing back the way they'd come. It flew not far, struck bare rock and spun away downhill. Andrew screamed at the sky.

Andrew climbed as if possessed. This part of the range was new to them all. The plants were gone; it was naked rock. In the weird light they could see him far above, while Jemmy moved about helping the slower climbers and the ones who froze in fear.

Dennis Levoy was sliding. He'd lost the crack they were following. It was out of his reach now and he couldn't even scream. Jemmy scrambled down to reach him, but Dennis was sliding faster now, still silent, naked against a slick slope that wouldn't hold him. In the acid light Jemmy saw Henry flatten himself to avoid being knocked off. Dennis bounced against him and snatched at Henry's ankle. Henry kicked him free. He was falling, falling, gone.

Dennis had been naked. Jemmy felt shamed that he'd thought to look, but he looked around and ticked them off: his own and five other sets of windbreakers and shorts, all climbing well.

A rift in the blazing clouds showed as a black canyon and a terrible light within. Blinded, they froze against the hillside, under a blazing eye in a black sky.

The rift closed before they moved again.

As they climbed, the light crawled away from them, back toward the firebird ponchos.

Andrew was coming back down. "Not this way. Stop them." He edged sideways along the hillside and tried another path. Jemmy got the rest of them to where they could cling, and they waited until Andrew shouted.

Now the sky blazed upRoad, above the ponchos they'd left behind, lighting them until proles could come to see what they were. That ought to take hours. The Windfarm's felons climbed in the fringes of the light, with no firebird colors to mark them.

The bulge of the hill hid further heights. The crest receded like dreams. Jemmy tried to count heads. Ten plus his own plus Andrew should be twelve. He waited, and presently heard sobbing. Ansel Tarr, sixteen and skinny and shivering in the rain. Jemmy doubled back, cursing the slope he'd have to climb twice, and guided Ansel's hands and feet until they'd found the next split in the rock.

The next man he had to help was Andrew.

Andrew had spent the last day and night exploring, preparing. It wasn't surprising that he was exhausted. His glare of hate was hard to take. Jemmy tied the rope under Andrew's shoulders, then his own waist, and climbed.

They found a flat spot, and stood, and looked about.

Beyond was *down*. They could hear the whoops of the gatherers receding ahead of them. Only Barda and Willametta and Amnon had waited.

They chattered as they flowed downhill. They had their wind back.

Blazing clouds lit the way. There was valley below, and behind it another ridge. The slopes were steep, with a tangle of black and bronze and yellow at the bottom, and a glitter shining through. A glitter of water, not Road, Jemmy thought.

He didn't see any easy way to cross.

"That's not the Road," Henry said critically.

Andrew snarled. "Barda? If we follow the valley far enough, we have to hit the Road. We'll be moving toward the Neck."

Barda didn't answer.

"Willya?"

"Okay."

Andrew led off.

The bottom of the valley was all water and mud and Destiny thorn.

They crawled along the slope at the frost line. They were picking up stones and branches for weapons even before they saw the birds.

Two. They plunged out of the bush, uphill, silent, aimed like darts. Just beyond stone's throw they stopped suddenly, wings braked against the air. Turned and plunged back.

"We must stink of alien blood," Rafik said.

Andrew said, "Keep the clubs. Oh, man, I miss the prole gun!" He glared at Jemmy.

Jemmy said, "I should have given it to you and made you carry it."

"Carry it? But . . . oh. You *bastard*."

"Carry it back to where we left the ponchos and *then* throw it away. That would have fixed you."

Andrew was laughing, much against his will. "No birdfucking allowed!"

"It's the law!" shouted half a dozen voices.

The line straggled to a halt. The valley ended in a dome of gray lava . . . or began there. It appeared they'd been moving upstream.

Jemmy asked, "Andrew? Anyone? What makes tubes?"

"Tubes?"

Jemmy pointed across at the opposite slope. Lava had oozed out of Destiny's core to form a pillow of rock half a klick high. A snake of gray rock flowed from it, widening and narrowing in pulses. A rounded break like a snake's mouth emitted a lesser tube like a snake's tongue, and that grew larger until it did it again, and *that* tube ran down into the thorn. Jemmy could see breaks where the tube had collapsed.

He said, "I hid out in one of those. Saved my life."

"Great. How do we cross? Why bother?"

Henry said, "About now the proles are looking at, what was it, a dozen empty ponchos? And they're trying to think of someplace else to look—"

"And we're all ready to collapse," Willametta said. "But we've got knives, Andrew. We'll cut through."

Barda passed out knives: she had eight, and Andrew got one, but she kept the biggest. Andrew's opinion had not been asked.

They sawed their way through the weeds at the bottom of the valley, wading through waist-deep water. Birds of all sizes fled in terror from twelve noisy alien life-forms and a rich stench of human blood from cuts and scrapes and scratches. They were well and truly exhausted by the time they reached the tube.

The sky went black.

The light had been glaring beyond the ridge, over the valley they'd left behind, for so many hours that at first Jemmy couldn't understand what had changed. But someone in the Parole Board must have guessed that fleeing felons might need light.

In a sputter of lightning they crawled into true dark. The tube was big. It might have held any kind of predator. Jemmy moved knifepoint-first, ready to back up fast, though he was third in line behind Andrew and Willametta.

It was a big tube, as wide as two people; wider in spots. Jemmy sprawled out and let himself fade. . . .

"Let me out! Let me out!" far away and garbled; and then a rustle.

Barda: "Anything wrong down there?"

"Just Denis losing his dinner."

The tube was quite smooth and comfortable, barring a little rainwater in the bottom. Wind blew through the big holes and kept it from being stuffy. Thunder roared from time to time, but he'd grown used to that. He could hear Willametta and Andrew making noisy love, both wild with the taste of freedom, their feet a meter from his head. That was almost restful.

Yet he couldn't sleep.

He heard Henry ask plaintively, "Did *anyone* see an Earthlife bird?"

"We'd have known." Barda, three centimeters from Jemmy's feet.

Henry: "I'd kill a prole for a duck."

Ansel, much closer: "There's good eatin' on a prole."

"Is he right, Barda?"

"Oh, *shut* it, Henry. Even so, you all listening? We've *got* to find Earth-life food. If we still look like a dozen ghouls the first time any citizen finds us . . ."

"That's kind of what I meant."

Willametta, from uptube: "Barda, tell us more about this inn we're trying to get to."

"Wave Rider, we were going to call it. My older brothers, Barry and Bill, and I went off with a gang of workmen from Destiny Town. That left Daddy with Brian and Carol. We knew Daddy'd work them hard. We hated to leave them.

"The Overview Bureau used to be antsy about people messing with Otterfolk, but they've loosened up some. Daddy got permission some-how. We built not far from shore. We brought a specialist to teach us how to deal with Otterfolk for fish. I don't think Daddy could ever have loosened up enough. You have to swim with them. They like to play."

"You like that, Barda?"

"It beats what else we were doing. Digging a foundation. Pouring stone. We were starting to build the frame when Daddy sent me off to Romanoff."

"The other best restaurant."

"Jeremy, I grew up knowing how to cook the Earthlife fish from Swan Lake, but Daddy thought seafood must be different, and *Destiny* seafood . . . anyway, I went. Wide Wade's School of Destiny Biochemistry and Cuisine is attached to Romanoff. The best students end up there.

"And while I was at Wide Wade's, I got word that Bill ran away with the money for the workmen! Daddy was in a rage and I was supposed to go back to the Swan. So I ran too. And I never saw any of them ever again until the tribunal."

"I've been in the Swan," Duncan Nicholls said.

"No way," said Barda.

Willametta asked, voice raised to talk past Jemmy, "Barda, how far away is this shoreline site you picked?"

"Seventy klicks from Destiny Town, where the Road dips almost down to the water. About that far from here, I guess. Willya, I don't know how much of it they built."

"Well, there's ten of us, and you tell us how to do it, and Jeremy can make us a pit barbecue."

"If we can get there," said a voice. Another told him to shut up. Jemmy stopped listening. He was half-asleep, and so were the rest of them, and anyone still awake wouldn't be making sense.

He dozed. The voices had all gone quiet. All but—

"It's at Swan Lake, between the Road and the shore." Duncan.

"Daddy wouldn't let you in the Swan." Barda, scornful.

"Harold Winslow? He wasn't there."

"Who was?"

"Nobody. Barda, it's just a shell. They took out the ovens even, and the chairs and tables. I hid out in the Swan while they were looking for me after, you know."

"How'd they catch you?"

"Got careless. Twice. I mean, I thought I'd hide out for a while and then hit the Road with the money and settle down in Terminus. But I didn't think of speckles. So I got speckles-shy and careless and got caught fishing off the dock."

Jemmy asked, "Duncan, do you have any idea where the Winslow family went?"

"How would I?"

"Well, the proles might have said something."

"Nope."

"Barda, it strikes me that maybe your daddy just left the Swan and went off to finish Wave Rider."

Silence.

Jemmy asked, "Who else would take the ovens?"

"Is Andrew awake?"

"I don't think so."

"We'll tell him in the morning."

✳ 24 ✳

The Ridges

We could build clocks that keep a Destiny calendar and Destiny time, but there's no point. The Spirals sell clocks by wagonloads, and we all use them. On Earth it's some slightly different date plus the lightspeed gap, and that doesn't matter either.

—Hillary Miller, first mayor of Terminus

In the morning they crossed the ridge and found another valley. They hacked and waded across.

And another behind the next ridge, but *Cavorite* must have seared and seeded this land. They yelled like maniacs to see green trees and grass covering the slopes. Black and yellow-green ran along the bottom, Destiny life seared away and then returned.

Felons scattered to hunt. Andrew kept others to dig a pit with their hands and to cut Destiny wood with kitchen knives. Jemmy Bloocher and Barda Winslow fought sporadic flurries of rain to make fire.

Before night fell they had cooked a pig, four rabbits, a small bird Ansel caught by leaping at it, and a man's weight of green bananas.

Gorged stupid, the dozen escapees lay on a sloping hill and looked at each other. Andrew Dowd said, "It can work."

Someone was talking about staying here.

Jemmy could have slept through that if Andrew hadn't begun shouting. *Where will the Parole Board look first? Where . . . more speckles? crazy bastard . . . had a plan . . .*

He tried to ignore the sounds, but now Ansel was shouting back. "Not forever! We stay here till the Board gets bored looking for us."

Andrew: "I know where the caravan is now! When they get to the Swan we've got to be ready. Merchants won't wait."

"If we settle here, the Board will quit after a month. They don't *know* we've got a speckles stash—"

"Speckles rots!"

"What? What are you saying?"

Barda: "Ansel, speckles gets a splash of radiation before it goes on the Road. They do it in the Parole Board complex. Didn't you know?"

"You planned this *knowing*—? Wait a minute. Andrew, how long does speckles last if nobody zaps it?"

"No idea."

"You don't even know it's to preserve the speckles, do you? It might be they don't want fertile seeds getting out—"

"That's birdfucking crazy!"

"Who died and made you prole?"

"Shut up! Shut your face or I'll turn it inside out for you!"

Barda was on Andrew's arm, whispering, while Willametta stalked off in a rage.

Jemmy spoke as she passed. "Willya."

She dropped beside him. She said, "They're all crazy."

Jemmy said, "Sure."

"Andrew too. Idiot. If he'd just let them talk."

"He still thinks he's a trusty, Willya."

"What's your take on this, Jeremy?"

Jemmy said, "We had a plan. Then we had another plan. Plans are cheap. I've thrown away a lot of plans. I like—" His arm swept about himself. "—*this*. We can hunt!"

"You'd stay?" The ragged clouds permitted glimpses of stars, but it was too dark to see more than shadows. She moved closer, to see his face.

"No, I mean we can keep a restaurant supplied. If they seared *this* valley, *Cavorite* must have seared and seeded every valley between here and the Road. They're all ready to be hunted. I saw—"

"Ah." Relieved, she nestled against him.

He asked, "Does Andrew—?"

"Too many men, not enough women, and a woman who gets pregnant goes free. Any man who tries to hold on to a woman gets taught different."

"Unless he's a trusty?"

"By that time, he knows." Somehow they'd come to be lying side by side, their backs against the long damp grass. Willametta said, "I haven't seen stars in two years."

"Me . . . well. Days."

"Be a restaurant. It sounded crazy when you said it."

"Caravans build a new restaurant every evening, and I was the one who did the building. When I see the Swan I'll tell you what I think. Maybe it's fallen down."

"What do we do then?"

"*I* can't stop until I've seen Destiny Town."

She sat up abruptly. "Crab shies aren't allowed on the mainland," she said. "You *know* better than to go into town without an identity, Jeremy."

Crab shies?

"How would I pick up an identity? What identity? I mean, with this accent."

"You could be a merchant child."

Jemmy chewed that. He'd have learned the Crab accent while traveling with the caravan . . . wait. "Willya, there weren't any children on the caravans."

"No. Jeremy, if a merchant gets pregnant on the Road, she's bound to be home before she has the baby."

"Then what are we talking about?"

"Well, merchant men make children along the Road too. The children stay where they're born unless something happens. You could have been picked up at two or three years old."

"That ever happen?" It sounded like a children's story.

"Ask Duncan Nick. Nicholls."

"Duncan doesn't have any accent."

"He lost it." She rolled over onto him. "You going to talk all night?"

He did wonder, afterward, why he had been so favored. But Willya, her breath easing, whispered, "What did you see?"

"When?"

"You said—"

He remembered, and smiled. "I saw green beans growing up cornstalks over most of a hillside, but they're not ripe yet. In a few months we'll get our veggies here too. I've been looking for potatoes. We can bake bananas—"

At dawn the felons were all over the place. Andrew whistled to gather them up.

Winnie was talking to Barda, low and fast.

Barda listened, then summoned Andrew.

The rest straggled in. Winnie looked exhausted already, and two were still missing: Ansel Tarr and Asham Mandala. Andrew looked like bloody murder.

This would be easier, Jemmy thought, if he had bread to offer instead of leftover pork. He said, "They'll catch up. Once we're on the ridge they'll see us. Being seen from the sky is the problem."

"Always ready to spot the problem, aren't we, *Jemmy?*"

"Mmm? What am I missing?"

Barda said, "Tell him, Winnie."

The slender dark woman spoke in a fast monotone. "They wanted me to go with them. Asham had my arms but I bit Ansel's hand and started screaming, I think I kicked him a good one too, and I pulled loose. They wanted me to stop yelling and let them go, and I saw Asham had one of the knives so I just ran back here. But they're gone."

"And you didn't tell me," Andrew said venomously.

"We can't wait," Barda said.

"Barda, they've deserted me!"

Andrew and Barda were still keeping their voices down, though Amnon and Henry had moved into earshot. Jemmy risked saying, "Some of us still think you're the trusties, you know? And some of us have noticed that there aren't any proles to say so. Andrew, when you tell *all* of us to stop talking about anything but the plan, who is it that stops talking? Just the ones who say you're right, right?"

"Your point?"

"Keep us talking or you'll lose more."

Andrew sighed. "But if I let *these* birdfuckers go—"

"Did they get our speckles stash?"

"What? Turn around."

Jemmy turned. Andrew opened Jemmy's pack and looked in. "Still there. Wait." He fished the bag out, opened it, looked, sniffed. "Still there. What are you playing at? Did you think they could get it away from you?"

"It was the only thing they could take that's worth anything, and they don't have it. Let them go."

"No!"

Henry said, "We can't catch them. Earth's sake, would you have chased them in the dark? When they do show up in a few days, speckles-shy and begging for their brains back, they'll be a horrible example."

Andrew snorted. Barda said, "We'll be restaurateurs by then. They'll have to be hidden fast."

Jemmy saw Andrew bite back his answer. *Killed! We're planning a charade, and a speckles-shy might blurt out something deadly.* Jemmy looked for alternatives . . . and Andrew saw his nod.

Ten were left.

Over the ridge was another valley, Destiny life along the bottom, Earthlife running up the slopes, birds that hovered like hawks. The sky was tattered clouds and fluttery winds that would not support heavy Destiny birds. Those birds must be Earthlife.

Ten felons hunted and feasted on burrowing creatures. It seemed strange to be eating at noon. Merchants and yutzes didn't do that either. Their intestines had forgotten about meat, and some were having trouble. They talked as they lay about the slopes, and continued as they moved on.

"I signed a contract I shouldn't have," Andrew Dowd said. He was walking off his anger. He walked *fast*, and Jemmy matched his pace just to see if he could.

"Didn't you say you were being robbed?"

"Robbed, yeah. They were my partners."

"I had the idea they were holding you at gunpoint."

Andrew only grinned over his shoulder.

But he'd certainly implied . . . "Were they trying to kill you?"

"The courts are screwy, Jeremy. I wasn't sure I'd get justice."

Jemmy dropped back by a little. Andrew was half-smart and dangerous . . . and maybe his own record was no better.

"I don't remember any of it," Duncan Nick told Jemmy. "My mother got killed when someone got careless with a weed cutter. My aunt and uncle, they already had Marie. Now Momma was dead and suddenly they've got four, and I didn't look like the others. Daddy already knew about me. When the summer caravan came by, he took me. Carnot wagon. Maria wasn't any too pleased."

Jemmy guessed: "Your stepmother?"

"My older sister."

"Is that when you saw Mount Canaveral?"

"Oh, I wasn't much past two. Funny I remember anything at all. But I saw Mount Canaveral when some of us went swimming and fishing at Swan Lake, years later. Winslows chased us off."

"So the restaurant was still going?"

"Then. I was only thirteen." Duncan looked around him. Barda Winslow was trailing, well out of earshot. "So me and my two friends, we went back to the Swan six years later. But it was empty. So we went through three of the big houses on the Nob and hid out in the Swan. I suppose you'd think I was crazy, a Crab shy forgetting about speckles."

"I can't imagine it."

"But I grew up here. Hereabouts, not just in Destiny Town but *everywhere*, speckles is free. We don't need much. Earthlife animals have nerves too, you know."

"So?"

"Hey, Willya?"

"What?"

"You told me once. Why is it that we don't have to worry so much about speckles? The Earthlife and Destiny life grow together . . . ?"

"Yes. Jemmy, these valleys are all Earthlife and Destiny mixed. It's like that around Destiny Town too. Earthlife animals learn to eat Destiny plants that secrete potassium. The ones that don't, get stupid and die. The Crab isn't like that. Nothing's like that unless it's near the Winds. See, the potassium has to *be* there."

"Willya, how did caravans get started?"

"Don't know. Lucky for the Crab shies, though, eh?"

Barda thought it over while she walked. "I know some of what's in the lessons," she said. "A little. Daddy didn't give us much time to learn."

"But you've got tapes and computers? Like in Spiral Town?"

"Sure. You can't get to them, though. They're in the libraries, and you don't have identification."

"The caravans—"

"They keep the Crab shies going."

"Why?"

"Jeremy, you're one yourself."

"I know, but why? When there were only two hundred of the first settlers and another fifty children, why not move us then?"

Barda walked silent for a bit. Then, "Hell, why not? I never thought of that. But the stories—"

She'd trailed off oddly. Jemmy asked, "What do they say about us?"

"You had to be fed by hand. You were meaner than snakes—I mean your ancestors, of course. Couldn't move you then, I guess, and they tried speckles on a few of you and you must have brightened up. Jemmy, I guess they got tired of you."

Speckles-shy.

Two hundred adult-sized angry infants who had to be fed, clothed, washed, toilet-trained. The lucky ones who recovered would be more or less ambulatory but no damn use to anyone. Transplanting two hundred Jael Harnesses would be a nightmare.

Jemmy was, he discovered, crying. Destiny Town had the planets, and Spiral Town was left to savagery.

He dropped back so that Barda wouldn't see tears, and he said, "Without speckles we would have died. They *must* have brought speckles. They could *watch* us getting well. Why not move us then? Now they have to *keep* bringing us speckles."

Barda shook her head. "It's stranger than you think. You talked to Duncan?"

"Yeah."

"There were only forty in *Cavorite*, right? And two died early. Now it's two hundred years later, and the merchant women almost always get pregnant on the Road, and the men leave children too. They do it to keep the gene mix. But why go so far? You tell me."

Now Jemmy could picture the settling mass of extruded mountains pushing the flat land away, until from the sky it would seem to run in parallel wrinkles. They crossed wrinkle after endless wrinkle. At evening they crossed another ridge—

And the Road was below.

Heads lined up along the edge of rock, showing nothing more of themselves, looking down.

There was nobody on the Road.

It was another valley, another wrinkle, with another ridge beyond. The Road was one edge of a fast-moving stream lined with Earth-green bushes. Jemmy's view to the right showed no more than Road and river running on, dipping and reappearing, finally curving out of sight.

Left, the ridge ran two or three klicks and then splayed out into a flat-topped peak. Andrew whispered, "Where are we, Barda? Is that Canaveral? I've seen pictures. Not from this angle—"

"It's Mount Canaveral," Duncan Nick said. "The restaurant was just past . . . it must be half a klick this side, just around that curve. The lake too."

They spoke without looking at each other, their eyes on the Road. Andrew said, "An hour's walk and it's getting dark. Damn, if anyone saw *ten* of us sneaking up on an empty building . . . okay. The rest of you wait here. Stay the night. Barda, it's you and me. Whatever we find down there, you're the owner, or the owner's daughter. I'm your husband—or not yet?"

"Not yet," she decided. "Lovers, but I want Daddy's approval. You want to meet my parents and it has you a little scared."

"What if they're not there and someone else is? Do I threaten to call the police?"

"For Earth's sake don't lose your cool until *I* do!" Barda hissed.

"Okay."

"We're too far from anyone else. Daddy kept guns. If it's Daddy . . . keep your cool."

"Ready?"

His better judgment told him to be quiet, but Jemmy said, "Not you, Andrew."

Andrew turned. Jemmy said, "Don't take it wrong, but you look as crazy as a pigeon in a fool cage. Grow some meat over your cheek-bones, soften those eye sockets, you could pass. Not now. I'd say Duncan. He's gaunt, but at least he *knows* the Swan."

Barda Winslow looked at the men and women lined up along the rock crest. They waited her judgment.

She said, "You, Jemmy."

There was nobody in sight. They scrambled down to the Road. Jemmy looked at the fast-moving water. He asked, "Can you swim?"

"There's a bridge. Now we just walk, right? A little tired. We've been swimming."

"Where are our towels?"

". . . In the pack?"

"Good."

"Now, you might see a bus go by."

"Bus?"

"If you see a box full of people being pulled by a tug, and they're looking out the windows at you, just look back. I'll wave it on."

"Tug?"

"Tractor. Pulling machine. You see them a lot. Back at the Windfarm, that was a tug pulling the speckles cart."

Oh, *that* was a tug. "A flat metal thing that hugs the ground? Hip high. The top is Begley cloth?"

Barda nodded.

The light had faded to a silver circle above the west: Quicksilver light blurred by haze.

The bridge was wood. It wasn't in good shape, with only one handrail, and it shook as they crossed.

The Swan loomed, a lightless shadow against a hillside, twice the size of Bloocher Farm. Brenda's jittery voice led him toward it. "That bridge will need some serious repair. Place hasn't collapsed; good. What do you think, go in the front?"

"Is there a bell? Bloocher Farm had a bell."

The front door was twice a man's height. Barda waved her arms about. "The bell rope's gone. I think Daddy's gone too, and he took the bell. *Daddy, it's Barda!*"

They listened. Barda whispered, "No lights. The sign is out. You don't close an inn at night. You just charge higher if they wake you up. *Daddy, it's Barda! I've brought a—*" A nice hesitation. "—*friend!*"

Nothing.

Barda pulled and pushed the door. "Locked. Come on around."

The kitchen door was lower and wider, wide enough to pass a cart. Barda pulled and it swung open. "The lock's broken."

Jemmy suggested: "Duncan?"

"Sure. Well, come in. Here." She hooked her fingers into his waistband and led him. There was nothing else to guide him, but Barda moved by memory and scent.

"Not even night-lights. Daddy must have taken the guide spot with him. Kitchen," she said, and he smelled old food smells and smoke. "Dining hall. Wow, he took the tables and chairs too, and the carts. Stairs here. Watch it! There was a banister. Stay along the wall." And, "These were the guest rooms."

"Sounds good to me."

But she kept moving, down to the end and another flight of stairs. Then a strange smell, flowery—"My room. Watch your feet."

He'd kicked something. "What's *that?*"

"Don't know. Clutter. We'll have to sleep on the floor."

"No wind? No rain? And they left us a rug. I like it."

✳ 25 ✳

The Swan

Quicksilver's year runs three months and a bit. It rises as much as an hour before sunrise, or sets up to an hour after sunset: as bright as Mercury from Earth. I miss the Moon.

—Henry Judd, Planetologist

Andrew hailed him from the crest. Jemmy stopped on the bridge and waited while Andrew bounded down.

"We tracked you," he said. "Thought you might need help. And we watched a bus go past."

The others were already climbing down. Three more in windbreakers, followed by four scrambling down in naked haste, exposed in brilliant sunlight. *Become a restaurant? We're kidding ourselves—*

"How's it look?"

"Lot of work," Jemmy said. "I don't *see* everything Barda says needs doing, but there's a lot."

By morning the damage was easier to see.

The bridge might have been a century old. It was new enough that big trees had been cut to build it. On Earth there had certainly been life-forms that ate wood, but here it would last forever. The wood was sound, and thick, and moored in poured stone: sturdy enough to support a caravan. It sagged in the middle. Water had poured over it in a spring storm, or several, and taken the handrail and some paint. Patches of paint lined the edges, still glare-bright.

"Needs propping," Andrew said. "One big beam right in the middle."

A wide sheet of clear glass wrapped the front of the inn in a half-cylinder, framing the dining area. Several smaller windows were broken.

246

The bed left behind in the Captain's Suite would have been too big to move. They could clean up the Captain's Suite for display. The thick rug in Barda's room would be bed for them all.

"And of course the sign is out," Andrew said.

There were outhouse toilets. The one with a woman's silhouette stank. "These have to be dug out," Barda said. "Daddy must have just let the fem's go."

A much bigger outbuilding was barred from the inside. Barda showed them how to slide a sawblade through the crack and lift the bar. "Daddy thought this would keep us out, but my brother Barry figured it out. Daddy's hiding place, right?" She opened the door and yelped in delight.

Harold Winslow hadn't taken everything.

They wandered through the place as if entering an ancient Texas politician's treasure trove. There were tools: no little stuff and nothing powered, but . . .

They put Amnon into the big set of coveralls and gave his trunks and windbreaker to Rafik Doe. Rafik claimed a long, vicious weed cutter, then reluctantly traded it to Andrew for one of the shovels; Amnon took the other.

There was a roll of cloth! A tablecloth with the logo of the Swan, a fluffy white bird sailing a pond that reflected the blue sky. Blue and green and pure white. Andrew's weed cutter sliced it into broad strips: loincloths for the nudes. Clothing at last.

They looked at half a dozen fragile wands as tall as a man. Barda wondered, "Now, why didn't Daddy take these?"

Jemmy said, "I've never seen anything like them." A breath would have broken them.

"Fishing rods," Rafik said.

"Not for ocean fishing!" Jemmy told them. "Barda, you dealt with the Otterfolk? Your daddy wouldn't throw a hook into somebody's dining room."

"Daddy might."

Rafik and Amnon dug a pit. Then six men picked up the old outhouse, hoarding their breath, and moved it to the new pit.

They were all wolfishly hungry by midafternoon, and Barda was trying to get them to dig out the other outhouse. Jemmy got her attention. "Pit. Fire. Hunt. Cook," he said. "Now."

"We can lose a meal, Jeremy."

"That's not it." Though he was getting hungry. "Willya, Henry, give me a sanity check here? The day anyone sees this restaurant going, we've been here for half a year. Yes?" Jemmy waved at a flat patch of ground. *Just look at our fire pit, sir! We cleaned it out last week and it's already full of ashes. We were so busy two days ago, it's no wonder we've run out of a few things."* He saw a few grins, and persisted: "But we don't have a fire pit. What if someone comes by *today?"*

"No chairs either. No tables. No silverware," Barda said.

"Start a list. We don't need silverware. No forks at a caravan stop, Barda. Everyone carries his own knife."

Andrew asked, "What about the buses?"

Barda waved it off. "A bus ride costs money. People don't take them very often. So, there's a restaurant here. Last time anyone went past, he didn't notice. . . . Jemmy, *two* months we've been here."

"Fine. But I've got to teach you people how to cook!"

The nudes had skirts and/or loincloths now, but that wasn't quite like being clothed. It seemed best to send them off to hunt and keep the others for digging.

They dug a fire pit long enough to feed ten. *Extend it tomorrow.* The men's ancient outhouse could imply an ancient restaurant, so *that* could wait. The fem's had been too rank.

Barda showed them where the truck garden had been, and sure enough, potatoes and carrots were growing in a maze of weeds that had been (and still were) spices. The patch was clean of Destiny life.

They watched Barda choosing spices for dinner. The rest got bored and wandered away, but Jemmy stayed and made her identify every spice for him. He waited until they were alone before he asked.

"Barda, isn't this a graveyard?"

"Sure. Three generations of Winslows."

"It must have half-killed your father to move."

She looked up. "One day I'll have to ask him. Heya, Jemmy, if I said, 'No birdfucking allowed,' do you think he'd answer?"

"He might know. Maybe the proles caught your brother. It's the *law."*

Barda stood and dusted herself off. "That should do it." She left, carrying spices in her rolled-up windbreaker.

When she was gone, Jemmy reached into his pack.

The hunters returned at dusk with something piglike, still alive and struggling. They left it tied up and settled for root vegetables. *Can't cook in the dark.*

In the morning Jemmy and a few others built up the fire and killed and roasted the non-pig. They got a cheer from the late risers. Afterward they extended the fire pit into an arc seven meters long.

The men got tired of sharing their outhouse. They dug another pit and moved the men's outhouse to that. "We'll call this place the Pits," Jemmy suggested. They jeered him.

He took men uphill to collect rocks. A Roadside caravan stop *had* to have an oven. He'd walk the Road and look for grain, and find a way to grind it. If that birdfucker Harold Winslow had only left some pots, they could have set a stew going! There were flowerpots in the tool-house, but no passerby would accept those as cookware.

They cleaned the long hall, and the first pair of rooms leading off it, and the Captain's Suite. On Barda's insistence they cleaned the suite of rooms at the end too, because someone might want it. There were in-door toilets! and old signs on the doors that said

OUT OF ORDER

"These have been down since I was a little girl. Daddy got tired of digging up the pipes, or else he ran out of money," Barda said. "There's a Destiny plant that just loves to block pipes."

In Barda's old room were chairs and a desk. They took the chairs down to the dining area. The desk was too big.

Looking up at the inn, you could see through the picture window, but you saw only ceiling. So it didn't matter that the place was an echo-ing emptiness. "Daddy took all the curtains," Barda told them. "They should be there. If you don't close them the sun can fry the diners."

Andrew shrugged. "We just don't let anyone in."

"Might work. But the window's filthy."

There was soap, but no rags. They cleaned the picture window with their swim shorts, amid considerable horseplay, then used more soap to get the shorts clean. The shorts came out of that amazingly well. *Settler magic.* Some machine in Spiral Town, some relic of *Argos* and Sol sys-tem, must have continued making clothing after Carder's Boat stopped moving.

Jemmy found a tree big enough to serve as a centerpost for the bridge. That could wait. They found endless useless junk accumulated in the dining hall and moved *that* out, and made brooms and swept the place out. But there were no tables and no chairs!

Barda's list was growing. "I really wish we had *any* kind of money. Nobody in his right mind would start an inn without funds."

"As long as it doesn't rain," Jemmy said.

"What?"

"We'll drag some logs down here for seats."

It took them all the next day. They chopped down trees, split the logs, set them around the fire-pit arc and adzed them flat on top. It felt de-cidedly fancy, a sanitized wimpy mock-up of a Roadside caravan stop, when they dined around the coals that night.

"Napkins," said Barda. "It doesn't work without napkins. Clean nap-kins."

There was no light but the coals and, briefly, Quicksilver. They felt their way to their beds. But in the morning Jemmy got Barda to show him the list.

poured stone, ~~5~~ 10 tonnes		~~1000~~ 2000
glass panes		700
silverware		200–1000
paint		400
chairs		up to 2000
tables		up to 4000
line wire		4000
soap		100
curtains		500–1000
advertising		???
napkins, paper		50/week
		OR
napkins, cloth	logo?	200 +
washer		5000
cookware:		
stew pots		
teapot		
tea		

"I'm guessing at the cost, most of the time. Even so, some of this doesn't cost much. Cloth napkins, we don't need to buy a washer if one of us will wash them out."

Five days after their arrival, the Pits was starting to look more like the picture in Barda's mind.

The felons too were starting to look less gaunt. Less pale, too. A day of sporadic sunlight wouldn't give anyone a sunburn, but they no longer looked like they'd been living under an endless black thunderstorm.

Of course they were too many, and three were in kilts chopped from a tablecloth. And if Jemmy Bloocher had thought of robbing their first customers for their clothes, and never mind the friends and relatives and proles who might come looking for them . . . then nine people who had been imprisoned for violent crimes would all have thought of the same thing. Something had better be done about clothes!

Buses passed twice a day.

On the fifth evening they sat around the fire pit and spoke their plans. "It's a wonder nobody's ever tried this before," Barda caroled. "It could *work*. Unless it rains."

Was she fooling herself? Nobody could see the flaws in the inn as well as Barda, not even Jemmy, who still saw only a mask over chaos. Andrew asked, "What else do we need to be a restaurant?"

Barda said, "Well, the sign, of course."

Jemmy asked, "Paint?"

She laughed. "Paint? No. We have to turn the sign on . . . like the Windfarm barracks sign. We need lights too. Jemmy, there's a way out to the roof, but it's blocked. Can you climb up there?"

The roof was three stories up. Nobody but Jemmy wanted to climb it, but it wasn't difficult. He found a weathered and muddy elegance.

He called down. "Barda? Three tables, twelve chairs. You didn't say it was a dining area."

"We never got crowded enough to use it. That's why Daddy closed it off."

"I don't see how to get them down."

"We'll get the door unblocked."

"Barda, I can see the door. It's barred on this side."

"What? Really?"

"Whoever did it must have climbed down afterward."

"Brian! He would've! And then Daddy never got around to unblocking it!"

Jemmy lifted the bar away and tried to pull the door open. "Stuck."

There was no chimney. From this height you could see . . . well, you could see enough Road from here to prepare for visitors, get the nudes under cover, and put Amnon on display in his coveralls. From the roof's back edge, through a notch in the ridge, water gleamed through a fringe of slender, straight Earthlife trees. Swan Lake.

He called down. "Still there, Barda? I'm thinking. If a client never sees us except in swimsuits and windbreakers, we *have to* serve fish."

"Daddy left because Swan Lake was fished out."

"Worth a try. Barda? You've got electric power." Beneath a surface of accumulated dirt, he was standing on a dark silver-gray surface.

"Did something light up?"

"No, I only mean half the roof is Begley cloth."

"Of course. How's it look?"

"It's covered with goo; we'll have to clean it off. And there's . . ." A metal structure as high as his head was sited on the silver-gray surface, where the sharp corner of the restaurant pointed toward the Road. Like the prow of a boat, Jemmy thought. He put his hand on the stained metal casing and asked, "What is this?"

"What's it look like?"

"Casing out of a foundry. It looks like an open hand, round base, splayed fingers."

"Antenna."

"I can open it . . . the inside looks like settler magic. Is this your sign?"

"It's the sign and the lights and anything else that takes power. See if there's anything missing."

"Oh, come on, Barda, I've never seen *anything* like this. . . . All right, here's a slot. Like it takes a great big three-pronged key."

"Fuck my bird! I'm coming up."

So Amnon pushed the door open and they all trouped out on the roof to see what everyone except Jemmy knew all about. They hovered around Barda while she opened the shell and looked in.

She said, "He took it with him!"

"It?"

"Birdfucker!"

Andrew said, "It isn't as if we could go off to town and open another account."

"That birdfucking list is getting *big*," Barda said. "Andrew, whose name would we use? Not mine!"

Andrew laughed. "We're all wanted felons except Jeremy. Jeremy doesn't *have* a name."

"Well, without a guide spot we don't have a sign, and without a sign we don't have an inn."

Guilda's Place in Spiral Town had never needed anything but paint. Jemmy asked, "Guide spot?"

He wasn't heard. "Maybe I can rig something," Duncan Nick said.

Barda made way for him. The shell opened at the edge of the roof. Two could look inside; no more.

"I was up here before, but I did *not* want lights," Duncan said. "Mmm."

"Let me see." But Winnie Maclean wasn't heard either, and she wasn't strong enough to push her way in.

So Jemmy asked her. "Guide spot?"

"It sends back a reflection," Winnie said. "The power beam from Quicksilver goes to four orbiting relays. The relays flash a beam, and all the guide spots flash back. Then the beams focus on all the guide spots. It's a frequency Begley cloth can turn into power. But you buy your guide spot from City Hall and then you're in the records and City Hall keeps track of how much power you use."

"So there's a record in a City computer, and it says this is the Swan," said Denis. "But these things can be hacked."

Barda edged away from the power collector so that others could look it over. Duncan's and Denis's heads and shoulders disappeared inside.

"The Winslows must have retired the account when they moved," Winnie said.

Barda laughed suddenly. "Not Daddy. All the way to Destiny Town, when he's going the other way? I bet he just took the guide spot along and bought someone else's power collector."

Most of this was beyond him, but Jemmy caught that datum as it went by. "You mean the City thinks he's still the Swan."

"I'm guessing, you know."

"So if you got it going again—"

"I worked for a power company," Winnie said. "Let me try."

"The City would just see the Swan using more power? Your daddy would pay a bigger fee. Would he notice?"

"Oh, sure, and complain. But . . . couldn't complain to the City, could he? They like things neat in the City."

"*If* he didn't switch accounts."

Duncan Nick moved out. "It's hopeless," he said. "I could make it work if I had some number-four line wire."

Winnie moved in beside Denis. They whispered crypticisms, their heads hidden. "Don't need number four . . . any gauge line wire . . . isn't that what they use to wire a kitchen? No, it's thinner. . . ."

Watching them wasn't very interesting. They weren't doing anything.

The men picked up chairs and tables and wrestled them inside and downstairs and into the main dining room.

There were chickens in the woods. They were fast, hard to catch. But on the fifth day Winnie found four nests: scrambled eggs for all, cooked in the pottery pots.

On the seventh morning, Willametta saw the bus stop and let people off. Blind luck that she happened to be looking through the picture window. Andrew had set a guard, but he hadn't been taken seriously.

Two men, two women walked across the bridge carrying fishing poles.

Willametta moved about the house whispering the news. Nudes to the upstairs rooms. Amnon to work the garden.

The strangers were in their teens. They wore tiny swimsuits and skimpy vests with lots of pockets. What they saw was Amnon in coveralls, and four older folk in out-of-date short-sleeved windbreakers, carrying poles. Jemmy was one of those.

"Yes, we're reopening the restaurant. Just for dinner. We'd be happy if you'd pass the word."

"What have you got for breakfast?"

"We don't have flour yet. Cold chicken? Tea?"

They turned that down. One man said, "You should open for breakfast too. They come to Swan Lake to fish, you know, and this is the only way in. Cook their fish for them in the evening."

Amnon stayed. Jemmy took the rest to the lake. Behind him he sensed frantic action held leashed.

At the shore they separated. The inlet to Swan Lake was easy to wade. Jemmy tried to keep an eye on the little group on the far shore, but they weren't spending all their time fishing. They let a little tent inflate and spent some of their time in there. They went exploring through the trees.

Earthlife bushes and grass and trees. Earthlife fish. Before noon the felons had caught two dozen fish of three varieties, none of which Jemmy recognized. It made sense to go home then, and they did.

Jemmy dreaded that Andrew would see what he saw: four teens on foot who might have disappeared anywhere between here and the City, with clothes on their backs in current styles and money in their pockets. But he couldn't stay to protect them.

They returned to a great light.

Above the restaurant's roof a flame rose and fluttered in the shape of a Swan.

Jemmy was relieved to see Andrew grinning up into the lighted dining-hall windows. He lofted a mess of fish and got a nod. He asked, "How did you do it?"

"I don't know. Winnie and Denis pulled a nest of line wire out of the ceiling in one of the rooms. You know what that is, a thread of super-conductor in a rubber tube? They'd have been electrocuted if the roof was clean, I think. Nothing worked till they found some silver thing Barda hid in her room and pounded it into shape. But—" He waved. "They got it going!"

"Shouldn't we turn it off? Or are we open?"

"We're open. Let's see, we'll keep that room locked, and clean up the roof so we get more power. All the lights are way too dim. But you, Jemmy, you get a pit fire going. When those kids come back we want to cook their fish for them. And show somebody how to clean fish! *Henry!*"

The visitors stayed for dinner.

Jemmy was a chef on display, with a Road accent, self-consciously not a Spiral Town accent, and, "My merchant father picked me up from the dairy when I was a little boy. . . ."

What the Swan lacked became much clearer. Bread, potatoes, lettuce. They'd have asked for a room until Barda told them there weren't any working toilets. Then they opted for their tent by the lake.

Then they tried to pay the chef.

"You pay Barda. She prefers to keep track." Jemmy sneaked a peek at Destiny Town money before they turned away. It was a hologram imposed onto thin paper.

Barda took their money. They climbed uphill with Swanlight behind them. And Barda gave him an intensive course in how to identify, count, and change money before she let him go to bed.

✳ 26 ✳

The Last Climb

We were chosen for genetic disparity. Now our numbers are down by one-third and we're scattered from Base One to the Winds! How are we going to avoid gene drift?

—Grigori Dudayev, senior M. D.

Next morning was a bleery-eyed scramble. They didn't have to look like a restaurant as long as they didn't look like a prison camp! Four visitors would be returning through here . . . any minute now . . .

They appeared near noon. They'd stayed to fish up a breakfast. Jemmy guessed right: he had coals going, and he'd saved a dozen of Winnie's eggs and several big mushroom caps.

The fishers wanted tea, and were mildly put off because it was herb tea, licorice picked from the spice patch. There was, of course, no bread. Admitting that was embarrassing.

After they were gone Rafik told Barda, "You could have charged them more."

"They'll talk. We want customers," Barda said. "What is an inn with no guests? A birdfucking halfway house!"

Jemmy asked Rafik, "How much whole-wheat flour would that buy?"

"Sack and a half. Last night's take would buy five or six. But we could have charged more," Rafik said, and Andrew's face was growing red with his laughter.

It was a trivial sum, of course. Barda's list had grown:

one full set of decent clothing	600
poured stone, 10 tonnes	2000

glass panes	700
flour	100
silverware	200–1000
paint	500
chairs	up to 2000
tables	up to 4000
soap	100
curtains	500–1000
advertising	???
napkins, cloth	(logo?) 200
washer	5000
cookware:	
stew pots	50
teapot	20
butcher's table!	1500 or make one
tea	
guide spot and power account	8850
line wire	4000

When Jemmy went to fetch wood for the pit, Andrew was there. "I found grain," he said.

"What, you mean before we crossed the last ridge?"

"Well, yes, in that last valley, but not where you were. We followed you on the ridge. Just before the sun came up I was looking back. It was all yellow. Earthlife yellow. It's not far from the Swan. I can show you."

"What kind of grain?"

"Two or three kinds. I went back to check, day before yesterday. Grain. Why would the settlers bring anything that looks that much like wheat and isn't?"

Jemmy thought it over while he and Andrew collected deadwood. They'd been here nine days, and they hadn't had to chop down trees for firewood, but the day would come.

He said, "Then all we need is a mill."

"I'll show you next time I go out, you want to come." Andrew moved off, dragging a log.

There was just too much wrong with that.

Grain: right. Barda's daddy, or his daddy or his, *would* have planted wheat and rye around the Swan. But it was a great find. Why wasn't Andrew taking the credit in his usual booming voice? Or demanding some favor in return? And when had he had the chance to check it out?

He found Willametta on the hill above the Swan. "Willya? Did you see any grain hereabouts before you got to the inn?"

Willametta looked around. Her windbreaker had become a bag for onions and mushrooms. "I didn't."

"Did Andrew?"

"No. Why?"

"Any idea where Duncan's got to?"

She'd seen his worry. "It's all going fine, isn't it? Why are you turning weird now? I haven't seen Duncan Nick since breakfast."

"Maybe I started weird. How would you like to go to Destiny Town?"

"What?"

"Somebody has to buy stuff. It sure isn't me, not with this accent!"

She smiled. "I guess I could stay out of trouble. Do I look like a living woman now?"

"Close. Let's test that." He took the bag she'd made of her windbreaker and set it down.

"Jeremy, Destiny people won't *see* this much of me."

"Speaking for the felons assembled, we're relieved to hear it."

Conversation deteriorated.

Winnie looked into the wood, grinned at them, and passed on. Then dashed back, scooped up Willametta's windbreaker, and ran away laughing. They were in no condition to chase her down.

Too many of them had spent too much of the day arguing possibilities. Nevertheless the arguments had culled Barda's list into what they needed most that cost least. By the red light of evening's coals it had all evolved into a plan.

Someone was going to have to go into town.

At some point that person had become Andrew.

He was going alone. "You were right, Jeremy. One of us is just skinny. Two together look like walking dead."

"Our bones aren't showing through so much now," Jemmy agreed. "You can pass. Most of us could."

"But not you. You'd make a mistake."

"Not Barda either. Barda, the places that sell supplies for an inn would all know your face."

Barda grinned. "They'd all tell me how wonderful I look. All that lost weight." She looked down at her windbreaker. It was too dark to see food stains, but she said, "I'd kill a prole for a stack of napkins."

"How high?"

Felons were tottering off to their beds. Duncan Nick wasn't among them. Duncan hadn't come to dinner. Jemmy hadn't seen him since breakfast. It bothered him most because he'd been expecting it.

Andrew said, "Come with me at dawn, I'll show you where the grain is."

He'd been expecting that too. "Not dawn," Jemmy said. "I'll clean up from dinner and set up breakfast first. I'll start after that and catch up."

They went into the inn. They left the hall lights on all the time now. Unbelievable luxury, and Spiral Town saw none of it. Felons and merchants took it for granted, and nobody wondered why, nobody but Jemmy Bloocher.

The ninth day had a lid of dark clouds.

Jemmy watched Andrew leave. His pack looked heavy. Jemmy waved; but there were things he had to do before he set off after Andrew.

Cleaning out the pit wasn't one. Those ashes would get to be too much of a good thing, but for now they were authentication of the restaurant's age.

There were squirrels and songbirds about. They did some of the cleaning up of spilled food. When Jemmy, Amnon, and Winnie finished the job, they left scraps in the wood.

Curious looks followed his departure. His pack was light. He'd hidden the gathering's trove of speckles. He didn't want to be carrying *that* down the Road.

He crossed the bridge and moved immediately to the center of the Road.

The river ran on his right, chuckling unseen. Jemmy moved briefly to its edge: a curve of melted rock flowing straight down into rushing water. He moved back to center. He'd considered climbing to the ridge, but that would have slowed him, and . . . he could be overreacting. Seeing murder in every face.

Willametta was no creature of evil. She would have been free of the Windfarm in less than a year. She'd followed Andrew for love, it seemed.

And Winnie's story, told by others, was that she'd killed a man because it was the only way to be rid of him. She had scars and broken bones to show for their time together, and he'd stalked her after she ran to Destiny Town. Maybe Destiny justice would have imprisoned him. Maybe she'd kill quicker next time a man gave her a hard time. She was probably no threat to a man like Jemmy.

Barda would never do anything to hurt the Swan.

But the Windfarmers *were* felons. Duncan Nick was legitimately a thief, and Dolores's first impulse had been to use a prole gun on the toolshed, and Andrew Dowd—

Murder in every face.

The Road straightened after a time. Now Jemmy could see several klicks ahead, though a dip hid part of it. Then he was over the dip, watching Andrew hike along the river's edge. Now, by a small black-bronze tree, he stopped and looked down into the water.

Then moved on.

Jemmy followed. Andrew must have expected Jemmy to start later. He hadn't looked back. Jemmy lost him around a curve, and couldn't see him when that stretch of Road reappeared.

The Road stayed a steady twenty-five meters wide, with a jagged bluff on the left, river and bluff on the right.

Where he'd seen Andrew stop, Jemmy, with his breath gone fast and the hairs rising on his neck, edged to the water and looked down.

The rock was split. A Destiny fisher tree's oversized roots were prying the rock apart. Jemmy moved back to center and, after a moment, kept walking.

Left and ahead, the red rock turned ragged and jagged: a steep slope with deep cracks half-filled with loose landslide-shattered rock. Okay. Jemmy called, "Hoy, Andrew!"

No answer came, but Jemmy turned in a quick circle, and Andrew was ten meters behind him, laughing. "How on Earth did you get past me?"

"Don't know. Did you stop for lunch?"

"No, a quick dip." Andrew strolled toward Jemmy. But his hair was dry, and Jemmy turned and ran straight at the red rock cliff.

Finding Andrew behind him had been a shock, but he'd already picked his path and he took it now, straight up the cliff, avoiding the loose rock. He didn't look back until he reached a flat spot as wide as his foot. Andrew was just below him and climbing fast, his pack swinging like something heavy and broken.

Jemmy climbed, breathing hard through a grin. He'd done this the whole length of the Crab. He could see his path, and there wasn't any better on this stretch.

A hundred and twenty meters up, the rock turned sheer. He edged sideways toward a heap of shattered rock standing at a forty-degree slope. He paused there to glance back.

Andrew paused too, blowing hard, teeth showing in a laugh. He shouted, "I thought you brought the lunch!"

"Just a watermelon," Jemmy called. "Hope you brought a knife!"

"You bet!"

"Seen Duncan lately?"

"Lately, yes!" Andrew lunged toward him, panting like a bellows now, across red rock and onto red scree. Jemmy climbed with some care. He thought he could climb faster than Andrew, but a slide would be bad . . . might be bad for Andrew too, but the game was to *live.*

The peak of the rockslide was sheer again but for a notch of sorts, a setting for his feet and a hold for his left hand. Jemmy set himself before he looked back.

Andrew was far below and making little progress.

Jemmy threw a rock at him. Then another, and another, without waiting.

They fell in front of Andrew, all three. He wasn't throwing hard enough, but his aim was good. Andrew screamed something foul . . . fowl, actually. Jemmy caught the echo.

Jemmy screamed back, "It's the law!," and he set himself and hurled. Andrew threw too, but his rock fell far short. His second throw started him sliding, and he flattened himself against the scree and tried to stay there. Jemmy's falling rock hit him—somewhere—and so did the next, and Jemmy threw three more before he had to stop for breath.

Andrew was sliding. He couldn't stop. Jemmy hadn't planned on that.

By now Andrew Dowd might have come to believe the unbelievable: that Jemmy Bloocher could beat him at climbing. If the slide didn't kill him, Andrew would have a chance to rest, to hide, to run now and kill him later.

There was just no help for it. Jemmy spread himself as flat as possible and crawled backward down the scree.

Andrew was out of sight. He couldn't have edged off the scree, though. Last time Jemmy saw him, those rocks were carrying him right to the bottom. Now Jemmy edged off to the side, onto solid rock, and looked down. Andrew was far below.

Jemmy began throwing.

Andrew got a little farther. But the rocks were hitting him, and he *had* to strike back. It was in his bones. He scrambled backward and reached bottom in a near landslide, crawled out from under, braced himself against a rock projection and started throwing.

It was not a fair contest.

Andrew gave up: turned his face to the rock and took the hits, and suddenly leapt up and threw three, and curled up again. Jemmy, with his arm hanging like a lead weight, started down.

He hadn't picked the quickest path this time, but the route that would keep Andrew in sight. Wherever he could stop he threw a rock. At the end he was walking toward Andrew, *knowing* that Andrew would uncurl and charge him with that great weed cutter they'd found in the outbuilding. He stopped out of knife's range and threw rocks from point blank until he knew that Andrew was dead.

The weed cutter was under him.

The pack wasn't on him. He pulled Andrew's body out of sight from the Road, rolled some rocks over it and left it there.

Jemmy found the pack when he'd nearly reached the Road. Andrew hadn't tried to hide it. He never expected Jemmy to live to find it, and he'd wanted to be rid of the weight.

Winnie and Amnon were doing nothing much at the bridge. Jemmy stopped in the middle and spilled the pack in front of them.

Winnie said "Yeep!" and covered her mouth. Amnon said, "What in . . . isn't that *Andrew's* . . . no birdfucking allowed."

"It's the law. I thought you'd better see this," Jemmy said. "I don't recognize most of it. Is *this* what I think it is?" He held up a stack of thin paper printed with holograms: little windows into a composite view of Sol system, sun and planets and moons blazing against black.

"It's money," Winnie said.

Jemmy fished among half-familiar things. A wide silver belt buckle. Handfuls of rings and ear crescents, jeweled and elaborately shaped. A tiny statue group: old men and a kibbitzer around a chess set, in inset jade. A malachite cube. "What's this? And this, and this?"

"I never actually saw—"

"That's a phone."

"Oh."

"And I think that's a book, an old holy book. And that's a lighter."

At a touch, a point on the lighter turned white hot. Jemmy kept it. "All right. We have to give the rest of this to Barda. Will you come with me?"

Amnon said, "We're supposed to be guarding—"

"I'll stay," Winnie said. "You go, Amnon."

"That's Andrew's pack," Amnon said.

Jemmy repacked the pack, holding out the malachite cube and two ear crescents. He said, "Not anymore. Andrew tried to kill me. I won."

"Andrew's *dead?*"

Jemmy looked at Amnon. He hadn't considered the big man a threat. "How do you feel about that?"

Amnon rubbed his jaw. "I guess we all knew he'd try to kill you. That stuff with the prole gun. You won?"

"Yeah. Winnie, here." He gave her the ear crescent and helped her fit it. "You shouldn't wear it much. Maybe not at all. In Destiny Town they might know where it came from. Here, well, you know."

"Thank you." She kissed him.

Once upon a time . . . twelve days ago? . . . Amnon had handed a monstrous weapon back to Jemmy. And Jemmy *had* to trust someone. "Amnon, I want to look uphill for . . . something, and then I want to talk to Barda. Will you come? I'm afraid to be alone."

Jemmy stopped at the big outbuilding. He'd hidden the communal speckles and some personal stuff in the bushes around back. He collected them now, and picked up a shovel.

Then up toward the lake.

The fresh new outhouses were closer to the inn than the old ones. Jemmy wondered if that was a mistake. Today they were conveniently close. In a few years, when they got ripe . . . or when the pit began leaking into the groundwater . . . and so his mind was led to the old outhouse middens.

Here, the men's. Now, where had the fem's gotten to? His nose led him to a patch of bare earth. He called, "Amnon, did someone set you to filling this in?"

Amnon shook his head. He was standing well back.

Now, who would have done hard labor here without first trying to get Amnon to do it?

Jemmy dug. The smell drove Amnon farther back.

He hadn't dug far when he uncovered a hand. He cleared enough to find Duncan Nick's face. The shovel set the head flopping loose.

"Amnon, his throat's cut. Take my word?"

"Sure!"

"I want to cover this up and leave it alone, at least till we talk to Barda. Got a better idea?"

"Want help?"

"No. You do everything else around here." He shoveled the dirt back. Not too deep. Now where was Amnon? Standing well back, maybe retching a little; trying to ignore the whole scene, stench and all.

Jemmy stooped over his pack. His back was to Amnon. He fished into the speckles bag and flung a handful of speckles over the mound;

closed the bag and swung the pack onto his shoulders in a smooth turn that brought Amnon into view. Amnon had noticed nothing.

"Amnon?" He gave Amnon the malachite cube. "You heard what I told Winnie. Don't show it around."

"Okay. What if I wanted the rest of what's in there?"

Jemmy laughed. "Well, you've already got a shovel."

You had to trust somebody.

Barda was in the kitchen, and every cabinet was open. "Just wondering where to put things," she said, and looked around. "Isn't that . . . ?"

Jemmy spilled the contents of the pack across the kitchen floor. "You tell me. Is that Duncan's loot?"

She stared. "No birdfucking allowed!"

"It's the law."

"Yes. Yes, of *course* it must be . . . that birdfucker must have hidden it here, and then they took him off to the Windfarm. Of *course* he wanted us back here. With just the *least* of that we could have . . . Jemmy, tell me what happened."

Jemmy told it. Barda listened with a face like stone. At one point she asked, "Andrew just *strolled* toward you and you scrambled up a cliff?"

"I did."

"But *why?* I mean, *yes*, I remember you argued about the prole gun, but we *all* stopped him killing the ones who wouldn't go. Jemmy, what will we do without Andrew?" Barda wondered miserably.

She looked up. "Sorry."

Jemmy said, "Here's how I saw it. Andrew can't kill the chef and still keep the Swan going. What would he have if he didn't have the Swan?"

He waved at the treasure heaped on the floor. "Every time you cried about not having the money for something to make the Swan a real inn, I saw Duncan Nick not saying anything. The rest of us all said something inane. Duncan Nick and his friends with no names hid out here after they robbed some houses. One of them might have it, or your proles might have the loot, or they gave it back to the owners. Or maybe Duncan Nick hid it at the Swan. And maybe Duncan told you in private . . . ?"

Barda shook her head.

"Or told Andrew? Then you'd have money and we'd all be set. But that isn't what happened. Duncan took seven days to get himself a little less pale, a little better fed.

"Now, Andrew knew Duncan much better than I do. If *I* could see all that, *Andrew* might just wait for Duncan to grab the loot and run.

"I saw Duncan missing for a day. I saw Andrew set off for town to buy supplies. They'd have to come back in his pack, of course. So why was his pack already full of heavy stuff? And he'd set me up to join him, alone. He was clearing up a loose end, Barda."

"So you lay in wait."

"Barda, *he* was lying in wait, and I thought I knew where, and I *still* missed him. He must have been under the roots on the fisher tree."

She studied him a little longer, then said, "You're rich now. You could . . . why didn't you run?"

"Where?"

"All right. Thank you. Thank you for bringing it all back."

"Duncan's in the old fem latrine pit with his throat cut. We covered it up again. It's none of the Parole Board's business."

"No."

"Someone still has to go in and buy supplies," Jemmy said. "Amnon and Winnie?"

"You told them both about this. Why?"

"I wanted someone with me when I brought you this. I thought maybe you'd do anything for the inn."

"Such as?"

"It's early," Jemmy said. "I'm going to get some fish for dinner." He set Andrew's pack beside the loot of three houses, and left. Barda's eyes bored into his back.

He still didn't *know*.

If Andrew was to be sent to Destiny Town with everybody's money, then Andrew had to want to come back. He had authority here, and nowhere else. Still . . . would Barda have offered him more? Say, the life of a man who snatched a gun away from him?

Jemmy didn't know, and it wasn't ever going to matter.

He passed a few people, and waved and went on. The men's old cesspit hadn't been filled in. Jemmy stopped and sprinkled speckles around the edge, and was reminded that he couldn't leave yet.

When he reached the lake, Willametta Haines was perched on a perfect rounded white rock, fishing. Jemmy took up position beside her. He handed her the speckles bag. "Would you take this, please?"

"Why? You're the chef."

"Accidents happen. I don't want to get it wet."

She took it. "What're you doing?"

"Going to circle the lake."

"Want company?"

He said, "Sure." Then he handed her an ear crescent, a tiny snake made of silver wire.

"Where did you get this?"

He fitted it onto her, and then he told her.

She scrambled backward. A safe distance away, she threw the ear crescent at the lake water and ran.

He waited until she was out of sight. Then he kept walking, around the lake and uphill. He kept the pole, awkward as it was. There would be lakes and rivers.

He didn't expect to be hunted. *Jemmy Bloocher disappears after admitting that he's killed the trusty.* Did he run? Or did someone take offense? Who cares? But anyone who tried to follow Jemmy would surely expect to find him on the Road.

Uphill he climbed. Swan Lake nestled in another wrinkle in the fabric of the land, another crest with another valley beyond. From the crest he could look into the next valley. Earthlife colors, then Destiny black along the bottom, then Earthlife again.

That day and the next three, he stuck to the crest. He made forays into the valley to hunt and gather. In time he descended to the Road. When he met the caravan he was welcome: he had money. He'd saved out half before he gave the rest to Barda.

✳ Part Three ✳

✳ 27 ✳

W a v e   R i d e r

The Otterfolk enjoy boat rides. We want to try a mixed crew.
                    —Willow Granger, Xenobiology, *Cavorite*

Jeremy Winslow had shaped a reclining chair for himself out of sand.

Out beyond the waves, blue and white water sparkled and flashed. A tiny pale shape bobbed up and down. Chloe was sitting on a board with her back to Jeremy, surrounded by small dark shell-topped heads.

It was off season. Wave Rider's clientele might think that they came for the Otterfolk, but they came for each other's company too. When a caravan wasn't in, nobody else came either. The folk who tended Wave Rider could all relax a little.

Only a little. Entropy ran fast at the shoreline, and Barbara Barenblatt had brought a large family: a husband, four young children, and a sister doubling as baby-sitter, all in the three-back suite. Barry and Brenda were cleaning it up while they were out; Brenda's husband, Lloyd, had gone yesterday for supplies, and he'd seen Karen tending a cauldron of soup.

And Jeremy was nursing a twisted knee, but it wouldn't keep him idle forever. He was shelling peas under a net to keep sand out. His hands moved without distracting him much.

Out beyond Chloe, the water humped. Chloe saw it. She was paddling, turning. Small heads popped up around her, a dozen, twenty. The hump in the ocean rolled toward her. Chloe paddled madly. Jeremy watched, nodding. Good, good, you're on, good, stand *now*.

She stood. The board slid down the water slope in a flurry of Otterfolk. When Chloe veered they all veered.

No surfboard *ever* hit an Otterfolk.

The wave was breaking, and she skimmed away under the falling water. Otterfolk got lost, or let the wave roll over them just for the hell of it. A few were almost keeping up.

She looked good, his sister-in-law. He'd taught her to ride these waves. He'd be riding again after his knee healed. At forty-seven years of age, he couldn't expect that to happen fast.

Behind him, not loud, Jeremy heard a metallic thump and a high-pitched *yip*.

A moment to realize how queer that sound was. Another to wait for the yell of reassurance that didn't come. Then he was hop-running up-hill, cane stabbing sand, right arm windmilling for balance.

He saw Karen, and he bellowed, "Barry! Brenda! Help!"

Karen had set the cauldron in a frame above the pit, in the sand below Wave Rider. The cauldron was on its side. He could see where chowder had spilled down Karen's right side, shoulder to hip and elbow.

"Barrbarrbarreee! Brenbrenbrendaaa!"

Her face was twisted in terror. Why wasn't she screaming? He shied from the answer: the nerves must have been seared lifeless. He got under Karen's shoulder, her *left* shoulder, just as she started to collapse. His own scream rose to incoherent agony as his knee buckled under her weight.

Brenda came running.

Jeremy was down on his knee, still supporting Karen. "Don't touch her where she's burned! Get under her *here*, here where I am, okay?" He transferred his burden. Karen was moaning. She'd started to realize how bad it was. She wasn't able to stand.

"Get her up to the inn!" Jeremy limped uphill, up sixty meters of old wooden stairs, shouting every few steps. "Barrbarrbarreee!"

"*What?* I was stowing meat and veggies." Lloyd was back.

Good! "Get ice! All the ice! Karen's been burned! Barrbarrbarreee!"

Lloyd disappeared.

Jeremy continued his hop-jump progress up the stairs from the beach, through Reception and into the kitchen. Lloyd had poured several pounds of ice over a towel in the sink. He rolled the towel up and rushed past Jeremy.

Brenda and Karen had reached the landing outside Reception. Karen was whimpering; her eyes rolled. A patch of skin on her upper arm had *slipped*. Lloyd and Brenda eased her down to the wood floor and settled the ice-filled towel across her. Jeremy slid a pillow under her knees.

Brenda asked, "Did you call anyone?"

Call? "Lloyd—" *Phone?* "No."

Brenda ran inside.

Karen wanted to hold his hand. He told her, "Don't worry. Brenda must be calling the City. What happened?"

"It was tipping over. I tried to stop it."

"Should have called me."

"No time. Your knee."

"Someone."

"I know." Her eyes closed, her hand went slack.

He found Brenda in Reception talking to the settler-magic box in her hand. "Karen Winslow. Wave Rider Inn. Got it?" The little projector behind the desk flashed white-on-blue print into the air and she said, "Yes. I'm her daughter, Brenda Winslow, but she'll probably come in with Daddy, Jeremy Winslow. That's right—" The air blinked ruby script at her, and she frowned. "Daddy? When were you born?"

"Twenty-seven eleven." The truth. He didn't know a better answer.

"Where?"

"Skip it."

"Haven on the Crab, *I* remember. Daddy, they're having trouble finding your credit references."

Jeremy Winslow didn't answer. Brenda said, "You came here, so you took Mom's name. Would they have your name from before?"

"I hope not."

"Jeremy Hearst. Dad?"

"They won't find me."

His daughter gave him a long, hard stare. Then she told the phone, "Try Barry Winslow. Uncle Barry, Karen Winslow's brother." The screen flashed. "Yes, that's right. Daddy, see if you can find Uncle Barry!"

Jeremy hop-jumped away. He heard Brenda's voice continue behind him. "Yes, I'll have him phone and give you a reference, but send an ambulance *now*. She's burned over half her body! When can we expect . . . ?"

Barry was up two flights of stairs, making dust. Jeremy had to go up after him. Wave Rider had a high noise level. You got to where you barely heard the crashing waves, but you couldn't hear someone shouting either.

Barry moved fast for his age. Jeremy followed him down slowly, favoring the knee that hadn't worked right since the surfing accident. When he was alone, he let his face have its way.

His face wanted a twitching, teeth-clenching *rictus sardonicus*. His hands wanted to tear the banister apart. What was he going to tell Brenda? Or, when he must, *Karen?*

Whatever he told his daughter, he'd have to tell them all. Barry and Chloe would demand to know what was up, and they weren't just his in-laws, they owned part of the restaurant. He didn't see his other children much.

Harlow? Earth, he would have liked to talk to her! His stepmother-in-law hadn't quite got along with Harold's children. After Harold's death she'd sold them what she owned of Wave Rider, not quite of her own choice. She ran a candle shop in Destiny Town itself, out of Jeremy's reach.

When Karen had survived this horror, *she* would have to know.

So he'd better build a story, Jeremy thought, gripping the railing as he limped down the stairs.

He'd *had* a story. It had bought him twenty-seven good years.

They were clustered around Karen when he got down, trying to explain the matter to Chloe and six hotel guests. Asham Barenblatt offered to use his credit reference, but Barry was already on the phone giving his. Karen had been given pills. The way she looked frightened him.

Brenda looked at him and said, "Daddy, the ambulance will be hours getting here. I have to pack. You should pack for Mother."

"I told Medical the same as you used to tell *us*," Brenda said. She moved briskly about Karen's bedroom, stuffing clothing into the case with unnecessary force, not looking at her father. "Born at *Haven* on the Crab, little place with *six* families. Your mother, *my grandmother*, died. You were *three*. Your father came by with the spring caravan and took you. Randall Hearst of Hearst wagon. But Medical's got no record of any of that!"

"It's fiction."

"Didn't you tell Mother there was no documentation? Father dead, stepmother never got to it?"

"It's fiction. Randall Hearst, he's a merchant I barely met when we traded off at the Neck. He wouldn't know me . . . well, he might. Haven's real. Carnot wagon's real too. I'm from Spiral Town."

Brenda hugged a double armful of blouses to her, and stared. "You mean *literally* Spiral Town?"

"Literally."

"Nobody leaves Spiral Town."

"I had to. I shot a man. It was an accident. . . ." He told her the tale. Marriage in Twerdahl Town. The caravan's long, leisurely trek down the Road. The quick, terrible trip back. Adrift aboard Carder's Boat. . . .

There were tears running down Brenda's face, but she'd finished packing. They left the cases in the hall and crossed to her own bedroom.

He spoke little of the Windfarm, but she knew more. Every child of the mainland studied speckles biology and the biology of the Winds.

When he told of birds killing Shimon, she held her breath. When he came to the fight with Andrew, she was looking at her father with horror and fascination.

"You *killed* him?"

"Yes."

"How?"

"I threw rocks."

He wasn't proud of giving away Duncan's twice-stolen loot. He skipped that, and he skipped over what he'd done with the speckles, though he'd already told Brenda enough to put him back in the Winds. He said only, "I kept out a handful for the Road and gave the pouch to Willametta. Then I walked out. Four days later I was looking down from the ridge at the autumn caravan. It was down to six wagons pulled by tugs. I bit my tongue trying to look nonchalant. They'd have arrested me anyway, scruffy as I was, if I hadn't had the fishing pole and fish to share around.

"I bought some clothes and a haircut and a bar of soap, enough to make me look civilized. I went on up the Road to the Wave Rider and asked for a job. Your grandfather turned me down."

"I thought—"

"No, he turned me down. I knew a lot about Harold from listening to Barda. I thought I could push his buttons. But your grandmother had died and Harold was married again. Harlow met me at the door. I thought she must be Barda's sister Karen. Maybe Harold Winslow didn't like how I looked at his wife.

"So I camped on the beach a little down from Wave Rider. I set up a pit barbecue. Ate a couple of meals at Wave Rider while the money held out. I swam with Otterfolk—"

"Weren't you afraid they'd remember you?"

"Otterfolk don't travel. I'm not even sure this bunch could *breed* with Otterfolk around the curve of the bay." But he'd learned that much later, and he added, "Sure I was nervous. But they didn't know me and they liked playing with me. Harold's family, they never got time. It's part of the bargain, Brenda. They like us. They're interested. They want to play with us.

"I think Harold's poor overworked family nagged him into hiring *someone*, and I was there. Temporary, he said. He kept boards for guests. I taught Harlow how to ride a board, then some of the others tried it—"

"And you told them a story."

"Yeah, I told my tale of a caravan trader and his Roadside son, and I stuck to it. Brenda, I know what happens to anyone crossing the Neck.

They shoot him. I do not know what they do to an island shy who lives among them for twenty-seven years."

There was noise outside the windows, from the Road. They looked out. A tug pulled up towing a boxy vehicle marked with a red cross.

Jeremy hop-limped down the stairs in Brenda's wake.

They were carrying Karen out. She was quiet . . . she looked dead. The medics stopped so that he could see she was breathing: raggedly, but breathing.

"No, Daddy's not going, I'm going with her," Brenda told them. She put the cases in the ambulance alongside Karen's stretcher, and Lloyd added his. Lloyd was going with his wife.

Brenda asked, "Can't you visit us?"

"No." There were others listening, so he said, "I've got to take care of the inn."

Chloe and Barry began to assure him that they could handle that, it was slack season, they didn't depend on the cookpit . . . but Brenda and Lloyd climbed into the ambulance, Jeremy waved it away, and it moved off.

Asham Barenblatt and his family boarded the outbound bus the next day.

Jeremy wondered where they'd stay. Outbound was the spaceport itself, and beyond that, the caravans. Barbara Barenblatt worked at the spaceport that was somewhere up the Road. She couldn't leave during the fine weather season.

There must be facilities for rebuilding the wagons. Maybe they'd stay there.

Now the inn was empty of tenants. They closed all the upstairs windows pending the next caravan's arrival in fourteen days. Chloe and Barry took up the slack. Nobody expected very much of the pit chef, but he could cook for the rest.

For years Jeremy had watched shuttles streak overhead like slow and vivid meteors, until one day Karen told him that the spaceport was just around the bluff to the east. All he had to do was paddle out on a board, and watch.

The shuttles always came out of the west, always came down tens of klicks short of the Neck. Jeremy remembered seeing a takeoff when he was nearing the Neck; but yutzes who thought they'd seen spacecraft reentering above them on the Crab had seen only meteors.

The shuttles came down on inverted, nearly invisible flames that flared yellow when they touched the water. Then a boat went out with a line, and the craft, bobbing like a top, was winched to the beach where tracks and a pair of big bulbous structures waited.

Jeremy couldn't get any closer because people in boats would come out to yell at him.

Barbara Barenblatt wouldn't talk about what she did there. Asham wouldn't talk about it. But Jeremy had mentioned his pilot stepson to the Barenblatt children, and maybe they knew something . . . and now they'd gone.

Guild secrets. The spaceport stretched from the Road to the beach, Jeremy believed; but a high wall hid all of that from the Road, and boats guarded the beach. They didn't like gawkers from Wave Rider risking cremation under a shuttle flame. The far side of the spaceport was a long white line of beach, just visible some days, and then, invisibly far, the Neck. Caravan country, and they didn't want company either.

He knelt at the edge of the pier, water lapping just below his knees, and reached out with a slice of sweet potato. Three flattish heads popped up.

"Winston," he said, and one of the Otterfolk took the sweet potato. Short arms, wide hands with four thick, short fingers.

Jeremy curled and uncurled four fingers, thumb withheld. *Four fish.* He concealed all but the tips of a finger and wiggled those. *Shrimp.*

Winston disappeared without acknowledgment.

He couldn't ride the waves, or even ease off the dock and swim, because they'd swarm around him and bump his leg. When the Otterfolk were happy with him, they'd try to surprise or delight him. Today they'd bring whatever fish were nearest.

He couldn't surf out to watch the shuttles land. Time he gave that up anyway. But what was there to do here but worry about Karen?

He went back inside to a ringing phone.

Jeremy had never gotten used to the phone. He almost never answered its flash and bell. He was only the pit chef, after all; he owned no part of Wave Rider. Barry and Chloe had bought out part of Harlow's share—

Never mind. In the absence of Karen and Brenda, they expected him to answer. "Wave Rider Inn, speak to me."

A young man's head and shoulders, half familiar. Man's voice. "Who've I got?"

"Pit chef Jeremy."

"Karen's man? Brenda talked to Eileen. Yesterday. Dreadful thing. Anything new?"

Jeremy knew him now. Johannes Wheeler had married his eldest daughter Eileen.

Jeremy tried to think: not easy since Karen's accident had shattered his world. "Let's see, they took her to the hospital day before yesterday, and Brenda called this morning. They're treating her as a burn patient, I guess. I don't know medical terms. *Cultured skin transplant?*"

The cameo bust of Johannes stared at him. "Means she's lost huge amounts of skin!"

Jeremy settled to a squat so that he wouldn't faint. Johannes must have noticed. "Hey, hey. They mean *superskin.* They're putting skin *back* from the cultures in Medical. She'll grow it back, Jeremy!"

"Grow it back."

"Why aren't you with her?"

"Somebody had to take care of the inn." Jeremy remembered that these two had bought out part of Harlow's piece of Wave Rider. "Then again, the Barenblatts are gone. Now it's just us."

"Can you handle it?"

"Just barely, with three of us missing." *Tell Eileen I can't come to Destiny Town.*

"Well, I can't get away, but we wondered if Eileen should come early. No? Well, you've got our number. And Brenda says her mother is calling for you, and she says they've found your records."

"*My* records?" Earth, he felt stupid. Karen was half his brain. But what could she have meant?

"You were having trouble with your credit record, I guess, but Brenda says it's all straightened out. Look, if you can get to the hospital, I think you should, and soon. Karen's been asking for you, and Brenda sounded scared."

After he hung up, he stood staring through the empty space above the phone projector. They *found his records?*

Did he dare call Brenda and ask? Brenda was staying with Harlow. They'd given him the number.

. . . Better not. But he knew how to summon a credit check! He typed in

Jeremy Winslow   @99.200@

—a reasonable price for a meal for eight.

Green.

Somehow he was in the computer.

He used the phone once more, to get a schedule for the next bus to Destiny Town.

✳ 28 ✳

D e s t i n y   T o w n

Most species on Earth aren't adventurous. They occupy one habitat, and if it fails, they go extinct. The Otterfolk shouldn't have surprised us. . . .
Maybe most intelligent species can't travel.
—Wayne Parnelli, Marine Biology

A big square bus and the tug pulling it came the next morning. A swing of his arm flagged it down, a gesture Jeremy had seen a thousand times, and never used himself. He climbed up into a box full of indifferent strangers, stowed his backpack, chose a seat.

As soon as Jeremy was settled, it took off at a scary fifty klicks an hour down the Road, straight into the horizon.

When the caravan was in, Wave Rider seethed with strangers. They didn't press this close, though, because too often he was holding something sharp or something hot. At the pit, his word was law, and any strangers about him were in his charge. Here . . . The bus was no more than half-full. They weren't staring, they weren't hostile, yet he couldn't meet their eyes.

He looked out the windows. He got used to the speed and the shaking, and even dozed for a time.

He woke afraid that he'd missed the Swan. But when the bus stopped an hour later, he recognized the bridge. It had a new handrail and new paint. It still sagged almost to the water under a big painted sign: CORSO'S CAMP WAIKIKI.

Six older children crossed the old bridge to the bus. They chattered as the bus moved on. The passengers paid not the slightest attention to a landslide slope not much farther on, site of an old climbing accident never discovered or long forgotten.

277

*   *   *

Terminus was bigger than Twerdahl Town. The buildings were old and blocky and oppressively massive, like nothing he'd seen short of the Windfarm. Still, the town wasn't dying. A street fair was buzzing along the Road. The bus stopped to let a dozen people get off, and near as many got on.

Another hour passed. Here were more houses, then a line of stores. Side streets multiplied. The bus stopped frequently, and now it was easing through foot and bicycle traffic.

You're supposed to have seen it all before.

Nothing he saw stood above three stories. Newer structures had a lighter feel, but as the bus moved deeper into town he saw massive blocky buildings like those in Terminus. It was as if *Cavorite*'s crew built to withstand some terror left behind on old Earth. Coriolis-driven storms spun off from the Winds. Earthshakes.

Guessing, he was guessing. But he was close enough to taste the answers. All the answers! Ticking in the back of his mind was the certainty that he was nearing the end of the Road. How could he have lived so close for so long?

Stop staring!

He'd grown up with as much variety, if not quite the same styles. When traffic slowed, he looked for the oldest buildings to encroach on the Road as they did in Spiral Town.

The shops along this part of the Road were marked by signs; few had holograms, and those were faint in daylight. The glowing ghost of a man-high fur hat caught his attention. The hologram letters were too dim to read, but there was a painted sign too. ROMANOFF.

The Road curved gently right, then gently left. Still the buildings stood well clear of the Road.

Jeremy suddenly realized that he was looking up at the curving hull of *Cavorite*, so close that he couldn't see the top, but only what he had taken for a cobbled wall: the lander's lava-spattered ground-effect skirt.

Other passengers were staring too. *Cavorite!*

The end of the Road was a loop, and *Cavorite* was the middle of it. Like *Columbiad* in Destiny Town, the lander stood among smaller structures, in a lava dish of its own melting. There was a fence around it.

Traffic was clogged here, but only because there was so much of it. Nothing blocked the Road. Building must have been restricted from the beginning.

He had wondered whether it would be safe to ask directions. No need. Faded holograms marked three buildings of ancient poured stone, all with big glass windows. *Medical, Medical, Medical.*

The bus stopped. With his case on his back and a cane in his hand, Jeremy climbed down to the Road.

Closer, he could read more.

Medical: Reception and Records
Medical: Intensive Care and Surgery
Medical: Outpatient and Recovery

He stagger-stepped into the leftmost building.

A narrow-faced woman his own age looked up. What she wore was likely a uniform, white with scarlet markings:

Lisa Schiavo
Reception
Duty Doctor

He was the last thing she wanted to see. "Patient?"

He said, "I'm here to see Karen Winslow."

She repeated, "Patient?"

"Yes. Emergency, burn patient, four days ago."

"Family only." Her brows furrowed: puzzled at the Spiral Town accent that he'd thought long lost.

"I'm Jeremy Winslow," he said more carefully. "Karen's husband."

She said, "Okay. Okay. We're all speckles-shy here today, and the reason is, the computer went out about quitting time yesterday." Her hands shuffled a stack of printouts, helplessly. "We spent the whole morning trying to keep track with notes on paper. Now we're using the library computer, and that's where you'll find out where your wife is. Through that door and up three floors. There's a lift. Wait. What's wrong with your leg?"

"I hurt my knee surfing."

"Really. Wonderful. *Brendan!*"

Nothing happened immediately. Schiavo said, "Sit *down*. How long ago?"

"Almost three weeks." He sat down.

"Is it healing all right?"

"I suppose."

"Come back after you see your wife. I'll have Brendan scan you. Here." She handed him a card. "Your wife's name, address, age, and whatever you remember about her medical history."

Jeremy began writing.

A barrel-shaped man jogged in. *"Ja, mein Führer!"* His uniform was very like Schiavo's, with a label that read:

Brendan Shaw
Surgery
Duty Doctor

"Brendan, want some exercise?"

"Run up to the library?"

"Yeah, find out where they're keeping a burn patient and get her status. Karen Winslow. You *could* take the lift. Who'd know?" She took Jeremy's card, glanced at it, handed it to Brendan.

"I go, effendi!" Brendan jogged out, knees high, arms pumping. He slowed to a walk while in Jeremy's sight, but not Schiavo's.

Schiavo handed him another card. "Fill one out for yourself too." Jeremy filled out what he remembered from his credit rating. Put it in his pocket. Closed his eyes. . . .

Brendan's voice jolted him awake. "Winslow? We've got her in Intensive. Out the door, turn left, it's the next building over, fourth floor, Room Four-ten. Her doctor's Nogales, but she's home today. Come back after you see your wife and we'll scan your knee."

Karen smiled. "Jeremy. Can't move. I can't disturb the skin."

"All right." He went around to her good side and she gripped his hand. The sheet didn't cover much of her. They had her hands tied . . . loosely, and padded, but she couldn't reach herself. The skin over half her body was shiny and patchy. It made him queasy to look, but he could well understand why nothing should touch her skin.

"So good to see you, Jeremy. What kept you?"

"They couldn't find my credit record at first."

Her eyes doubted him. He'd always wondered how much she'd guessed.

He told her how matters stood at Wave Rider. No customers, and a good thing too. Himself, walking around brain-dead with worry. The Otterfolk were getting bored; what they brought in was skimpy. Nine days until the caravaners arrived. She listened . . . dozed. . . .

There was a hand on his shoulder.

He'd gone to sleep with his cheek on Karen's good arm. "Lloyd?"

"Don't wake her."

Karen's hand was slack now, and he disengaged. Their youngest daughter's mate said, "I'll take you back to Gran Harlow's place. It'll hold four for one night."

"Can't go yet. The doctor wants to look at my knee."

"About time."

* * *

Medical was the strangest, scariest place Jeremy Winslow had ever been. He hoped it didn't show. *You're supposed to have seen this before.*

He told Brendan Shaw, "The waves were rolling in from *way* out there. Little shelled heads all around me. I hadn't been out for weeks because the caravan was in. They like it better when you take chances, you know? I caught this *beautiful* curl and rode it till my knees turned to water, and then let it break and carry me till the board hit sand and I lit running. I twisted my knee running in sand. Just too tired."

Brendan Shaw had a hand scanner. He moved it around Jeremy's injured knee, and a hologram showed him the inside. He said, "Well, you tore the meniscus."

"Will it grow back?"

"No." He moved to scan the good knee for comparison. "The meniscus isn't alive, exactly. Your body grows this spongy cushion in your knee joint, and it only grows once. Now there's a piece floating free. When it gets between the bones, that hurts."

"Too right. Can you sew it up?"

Brendan wrapped a blue pad around Jeremy's knee. Jemmy grimaced at the cold, and Brendan grinned. "Yes. First we chill you down. I need to wheel some equipment in here. The groper, a fiber-optic probe, the stitcher, some help . . ." He was thinking out loud. "After that cools a little we'll poke some fiber optics into your knee and look around more. Then we'll position the torn part, which has to be done by hand, sorry, and paint the edges for the stitcher so it can sew them shut. That's not real paint, it just marks them in memory. You got a card for me?"

Just like that? Jeremy's teeth were clenched. The cold burned him, but fear did too. But if he put this off, he'd spend days getting his nerve up . . . card? In his shirt pocket.

Brendan took it. "Lie down and I'll put you out. Or I could give you a local, but most patients don't want to *be* here when this is happening to them."

No telling what he might blurt out while he watched things being poked into his knee. "Put me out."

"Safer, actually."

Jeremy closed his eyes as Shaw settled a skeletal metal structure on his head. Wet pads touched both eyes and the nape of his neck. "Three hundred years old if you figure it was built on Earth, but it still works. Local anesthetic would be a drug. Much cruder."

Jeremy woke up hurting. A bulky cast held his leg stiff and a little bent. A young man handed him pills and a mug of water. Brendan said, "Aspirin. You're not allergic."

"Good. All done?"

"Oh, yeah, two hours ago. You looked like you needed the sleep. Here. Do you know how to use crutches?"

"No, I've got my stick."

"No, use crutches for a few days. Try standing up. Now, the trick— you okay?—the trick is to never put your weight on your armpits. The crutches go there, but your weight is on your arms and hands. Crutches move first, then your foot. Steady. Try it again."

"Where's Lloyd?"

"Let's go see."

Brendan darted down a hall. Jemmy followed. Crutches, right foot, crutches—he felt unstable. His knee hurt like fury. Brendan darted back. "Lloyd Winslow? He's got your pack too."

Lloyd saw Jeremy come in and started to laugh.

The bus stopped in the middle of a block to let them off. Lloyd was chattering. "We thought we'd take you to Romanoff's for dinner tomorrow. After twenty-seven years eating your own cooking? But it's eight blocks from Medical."

Jeremy's wife's father's second wife was Jeremy's age. She was dark with black kinky hair, white showing through now. Her beauty had refined itself. Why she'd married old Harold was something he had never asked. She was too good for him.

Twenty-seven years ago the vision of Harlow standing in the doorway of Wave Rider had gone straight to his glandular system. He'd held himself polite and diffident, a pit chef looking for a job; but what had she seen in his eyes? He'd never asked.

Had Harold been relieved when Jeremy married Karen?

Today . . . she was not much changed, but he knew what she saw from the dismay in her eyes. A young man grown old, fatigued and in pain.

"What on—? I think you'd better have the downstairs," she said. "Used to be an office."

Harlow leased one quarter of a big two-story building of poured stone. The old office was big enough for a bureau and a big futon—big enough for Brenda and Lloyd, but they'd moved upstairs—and an old computer with a dark screen.

Anything he did to his left leg hurt. He crawled down the crutches, maneuvering around the leg's rigidity until his back was on the futon. He didn't move again until Brenda woke him for dinner. Getting up again . . .

Could be worse. He might have lived as a cripple, forever waiting for his knee to heal.

Lloyd's laughter chopped off when Jeremy entered. He said, "Sorry. But they were going to *look* at your knee. You went away with a limp. Next thing, you're staggering in on crutches with your whole leg cased in concrete! It's everything I grew up knowing about Medical. I shouldn't have laughed, Jer, but I *hate* that place."

"I share your pain."

Lloyd laughed wildly. "Well. You're here. Should we go home in the morning?"

This was the part-owner asking the pit chef: *Is there anyone left to run the inn?* Jeremy said, "We're empty. You could take another day or two."

"How's Mommy?" Brenda asked.

Jeremy took his seat. "Hanging on. Brave. Brenda, *I* don't know anything about Destiny Town medicine. You tell me. *How is she?*"

"I could lie to you?"

Only one answer to that. "Sure."

"Daddy, she got badly hurt. We're not wizards. Superskin is old settler magic, but it still has to grow on her."

He'd *known* she could die.

He couldn't speak of that. So: "Brenda, dear, how did they 'find' my identity?"

"Ask Gran Harlow."

Harlow said, "I wrote it in. That computer you're sleeping with, it died before I moved in here, but one of my friends got it going. Brenda told me what to say. Are we likely to be caught in an inconsistency, Jeremy?"

"That story held up for twenty-seven years," he said.

They all seemed to be studying him: a sudden stranger. Harlow asked, "Was it supposed to?"

"What d'you . . . ?" Then he understood. "Harlow, I wasn't sure what I wanted. I needed refuge. I didn't know what was *possible*. Maybe I'd follow the Road the rest of the way to Destiny Town and see where *Cavorite* ended. Maybe I'd go home. Maybe there was a way to serve time in the Winds and come out as a citizen. I didn't know how to *do* any of that, but I thought I knew how to keep a restaurant and get some breathing space."

"So now you've seen *Cavorite.*"

"Yes." He looked at Harlow in wonder. He hadn't known it, here in his bones, until now. "I've seen *Cavorite*. I've seen the end of the Road. Harlow, thank you."

"Is that a big thing?"

"Harlow, what we learn is all wrong. We're told that the Twerdahl contingent got bored. *Cavorite* went off with all the wealth of the colony and was never heard from again, just like *Argos*. I followed the Road all the way down to the Neck, and I found it again in the Winds. *Cavorite's* crew saved Spiral Town. They set up the Windfarm and worked it to grow speckles. They set up the caravans to keep the speckles coming."

"They did more than that," Brenda said.

"Ah?"

"Daddy, do they have teaching machines in Spiral Town?"

"Sure."

"There's a computer in Medical, in the library. Look up *speckles*, Daddy."

✴ 29 ✴

It's the Law

Cavorite calling Base One. We remain camped halfway along Haunted Bay. We've found aquatic animals like little armored Volkswagons. They like to pull things. The sophonts' language seems to be mostly body language. Most of us have swum with them, and Parnelli has made a surfboard.

Will somebody please talk to me? Are you all right? It's been two months since I talked to anything but a damned recording.

—Oliver Carter, Ecology

Moving only her eyes, Karen watched Brenda help Jeremy into a chair. She said, "That limp's getting worse, isn't it? You should go to Medical."

Lloyd laughed himself into tears. They told Karen what had been done to his knee. They talked about Wave Rider, then about his first return to Destiny Town in twenty-seven years. Had he been to see his old home?

Under Brenda's censorious eye he told Karen, "I haven't been anywhere. The bus this morning was a nightmare. Lloyd and Brenda had to get me on and off. I don't think I want to visit *anyplace* before I heal a little."

"Not even *Cavorite?*"

Those first few years he'd talked of burning lights settling on the sea just out of sight; of space and *Argos* and *Cavorite*. Spaceport personnel ate at Wave Rider, but Harold didn't want the pit chef bothering them. In time he dropped the subject. But Karen remembered.

He said, "For *Cavorite* I'd walk on my hands. Would they let me in?"

"I don't know."

"Can just anyone get in there?"

Lloyd said, "Brenda went."

285

"Mustafa took me through," Brenda said. "Pilots get in. Mustafa came to visit while he was in training and I was at Wide Wade's, Daddy. I used to wonder why you never came. If you ask—" She caught herself.

Yes, he could ask his wife's son the shuttle pilot to guide his stepfather through the old lander. But it *was* a risk.

He gave Karen a hand massage, both hands, he and Brenda trading chairs. When he had put her to sleep, Brenda stood up. "When are you going to tell her?"

"When she isn't on drugs. When I figure out how to tell her about her sister Barda. When I think it won't kill her."

"Look up *speckles*. We'll see you at dinner."

He tracked down Dr. Nogales in a third floor office.

> *Rita Nogales*
> *Surgery*
> *Surgeon and Anesthesiologist*

She was reading a computer screen. Jeremy told her, "Karen doesn't look good."

"Karen Winslow?" She tapped at a virtual keyboard. The configuration jumped: a torso with highlighted internal organs, then with highlighted patches of skin; a requisition form; a block of text. Nogales hadn't looked around. "You wouldn't look good either if you'd scalded seventy centimeters of skin off your body. Your wife?"

"That's right."

"We put superskin on. We wait. It's a life-form, you know. Human genes trimmed in some lab in Sol system to make it a universal donor. Wonderful stuff." Now she looked up at him. "We wait. It attaches itself. Eventually the patient gets up and goes home. There are old guys walking around with superskin faces and hands. Women too. You can just barely tell."

He knew her. Narrow head, narrow nose, yellow-brown skin, and Oriental eyes: handsome, but an impatient, angry woman.

He couldn't quite remember, and he couldn't just stare. "I know you've got her on drugs. Is she in a lot of pain?"

"Would be. She's taking Novabliss. With that in her she's happier than you are." Her eyes widened in shock. "No birdfucking allowed!"

Oh.

There being nowhere to run, he said, "It's the law."

"I didn't know you till you smiled. Jeremy . . . *Jemmy*."

"How's Dolores?"

"Died."

"Damn!"

"*I* got pregnant. A man killed her after I wasn't there to protect her."

"Anyone I know?"

"No. I'll know *him*. Everyone comes to Medical sooner or later. *Winslow*, like Barda? Married Barda's . . . sister?"

"Right."

"Clever. Jeremy, anyone could find out I served time in the Windfarm, but I don't call attention to it."

"Sounds good to me."

She was still studying him. "*That's* right, you're a Crab shy! How on Earth did you get here at all? Fake records. What's with the knee?"

He told her. She nodded, nodded, used her keyboard. "Okay, it says you're real, and your credit is midlevel. You can buy dinner but not a restaurant."

"Can I go to the library?"

"The computers see you as a surgery patient. You can use the library while you wait for a doctor. I'll take you away from Brendan, and I can't fit you in for . . . is six hours enough? Then I'll look you over and we can talk."

Lisa Schiavo was on duty in Reception and Recovery. Jeremy watched her for a bit. "Got your computer back?"

"Winslow. How's, ah, Karen?"

"Dr. Nogales won't make any promises."

"She's good that way. I mean, I'm sorry it's bad news, but Nogales won't lie. How's the knee?"

"Dr. Nogales wants to look it over later today. Doctor, is everyone here a doctor? Aren't there any nurses or aides or—?"

"*Doctor* means you're doing something to run a hospital. It's courtesy. Like in a restaurant, saying *Herr'ober* gets you someone who can bring you food or clean your table? It used to mean *headwaiter.* But patients get put on diets, so even the commissary chefs are doctors—Winslow, I've got to work."

"I'd like to wait in the library if you're not using it."

"Log on with your credit ident. Doctors get priority."

Up three floors. Lines of office doors along a corridor, all labeled, all closed. At the end of the hall, an open door.

LIBRARY

He found a dozen comfortable chairs and five screens. One wasn't working. Four were in use. One user looked wasted: his eyes had a glassy look. Patient. Three looked healthy and busy: doctors.

Jeremy sat down and waited placidly. He'd waited twenty-seven years.

The patient nodded off; rapped his forehead on the keyboard, jerked up to see gibberish. Staggered upright and went away.

Jeremy took his place. As his fingertips touched the keyboard, Jeremy's eyes stung with tears, abruptly, unexpectedly. The home he'd lost again and again was his at last. He was back in Spiral Town, eight years old again, and it was time for school.

All *right*. There were things he'd always wondered about. The teaching programs never had enough to satisfy him.

CRAB

There were hundreds of Earthlife varieties. Jeremy could pick one or two that resembled the Crab Peninsula.

OTTER

Earthlife: a mammal, streamlined, with bristly hair. It looked nothing at all like Otterfolk.

OTTERFOLK

Kismet tegumentum lutrahomines, the first intelligent species ever found off Earth.

Otterfolk were curious about humans.

Cavorite's crew loved that. They ran their Road well above Otterfolk beaches for fear that those who came after would meddle. Jeremy found references to species gone extinct because they attracted human attention. But they'd done some meddling themselves.

They'd taught the Otterfolk how to cultivate Earthlife fish and crustacea, and traded them simple tools for fish. That was a success.

They'd set up a cooperative exploring team.

Reference:

OTTERFOLK*EXPLORE*CLIFFSIDE

OTTERFOLK*EXPLORE*BEACHES

The Otterfolk enjoy boat rides. We want to try a mixed crew. Arundez has designed a suitable boat, a catamaran with nets we can drop to block off the central well so that otterfolk can swim during a voyage. . . .

They'd gone exploring together, along the coast and off the back side of the Crab, above and beneath the sea.

Destiny sunlight, reddened and deficient in ultraviolet, still caused skin cancers and blindness in Otterfolk.

Sea life outside Haunted Bay poisoned them. Or attacked them: there were predators worse than lungsharks.

In unfamiliar currents they followed the wrong smells and got lost.

Lower salinity hurt their skins and made them vulnerable to parasites.

To avoid bringing back a nasty skin parasite, the contact crew had euthanized ten Otterfolk and burned the boat.

EUTHANIZE

Kill.

It bothered Jeremy, but the Biology crew had been horrified. Not just the guilt, not just the deaths. An intelligent species that couldn't explore! To men and women who had conquered space—

And seen space ripped from their grasp—

That was obscene.

He flinched from the next entry—

KAREN WINSLOW

Patient records are restricted. Access code?

—relaxed, and tried—

ARGOS

Familiar stuff.

Half a thousand colonists had left Sol system in cold sleep, with twenty crew.

Cold-sleep techniques were two hundred years advanced beyond Avalon's time, but the major advances were diagnostic. Colonists damaged by cranial ice crystals would be, ah, euthanized. A crew member wakened during the voyage must remain thawed.

Far too many were damaged. Three hundred and sixty-six sleepers arrived, and *seventy* crew. Fifty sleepers chosen for skills learned in deep space had been revived to deal with an emergency.

Most of the fifty had lived their lives off Earth. They'd grown up using the resources of an entire solar system. They had flown *Argos* across light-years to a system yet untouched. Asteroid and gas-giant mining techniques were centuries old. Their faith was in *Argos* and their own skills.

They'd expected the colony on Destiny to fail. Destiny's ecology, after all, would have its own agenda.

On arrival, they mutinied.

ARGOS*MUTINY*TRIAL

The facts weren't in dispute. A trial hadn't struck him as silly when he was a boy. Base One's tribunal had found them guilty, and so what? By then the mutineers were elsewhere in the solar system. Their judges were marooned, owning two landers and whatever gear had been judged useless by an exoplanetary community. They were barely able to reach orbit.

ARGOS*DEBRIEF

He'd been through these too: memoirs by crew who chose to remain

with the Destiny colony. Wait, these files had more bulk than Base One's
memoirs. It must include material written after *Cavorite*'s departure. Try
ARGOS*MEMOIRS: TWERDAHL

Restricted material. Access code?

No birdfucking allowed.

ARGOS*SIGHTINGS

Ye gods! Destiny Town had an orbiting telescope!

The Cyclops telescope had gone up a hundred and ninety-one years
ago. First sighting of *Argos* came ten years later; first *verified* sighting,
eleven years. *Argos*'s drive flame was not bright; *Argos* without it was
invisible. But the *Argos* drive flame impacting an asteroid was brilliant
and unmistakable . . . for whatever that was worth. Destiny Town could
only watch. *Cavorite* could reach geosynchronous orbit, but not the
moons, not the planets, not the stars.

Cyclops telescope watched *Argos* establishing a base on the
dumbbell-shaped asteroid called Blake, and verified that *Argos* had kept
faith by this much: they had seeded Quicksilver with a photocollector
factory.

QUICKSILVER*SUNPOWER

In 2689, approaching two centuries after its emplacement, that first
little self-reproducing factory had multiplied enough to be noticed. A
bright patch was visible on the innermost planet, and a trickle of power
was flowing to Destiny.

Power was also being directed toward *Argos*.

Today—2739—Quicksilver's sunward face was covered in silver.
Along the Crab they never knew it had been different. But power flow
toward *Argos* could no longer be detected.

Jeremy kept returning to the blueprints for the self-reproducing factory. Shape of a turtle, mass of a man, size of a small boy. There was a
name for such things: what was it? A factory that could be directed to
make more of itself.

Von Neumann device.

Argos's mutineers had no faith in the planetary colony. Time might
have justified that to their descendants. The colony on Destiny had done
little in a quarter of a millennium. Wait, hadn't he seen a file—
ARGOS*SIGHTINGS

Yes. The last sighting of *Argos* in flight was in 2680, fifty-nine years
ago. And the flow of power from Quicksilver had stopped.

Did *Argos*'s crew still have descendants?

SPECKLES (*FATUM VENTUSI HERBAAE*)

The list of entries ran on and on. What on Earth was

SPECKLES, see also Fatum mortem parnelli
FATUM MORTEM PARNELLI

Destiny krill is a multicelled microscopic life-form that uses photosynthesis, but swims free.

Even on Earth there were organisms that crossed the line between plant and animal.

F. mortem parnelli lives in every part of the ocean thus far explored. It is clearly of the speckles family (*Fatum ventusi herbaae*), though speckles is entirely a plant.

May one speculate? Future archeologists will find the fossil record of a krill eater—one pictures a Destiny blue whale with shell and shellcap—that plowed this world's seas until M. parnelli learned to secrete deadly metals. The krill poisoned them to extinction. Later a Mortem variation evolved on land.

The crucial point here is that Destiny krill secretes potassium. When it dies it sinks to the bottom of the sea. There the potassium remains. After billions of years of that, we find no potassium in Destiny sea salt, and that is why we will die.

—Wayne Parnelli, Marine Biology

Fatum mortem, he'd called it. Destiny's death. Scared the hell of out him, did it?

Jeremy had wondered . . . every child wondered . . . why *Argos* came to Destiny without the means to keep settlers alive. How could the ancient wizards of Sol system have been so *stupid*? But if oceans on Earth had all the potassium they needed . . .

Jeremy almost laughed. That must have been a *nasty* shock.

Look up speckles, but there were so many files. Be selective. Search:
SPECKLES*FARM

A line of sporadic volcanoes four hundred klicks long. Tornadoes. Metals . . . potassium refining . . . speckles . . . thorn trees and thorn weeds, ground-hugging animals and windbirds, a varied and intricate ecology evolved within the Winds, each new species needing classification and further study.

And: If speckles can be farmed elsewhere, we must still extract potassium to feed it. Why bother? We'll grow it here.

Cavorite's course matched his guesses, but what had Brenda meant? *They did more than that.* More than refine potassium, then discover and cultivate speckles, in an endless howling storm full of thorn birds? Then race home. . . .
SPECKLES*TWERDAHL*BASE ONE

He read on, while afternoon darkened to evening.

*   *   *

Base One had delayed *Cavorite*'s departure, had afflicted them with a long list of projects, had repeatedly tried to cancel the expedition. The first settlers had not perceived any need for haste.

A nasty shock, as Jeremy had guessed, following the nasty shock of *Argos*'s betrayal. Base One was in denial.

But, though sea salt would not sustain Base One, Earthlife animals made nerves too. They were good at secreting potassium. Ancient kings had learned to confiscate manure piles at the first sign of war, for nuggets of saltpeter to grind up for gunpowder. But saltpeter—potassium nitrate—could also be ground into food.

So *Cavorite* drifted down the coast at a snail's pace, leaving a snail's trail of molten rock. They would fulfill all of their mission: seed Earthlife wherever they went, pause to sample local life, look for places a village might thrive, investigate signs of what might be intelligence. Let the ungrateful bastards wait and wonder. *Cavorite*'s crew could take their time.

In due time *Cavorite* returned to Base One emptied of Earthlife seeds and infant animals, and loaded with samples of rock and Destiny life, maps, refined potassium and speckles.

What had gone wrong at Base One?

They found plumbing redirected to sterilize sewage with heat, then vent it above croplands. That would have done the job, if the job had been more than ten percent finished! Maybe they were stopped by the stench.

Livestock implied manure. Manure had even been raked into heaps, but the heaps lay untouched. Nobody had picked through them for saltpeter. Then again, there wasn't much. Potassium must first be put into fertilizer to feed the grass! *Grass* didn't make nerves.

As their intelligence dropped, had they forgotten what was at stake?

Cavorite's crew might speculate, but there was nobody to ask. There were nobody at Base One who could still talk coherently.

The records that followed were nearly incoherent with medical jargon. Here Jeremy sensed a rage shared but never expressed. Twerdahl's crew had fed and washed and dressed their former colleagues, dressed the sores and treated the illnesses caused by dirt and randomly deposited sewage, and cleaned up after them until they grew to detest them.

Jeremy found reference to discipline problems, and murky speculation as to what constitutes rape and consent, theft versus custody, murder versus euthanasia, for people who had ceased to be people.

This wasn't in the teaching tapes at Spiral Town! But Barda Winslow had tried to tell him.

Some of the sick ones recovered some of their intelligence, some of their memory. Not all. Central-nervous-system nerves, once dead, don't grow back.

Cavorite's crew came to realize that *they* had become the primary colony on Destiny.

They founded Terminus far enough outside the Winds to escape the continual howling—

"Move it," someone said. Before he could react, someone was handing Jeremy his crutches and lifting him to his feet. "Set?"

"Ah—" *Wait, I want to look up—*

The man sat down. A doctor. He erased Jeremy's file and called up something else.

—Caravans!

If Jeremy's sudden rage showed through, the doctor hadn't seen it. Jeremy was on crutches and still getting his balance, and that was as well. He had time to visit Karen before he saw Rita Nogales.

Karen was awake but a bit fuddled. He tried to tell her what he'd learned about speckles, *Cavorite*, *Argos*, the Windfarm, Destiny Town. She listened. She tried to comfort him, as if he'd suffered a personal injury. Presently she fell asleep.

"Looks good," Nogales said, turning the luminous interior of a human knee before her eyes. "A doctor like Itchy Wald does a neater job, but he spends too much time probing around *in* the joint. Trauma. Brendan is *brisk*. So, stay on crutches and don't do much walking for another day, then maybe we'll take the cast off."

"Would you look in on Karen before you go?"

"Sure."

He started to stand. "I should catch a bus—"

She said, "Wait, wait, wait. You owe me a story."

He sat down. "You owe me, I think. Andrew was going to use the prole gun on you all."

"*No birdfucking allowed!* I *knew* that speckles-shy birdfucker—"

"It's the law—"

"Go *on.*"

"I was expecting it, Rita. He turned around and I yelled and jumped him. The rest piled on. Of course he tried to kill me later. . . ." He told

293

her more than he'd told Brenda, but again he left out the speckles.
". . . I *did* it, I made them into a restaurant before I had to leave, and
now I knew how!"

Running from the Swan, Jemmy Bloocher might have begged a ride
from the inbound caravan. Go to Destiny Town, the end of the Road,
Cavorite. In the instant that was possible, he'd remembered what the
Windfarmers had called him.

Crab shy. A stranger in a place where he didn't understand the rules.
He'd done that before. And generally messed it up.

He'd gone outbound instead.

From Barda's description he'd had no trouble finding Wave Rider.
"All I had to do was get Harold Winslow to give me a chance."

"The daughter?"

"Karen? She was two months pregnant when I got there. She never
told me who. Maybe I've served him dinner. Maybe not. Turnover's high
in the caravans, or he might be from the spaceport. Rita, are you thinking
I *targeted* the innkeeper's daughter?"

"Didn't you?"

"No no no. I only wanted to make myself a pit chef. I wasn't staying.
And Barda didn't know *Harlow. She* worried me. Karen was just the
little sister. Then we, I started noticing her, we started talking while she
was pregnant with Mustafa."

"Tell me about her. She's my patient too. I can tell by her skin, she
gets a *lot* more sunlight than most human beings."

"Karen was the one who talked to the Otterfolk before I came. She
swims, and Wave Rider has a pier; she didn't have to bull her way
through the waves. She gave birth in the water. Later I taught her to
surf."

"But Otterfolk don't talk, do they?"

"Karen taught me to read their dance. That's her word, dance." He
talked about Karen and himself. He was never boss at Wave Rider. He
never owned any part of the restaurant. Any investment was emotional.
Karen had never demanded that he show ambition.

"She has you by the balls."

"They're still there."

"Show me."

He shied off. Rita laughed.

He'd stayed nearly faithful. Pressed, he admitted four affairs in those
twenty-seven years. As for Karen, he was sure only of a wagonmaster
who may have been Mustafa's father. He was an old man now, and
Mustafa flew the orbital shuttles.

"*Yeah*, you weren't staying. Twenty-seven years?"

He didn't laugh.

She said, "I'm a real doctor now, a surgeon. It's what Dolores wanted to be. When she, when that birdfucker—"

"Dolores had empathy."

"She couldn't stand to cut a person open. For me that's the easy part. Wanting to fix something broken, that's easy too. Jeremy, if Medical knew I was in the Windfarm, they might ease me out. Might not."

"I'd be in worse trouble than you." *They'd kill me*, he *didn't* say. Reassure her, yes, but he didn't want Rita Nogales thinking in terms of extortion.

"Well, I'll go look in on her. Anything else you want," she shrugged and didn't finish.

He found Harlow, Lloyd, and Brenda waiting in Reception to take him to dinner.

✳ 30 ✳

H y d r a u l i c ✳ E m p i r e

We have to stop meeting in Cargo/Rec. It's gotten too small. The grand-children are growing up.

—Anonymous

Cavorite was just across the Road.

Jeremy stood rapt, until he realized that they were trying to help him sit down on a bench. Lloyd said, "We'll get a bus pretty soon."

"It's only eight blocks? Let's try it." Jeremy turned away and began his swinging progress. Crutches then foot. Crutches, foot.

Harlow said dubiously, "If it starts to hurt—"

"What's it like?" Jeremy asked.

"*Cavorite?*"

"Yes."

"Two stories tall, and you bump your head a lot, Daddy. Everything's near the base," Brenda said. "Rooms, cargo, motors and pumps and cooling, even the system that makes fuel and air. Everything that has any mass. The upper part is all hydrogen tank."

"They build the new shuttles the same," Harlow said.

"I know."

You want every part of a spacecraft as light as you can make it, see? Tanks you can make into frothy-walled balloons. Motors, you can't lighten those much if you want to run them a few hundred times, and motors have to be at the aft end. Now, the cargo, one trip you leave it in orbit, the next you're bringing it back for repair. You never know where your center of mass will be coming home, so you don't know how the ship will fly unless you put the cargo hold where the motors are. Now most of your mass is at the tail. It's going to fly butt first coming back, so you beef up the tail against reentry, and you might as well pile all the rest of the mass there too.

"Mustafa had a test coming up," Jeremy said. "We all had to hear him lecture."

And the new shuttles aren't fusion, they run on kerosene and liquid oxygen, so they have to be really light. They come home like a silver birthday balloon weighted at one end. So even if the motors don't light at the last second, it doesn't crash, see, Daddy?

He and Mustafa never said *stepfather, stepson* to each other. He'd learned more about the shuttles before Mustafa's tests. . . . They fueled the shuttle right on the beach, electrolyzing seawater then liquefying the hydrogen and oxygen (those rounded structures!); then ran it up those tracks.

The fur hat blazed ahead of him, brighter than Quicksilver or any moon. Crutches, foot, crutches, foot. A pit chef developed massive arms. Jeremy was in the swing of it and outrunning the others by the time they reached Romanoff's.

He stopped, blinking in the hatlight at a flight of stairs. "This I'll have to take slow."

"No, Daddy, they've got a lift."

Romanoff's dining hall was an awesome sight, ablaze with holograms of chandeliers, the kind that had candles in them. The headwaiter moved them through the crowd with some care. The restaurant was laid out in levels, with steps up or down every few meters. Jeremy was watching his feet and the crutches. He didn't get a chance to gawk until they were seated.

Tables of half a dozen were common. Families shared dishes around, just like Spiral Town families. A young couple turned out, at second glance, to be a stunning young woman and a creaky older man with a startling young face of superskin.

Harlow asked, "How's Karen?"

"Hanging on. Dr. Nogales has her on Novabliss for pain. And she wanted Karen's life story."

"What's she say?"

No birdfucking allowed. Something about Romanoff's made it impossible even to whisper that. "She didn't make any promises. Brenda, you sent me to the library—"

The waiter came. Jeremy asked him about some menu items and the man got bogged down in questions. He went to get the chef.

Several minutes of shoptalk ensued, much to his family's amusement. The cuisine sounded like Spiral Town, but Chef Simonsen knew pit cooking. He had been a merchant on Hearst wagon.

Jeremy realized, barely in time, that Jeremy Hearst had not! *That* Jeremy, raised in Destiny Town, had learned pit cuisine from a Spadoni wagon merchant and from lessons filed under CUISINE*BARBECUE. *That* Jeremy was an apprentice learning from a master.

His family listened to this line of fiction with much interest.

Simonsen went back to his kitchen. Harlow had ordered drinks, and Jeremy sipped something fruity and alcoholic. Brenda asked, "About the library—"

"I spent the whole day there. We were never taught that our ancestors were mindless idiots for eleven months! *More than a Destiny year!*"

Brenda began to turn pink. Harlow asked, "Shake you up?" She was not quite amused, and not shocked.

"*You* knew."

"Every child learns that."

"Brenda? You? The other kids too?"

"You all got well. Daddy, *you* haven't changed."

But Jeremy Winslow's children knew him as a Crab shy who worked the pit at Wave Rider. The wonder was that they gave their father any respect at all.

"You'd have died without us," Lloyd said casually.

"Sure, we owe you. My ancestors owe yours. But I think they robbed us too."

"*Robbed—?*"

Dinner came: communal dishes, separate plates. Lloyd waited until they had served themselves. Then he repeated, "*Robbed* you?"

Jeremy pointed up at the hologram chandeliers. "Settler magic all around us. *Megas* of electric power—"

"That's from Quicksilver," Lloyd said.

Jeremy said, "That's power beamed from Quicksilver to relay satellites to guide spots all over Destiny Town and way beyond. They could be sending power to Spiral Town too, couldn't they?"

"We could reset them," Harlow admitted.

"I see a lot of tugs—"

"There's just one factory, Jeremy."

"Lloyd, it's nearly the same design as the power plants on Quicksilver, or a Begley cloth weaver unit seen under a microscope, or Destiny Town's Varmint Killer. It's unmistakable. Your tug factory was designed in Sol system. More to the point, it will accept a signal to reproduce itself."

"I don't actually know that."

"*Cavorite* made a lot of trips in eleven months. Speckles to Spiral Town, home with a loaded cargo hold every time, right?"

His family was embarrassed. Jeremy kept his voice down. "I can *see* it. Your ancestors stripped us. There's nothing of settler magic left in Spiral Town but," now he came to think of it, "a handful of computers, a paint machine, thousands of electric lights, the Road, Varmint Killer, and a cave in a hillside where Begley cloth comes from," and he couldn't suppress the smile.

Lloyd smiled back. "Quite a lot."

"Well, that cave was just too big to steal, I guess, and the rest isn't valuable enough."

Harlow said, "Jeremy, suppose you're right, suppose *Cavorite* carried some communal supplies away from Base One. You *did* survive."

"So far. Harlow, they took too much. Everything's wearing out."

"Mmm."

Was he annoying his family without reason? It wasn't as if he'd evolved any kind of answer. He turned his attention to dinner.

The food resembled Spiral Town cuisine, with an emphasis on sauces and potatoes and a variety of salads, light on the speckles. Hey, this *wasn't* a potato. Shreds of black in the pork-and-broccoli, yellow-green in the duck dish, were certainly Destiny spices. There were spiky yellow-green disks in a brown sauce: more Destiny plants, and his family was careful cutting off the rind.

Jeremy's taste and belly and intellect feasted all together. *What flavors has Simonsen matched here?*

It became a lively family discussion. *He's done something to these almonds. How can our kitchen do this? and this?*

He could see their relief. *Jeremy was being difficult, but we got him to change the subject.*

But who else could he ask?

He had questions. His family had pieces of answers, if there were answers. His family would protect him, knowing that Jeremy Winslow was fiction.

"Otterfolk," he said. "They drove *Cavorite*'s crew crazy. Leaving Haunted Bay kills them. Here's an intelligent species that can't explore. What's intelligence for if not for seeking knowledge?"

"They're happy," Brenda said.

"Jeremy, we all read those old records," Harlow said. "One point

Daryl Twerdahl made. The Otterfolk knew some of them were dying, but they kept coming back for more. The ones who lived had tales to tell . . . however they tell tales."

"So they'd die to learn more, but they can't," Jeremy said.

"Daddy, they've got *us*. We can show them things."

"Here's my point. Feeling the way they did about the Otterfolk, and knowing what *Argos* had done to them, how could *Cavorite*'s people take away our access to space and leave us marooned?"

Lloyd said, "We had *Cavorite*. You had *Columbiad*."

Jeremy thought it over . . . and Lloyd was right.

He said little after that. He listened to in-group chat from his family, and a few tantalizing snatches of conversation from tables nearby.

Dessert was a mountain of fruit and sorbets. Chef Simonsen brought over a bottle of a sweet wine and poured them thimble-sized glasses. "Tasting wine isn't one of my skills," Jeremy admitted.

"You should start," the chef said severely.

Jeremy heard a big bell's *bong* before they had finished. "Ten minutes to bus time," Harlow told him.

He paid the bill just like a citizen, by speaking his name and a number to their waiter. Then he tried to get up. *No birdfucking— Forgot.* They had to help him to his feet, but he was all right with crutches under him. He wondered if a tablespoon of wine (and a fortified fruit drink) could have thrown his balance off so badly.

In the morning the house was empty. But Jeremy remembered Harlow standing over his futon, looking down at him from what seemed a vast distance.

"Tomorrow, look up *hydraulic empire*," she'd said.

Karen turned just her head with a delighted smile. "Hi!"

"Hi. Did Nogales take you off the Novabliss?" She seemed far more alert than she had yesterday.

"Don't know. Nogales . . . Rita? My doctor? She says I've got to stay out of the sun for a while. *And* the water. Till autumn!"

"Long time."

Karen said, "It means I can't help you with the pit."

Her hands were still bound but her shoulders moved restlessly. Karen still looked patchy. Better along her ribs and hip, but her shoulder and breast were worst. One big grayish patch of skin had sloughed off her shoulder onto the sheet. Jeremy wondered if he should remove it, or put it back. What was underneath was puffy and red touched with purple.

He said, "You can't talk to the Otterfolk either, and that's the fun part. I should have my knee back before the next caravan. I want to try some things in the kitchen. If any of it works out, we'll be working there instead of the pit—"

"Ah-hah! Brenda got you to Romanoff's!"

"Lucky guess."

"Yeah?"

"Brenda and Lloyd and Harlow took me last night. We're all staying at Harlow's—" except that Lloyd and Brenda went back this morning, and he chose not to tell his wife *that*.

"We had a good life, didn't we?"

What? Where did that come from? "So far so good," he said cautiously. *And every bit of it stolen.* He could put off telling her that for a little while yet.

"I used to wonder. Did you and Harlow?"

He didn't ask, *Did we what?* He spoke the truth while he had the chance. "Yes, while you were carrying Mustafa. We were careful. Your father never caught us."

"Mmm."

"But never after we were married, Karen."

"Good." She shifted a little. "It itches." She shifted again. "Burns. What did you call it? Novabliss? If you run across Dr. Nogales, I need some."

He found someone with a label and told him that Karen needed a doctor. That might get something done, but Rita Nogales should see her.

He looked into some rooms. He stopped at Reception and spoke with Lisa Schiavo. Then he went to the library, the obvious place to wait for a doctor.

CARAVAN
Again, a multitude of entries.
CARAVAN*MAP

Three klicks of the Neck and a twelve-klick stretch of land between the Road and the ocean were all shaded in tan. Call it twenty square klicks: all property of the caravans. A scatter of rectangles and a sprinkling of square dots just the far side of the spaceport (yellow), and another scattering just short of the Neck, and no other buildings in between.

To the west the Road ran off the map, and Jeremy wondered—
WINDFARM*MAP
restricted material. Access code?
WINDFARM
restricted material. Access code?

DESTINY TOWN

That was well mapped, with a zoom feature. He could sketch the details of Jeremy Hearst's life onto this. He should! But it felt too much like work, and there was something he wanted more.

CARAVAN*CARGO

Nothing. Wrong word?

CARAVAN*EXPORT

Nope.

If he knew *exactly* what wagons carried and what they needed, he'd know how to deal for it. Try:

CARAVAN*2739*REPLACEMENTS

Bandages. Whiskey considered as medicine. Paint from Spiral Town, oil from Twerdahl Town, silver fern tea from the Shire. Did the caravans carry high-tech medicine? It wasn't listed, and he'd never seen such. Not for yutzes, at least.

Ammunition, guns, gun oil and cloth, the cylinder on the little reboring thing in Tucker wagon . . . shark guns and tools to maintain them. Nothing about Spadoni or . . . he didn't *know* a proper name for "prole guns."

Better *not* try CARAVAN*SPADONI*SUPPLIES. A computer might be told to alert somebody. Try

CARAVAN*2739*SALES

This year's outgoing. Speckles and spices. Basic farming and cloth-making tools, and some half familiar terms that were also tools. Cookware: *not* the magical stuff nothing sticks to. Toys and shells and other luxury goods. Preserved meat, root vegetables, spices, some of which had been sold to Wave Rider. Nothing much to learn.

CARAVAN*2739*PURCHASE

This year returning: clocks and paint and Begley cloth. Spices again, and salt. Shire tea. Smoked fish from Haven. Whiskey, liqueurs, and cheeses. Wave Rider kept some of these in stock.

For twenty-seven years he'd watched and eavesdropped on caravan merchants, merchants from Terminus and Destiny Town, and the Winslow clan. He had a very good idea what passed along the Road, and Wave Rider was involved in all of this. Except—

Prole guns. Replacement, purchase, maintenance: nothing at all.

And speckles. If the route involved middlemen, he'd have seen something. The sterilized seeds must go straight from the Windfarm to wherever along the Road they did their loading.

He went back to CARAVAN and opened

ORIGIN*CARAVAN

In Will Coffey's vision, now more than two centuries old, caravans were not for commerce, not for making wealth. They were a way to deliver speckles to Spiral Town. The impression would be that Spiral Town was the peak of civilization on Destiny; that sophistication dwindled with distance down the Road.

We've been swindled. The greed of merchants, is that a lie too? or a game the merchants play to entertain themselves?

A later entry: The caravans are working! They serve as recreation for some, for some a way of life, a forum for courtship for some, but for all a hedge against the danger of inbreeding. They allow us to learn more about the only other sapient species ever found. They maintain the stability of our control experiment.

All that vastness of stars staring down at us, and it's just us and the Otterfolk? But Argos *might have heard more from Earth by now.*

—Control experiment?

Base One, now Spiral Town, was to retain technology that was too heavy or fragile to transport. Visiting caravans would purchase the use of what they hadn't already stolen: paint and clocks and Begley cloth and, in later years, handcrafted work. . . .

A generation later they teased the paintmaker system into duplicating itself. On their next circuit they bought the duplicate from puzzled Spirals.

They didn't bother with the clock factory, but they tried it again with the Begley cloth weavers.

Jeremy read the results in bitter amusement. The little mechanical spiders in the walls and roof of the Apollo Caverns could be snatched by handfuls. Spirals never interfered. But they wouldn't dig anywhere else! Of course it was a safety measure, a part of their program. One wouldn't want mechanical vermin eating caverns into every hill and mountain on Destiny. But where was the damn code? Stored in the teaching tapes? Or lost with *Argos?*

CARAVAN*GENEOLOGY

A handful of listings.

CARAVAN*GENEOLOGY*Shire

restricted material. Access code?

CARAVAN*GENEOLOGY*Twerdahl Town

restricted material. Access code?

CARAVAN*GENEOLOGY*Tail Town

restricted material. Access code?

Somebody somewhere was keeping genealogical records, and keeping them hidden.

He'd seen an ominous degree of continuity in the families that held the wagons. He remembered three generations in ibn-Rushd wagon. Outsiders not welcome? How could he learn?

303

*   *   *

AVALON

restricted material. Access code?

SPACE*SHUTTLE

Designs, vidtapes, test results, wow!

Six crashes in fifty-one years. No deaths mentioned. A vivid description of the tenth flight by the first humans to orbit. *Say what?*

He'd read it and failed to believe it. He had to go back for it—

The shuttle didn't have a pilot on board.

It was flown by onboard programs and a pilot on the ground. A box of varied design but rigidly exact size fit into the shuttle's rectangular cargo space. One such box was a cabin for two passengers and an array of tools.

Passengers had flown twice. That first pair of women went up to repair a satellite. The second pair . . . something political.

Jeremy felt massive disappointment. Had Mustafa ever *said* that he'd gone into space personally? He couldn't remember. But he'd daydreamed, from time to time, of persuading Mustafa to help him stow away aboard a shuttle. The space wasn't even *there*.

Harlow's words didn't make sense together. Maybe he'd remembered wrong. Try it anyway:

HYDRAULIC*EMPIRE

A political entity that controls its citizens by controlling the flow of water.

"Fuck my bird."

"What?"

"Sorry."

It was no trivial thing. Thousands of years of Eastern despotisms had been of that nature. Water was life. Dig a canal system, guard the canals. If a town opposes the government, block the canals, dam or pollute the river, confiscate the wheat or rice.

Two towns in a drought? Strip one of food, send it all to the second. Gain the second town's support; make deadly enemies of the first, but it won't matter, they will die.

Hydraulic empires never died. No matter how far they slid into decadence, they lived on until destroyed by barbarians beyond the border.

Hydraulic empires grew with the rising level of communications and transport. On Earth a moment came at which one government could rule the world, forever. Afterward the United Nations controlled not just water, but communications via comsats, electric power from sunpower satellites, and every resource that could be labeled "limited." The United Nations in its last days had launched the Avalon expedition—

Last days?

He skimmed, picking it up little by little.

Ah. They'd grown their own barbarians. They'd been brought down by a coalition of populations throughout the solar system, each as great or greater than the population of Destiny. There followed two hundred years of stagnation before one civilization stretched from Sol to the far comets, one empire with a stranglehold on . . . what?

Reading between the lines—

Everything. The Web controlled everything that flowed. Water, hydrogen, information, diet supplements, placement of orbiting habitats, and kinetic energy. Especially kinetic energy. What moved through interplanetary space averaged twenty klicks per second. Fusion explosions were nothing compared to that. Every habitat in motion within Sol system was assigned its orbit. Keep to it or be treated as a meteor.

In a spasm of creativity the Web had launched *Argos* and a third expedition—

restricted material. Access code?

The thrust of the lecture was that Sol system had become one vast resource-control empire, sluggish, but able to make long plans. There weren't any barbarians because there was no outside. A million years from now it would still be in place.

Outsiders and their barbaric ideas would not be welcome in Sol system.

There was no home to return to.

"Jeremy."

He looked up. "Rita! Karen's itching like crazy. Did you take her off Novabliss?"

"I cut the dose as per your suggestion."

"Right, and it's great to hear her making *plans* again, but now she's itching—"

"I'll go see her. Come along."

Rita's tendency was to outrun him, and what the hell, he knew the way. But she glanced back and then waited. "How's the leg?"

"I did eight blocks last night."

"I guess we can take the cast off after we see Karen."

"I've been reading about hydraulic empires."

Silence: she was fishing through her head. "Sol system? That old tenth-year lecture? It's a reason why we can't go back, but that's just mind games, Jeremy. Anyone can think of reasons why we shouldn't do what we can't do anyway."

"Suppose a government didn't control water. Just speckles."

A disgusted look; then Rita Nogales walked away from him. She held the lift. They descended in silence. She walked away from him again, outside, in, another lift, and he reached Karen's room a good ten minutes behind her.

It was too active. Something was wrong. Four doctors crowded the room, and one left at a half-run. Jeremy backed against the corridor wall and, resting on his crutches, waited.

Rita Nogales noticed him and came out. "Jeremy, did Karen have trouble controlling her weight?"

"No."

"Damn."

"After all, we live at Wave Rider. She just eats a lot of Destiny sea life if she needs to lose a few kilos. So do I."

"Was she doing that a week ago?"

"I don't know."

"All right. Right now Karen's getting all the attention she can stand, right? The whole damn hospital's worrying about her. They don't need a twitchy husband on crutches getting in their way," she said, and walked away fast. Over her shoulder she added, "Go eat. Go home. Go read, but don't block any doctors."

Now there were two doctors in there with Karen. One saw Jeremy still there, and came out. His label said *Malcolm Evans*. He was having trouble keeping his smile on.

"Don't let all this . . . activity worry you," he said. "Karen is rejecting superskin, that's all, but it's not supposed to happen. Maybe this batch threw off a sport. Clinics keep batches of superskin all over Destiny Town and on up the Road. Nogales is off to get a different batch for, uh, Karen, and Walther is phoning patients who got superskin from Batch One, so you can s—" Evans caught a gesture from the other doctor and turned away without finishing the sentence.

CONTROL*EXPERIMENT

Jeremy couldn't concentrate. He had to read it twice, though the idea wasn't complicated.

A population to be experimented upon would be split. The control experiment was the group to which nobody did anything. These were the rats that didn't ingest carcinogens, didn't have to run mazes with traps in them, weren't bothered by flashing lights or loud noises. The

patients who got placebos instead of medicine. You watched for differences between the control group and the experimental group.
CONTROL*EXPERIMENT*Base One

> The lives we're trying to carve from this wilderness would be a risk even if Argos had not deserted us!
>
> Base One is thriving, they tell us. They're living according to the guidelines laid down for Argos Project in Sol system. Isolated on a peninsula with the Neck blocked, they're safe from whatever Destiny life might throw at them, with one horrifying exception.
>
> *Fatum mortem parnelli* is our prison. We must live within range of the planet's only known potassium source, inside a maze of twisty little Destiny ecologies, all different. Granted that nothing has come after us yet: the lesson of Avalon seems clear enough. Trust nothing in an unfamiliar environment.
>
> I propose to designate Base One as a control experiment, where the primary experiment is Terminus. Establish an Overview Bureau. Give it authority over the Crab: Base One and Haunted Bay and whatever communities arise elsewhere. Whatever risks we take here, the larger population will survive provided that we can secure the Crab's speckles supply. . . .
>
> —Will Coffey, Hydroponics

Idiot. How could he conceivably expect to do that? The caravan system—Coffey's proposal—was only as good as the Windfarm and Terminus. If either failed—

Terminus hadn't failed; it had fissioned. Destiny Town was thriving. But what of Spiral Town?

A couple of generations of a control experiment might have made sense. Two and a half centuries later, why on Earth would they still need a control experiment?

He'd come to the library looking for distraction and found this!
OVERVIEW BUREAU

—was two doors up from Medical. They still had charge of the Crab, Spiral Town, the Road towns, Haunted Bay and Otterfolk and all. He could walk there, but why bother?

A government bureau was not likely to give up its authority over anything. From Destiny Town's viewpoint, bringing Spiral Town into civilization would only risk the flow of Begley cloth, clocks, and handicrafts down the Road.

Destiny Town hadn't failed. *The Windfarm would!*

Twenty-seven years ago Andrew Dowd would have killed all the prisoners and left nobody to harvest the speckles. Dolores Nogales had wanted to shoot up the toolshed. There would be other revolts, other escapes.

When the speckles flow stopped, it wouldn't be Destiny Town that went speckles-shy.

Jeremy made his way to Karen's room.

Only Rita Nogales was on duty. Karen was asleep. Her burns were covered with new patches of superskin.

Jeremy took the bus back to Harlow's.

✳ 3 1 ✳

L i e s

Whatever risks we take, the larger population will survive, provided that we can secure Base One's speckles supply. . . .

—Will Coffey, Hydroponics

It was an invitation to disaster, cooking a dinner in someone else's kitchen. It worked partly because he had Harlow to tell him where the tools were kept.

There was that one moment of disorientation when Harlow began taking vegetables, bacon, and a calf's liver out of half-invisible envelopes all the same size. He lurched over to study the things.

"These come out of a machine that used to be mounted in *Cavorite*," Harlow said, laughing at his astonishment. "Thousands a day. We feed it sand. We feed the bags back in too. Don't you have . . ." She trailed off.

He said, "Speckles pouches. Merchants sell speckles in these. I never saw them used for anything else."

She nodded. Then she showed him how to make meringue shells. They cut fruit into the shells.

"Men lie to their wives," Harlow said. "Women lie to their husbands." She sipped at her brandy.

Brandy wasn't familiar to Jeremy, and he thought he was being cautious with it. He said, "I've gone through this in my head. Scripted it, my lines, her lines. I'm not who she thought I was. I'm a Crab shy, right. I killed a man and had to run, right. I was in prison, right, but never convicted of anything. I didn't hurt anyone getting out except Andrew

Dowd. I can say all that, but, Harlow, how can I tell Karen that I knew her sister?"

"What? Oh, *Barda.*"

"Barda was a trusty when I got to the Windfarm."

"I never met Barda."

"We escaped together. Brenda must have told you the rest, we helped her run the Swan—"

"Barda told you about *us?* You already knew us? *Karen?*"

They were dining by firelight and an awesome variety of candles. Harlow was mostly shadow. He couldn't make out her face. "Not you. You were a shock. Harold, though, and her mother, Espania Winslow, and Karen as a little girl. Harlow, when I last saw Barda she was all right. I never told Karen that. When did Karen last see her?"

"At the trial, when they took her away. It was just Karen and Barry and Espania. Harold didn't go. Did Barda tell you what she did?"

"No."

"Poison. The whole second class at Wide Wade's. Two students died."

"The *proles* had to know that," Jeremy realized. "The Parole Board decides who does the cooking. That's why they made her a trusty!"

"You think that's *funny?* And you knew what happened to Barda and never told Karen? Jeremy, you . . ." She trailed off.

He said, "Barda got as far as the Swan, but after that . . . and the longer I waited, the harder it was to say anything. Now it's twenty-seven years. Harlow, I'll lose her."

"Leave it out. Tell Karen you escaped from the Windfarm. Don't tell her who came along." She watched him absorb that.

"No Barda?"

"No Barda. So how did you get to the inn?"

"Let's see. If *Barda* didn't tell me about Wave Rider . . ." He played it through his mind. "I didn't know it was there. I was . . . running home? Back across the Neck. If I meet a caravan, I'm dead. Here's an inn. I can cook. Merchants don't notice a chef. A week later I've heard too much. Nobody but a merchant gets across the Neck alive."

"At least it doesn't sound so . . . premeditated," Harlow said. "Why *did* you come here?"

"Mmm?"

"Carder's Boat. Jeremy, you were nearly home. With your board and your gloves you could have crossed the weed, straight to shore. That would put you on the beach at, at the inn there?"

"Warkan's Tavern. With Bloocher Farm right next door. Yes. Harlow, they would not have been glad to see me."

"Who would? But they'd take you in. Why did you throw your life to the ocean currents?"

"How did you get to know me so well?"

"I pulled you under the surfboards twenty-six years ago."

"Repeatedly. It comes back to me."

"But I *don't* know you. Even Karen didn't know you. Why didn't you go home?"

"I had to know where *Cavorite* went."

Harlow laughed in the dark. "Jeremy!"

He tried to tell her, but he barely remembered himself.

Cavorite's path was the path of humankind, from the stars down to Destiny, to Spiral Town, on to the mainland, and out again to the stars. Jemmy Bloocher was tracing the path of *Cavorite*, and he was looking for a home.

When he killed Fedrik he'd blown his home apart. He'd left Spiral Town, then married and settled down the first chance he got.

Tagged by the caravan, he hadn't resisted. There was the Road, and he followed it, donning the life of a caravan yutz like a well-fitting glove. He'd never taken it off until his life was threatened. After that . . . there was joy in learning and exploring, but his roots waved in the air. The farther he went, the less he was tied to anything at all, unless it was to Loria Bednacourt.

Rejected by Loria and by Twerdahl Town . . . he'd gone mad.

Still mad, perhaps, he'd rebuilt the life of a pit cuisine chef from nothing more than escaped felons and the abandoned wreck of an inn.

When that collapsed in blood, he did it again at Wave Rider.

And he settled in as Wave Rider's pit chef, and forgot *Cavorite* for twenty-seven years.

"I knew where *Cavorite* was," he said. "It was just down the Road, and a bus every two days, but anyone who asked me to pay for something would know I didn't belong. They'd put me back in the Winds, or kill me. After a while I stopped thinking about *Cavorite*. I burrowed in and spent twenty-seven years half-asleep. There's a civilization out there, Harlow! Spiral Town and the Crab are all barred from it! And I forgot. I just forgot.

"Then Karen burned herself," he said, "and here I am."

"And now what?"

He couldn't tell her what he'd decided. He didn't know what she'd do. Harlow was of Destiny Town. He was of Spiral Town, and he'd learned too much.

He'd learned what it really meant to be a Crab shy.

He'd learned about the Overview Bureau.

But he could tell her a little. "I can't stay here forever. As soon as Karen's better . . . back to Wave Rider, I guess. I want to stop at the Swan. Maybe I can figure out what happened to them. To Barda."

"Want company?"

"Sure." His mouth had run ahead of his mind. "Don't you have a shop to run here?"

"I can get Belle Kuiger to cover, with a few days' notice. You'll be shorthanded, come the caravan. I can help. I miss Wave Rider, Jeremy." She reached across to take his hand. "I miss you."

He was Harlow's guest, and everyone else had gone home. Best to be wary here. He asked, "Why did you leave? I always—"

"You didn't *notice* what was happening?"

"Dominance games, you and the rest of the family. Property rights."

"Harold's brothers and sister didn't like it when Harold married me. They waited it out, but when Harold died, he . . . didn't leave a will. They could hassle me, I could hassle them. It just looked better to let them buy me out. And you, you didn't do anything."

"With what?"

"You were just the pit chef, weren't you? But I thought you had some . . . authority. Karen, *she* sided with her brothers."

"Will they want you at Wave Rider?"

She settled back in her chair, the firelight behind her. "I'm sorry, I wasn't thinking. Still, they might want the help, with Karen in Medical and you in a cast and the caravan coming."

He got himself onto his crutches, a little off balance: the brandy. Harlow wrapped herself around him for a deep kiss. "Thank you," she said, and held him steady until he had his balance.

He hadn't felt *this* since Karen burned herself. The flash of lust had knocked him off balance, but his breath was coming back and his mind was catching up.

He made his toppling foot-crutches-foot way to bed. Maybe Harlow hadn't noticed. Any man could miss a signal.

Lisa Schiavo told him at Reception. Karen was dead.

"But, but . . . What *happened?*"

She was reading it off her screen. "Karen Winslow had a severe allergic reaction that led to a heart attack. Mr. Winslow, a human body is really very good at doing unexpected things."

"But . . . they had the other batch of superskin—"

Schiavo didn't seem to be used to this. "I'll l-let you talk to Dr. No-gales. Why don't you wait in the library?"

Crutches took his attention until he'd reached the library. What now? The computers were all occupied. He sat down.

Dead?

Not Karen: someone else. Scores of patients must be wearing trans-plants from that bad batch of superskin. Picture them collapsing every-where, like a plague. Mixups would be routine. . . .

Nah.

He'd never be able to tell her . . . never *have to* tell her. . . .

A patient got up and left. Jeremy looked at the vacated screen. He'd learned all he cared to of *Cavorite.*

No, wait—

LAW*CARAVAN
ref Overview Bureau
LAW*OVERVIEW BUREAU
Restricted material. Access code?
PASSENGER*CARAVAN

Nothing.

You wouldn't just hail a caravan and buy a ticket. Caravans weren't trans-port. They were a way of moving speckles, and they'd be filed that way.

Meanwhile, try
PASSENGER*BUS

One set of buses moved around the city, back and forth along the Road. You stopped it where you liked, the usual gesture and a lot of flex in the schedule.

Two buses ran from Destiny Town all the way to the far end at fifty klicks per. One started at dawn on alternate days, the other at noon. Both returned the next day, over and over.
NECK*MAP

He'd seen these pictures as a child: maps made in orbit by *Argos,* before the mutiny. A black-bronze-yellow forest ran thickly down the fat side of the Crab, sparsely down the narrow side, joined at the Neck and ran on into the mainland.

But this next was more recent, taken by the Cyclops telescope. The Road was in place. Chugs were pulling thirteen wagons. Amazing, how much detail showed below the water. Crude Otterfolk cities, built hefty to withstand currents . . . not cities at all, the text said, but walls to guide currents and precipitate sand, to provide refuge for Destiny fish and extend the Haunted Bay environment by a little.

The back of the Crab was all cliffs. The sea bottom dropped straight down.

What had he hoped to see? There was no way across the Neck save with a caravan.

SWAN INN

Open: May 2651. See crime files case 2708–10. License terminated: May 2713. Current site: Corso's Camp Waikiki, children ages 5 to 12 Earth.

Those dates: Harold Winslow must have noticed he was paying for too much electricity. He'd terminated the Swan's power license a year after Jeremy reached Wave Rider. How had Barda and her crew survived that? And now it was a children's camp.

And buses stopped. He'd seen that.

CRIME*2708-110

That was the record of Duncan Nick's arrest. Caught hiding out at the Swan, sent to the Windfarm, the loot never found.

What Jeremy had in mind seemed possible.

He'd started to cry.

They were all looking, and the hell with them. He let it come. *Karen, I don't want to go!*

A doctor got him onto his crutches and led him out and sat him down in an empty room.

Rita Nogales found him there.

"All right," he said, "what happened?"

"That's still under debate. We lost her, Jeremy, but the problem may not stop there. If Batch One—"

"As I—"

"—went bad—yes?"

"—understand it, Karen rejected Batch One, so another batch was found—"

"Hope Batch, from Hope Clinic. Last night she rejected *that* and went into a coma. They loaded her with antihistamines, but she was dead by the time I could get here. We couldn't resuscitate her.

"Jeremy, there might be something atypical about Karen. Too much sunlight for too many years, too much of something in Destiny seafood or just *Haunted Bay* Destiny seafood, or . . . something genetic. Anything. Then again, maybe Batch One is bad. Karen reacted to it, and it set her up for a reaction to *any* breed of superskin. We need to know. Jeremy, we're doing an autopsy."

In Spiral Town there would be no question that the community held title to a lifegiver. "Do what you need to. Can I see her?"

"Of course, but—" She hesitated. "—I don't recommend it."

Of course it was his duty to . . . but Rita Nogales was shrinking back in her chair, withdrawing from him. With that for a clue, his mind showed him more than he wanted to see of what Karen must look like.

"All right."

"Shall we take that cast off you?"

"Fine."

He rested on his stick for a time, looking across the Road, considering how he might get inside *Cavorite*. Then he flagged the bus and boarded it.

Back at Harlow's he called Wave Rider immediately, getting Harlow to place the call.

Brenda picked up. "She's dead, isn't she?"

"How did you know?"

"Oh, Daddy!" and she wept.

"The damn trouble," he said, "is Medical looks like the power of life and death written in stone. Brenda, Nogales still doesn't know just what killed her. I should come home—"

"No, Jeremy, you'll have to stay a few days."

That was Harlow. He looked around. "Why?"

"Legal reasons, and to bury Karen."

"Brenda, I have to stay a few days."

"All right, Daddy. Call and tell us when the funeral is."

Harlow showed him how to hang up. He said, "Legal. Why?"

"Because you'll inherit Karen's piece of Wave Rider."

That jolted him. "I never asked about a will."

"She told Brenda and Lloyd where to find it."

"What does Karen own?"

"I think one-quarter, but it wasn't any of my business."

"This'll make me conspicuous, won't it, Harlow? Somebody will be putting new information in a file marked 'Jeremy Winslow,' who is fiction."

"It's fiction, but I wrote it, Jeremy. Trust me."

The next day Medical released Karen's body. They arranged a funeral for the day after. Funerals weren't important events in Spiral Town.

But Brenda came, and Mustafa, and Rita Nogales. They buried her with black pepper and lemon trees at her head and feet.

The children and Harlow stayed with him while he talked to Nogales. "Thanks for coming. I know Karen would appreciate—"

Nogales rode him down. "The autopsy showed some abnormal chemistry going on," she told them with a touch of belligerence. "Some of us think it's Destiny seafood. People have been losing weight that way for a long time, we don't really know how long. I do it myself, but we damn sure didn't *evolve* to eat it. Have you *any* idea if she was eating—"

"Mother and I had lunch together," Brenda said quietly. "Avocado and seafood, surf clam and Earthlife crab."

"Mayonnaise?"

Jeremy listened as Morales quizzed his daughter like a felon. She went away mumbling to herself. Rita Nogales was a solver of puzzles, like Jeremy himself. If he'd known that . . .

Well, then what?

Two days later, Jeremy Winslow, born Hearst, owned one-fifth (not one-quarter) of Wave Rider.

Jeremy read through a thick file of data, and learned more of the restaurant than he'd learned in twenty-seven years. Karen's three siblings held another fifth each. The last piece rested with an entity that called itself *Andy's Bank.* "Investment outfit," Harlow said. "They bailed us out with some money just after we opened."

In Spiral Town the law would have dithered for much longer; sometimes years. He said so. "It's communication," Harlow answered. "That, and an attitude. The law doesn't like ambiguities. If they'd found any discrepancies in the history of Jeremy Winslow, they'd be on your tail already."

"So I'm real?"

"Real and a man of property. Let's celebrate."

"I want to be on the bus at dawn."

"*Dawn?*"

He couldn't sit still. He paced, leaning on the stick, careful with the knee. "Now, here's my plan. Dawn bus. I want to get off at the Swan, that'll be about midmorning. I'll flag down the noon bus and get to Wave Rider after someone else has finished making dinner."

"There's a noon bus?"

"Why don't you take that one, Harlow? Meet me at the Swan? We'll go on to Wave Rider. In a day or so we'll know if you and the rest of Karen's clan can get along."

"No, I'll . . . dawn bus. Early dinner?"

"Good. What are the neighbors like?" But Harlow didn't have friends she could invite at short notice.

She had not repeated an invitation that might have been only his imagination. Nonetheless that seemed ominous.

*   *   *

His leg was healing nicely. He was able to get around the kitchen without the cane. He packed for tomorrow's bus trip, and then they spent the afternoon building a dinner for two.

(Speckles pouches all over the table. All the same size, big enough for a head of lettuce, sold with half a cup of speckles in the bottom. He'd thought the merchants were being stingy. Never wondered if they just didn't have a choice.)

She opened what she called a half-bottle of wine, and tried to make him see what made it superior to whiskey. It was weaker, anyway. Again, he thought he was being cautious.

Harlow hadn't played among Otterfolk in years, nor visited the inn, and he had stories to tell her. He told her what "It's the law!" was about. He got her to telling tales of Destiny Town, and he told her about playing with Varmint Killer in Spiral Town.

He knew he'd drunk too much when he tried to stand up. Harlow got under his shoulder and led him to bed. She was weaving more than he was.

She got him down to the futon. Then she asked, "Shall I stay?"

He said, "Of course, woman, it's your apartment," being more obtuse than should be required of any man; and he let his eyes close and his mouth fall open. He knew no more until morning.

✳ 32 ✳

The Windfarm Innkeepers

Not you, not your family, your guests, passing strangers, nobody goes near the Otterfolk birthground. Understand me, Harold?
> —Georges Manet, Overview Bureau

He'd leave without her, let her take the noon bus, if he found her asleep. Leave her a note . . .

But she was bright and perky and handing him a mug of tea in the predawn dark.

Backpacks. Cane. The walk to the Road loosened up his stiff knee. Apollo finished rising. They flagged down the bus. Harlow pointed out sights as they moved out of Spiral Town.

She was asleep before they reached Terminus.

Too soon, she woke. "Mount Canaveral!" she crowed. "We used to launch *Cavorite* from here. Land by the ocean, refuel, fly it back here to load up."

"Ever see this yourself?"

"No." She squinted up at the mesa rim. "How's the knee?"

"Not that good. That looks like quite a climb."

The bus rolled on. Harlow asked, "Whereabouts did you and . . . Andrew . . . ?" and didn't finish.

The bluff was in view. Andrew might still be there, bones picked clean and maybe scattered. Jeremy pointed well past it and said, "Far side of the Swan, on the same side. Andrew would have gone out the same way I did."

Here was the bridge. They signaled to stop the bus, donned packs, and got off, Jeremy leaning heavily on his stick.

Like the bridge, the Swan sagged a little. Lights glowed inside, though the hologram sign wasn't lit. The pit barbecue smelled of recent fire.

Children were all over the place, mid-teens commanding hordes of youngsters with moderate success. They looked too busy to talk. Jeremy and Harlow went in looking for an adult.

Alexandre Chorin was a little old, a little heavy, a little slow to be chasing after children. It was easy to see him as hiding from the noise, here in the shade of what had been the Swan's dining room and was now littered with games and toys. But he seemed glad to see them, or anyone.

"Jeremy's grandchildren will be old enough soon," Harlow told him. "We thought we'd stop off and look."

"I used to fish here," Jeremy put in.

"We still do," Chorin said quickly. "The lake perch are nice. There's a pit barbecue we use sometimes."

"But then there was that trouble and everyone stopped coming," Harlow said.

Jeremy: "My children missed this entirely. Fishing at Swan Lake— It's still *Swan Lake?*"

"Oh, yes."

Harlow: "Do the children know—?"

"Oh, yes, it's one reason they come. Duncan Nick? The city planted an oak over him. It's just up the slope."

"Oh."

"You can't miss it. And there are horror stories about the *Windfarm innkeepers,*" in a hoarse whisper. "There's no knowing how many people stayed here overnight and weren't ever seen again."

"Well," Harlow said, "I'd have thought *one* felon would have babbled stories. How many were there, a dozen?"

"Five, the caravaners say. All gone when the proles came. If you go up to Swan Lake, you can see how easy it must have been to get into the hills."

Jeremy had found a brochure. Day rates. Rates for stays of a week. List of what a child should pack. A map.

"What's it like, staying here? May we look around?" Harlow asked.

"Of course. Outside too. If you're going to the lake, take some fishing poles."

*   *   *

They went upstairs, pro forma. Harlow went into the nearest room and bounced on a tiny, carefully made bed.

"Nice move, but I didn't leave anything up here," Jeremy said.

Her hands smoothed out the bed. "Any interest in anything?"

"Just the roof. Two floors up."

"You rest. I'll go up. What should I look for?"

"Well, the guide spot's working, but see if it got damaged. The floor's Begley cloth; see if it's been kept up. Look around at the view, all directions. Harlow, it's probably not worth the effort—"

She laughed and went, feet quick on the stairs.

Jeremy went into the men's bathroom. He tried the taps. They'd got the plumbing working again! He used a toilet, then stayed there, private, thinking.

Harlow was staking a claim.

Jeremy Winslow was in mourning! But set that aside, because it was twenty-seven years late to tell Harlow to get lost, and innuendos were getting harder to miss, and that wasn't the problem anyway. He needed to get out of Harlow's sight! For . . . seven hours would have been great. Half an hour would do . . . might not. He'd be climbing all over a hillside.

He'd see the hill from the roof.

She met him on the stair. "What?"

"I thought I'd look for myself."

"I never *stared* at a guide spot before. Somebody whacked the casing with a crowbar, looks like, but it must be working or there wouldn't be lights. The Begley cloth's new. What else?"

They walked out on the roof. Jeremy opened the powerhouse casing and looked in. "That's a new guide spot too. It was a snarl of line wire when I left here." He turned in a slow circle. "That way is Swan Lake. The proles think they went out that way. But that way—look across the Road." She nestled close to sight along his arm. "That's how we came, and there are valleys where we could survive for weeks. Mr. Chorin didn't say the caravan sold them clothing, but I bet they did, a *lot*."

A proud oak stood above the hillside, easily a quarter-century old. Duncan Nick's oak, where the women's cesspit had been. What was that growing around its base? To Jeremy's eye it stood out like settler-magic paint: greenery tinged with yellow, and orange flecks on black.

From the oak he traced narrow paths to a thicket of growth, green-and-black shadows with touches of orange. The other ancient cesspit. Broader paths led from Duncan Nick's oak down to the lodge, and to the lake, and east to the ridge—"Another way out," he said, pointing—

and to a stand of fruit trees that must have replaced the old spice garden, with a hint of orange in the shadowed green-black around the trunks.

"You think Barda got away," Harlow said.

"She could have. I can . . . could've . . ."

Harlow hugged him from behind, chin on his shoulder. He plunged on: "Could've told it to Karen that way. Still can. Karen had . . . Barda has brothers." Suddenly he knew what to do. "We've got four hours. Shall I show you how to fish?"

Alexandre Chorin stored their backpacks behind the desk for them, and rented them fishing gear all assembled for instant use. "Do you use flies?"

Harlow stared. Jeremy knew just enough to say, "Harlow, it's a lure you float. Mr. Chorin, have you got actual bait?"

"No. Try digging in the orchard."

"Okay."

The graveyard-turned-spice-garden had turned fruit orchard. Speckles grew all through it, sparsely, as if a gardener had failed to weed them out. Jeremy studiously ignored them while he dug for earthworms.

There were children all along the near shore, fishing, throwing frisbees, batting at a ball tethered to a pole. A worn, transparent tent sprawled loosely along the south side of the lake, with room for twenty or thirty underneath. Six growing Earthlife trees had become the tent poles. Destiny trees had been chopped down to make room.

Harlow said, "The way the buses run—"

"Yeah." Kids would *have* to stay overnight; hence the tent.

By silent agreement they walked around the north shore until most of the activity was out of sight and hearing. They took off their shoes. Harlow didn't flinch from putting worms on a hook. "You can use anything organic, but we didn't bring anything," he told her. They flung the lines a fair distance out, and waited, drowsy in the sun.

Reasonable time passed, and nothing struck.

Bare white rock stretched far into the lake, coming to a point a meter above deep water. Jeremy walked out onto it, set his cane down, and, carefully balanced, flung out his line.

Waited.

A fish struck. He pulled it in.

Harlow came to join him. She maneuvered to put them nearly back to back.

Moving to make more room, he stumbled, started to fall, arms windmilling. She reached and had him, and pulled. He backed into her hip, hard. She lost her balance and splashed into the lake. He barely saved himself from going after her.

The rock fell off steeply. Jeremy went down on his belly and reached for her hand. She could swim, of course. She swam over and, with his arms to anchor her, walked up the rock.

Her clothing clung to her like paint. The sight of her froze him like a rabbit in torchlight. The words he'd planned to say evaporated.

She was furious. She started to say so. Instead she looked into the heat of his stare, and then began to pull his shirt open.

He pulled them together. No other response ever crossed his mind until much later.

He felt so incredibly good.

She curled against him and said, "Tell me you didn't throw me in the lake just to rub up against me."

He laughed like a maniac. Then he said, "I swear to you by everything I own, I did not."

"Right. Good."

There were children just out of sight; they deemed it better to ignore them. They sorted through their clothes, looked them over critically, put them on anyway. Jeremy asked, "Did you bring a change?"

"Sure. You?"

"Course."

He used his pole to fish her pole off the bottom. They walked back down to the lodge, dripping. She'd got his clothes almost as wet and muddy as hers.

Alexandre Chorin's chuckle kept bubbling through his self-restraint. He had towels for rent. They retrieved their packs and went upstairs.

MEN   WOMEN

Change together in one room? Harlow's suggestion was a wiggle of her eyebrow; his answer a quick headshake. They went in separate doors.

Jeremy spilled his pack, snatched up a shirt and shorts, stripped and put them on, rubbed a towel past his hair, stuffed his wet clothes into the pack, closed it, and was out. To hell with showering. Down the stair fast, but *limp* past Chorin and, "I think I want to see that oak."

"Just don't overdo it with that leg, Mr. Winslow."

He climbed the hill fast, digging his stick in and pulling himself up. He'd seen speckles growing around Duncan Nick's oak, but the oak was a bit conspicuous; and the graveyard grove, but that must get visitors.

His fragile plan had gone all to hell. Fall in the lake, go back to the lodge to change, anything for a moment alone with the speckles crop. Anything, but he hadn't expected—

He *certainly* hadn't expected—

Hadn't fought her off, either.

Couldn't. She'd wonder at his motives! Harlow was doing quite enough of that already.

Yeah, right. Karen, I'm sorry. I have to do this.

Here: the ancient privy, the men's. Ground-hugging bristly plants, with black stalks that split and split again to become orange thorns whose tips divided down to tiny, tinier, microscopic green needles.

These plants couldn't be ignored, even if nobody here knew what they were. Children must have tasted the buds. A cook who found speckles in the spice patch might try it on food. Did it taste like sterile speckles?

He'd brought two bags. He'd forgotten to bring a glove. He wrapped his hand in a silk scarf and took a pinch of tiny seeds and put them in his mouth, and chewed as he stripped the speckles plants.

Fresh speckles *was* a bit different. Try mixing it with . . . salt?

He filled the first bag and pushed it deep in his pack, and heard a rustle and knew it was Harlow.

He didn't look around. Had she *seen* more than one bag? He began stuffing the second bag. She wouldn't find the other unless she dug deep in his pack.

She was nearly breathing in his ear now. He said, "We will never have to buy speckles again."

"Is that what this is?"

"Don't you know speckles plants? Does anyone outside the Windfarm know what speckles looks like when it's growing?"

"There must be pictures in the teaching programs."

" 'Restricted material. Access code?' But prisoners do get released from the Windfarm."

"You're evading."

"We came out of the Windfarm with fertile speckles. We used them for cooking, so the chef got to carry them. I scattered them where I thought they'd grow. Now it's twenty-seven years later and I own a piece of a restaurant. Harlow, I never had to worry about how to keep a restaurant solvent, and now I know we lost a piece of the inn to people I never heard of—"

"They were there at the right time, Jeremy."

"Next time might be worse. So I thought I'd fall in the lake and collect a bag of speckles on the way down to get myself changed."

"Wasn't I supposed to get wet?"

"That would have worked too. If we *both* get wet, *that* doesn't work. If you get wet and then we rub all the water and mud into each other's clothes, *that* sends us both back together."

She smiled now. He said, "Look, I only suspect it's illegal—"

"You speckles-shy idiot, of course it's illegal! We can't stop buying speckles and still run a restaurant!"

"Of course we'll have to buy speckles. We'll get them from the caravans, just like always. But if hard times come, there's a bag of speckles—"

"How many did you bring?"

She'd seen. "Just the two."

"One would have done. Any bus can get us back here for more."

"Okay. Stashed where only you and I can find it. We don't tell anyone else."

"You didn't think you'd tell me!"

"It's a *crime*, Harlow. I thought I'd tell Barry, but as long as you know, that's enough."

That ought to get her.

And he saw that it had. Wave Rider had a secret, and none knew it save Jeremy and Harlow: the inner circle.

They arrived in time to scavenge the last of dinner. Three caravan suppliers had come early and were sharing a room. Otherwise the inn held most of Karen's siblings and children and in-laws. Everyone stayed polite, and presently carried Jeremy's and Harlow's backpacks up to separate rooms.

They'd discussed *that* on the bus.

Jeremy got to Lloyd before they gathered for breakfast. "What have you and Brenda told them about me?"

"About the Windfarm? Brenda and I won't tell them anything, Jeremy. We talked it over. It just wouldn't be good." Lloyd laughed suddenly. "And then you show up with Harlow!"

"She can help when the caravan—"

"Sure."

At least the timing was sweet. Whatever the Winslow clan remembered of their stepmother . . . however much they mourned Karen, now a lifegiver . . . whatever they thought of the pit chef who was probably rubbing up against his stepmother-in-law . . . they were shorthanded. It was late autumn. The outbound spring caravan was due in five days.

Over the next few days Harlow and the Winslow clan found some sort of adjustment. Jeremy didn't have to watch dominance and accommodation games. The trick was to stay outside. He tended the pit, and tried out some of what he thought he'd learned in Romanoff's, and upgraded his tools for the onslaught to come.

He tested his leg by swimming with the Otterfolk, reacquainting himself with them. If they noticed his game leg, that was all to the good: they'd guess why he wouldn't surf.

Harlow and Chloe surfed with them, riding waves in tandem. Harlow had returned to the board as if she'd never been away.

They'd need the Otterfolk's goodwill, to get fish to feed the merchants.

Harlow simply poured one bagful of speckles into their speckles shaker can. "It's the obvious place for it. The way we run the inn, everyone'll think someone else got us more speckles." He stopped her from adding the second bag, but he had no excuse at all.

A day later he'd found one. "Taste this."

She sipped. "Smooth. Grapefruit and vodka and . . . salt?"

"Secret recipe," he said.

"Speckles. Sea salt and speckles?"

They called the drink a Salty Dog, and the last bag of fertile speckles stayed in the bar.

Rita Nogales phoned. She had answers. *Fresh* avocado reacting to speckles in the mayonnaise, in Karen's and Brenda's mixed seafood dish, produced a mild allergic reaction that disappeared without obtrusive symptoms. Only a patient already sick was threatened. Avocado picked two days earlier wouldn't react. Hardly surprising if nobody had noticed in two hundred years.

Nogales was crowing, sure that anyone she talked to must be just de*light*ed. She could live with throwing away Hope Batch and Batch One, but *all* the superskin on Destiny? Jeremy was glad he'd answered the phone. Anyone else would have screamed at the woman.

Even he hung up in a black mood. Avocados . . . what a lousy, trivial . . .

With two days to spare, Johannes and Eileen Wheeler arrived with a wagonload of green and root vegetables pulled by two goats and a tug. "Hell of a lot of prep work for three days of pure madness," Johannes told Jeremy, grinning and slapping a goat's flank. "I expect you can use the help?"

"Yes. *Do not* introduce me to the goats." Johannes had once insisted on doing that before Jeremy put on his butcher's hat.

For a day, then, he and Harlow faced Karen's entire family. Then all four men went off to hunt and left just the women and the gimp. Jeremy didn't see any fireworks. They were being civilized. Eileen tried once or twice to involve her father in some kind of property discussion.

As for the separate rooms, "There's no point," Harlow told him. "We came here together. They know where you were staying. They don't know how long you fought me off—"

"Hey."

"We probably even *walk* like we're rubbing up against each other."

"You do. I have this deceptive limp."

"Jeremy, we're not doing them a favor here. People like to file people in subroutines. It's easier for them if they think of us as a couple."

Matters of courtesy be damned, the room would be needed. A day ahead of the caravan, Harlow moved into Jeremy's room.

He liked it. He dreamed of Karen and woke guilty, but with a woman in his bed, he could sleep.

They came at noon, announced by a cloud of dust.

A wagon was the length and width of a bus, but taller, and two tugs were enough to pull it. They numbered a full twenty wagons: no yutzes yet, but eighty merchants and perhaps twenty-five suppliers. They rolled past Wave Rider and out of sight.

In Spiral Town the caravan's arrival had been very like this.

Wave Rider had twenty-two rooms, and that had always been barely enough. Caravans carried tents, after all, and did not look for unnecessary expense. Wave Rider housed merchant families with elders and children. Merchants' relatives and businesses that dealt with the caravan were the caravan's supply line, and they *would* want rooms: they often doubled up. Romances and marriages had started that way.

Forty or so to be housed in twenty-two rooms. Over a hundred to be fed! Wave Rider geared up for business.

✳ 33 ✳

The Spring Caravan

The natives are irrelevant to humankind on the Crab. They're not as madly versatile as men.

—Wayne Parnelli, Marine Biology

There was no winter in Destiny's year. Removing winter allowed the other seasons to be almost the right length for the Earthtime clocks.

In order for the spring caravan to reach Destiny Town in spring, it must reach the Neck in autumn. Wave Rider hosted the spring caravan in early autumn, and the previous summer caravan carrying goods acquired along the Crab, three weeks later.

It was autumn now: the nights were cooling. Dionne, party of eight filed out onto the pier to watch the sunset.

Old Wayne Dionne traded in Terminus, selling carved and painted shells and similar goods collected along the Road by his family in Dionne wagon. Jeremy had known them for years. When they filed back toward the fire pit, Wayne called, "Jeremy, meet Hester. She's old enough for the wagons now."

"Hello, Hester." Wayne's granddaughter had grown tall, and kept the quiet smile. "Will any of you be staying, then?"

"No, the tent's enough for us. Just meals tonight and tomorrow. We wouldn't miss your cooking."

"I have something for you." Jeremy showed Wayne what he'd found on the beach west of here: a flattish shell nearly a meter long. Rainbows played along its inner face where Jeremy had polished it.

Wayne looked dubious.

Jeremy persisted. "It doesn't look like a back shell, does it? More like a skullcap? This at the end would be where the beak extension broke off."

"The beast would be huge."

Jeremy set it aside.

Wayne said, "No, sell it to me. Somebody might be interested, back in Destiny Town. Forty?"

Money changed hands.

Jeremy asked, "Wayne, what would you think of my joining a caravan?"

And he watched Wayne's slow grin. "Unlikely. Why would you want to at your age?"

"I never saw a caravan pit barbecue. Everything I know is second-hand."

"You do fine."

"Would I do better if I'd been up and down the Road?"

"Maybe."

"Would you want me in the cooking crew if you had to eat the result?"

"Maybe. Hester, what do you think?"

The girl smiled. Jeremy grinned back. Hester hadn't tasted his cooking *or* the Road's. Wayne wasn't taking him seriously.

Wayne wasn't a merchant.

Chloe and Harlow came out with the large salad bowl. Harlow stopped for a lingering kiss before going back in.

More merchants were gathering around the fire pit, or watching the sunset fade and the Otterfolk play. Merchants and suppliers did business here. Not many would bother to talk to the chef. Jeremy wore his pit chef's persona like a vividly painted mask, and of course the light hid him too.

Jeremy had persuaded Harold Winslow that he could run a pit barbecue. So Harold had run a strip of lighting along the deck's edge, above where Jeremy dug the pit. "My guests eat late," he'd said. In that electric blaze Jeremy hadn't been able to tell whether food was raw or cooked.

In two weeks it had become much easier than trying to judge by sunset-light. And in this blue-tinged light no merchant from Tim Bed-nacourt's past had ever recognized him.

"This is one thing you almost never get on the Road," an older man said, not to Jeremy. "Lettuce." He looked around for inn personnel. "You grow this yourself?"

"Half our back garden is planted in lettuce," Jeremy said, and kept the neutral grin as he recognized Joker ibn-Rushd, aged and weathered and gone a bit soft. He babbled on: "After all, it'd be wilted mush before it got here from the Terminus farms."

Joker was frowning in the harsh, blue-tinged light. Better not give him time to think about where he'd seen this barbecue chef. "I'm Jeremy Winslow, part owner. You're new here?"

"Not quite new. I'm Dzhokhar Schilling. My wife Greta, my daughter Shireen."

Jeremy clasped his hand and said, "Dzhokhar Schilling," careful of his pronunciation, because Jeremy Winslow had never called this man "Joker." "Hello, Greta. Hi, Shireen," more handclasps for the young woman and the ten-year-old girl.

Joker was saying, "We're ibn-Rushd. You buy our cookware. I've spent time at Wave Rider, but usually I eat in the restaurant. I see enough of pit barbecues!"

"But it's a new thing to me," Greta laughed. "For twelve years we've worked Dzhokhar's shop in Destiny Town."

Joker had married a woman fifteen years his junior. She was small, pale of skin and hair, a bit plain, too easy to overlook. Jeremy asked her, "You've never been on the Road?"

"No. Dzhokhar has been trying to prepare me."

Jeremy, trying to picture that, said, "We hear interesting rumors," suspecting he already knew more than he was supposed to, and less. Had Joker explained—

Joker grinned at them both. "Things not to be told."

The tuna must be cooked through by now. Jeremy drafted Lloyd, and together they turned it onto a platter and carved. The Schillings watched. Other merchants gathered to watch the show and to serve themselves.

Jeremy asked Joker, "How was that?"

Joker ate a mouthful. "Skillful."

"I have to ask. Everything I know about pit cooking, I learn by asking. I've sometimes thought of joining a caravan."

"Yes, I see." Joker was amused. "Try grilling your fish when something has delayed the wagons. Cook and carve by dying sunset light, and Quicksilver already gone. You'll know then what a caravan chef's first law is. 'Get more lights!' Stick with the lights, Jeremy."

Turnover was high in the caravans, but there were still familiar faces. Put Jeremy Winslow under blue light, dress him in white, age him, scar him: no merchant would know him from the past. But, even dressed in a merchant's flamboyant garb, Tim Bednacourt still might be remembered in daylight.

Of course he'd be crazy to go *now*. It was the wrong caravan!

After the spring caravan moved on . . . Harlow had fallen in love with Wave Rider, not Harold Winslow, maybe not Jeremy either. If Jeremy married her, she'd have his fifth of the inn after he was gone.

Come spring, speckles would be sprouting around the lettuce patch. He'd imposed that time limit on himself. Wave Rider was too public: a speckles crop couldn't be ignored for long. In early summer would come the outbound autumn caravan, and he must go.

But go how?

Hadn't he had this conversation once, long ago, with murderers trying to hijack a wagon? Nobody could cross the Neck alive, nobody could travel the Road, except with a caravan. Even a lone captured wagon would be attacked.

Tim Bednacourt had run the length of the Crab by keeping to the peaks no man had climbed. Now he was nearing fifty and he limped. Now he'd have a secure speckles supply; but could he still climb? Climb along the frost line, dip down for food and water, up and over to circle around any bandits. He'd even considered traveling up the narrow side of the Crab, but on the maps that looked lethal.

He'd need a way to cross the Neck. A boat, a surfboard: the currents ran the right way. He'd want a cockade, too. He hadn't found them growing anywhere.

What he was looking for was the least crazy way back.

And that was to talk himself aboard a caravan, if it was even possible. His family was serving dinner in the restaurant, out of earshot. He could sound out a few peripheral people, now.

The slow-cooking part of dinner was taking care of itself. Guests milled and sampled. Waver Rider's people milled and cooked. Jeremy joined a dozen guests out on the pier.

He knelt at the edge of the pier, water lapping just below his knees, and reached out with a slice of sweet potato. To the ten-year-old girl he said, "Shireen, go like this."

Three flattish heads popped up.

"Winston," he said, and one of the Otterfolk came forward to take the sweet potato. Short arms, wide hands with four thick, short fingers.

Jeremy handed sweet potato slices to Shireen. Shireen began distributing them to the other Otterfolk. Winston was still watching Jeremy.

Jeremy curled and uncurled just his fingers, no thumbs. *Eight, sixteen, twenty-four fish. Prawns, a double handful. One surf clam.* Fingers wiggled: *Don't bust your chops, we'll take what you can get.*

Winston disappeared. Tomorrow he would be back with what he

could collect, and would tell Jeremy what he wanted; but that was easier by daylight and while they were both in the water.

The little girl asked, "Jeremy, can I go in with them?"

"Depends. What are you wearing?"

"No!" cried Greta Schilling, unseen in shadow until now. "Tomorrow morning, yes, dear?"

"Yes, Mommy."

Greta turned to Jeremy. "We wear our good clothes for your first night's banquet, you know." Reproving.

"Mrs. Schilling, you flatter us."

"Please, I am Greta. Jeremy, is it safe for a child to swim with Otter-folk?"

"Absolutely. We depend on it. If we don't entertain them, they don't fish for us. Greta, I know that name. Shireen?"

"Her great-grandmother Shireen died twelve years ago. Dzhokhar and I, we both loved her. So I married Dzhokhar Livnah and gave her name to our first daughter."

It took Jeremy a moment to untangle that in his mind, but the implications—"So Dzhokhar settled with you? In Destiny Town."

"Yes, for twelve years."

And took Greta's surname, of course.

"His wife was with Armstrong wagon, you see, but she retired. Many merchants travel the Road for a time and then retire to a family shop. Dzhokhar could have married another merchant, but we knew each other—"

"Dzhokhar *Livnah?*"

"Yes. Why?"

"No, nothing." But he'd always assumed that everyone on ibn-Rushd wagon was named ibn-Rushd! Assumed that Joker was single, too. "I only wondered how a man named Livnah joined ibn-Rushd wagon."

She shook her head. "There are things I'm not supposed to tell."

If he forced too many merchants to say that too often, it would be noticed. But a caravan trainee was *exactly* who he wanted to question! He compromised. "Is there anything *I* can tell *you?*"

She laughed.

"No, really. I've been listening to fire-pit talk for twenty-seven years. They speak a secret language, but I've picked up a little. Ibn-Rushd cooks, and that *is* my language."

Shireen tugged at her mother's arm. "The fence," she said.

"Yes. Jeremy, we walked down the beach this afternoon, as far as a razormesh fence. The beach beyond, it looked nice. Private. There were shells. Can you get us past that fence?"

"As I understand it," Jeremy said, "if I could get you past that fence, you wouldn't see a restaurant here next year. That's the local birth-ground for the Otterfolk, Greta, and the Overview Bureau is very serious about that."

"Oh." She thought a moment, then asked, "After you fillet the tuna, where do you take the bones and head?"

"Soup stock. Everything interesting goes into the cauldron. On the caravans . . . you won't carry that size cauldron."

"Why do you shudder?"

He shook his head, thinking that a chef could always break off conversation for some convenient urgency—

"Is it true that we must get pregnant by men along the Road? And the men make the local women pregnant?"

"That's what they say. They say also that you merchants are almost inhumanly good at doing that with us mortals."

She dimpled. "I thought Dzhokhar might have been having fun with me. Well, I haven't had the training yet."

Most of the merchants had gone up the Road and the rest had gone to bed. The Winslow family cleaned up after them to some extent, then quit. Jeremy went up to bed. He could climb a flight of stairs, now, but not run up it.

He began stripping down, found he had some help. Harlow breathed in his ear. "So you want to join a caravan?"

She must have felt him lose his balance and wince as pain crunched in his healing knee. He said, "I've been thinking about it. Who told you?"

"Yvonne Dionne told me my husband was talking about hitting the Road. Yvonne and Wayne, the only thing between their shop and mine is a sandwich shop. Jeremy, were you serious? Is this a sudden thing?"

Still thinking as fast as ever in his life, Jeremy said, "Not sudden, but I never could have talked Karen into doing it, and just to get away from here—"

"But with that limp—"

"Oh, I can wait for the autumn caravan. I'll be healed by then." They were seated on the futon by now, and he took her face in his hands. "Will you marry me after the spring caravan leaves?"

"Well, I'd have to, wouldn't I?"

"What? Why?"

She laughed. "The caravans only take couples!"

"*What?*"

"You didn't know?" Still laughing. "But you asked me to marry you first. Good!"

He'd been thinking that she could vote his one-fifth share of Wave Rider. This blindsided him. "*Everyone* on a caravan is married?" What about Rian? and old Shireen? and Joker? Wait, Joker *was* married—

"Well, no, not everyone. A woman in her teens or twenties, or a veteran who wants to die on the Road, but only if they're a caravan family, Jeremy. Anyone else, it's couples. Otherwise there would be too many men, I guess. Local help is supposed to be *all* men."

He was still stunned. "Harlow, why didn't I think of coming to you before?"

"You may be an instinctive liar, Jeremy."

She was the answer all along, and he'd been dodging and weaving— "No, wait, I'm a Spiral. You're a girl. We almost don't talk to each other in Spiral Town. I thought I'd got that . . . crap out of my head."

"Hmmm."

"Can we get on a caravan? Will you come with me?"

She hesitated. "You know there are certain rules."

"I double-damned don't seem to know what they are!"

"We'd both be rubbing up against locals, mostly younger locals who can make babies. We'll be trained for that at the camp. I don't really know more than that, but I hear jokes."

"Sounds like fun?" He put a question in that, and she grinned. "We can still rub up against each other. I remember the ibn-Rushds did."

She said, "You know how to cook, but they'll train you to sit behind a counter and sell cookware and speckles."

"I've watched. Only watched."

"The third rule is very important. Keep the caravan secrets. Never tell."

"My darling, you seem to have learned a lot of what they never tell."

"I listened to merchants at Wave Rider for years before you came. I've spent more years talking to shopkeepers. A lot of them retired from the wagons, you know. Even so, I don't know anything deep. We'll have to persuade a wagonmaster that we can be trusted."

He thought. Smiled. "I could persuade someone that I *have* kept a secret. I could ask, 'What would happen if Spadoni wagon fell into the hands of bandits?' Better to trust me than someone who hasn't been tested."

"What does it mean?"

Doubtfully, "Should I tell you?"

"Jeremy!"

"Spadoni is where they keep the real guns. Tucker has the shark guns and ammo, the stuff the yutzes use. The yutzes don't see what's in Spadoni, and locals shouldn't have it, let alone bandits. If bandits stopped Spadoni, the whole caravan would have to deal with it."

"Any idea what those weapons are like?"

"Some—"

"Don't tell me. Don't tell anyone."

"Can we get in?"

"I don't know. Best if there's an opening on one of the wagons. Sometimes they're shorthanded. We can ask Walther Simonsen at Romanoff's. He knows you're the real thing. The spring caravan won't be back in time to do us any good, so there's no point in you talking to *them*. Talk to the suppliers."

"Yes. Harlow, thank you."

"Can Wave Rider do without us both?"

"We'll hire someone. I'd better tell someone where the extra speckles are. Brenda."

She was searching for something in his eyes. "I don't see why it's so important to you. Oh, damn, of course I do. I forget who you are. You want to go home."

That was true, and he nodded.

"Jeremy, promise me you won't do anything stupid."

"Like what?"

"Don't run away home when you get to Spiral Town. Disappearing from a caravan rouses all *kinds* of excitement. They wouldn't leave until they found you or your corpse. They could cut off the speckles to Spiral Town! Promise?"

"Harlow, I promise."

"Then I'll get us on a caravan."

From autumn to summer was a happy time. Jeremy Winslow paid attention. Look again, it might be gone.

No way could he board a caravan without a background check. He'd made a whimsical choice twenty-seven years ago, and now the computer had him as Jeremy Winslow born Hearst. What might Willow and Randall Hearst have to say to that?

He went back to Medical to get his knee looked at, and wangled two hours in the library.

Willow Hearst was dead: killed by overweight.

Randall Hearst had become an alcoholic. His periodic treatments were a matter of record.

Risk it.

Jeremy Hearst, born on the Road, was not a terribly happy child in

Destiny Town. He dropped out of Wide Wade's in adolescence, got into cooking anyway. . . .

He took long walks along the beach with anyone who would come. He swam. He didn't risk the board. Caravan merchants need their legs! Harlow said that the bus stopped at Baikunur Beach, where the shuttles were loaded; prospective caravaners walked twenty klicks further to where they'd be trained, and they dared not arrive limping.

There was a thing Harlow couldn't help him with. How could he get fertile speckles across the Neck?

Get them into a caravan: a chef *must* carry speckles. But *nothing* of Destiny Town technology crossed to the Crab. No caravan, no wagon, no man or woman crossed the Neck without a skin search, Harlow said.

Was that true?

He couldn't quite ask, but—"Harlow, they take speckles pouches. And the guns in Spadoni wagon aren't low-tech."

She shrugged.

At a guess: the rest of a caravan might be destroyed, but the prole guns in the #2 wagon must not fall into bandit hands. So phones or superskin or *anything* of settler magic would be kept in the #2 wagon too. And if a man couldn't get a pouch of speckles *in* there, he sure couldn't get one back *out*.

Jeremy considered a hidden pouch in a backpack.

He considered a trip to the Neck by surfboard: hide a pouch of speckles, pick it up after the search and during the leavetaking banquet.

He began playing in Wave Rider's kitchen.

In early spring Jeremy was able to say to Harlow, "Close your eyes. Try this." It was a sweet fruit jell cut to the size of a thumb and rolled in seeds.

"Delicious," Harlow said. She considered. "Sesame? Sesame and speckles." She laughed at his chagrin. "Nobody else would have guessed, Jeremy! I'm the only one who knows you get your speckles free."

"It's the sesame and honey that costs."

She looked at what she'd bitten in half. Pale brown sesame seeds, bright yellow speckles. "You should dye them."

Jeremy used a dark blue food dye, dilute. The tiny yellow seeds came out green as Earthlife grass. He could put green dye in the jell, or make a rainbow of colors. He dyed the sesame seeds red. He called it *festivity candy,* and then just *festivity*.

His only question now was whether dyed speckles seeds would sprout.

In spring, in the lettuce patch, they did.

And the autumn caravan departed at the height of summer.

✳ 34 ✳

The Autumn Caravan

We've found some animals that look like little armored Volkswagens.
—Grigori Dudayev, senior M.D.

Something about the position of the sun on his cheek brought Jeremy Winslow gently awake.

He was dozing upright in the driver's alcove. Harlow was driving. Behind them on the roof, Tanya Hearst kept watch with Steban, the new yutz they'd picked up in Haven. They weren't paying much attention.

In this territory, they needn't. There was farmland on both sides, and large houses sparsely set. People who feared bandits didn't build like this.

It was all new. This must have been wilderness when last he'd seen it. Jeremy wondered if he would recognize the New Hann Farm.

The sun: it was midafternoon, almost time to quit. A caravan doesn't hurry. If they didn't reach Warkan's Tavern tonight they'd make it tomorrow.

Some pointed structure poked up from the Road, too far ahead to make out.

Jeremy looked downslope, a mere half-klick to a strip of sand and then water dark with Destiny devilhair weed. It all looked strangely familiar. He still didn't know where he was until somebody far ahead shouted, "Warkan's Tavern!"

Angelo Hearst climbed up from the sales window to see. The word bounced down the caravan's length to Hearst wagon, and Angelo's bellow sent it on, while Jeremy stared ahead in befuddlement.

—Oh, of course, he'd been looking for Carder's Boat! which had been there forever, until—

He'd last seen Carder's Boat moored offshore of Tail Town. Haunted Bay fishermen used it as a dock. It had swarmed with children on the day the caravan rolled through.

He'd come home . . . but fifty meters past the just-visible façade of Warkan's Tavern, a slender triangular arch stood above the Road. *In* the Road. A gate, or a barrier.

Harlow was bringing the wagon to a stop. It took a while for the chugs to get the idea, but the message was welcome. Wagons behind were stopping too. The lead wagons wanted a little more space first. If you made chugs bunch up, they wouldn't bring in as much weed and wouldn't get enough to eat.

Locals were gathering on the hills above Warkan's Tavern. They knew: merchants did no business *now*.

Hearst wagon (#6) was at a halt. Harlow and Jeremy gave the reins the practiced *flip, flip, flip* that freed the chugs. A good trip: they still had all twenty.

The spring caravan had come back somewhat shot up. They'd found and obliterated a bandit nest, they said. Obliterated: maybe. Bandits hadn't bothered the autumn caravan.

The chugs drifted downslope.

Angelo dropped straight from the roof, showing off for his wife. Jeremy eased on down, then gave a hand to Harlow, who didn't need it, and Tanya, who didn't either. Wave Rider's pit chef always did that. It irritated Angelo and amused Steban.

On the roof Steban threw open the sides of the wagon, then came down to help the others deploy cookware. Miller wagon's people (#8) were doing the same.

The dark line of chugs had reached the sand.

Hearst wagon carried Tanya and Angelo Hearst, Angelo's grandfather Glen, and the Winslows. Five merchants meant room for only one yutz. Miller cookwagon carried three yutzes to make up for that. Glen Hearst made small concessions to pay off the debt.

Thus: the caravan would be here two nights. Not all could afford to dine at Warkan's Tavern or go into town, but it didn't take both cookwagons to cook dinner. Hearst wagon would cook on the first night.

The line of chugs flowed into the waves.

Jeremy and Harlow moved well together, unloading and deploying tools, hanging an ostrich and four chickens the hunters had shot. At this their steady efficiency and decades of practice made them the best in the caravan. Yutzes from all the wagons were gathering Destiny firewood and digging out the pits.

Something was bothering Glen Hearst. He spent less time supervising than in looking toward town, or the Tavern, or—

Far up the Road, two electric wagons approached.

Jeremy glanced that way from time to time as he worked. Atop one he picked out the glitter of Begley cloth. The wagons stopped short of the pointed structure, and men began unloading them.

The barrier stood just at the border between Warkan's Tavern and Bloocher Farm.

"Glen, what *is* that thing?"

"Never saw it before."

Hearst and Miller wagons had made all reasonable preparations for dinner, and no sign of chugs. The fires in the long pits were beginning to catch.

"Mind if I go look?"

"Set up the tents first."

Jeremy and Harlow exchanged glances. Jeremy hadn't meant *now!* There was time to break out the tents and set them up, but not to walk most of a klick, almost as far as Warkan's Tavern! Glen knew that. What had made him so touchy?

They busied themselves setting tentpoles and deploying tents and inflating pillows, until a long black line of devilhair weed rolled out of the sea. Then all the traders and yutzes dropped their work and returned to their wagons. As the chugs emerged pushing devilhair ahead of them, Hearst wagon's crew settled on the roof with a liter of lemonade and their guns.

The chugs fed placidly. Then they all broke off at once and rolled uphill.

Six long low shapes darted from the water, all at once and wide apart. Only six. A few guns sounded: overeager yutzes, quickly silenced. Four sharks stopped at the black weed.

Two came on. The caravan fired, one long roll of thunder. The two fell. Four sharks darted from the weed and into the next wave.

Two lay dead. Jeremy was pretty sure he'd hit one. A few yutzes were still firing into the shredded bodies.

It wasn't just Glen Hearst. The elders were in a fury. At dinner they gathered in a small, tight circle. They fell silent when yutzes came to serve them.

Harlow and Jeremy approached the circle and were rebuffed.

Yutzes did most of the work of serving dinner. Jeremy only had to get it off the fire while it wasn't yet charred. In dying orange light he stopped to look at one of the dead sharks. They were too chewed up to show detail. He'd look up LUNGSHARK if he ever reached another library.

The light was dying, and so were the coals. Jeremy set his pan of pureed cherries and gelatin where the heat wouldn't char it. He'd practiced that, and ruined several batches during the training period. He'd brought gelatin and honey and twenty pounds of seeds to roll it in. All along the Road he'd found fruit to make jell. Every batch of festivity was different.

Harlow was watching him. She said, "I think your festivity candy was what really put us here. It made us just that extra notch more desirable."

"You're very desirable." He kissed her.

Harlow gestured toward the circle of elders; lifted one brow. Harlow didn't *like* being treated as a child.

He said, "Maybe when you're *older*, dear."

"We're Glen Hearst's age! Let's eavesdrop?"

"No safe way. Love, the yutzes know how to clean up. Let's go look at that gate."

Warkan's Tavern was full of light and activity as they strolled past. At the edge of Bloocher Farm, they stopped beside the arch. It was poured stone in a cast-iron frame. It straddled the Road, narrower than a caravan wagon.

The chair beneath it was made of iron and poured stone, though lined with pillows. As Jeremy approached the man in the chair stood up, tall and massive, though armed with no more than a stick at his belt.

Harlow asked, "Are we barred from Spiral Town?"

The man didn't respond. Jeremy touched Harlow's hand: *Take it easy.* He reached into his special pocket for three thumbs of candy. "Try this."

When the man didn't react, Jeremy put one between Harlow's lips, ate one, then offered the other.

The man ate it. "Oooh. What is it?"

"Winslow's festivity candy. I'm Winslow. Are we barred from Spiral Town?"

"The caravans are. Yes, sir, merchants are too, unless you have special business. But you can go to the Tavern."

"There's a Carolyn Hope Hearst buried in your graveyard. I was a Hearst before I married. I'd like to visit her grave."

Harlow stared.

The guard missed that. He wasn't *seeing* Harlow. He said, "We haven't buried a lifegiver from outside in more than fifty years."

Jeremy said, "More like ninety for Carolyn Hope. Way too old to visit the Tavern, sir. You have one of our men, too, more recent. Father wasn't so sure of him."

The guard was massively embarrassed. "Sir, I don't doubt you'll be let visit your ancestors, but *I* can't, and not at night."

"When did the rules change? Since the spring caravan?"

"Yeah."

"If they did something awful, they never told *us*."

"Sir, I'm not sure I could tell you anyway." The man was nervous. He *must* have watched a caravan repel sharks. Everyone did.

The poured-stone triangle and the stone chair looked very permanent for so recent a thing. Cargo lay in piles just beyond, across the Road from the huge old elms that bordered Warkan Farm. A little heap of clocks. An array of pottery and glassware. Melons and squashes and oranges. Two great stacks of Begley cloth sparking with current. They must have brought it down from Mount Apollo in sunlight, uncovered.

Jeremy turned away, leading Harlow. He murmured, "He can't talk to a woman he doesn't know."

"It's birdfucking rude."

"You sound like a felon."

"I'll be one, after I murder the next birdfucker who treats me that way. What was that about a dead ancestor?"

He told Harlow, "I found her on that last trip to Medical. The programs gave me a lineage for Hearst wagon. Why not? I'm a Hearst, courtesy of Harlow Winslow. *Someone* in a caravan family was *bound* to have died in Spiral Town."

Quicksilver still lit the night while the caravan's elders walked the length of the caravan, talking to whomever they found. They found Maiku Lall bedding down his family beside Lall wagon, the medical wagon, first in line; and Harlow and Jeremy Winslow just passing.

"You sell no speckles tomorrow," Palava Lall said.

Maiku gaped at his mother. Glen Hearst quickly said, "That goes for us too. Harlow, Jeremy, speckles are not to enter Spiral Town tomorrow."

Jeremy didn't speak. Harlow asked, "Might one ask why?"

"Later," Glen said, and the group of elders turned downRoad. Jeremy noticed Govert Miller among them, back early from the Tavern. The roster of elders was complete.

The whisper of waves had a buzzing in it: the caravan was not asleep, but talking in their tents.

Glen asked, "Where have you been?"

Jeremy told Glen what they'd learned of the guarded gate.

Harlow said, "Caravans were founded to move speckles, Glen. This violates a trust."

"And so does that gate. We do more than deliver speckles," the old man said. "We supervise. The mainland takes risks, but these Crab shies live their lives the way evolution shaped us on Earth. Lots of farming, diet varies by season, not much medicine, not much industrial power—"

"Short life spans."

"Yes, all right, Harlow, shorter life spans," Glen Hearst said. "But they're safe."

If Jeremy was going to get his say, Harlow was going to have to say it. She tried. "Glen, humanity on Destiny is two hundred and fifty years old. Do we still need a control group?"

"You never do know in advance, Harlow. That's what a control experiment is for. Anyway, it's not just one anymore. When offshoot groups started moving down the Road from Base One, the caravans transported them. Whatever hurts any of them is a warning for the rest of us."

"We *know* what kills on Destiny. Speckles, lack of! The threat to Spiral Town is *us!*"

Jeremy feared she'd overdo it. In haste he asked, "Glen, what do we want from this?"

"They've barred us. In stages, over these past fifty years. No merchants past Peach Street. No merchants in town at night. One wagon to the market and one to Mount Apollo, then *none.* Now this. How the hell can we supervise a control experiment if . . ." He waved his arms in frustration.

"If the mice lock us out," Jeremy murmured.

Glen glared. "It's bad for them too! They don't see any sapient creature outside their insular selves. It stunts their minds."

Harlow said, "They're inbred, too, but that *is* policy—"

"So, we know what we want," Jeremy said. "What if we don't get it?"

"Oh, we'll get it."

"*That's* good. Because we're here for two nights if we get it or not. Chugs can't forage in one place more than two nights running."

"The Spirals know it too," Glen said. "Remember, sell anything *but* speckles tomorrow." He crawled into the tent to sleep.

Jeremy kept walking, and Harlow followed.

Wagons were wide apart. Between tents they could not be overheard. Jeremy said, "Thank you."

"It's a joy," she said, "watching you keep your mouth shut."

"You terrify me. Are you with Steban tonight?"

"Tanya snatched him as soon as he was on board. Don't you *notice,* Jeremy? Or was that a joke?"

"He'll have you both. If she's any good—?"

"Very. And beautiful. And already pregnant."

"He'll wonder what you've got to match her. Anyway, you're mine tonight, if I can get you relaxed. So what would that take?"

She was silent.

She was thinking about all the way back to Bloocher Farm, and watching him the way an armed yutz watches the sea.

Downslope to shore, then across the overgrown fence, then up. Likely enough he'd be shot as a burglar. . . .

Uphill would take him to the frost line. He'd crouch behind the brush like a nineteen-year-old, duckwalk past Mount Apollo and down into Spiral Town. The long way home, but Harlow couldn't guess who might give him refuge. . . .

Or he could procure Spiral garb, recover his Spiral accent, and walk past the gate in a clump of shoppers.

"I've promised not to go home," he told her.

"Right."

"Harlow, do you think I'd leave these old birdfuckers alone to decide whether to turn us all into speckels-shies?"

Harlow put her fingertips over his mouth. Damn, he was getting too loud. She said, "Now who needs relaxing?"

"Me."

"Well, come back to the tent."

In the morning the chugs went into the sea again. Ten sharks followed them out. Three lay flopping when the rest fled.

"Six last night, then ten. They're getting smart," Angelo said.

"Smart?"

"For sharks. The first night, there's weed close to shore. Morning, the chugs have to go deeper for it. Next night, deeper yet. Next morning, even farther. The sharks get a better and better chance to catch a chug or two."

"They don't get smart, just hungry. The chugs are taking their food, Angelo."

Thousands of Spirals had come to watch the shark-shooting. Now they descended on the wagons.

Yutzes were sent to fetch the clocks, pottery, glassware, fruit, and vegetables piled beyond the gate. The prices for these had been agreed. They were told to leave the Begley cloth alone. By noon it was sparking and spitting lightning, not safe to touch.

The Spirals bought what the wagons sold, and couldn't believe that they couldn't buy speckles too. Jeremy gave away handfuls of festivity to all the children. He'd cut and roll more tonight.

Merchants were expected to wear eccentric dress. Pockets were always in fashion. Jeremy had built a big pocket over his belly and lined it, and he kept a generous handful of extra seeds inside to keep the jelly candies from sticking. It gave him a lumpy-rotund look.

Come evening, the Hearsts geared up for Warkan's Tavern. As they laid out cookware and the yutzes dug their pits, Jeremy found himself crouching down behind his persona. The last time he'd seen Warkan's Tavern, he'd killed a man.

Here came a forest of black devilhair and a row of chugs pushing it. Time to board the roofs.

Far up the Road, two electric wagons approached Warkan's Tavern. Maybe Spiral Town only *had* two; in Jeremy's youth they'd had four. These were empty but for five men.

They stopped at the gate. Five soberly dressed Spiral Town men went into the tavern and emerged on the second-floor balcony.

The chugs left off burrowing in the black weed, and moved uphill. Sharks zipped up the sand. Bullets spattered them; two fled, seven burrowed into the weed, four sped after the chugs. A hail of bullets stopped those.

"Smarter," Angelo grunted, and relaxed.

Seven sharks zipped out of the weed all at once, into the waves before anyone could quite react.

Harlow asked, "What would it cost to wipe out lungsharks?"

"We almost have," Glen Hearst said. "There used to be more. It's a bad idea, though. Without sharks we'd pay less attention to shark *guns*. Locals tend to be respectful if they've seen shark guns in action. Bandits too."

Tanya asked, "Harlow, don't you like shooting sharks?"

"I really do not."

Tanya laughed.

Miller wagon was cooking dinner tonight, though Hearst wagon had helped set up. Jeremy and Harlow waited for Glen. The elders seemed to be waiting for . . . what? But a third of the caravan walked toward Warkan's Tavern, a growing crowd that included Angelo, Tanya, and Steban.

They stopped, milling a bit, when the dignitaries came out of Warkan's Tavern and walked toward the caravan.

Glen Hearst said, "I think that's *my* dinner."

Jemmy Bloocher's father had been of the Council, and the Council did usually take several wagonmasters to dinner. In his youth the caravans had come as far as the Hub. Later . . . but was it *normal* for the Council to come this far?

The Councilors were picking up elders from the wagons, not all, just some. Nobody from Krupp wagon, #2. Nine men reached Hearst wagon. One man took Glen Hearst aside and spoke to him, a casual and genial tone, words half-heard. "—Harry's Bar—"

Pat the special pocket: half-full. Pit chef Jeremy: obsequious, a bit effusive. First sight of Spiral Town: gape a little. Even Warkan's Tavern is impressive. Damn, you can see buildings poking up in clusters a klick away! He felt himself wanting to overdo it.

"—And you must meet our pit chef from the finest restaurant on the Road, Jeremy Winslow."

Not much interested, Chairman Greegry Bloocher stepped forward to shake the cook's hand.

"Jeremy, some of us have been invited to dinner by these good people, and I mentioned your dessert—"

"A recent invention, sir." *Spiral Town accent and a complacent smile.* Jeremy handed his brother a thumb of festivity candy. He watched Greegry's appreciation, and offered a handful to the rest. Harlow was watching him like a magician's hat.

"Why don't you come to dinner with us," Glen Hearst asked, "and bring some along?"

✴ 35 ✴

Spiral Town

Most cultures have understood that some are more equal than others. There were those who would not go to the stars, and there were those we would not take.

—Captain Arnold Cohen aboard *Argos*,
during negotiation

Electric wagons brought them back to the light and noise at Warkan's Tavern. Jeremy walked in behind Govert Miller. Harlow was with six other women on the women's side of the room. She saw him; he smiled; she dove back into animated conversation.

Jeremy looked around for company. He'd completely forgotten that he couldn't just sit down with his wife.

"There, Jeremy." Govert Miller meant a table of merchants, all men in their twenties, with one empty chair. Jeremy fielded one from another table and they sat.

Jeremy flagged a waiter and ordered drinks for the table, far too skillfully. The waiter was puzzled. Nobody else noticed. The elder Miller began an animated description of events at dinner for merchants from Miller and Hearst. Jeremy listened, picking up more than he'd been able to witness.

The Council had capitulated. They'd kept some tattered shreds of dignity, kept some surface concessions. Some had to be silent for the depth of their fury.

The caravans would roll into Spiral Town tomorrow. Begley cloth would be loaded. Speckles would be delivered to the Hub and sold to Spiral women. The gate? That was being dealt with.

Drinks appeared. Jeremy paid, fumbling a bit with the coins. He sipped vodka and grapefruit, being cautious with it.

"You're quiet," Govert said.

Jeremy jumped. He said, "I was wondering. We set things back the way they were . . . when? Twenty years ago? *Two hundred* and twenty years ago the caravans were a going concern. Already self-supporting, weren't they?"

Heads nodded, *don't really know*, and Glen Hearst at another table barked, "Right!"

"Self-supporting, and they carry the speckles, and even the Otterfolk get what they want out of it. That's what everyone hoped for in the first place. Isn't it about time we dismantled the Overview Bureau?"

The table burst into laughter. Jeremy looked down at his empty glass. *No birdfucking—*

Angelo Hearst said, "And we could raise the price of speckles through the roof!"

Govert Miller reproved him, elder to youth. "Angelo, each wagon puts its own price—"

"Couldn't we all set one price? Or, wait, let's say eleven wagons up our prices and only Miller wagon stays low? Govert, you'd sell all your speckles before we got to the Shire. After that they'd pay whatever the rest of us want."

Govert laughed. "Jeremy, he's got a point."

On another night they might have argued. How would Destiny Town cope if the Road communities knew the truth? Tonight wasn't that kind of night. Jeremy said, "Angelo, you win. I never thought of that at all!"

He saw the merchant women's table breaking up. He made his excuses and left in a cluster of elders.

Harlow saw him and waited. When he'd caught up she said, "I wondered if I'd see you again."

"You *know* why I couldn't get you in on this. Ever. Harry's Bar is men only. Remember the gate guard?"

She was ticked, that was sure. "Do women have places too?"

"Now, how on birdfucking Earth will I ever know that? You've been surrounded by Spiral woman all night! You'll be selling them speckles tomorrow. *Ask.* Then lie to me if you like!"

"What a concept."

"Fair's fair."

"Selling speckles?"

"Yes, the old ones came to some kind of agreement. I was too far to hear details."

"You enjoyed yourself?"

"*Oh,* yes. I took a whole big pouch of festivity, right? For sixteen of us and the chefs at Harry's Bar. Impressed hell out of *them,* and we spent some time talking shop. Pit chef Jeremy. They sat me at the far end from Greegry—"

"Greegry?"

"My younger brother, Greegry Bloocher, the Council Chairman. The tall guy—"

Harlow started to laugh. Then she said, "No offense, dear, but why did the Spiral Council *want* Jeremy Winslow?"

"They didn't! They held their tempers, but it was pretty plain."

She waited.

"Like making them come all the way out here with wagons. The caravans are playing mind games. Table for fifteen, we'll all sit down and pretend we're equals and talk business, only they've got to ride out here and *get* us, and then Glen Hearst rings in a loose cook! Now the table's a little crowded, and there are things no *cook* should hear—"

"What *is* this all about?"

"I was as far from the action as they could get me, and that suited me just *fine.* But the new gate is too much. They're tearing it down. The elders are talking like the Council rolled belly-up."

"Good."

"And I've been invited to visit the graveyard tomorrow. I can take my wife."

He felt her freeze under his hand. "Why did you—? Jeremy, I'm being obtuse, you must have people buried there. No, how can I come? Both of us can't be gone when the caravan leaves tomorrow! You'll . . . have to catch up later."

He saw in her eyes: *You've escaped.*

The burly Councilman was chewing a barely concealed rage. He couldn't make himself talk to the caravan elders. At least the chef could be kept occupied. He was Gwillam Doakes, and he didn't recognize Jemmy Bloocher.

Jeremy leaned on his Destiny Town accent. "You have a Carolyn Hope Hearst buried in your graveyard, William. I was a Hearst before I married. I want to visit my ancestor's grave."

Gwillam Doakes dithered, then called down the table to Greegry Bloocher. Greegry's downsweeping hand chopped off the request. "Yes, yes. Give my name to the gatekeeper. Get directions from him if you need them."

*   *   *

"No, dear, the caravan's going *in* tomorrow. Not very far, just around the first turn as far as the Outer Circle. The chugs can get down to the beach between the Tucker and Coffey holdings, along the runoff strip. The caravans used it for access when I was young. We'll let the chugs clear away some of their devilhair weed while they're there."

She relaxed: softened under his hand.

He said, "I'll go visit the graveyard afterward. Come or don't."

A breathy sigh. "Yes, of course, of course I'll come. Merchants never used to miss the Destiny Town graveyard. They say nothing grows there but Earthlife—"

"Right."

Neither of them slept well that night.

At dawn, before even the yutzes were up, there was a chattering sound from up the Road, like an enraged squirrel as big as a building. Jeremy lay in the tent, listening, trying to recall—

"Air hammer," Harlow said.

They got up and joined the caravaners on the roofs. Seven lungsharks tried their luck. Tents were stowed, chugs were hooked up, wagons were set moving, the sales windows were opened to throngs of Spirals who had come to buy. Jeremy and Harlow drove.

The gate wasn't gone. It lay flat in the Road, in a **V**-shaped recess cut into the old lava by an air hammer. Now it was hinged at the base. The wagon wheels bumped over it and rolled past.

"I just remembered," Jeremy told Harlow, "one of the reasons we closed Spiral Town to the caravans. The Road isn't wide enough for a wagon and team to turn around."

"That's going to be fun."

"No, that's why we go to the Outer Circle. It's where *Columbiad* landed when the landers were still unloading from *Argos*. They always came down on the same spot. Plenty of room there."

They rolled past houses Jeremy had known from his birth. "Warkan . . . Harness . . . Doakes . . ."

"Shut up," she suggested.

A quarter-turn around, ten klicks, brought them to another guard . . . the same guard. The wagons eased to a halt a little too bunched up, but that wouldn't matter today.

Inward, the shallow pool of refrozen rock was tangent to two loops of the Road. It was considerably larger than similar craters found along the Road. *Cavorite* and *Columbiad* had landed always within a centimeter of the same spot, guided down by settler magic.

Below was *Columbiad*'s runoff stream, a strip of bare rock that no-body had tried to farm in two hundred years. It ran a klick and a half to the sea. The sea was black with devilhair. The chugs would feed very well today.

Then again—"Today I think we'll get sharks," Jeremy said.

The chugs didn't mind stopping early. Through the long afternoon they ambled on down into the waves, rolled a black forest out, and began to feast. Not a child in Spiral Town had ever seen wagons this far into town, and they crowded round to watch.

The chugs left their dinner and started uphill just ahead of a wave of sharks. Jeremy heard startled laughter and nervous chatter over the rattle of gunfire. Damn fools. They could lose a few chugs here. He emptied his gun and reloaded in haste.

The guns left twenty-odd sharks on the rocky beach, and an awed silence among the watching Spirals.

Then Harlow may have misread Jeremy's triumphant near-snarl. Or not. Jeremy had never been sure of Harlow. She made some minor changes in her dress—still in the vivid style of a merchant woman, but not so apt for shooting sharks—while he filled his lined pocket with seeds and festivity candy.

Once there had been a hydraulic empire in miniature: the mainland's stranglehold on speckles.

No more. The next time a caravan tried such extortion as they'd used these past few days, they'd find fertile speckles growing over every garbage heap, every manure pit, every graveyard along the Crab. Where there was potassium, speckles would grow.

Argos had robbed Crab and mainland alike. Destiny Town had only *Cavorite*, Spiral Town had only *Columbiad*; neither could reach farther than synchronous orbit. Spiral Town had all the knowledge that *Cavorite* had taken for Terminus and Destiny Town, and the equivalent in settler-magic tools.

Destiny Town had built shuttles that would reach orbit. That was the first step, had always been the first step to the stars. Spiral Town could have taken that step, and had not. Speckles-shy for a year or less, they'd recovered; but they'd never reached farther.

No more whining about birthrights, then, or what the mainland owed to the towns along the Crab.

Jemmy Bloocher would *steal* the stars.

When children passed them on the Road, Jeremy gave them festivity. A growing entourage of children followed them through Spiral Town.

"One each," he told them. They didn't believe him. Maybe they just liked following a man and a woman walking together. It might have struck them—it would have struck young Jemmy Bloocher—as just a bit obscene.

At the gate that led to the graveyard, the children stopped. He gave them another piece each and escorted Harlow through the wrought-iron gate.

He saw newer graves marked not with holograms but with blocks of carved stone. The marker gun must have failed.

"People are staring at us," Harlow said. "Isn't that dangerous?"

"Nobody's ever going to recognize Jemmy Bloocher talking with a lovely woman."

"They might tumble if you don't stop acting like you've seen it all before!"

"I'll gawk a little then. How's this?"

He could guess where Carolyn Hope Hearst must be, from the date she'd died. Yes: here she was in the pecan grove, with a fading hologram to mark the trunk.

"Poor woman. The whole train was sick from malnutrition, and she was the one who died. The crops hadn't grown in yet, I guess." Jeremy pulled two thumbs of festivity out of his special pocket along with a smattering of seeds, and offered one to Harlow.

She said, "Is this respectful?"

"Sure. Collect some nuts too. There are lifegivers under those fruit trees: see the girls eating plums?"

They ate the candy. Seeds fluttered over Carolyn Hope Hearst's grave. Jeremy plucked two handfuls of pecans and pocketed them.

He chose a way out that led past a line of Bloocher graves. He didn't point out the names; he let Harlow discover them.

He noticed a boy and girl watching him, and offered them festivity. If he spoke to the girl she'd run, so he didn't speak to either. They both looked like . . . well, Bloochers.

So he didn't look up at their mother. She might know him. He watched them eat the festivity, and watched the seeds fall.